Kissing is the Easy Part

Kissing is the Easy Part

CHRISTINE DUANN

wattpad books W

wattpad books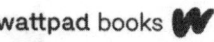

An imprint of Wattpad WEBTOON Book Group

Copyright © 2025 Christine Duann

Published in Canada by Wattpad WEBTOON Book Group, a division of Wattpad WEBTOON Studios, Inc.

36 Wellington Street E., Suite 200, Toronto, ON M5E 1C7 Canada

www.wattpad.com

First Wattpad Books edition: November 2025

ISBN 978-1-99834-192-4 (Trade Paper original)
ISBN 978-1-99834-196-2 (eBook edition)

Library and Archives Canada Cataloguing in Publication information is available upon request.

Printed and bound in Canada

1 3 5 7 9 10 8 6 4 2

Cover design by Mumtaz Mustafa
Images © Ann Haritonenko via Shutterstock
Typesetting by Delaney Anderson

To my sister, who read my first story
and asked what happens next

CHAPTER ONE

Flora

Nine failed attempts at small talk, five uneventful group dates, one tutoring session, and two shared classes—and now, maybe my last chance. Tonight, I might finally have a shot with Sean Foster.

One of Raymond Corbett's legendary parties is in full swing. The socially relevant slice of the junior class is here, which means Sean should be too. I owe it to myself to give it another try. Steeling myself, I step into the foyer.

The thick mix of beer, sweat, and cheap perfume hits me in the face. It smells like hope. Someone must have hijacked the playlist; raucous rap music pulses against the walls and through the marble floors, contrasting with the modern clean lines of the living room. But Ray's dad doesn't care what he does as long as he pays someone to clean up afterward. Everywhere buzzes with people clutching black Solo cups, shouting over the music, snapping blurry selfies as they spill through the open-plan house all the way to the kitchen. Still, no sign of Sean.

Raymond stands at the counter, and I make my way over—which sounds easier than it is in practice. Every few steps someone grabs my arm for a picture, a hug, asks me where I've been, and in return I squeeze hands and pose and dish out (genuine) compliments—*I love your dress! Your shoes are so cute!* By the time I reach the other side of the enormous room, my pulse is already racing.

"Don't worry, I invited him in person. Twice," Ray says. "He said he'd come."

Raymond knows all about my battles. New school year, new beginning, new party, same old crush.

When I first saw Sean Foster, we'd stepped into the hallway of Lakeridge High as freshmen. He wore minimalistic white sneakers and a gracefully aloof attitude, and his eyes were the most captivating kind of rainstorm. If my life were a movie, Sean would be next to me on the glossy poster, smiling like he already knew how the story would end. And it wouldn't be the kind of slow-burn romance in which the girl *finally* wakes up when she sees her best friend in a suit at prom, because for me, it was instant. I *knew*.

Sophomore year, he tutored our mutual friend Josie Wang in math. I weaseled my way into their first session. That afternoon, the only thing I understood was that my never-ending crush on him would go on like the numbers behind pi.

Over the summer, when he made varsity basketball, I joined the cheerleading squad to yell his name and mask my enthusiasm behind school spirit. Still, my cheering didn't catch his attention, so three days ago I tagged along with Josie and him to a movie, thinking we'd bond over caramel popcorn.

We didn't. Even though he was polite, he didn't laugh at my jokes. I got home after walking half a block because Sean refused to drop me off at my doorstep, claiming he couldn't make a U-turn.

Now, it's the first weekend of junior year, and I'm standing in the middle of Ray's kitchen, looking for Sean.

Pulling up a stool and sitting down opposite Ray, I sigh. "Madison says I'm too direct and it's scaring him off. She says when you're feeding wild animals, you don't wave your arms and run after them. Wait, lurk, and he'll come to me when he's ready."

"Apparently, Sean's the type of wild animal that would rather starve." Ray cackles.

"Exactly. Some guys need a bit of a nudge."

Or a snare for me to trap him.

It's time to launch one final attack against Fort Sean. More friends come up to catch up with us, and my phone doesn't stop vibrating with texts and mentions. Ray slides the key to his room across the counter. "You won't be able to talk to him with all these interruptions. Feel free to use the focus booth."

Ray's dad works at Microsoft, although I never know what his exact job is since he keeps getting promoted. Ray once told me how his dad goes to the office to *immerse* himself in the "collaborative culture," only to sit alone in a focus booth for six hours. Now Ray jokingly refers to his own bedroom the same way.

Jake and Dylan, also on the varsity basketball team with Sean, are sitting on the sofa. Waving goodbye to Raymond, I make my way over. Used cups are scattered on the glass coffee table, some half filled with beer. A cooler sits nearby, cracked open just enough to reveal a slosh of melted ice and a mix of crushed cans and bottles.

"Hey, have you guys seen Sean?"

Dylan looks up, the metal of his watch catching the light as he shifts. "Hello to you, too, Flora. He's around. He'll be right back."

"Want a drink?" Jake nudges the cooler open with his foot. It's just like them to hoard the entire stash, but Jake was voted Most Gorgeous two years in a row and gets away with everything. "We have Bud Light, PBR, a couple of Rainiers, and whatever's left of the Smirnoff—there he is."

When I turn, Sean emerges through the crowd, a water carafe in one hand and a bucket of ice in the other. His muted gray Henley is unfairly perfect—fitted just right, accentuating his lean build without looking like he tried. The color is a strategic choice, complementing the espresso tones of his hair. He sees me, and my heart speeds up. Dear god, he's such a beautiful, beautiful boy, even when he's in the middle of something so mundane.

"Sean! Join us!" I take the ice bucket from him, tug on his arm, and make sure to pull him down to sit next to me. Our legs brush against one another. His fingers are icy, and he slides his hand out of my grasp when he stretches his arm along the back of the sofa.

"Hey, Flora," Sean says.

"Took you long enough." Then I glance over. "Jake, know any good drinking games?"

Of course he does. Jake does a perfect bottle flip for no reason, then sets down a row of plastic cups and, with a sweep of his arm, pulls a few bottles from the cooler, adding them to the lineup. He gestures at the makeshift spread in front of us. "Here's how it works. On the count of three, we all point to a random bottle. If two or more people pick the same one, they have to drink. Simple."

He fills our cups with slightly flat beer to start. "Or we can say 'Go Wolverines!' before we pick—whatever works."

"Go Wolverines!" We chant in unison, then we all point. I don't even register which bottle I chose before I realize my finger is aimed at the same one as Sean's. Jake motions for us to drink, and I tip my head back and finish in one go. The beer's warm and bland. I slam down my cup. "Go Wolverines!"

The syrupy fruit-flavored vodka and the fizzy seltzer in the next two rounds are just as repulsive, and then something darker and harsher, a cheap spiced whiskey, burns all the way down my throat in that unmistakable way only cheap alcohol can. A small firework explodes in me.

Beside us, a group of girls initiate a dance-off. Jake laughs and his eyes light up. With a mop of golden hair and a dimpled smile, Jake's attractiveness is in-your-face, while Sean—Sean is filling up my cup with ice cubes, leaving almost no space for the beverage. Dylan catches this and snickers, shaking his head.

A new song blasts from the surround system. Someone must've turned up the volume. Where *is* the music coming from? My eyes can't focus. The scenes in front of me move in slow motion, like a movie playing frame by frame.

"Are you okay?" Sean asks.

I grin, then, realizing I'm showing too many teeth, close my mouth and reform it into a demure smile. A slight sense of wooziness kicks in, and my head feels heavy.

"How's everything? You folks having fun?" Raymond sails by, checking in on his party guests as part of his routine. Sometimes I wonder why he bothers throwing parties since he has no time to enjoy himself. All he does is rotate around the room, making sure no one's miserable.

"Awesome party. Thanks!" Dylan raises a cup. His bicep bulges against the fabric of his shirt. The airplane tattooed on his arm blurs.

Raymond places a hand on my shoulder, leans down, and whispers, "Please don't mess up my sheets later."

I laugh and shove him away.

Our drinking game resumes. I down two consecutive cups before Jake removes another bottle from the table, narrowing our choices. With fewer options, the odds of picking the same one as someone else spike. This time, I nearly knock over the bottle of peach schnapps when I try to point, but Jake catches it just in time. He pours us both drinks, finishes his, and nods at me. "Your turn."

My head snaps up. I reach for the cup in front of me.

Sean lays a hand on my forearm. His fingers are warm now. "Hey, maybe you should take a break."

"Game's still on. No mercy," Jake says.

"Don't go soft on us now," Dylan says.

Sean slides my cup out of reach. "You don't want a headache later."

"It's three times the penalty if you're going to drink for her." Dylan props his elbows on his knees, grinning. Pretty sure he made up that rule on the fly.

Sean presses my hand down, his touch firm but gentle. The veins on his forearm are so attractive. Without speaking, he picks up my cup and drinks—three in a row. His Adam's apple bobs as he swallows. Dylan and Jake exchange a glance and look over at me. My heart does a somersault inside my rib cage.

"Count us out the next round." Sean pours me a cup of water and presses it into my hand. His eyes linger on me when I chug it down, as if he wants to make sure I don't miss one drop.

Still in a daze, I dwell on the delicious fact that he said *us*. Hello, we're an *us*!

"Are you sure you're okay?" he asks.

I set down the empty cup. "I'm fine." This is the most positive interaction we've had so far, and the alcohol makes me brave. I have his full attention now, and I've got to act before I lose my nerve. "But it's too loud here. Let's go somewhere quieter. I need to talk to you about something."

Dylan lets out a low whistle. "Oh, *damn*. Sounds serious."

Jake grins. "Seany, are you in trouble?"

The room tilts when I stand up. Leather chairs melt into metal bar stools and faces and swaying bodies. My knees buckle, and I grab the air for balance, but there's nothing solid to anchor me.

Sean hops up and catches me by the elbow. I stumble over on my kitten heels and straighten myself. Taking a deep breath, I point the way and we make it up the stairs. Sean hesitates at the yellow tape stretched across Raymond's door. "It says Do Not Enter."

Raymond can be so *extra*. Ever since I met him at horse camp in second grade, he's always gone overboard.

"That's meant for other people. Ray's my pal. See, he's given me the key." Ripping off the tape, I unlock the door, and we step inside. The door clicks shut behind us and seals us off from the chaos downstairs. My head clears.

I turn the lock just to keep the outside world from barging in. A second to breathe, to speak without interruption. That's all I need.

"The alcohol helps . . ." I start. ". . . to work up the courage to talk to you."

"You need *courage* to talk to me?" Sean says.

As I lower myself into a single armchair and cross my legs, I make sure they're positioned at the ideal angle—forty-five degrees to the right, all stretched out, creating the illusion that they go on forever. Part of me feels invincible, like watching someone else perform, but the other part reminds me I've been crushing on him for too long, and this is the pivotal moment when we acknowledge our feelings.

"We've known each other for two years. We've hung out. More than once. And I thought I was being painfully obvious, but . . . you haven't made a move. I keep waiting for it to just *happen*, but since it hasn't—let me come right out and say it." I inhale, steadying myself. "Sean, I really like you. *That* kind of like."

My face burns. Sean holds my gaze for two seconds before he flicks his eyes to the door. Music filters in, a fast song about money and yachts. He clears his throat. "I wasn't expecting you to say that. You don't even know me that well."

"Maybe, but I can't stop thinking about you."

"Wow." He exhales a short laugh and shakes his head. "Thanks?"

Thanks? My scalp prickles as I wait for him to say more. Seconds drag on. "Is that all you're gonna say?"

"Flora, you're great. Really," he says. "But I don't think we'd work as a couple."

Everyone knows that everything before *but* is a setup for the hard truth. Before Sean, I was used to getting what I wanted. Attention, special favors, and anything shiny in a Neiman Marcus display window. Once, someone even gave up their parking space for me in downtown Seattle. But he's the clock striking midnight. He erases all my magic power.

"Can you sit down first?" I ask. "Let's talk."

There's nowhere else to sit in the room, so he chooses the foot of the bed. I get up and claim the space next to him, wanting to close the distance between us. Our eyes lock. His are a misty blend of blue and slate, the color of a winter sky before snowfall. Now he's mere inches from my manicured fingertips. So near, so handsome, yet I can't have him.

My supersuccessful parents say to always ask for feedback, especially in the face of failure. It's the key to improvement. "Is there anything you *don't* like about me? Help me understand why you don't think we could work."

Sean's eyes widen. Maybe other girls would have run away crying by now, but I'm desperate. He remains silent for a while before he says, "We don't have anything in common."

"How do you know? I'm into all sorts of things. No one's ever complained of not knowing what to talk about with me."

"I know you're—"

"I *want* to find out more about you. Maybe behind this mysterious, cool-guy facade, you're exactly like me."

"Mysterious?" Sean chuckles and a cute gleam gets in his eyes. "You're going to be *so* disappointed."

"Really?" I tilt my head, letting my hair slide down one shoulder. "You're not some broody guy who plays mind games?"

"Sorry to let you down, but once you know me a little better, you'll see. I'll bore you."

"No way."

"I study all the time. I don't have a—" My phone buzzes with yet another notification. He stops, taking his time to pick the right words. "—glamorous lifestyle like you do."

"Are you saying I'm shallow? I might not take eight billion AP classes like you do, but—wait. Is that why you dropped me from tutoring? Because you thought I was stupid?"

"No, I stopped tutoring you because you didn't need it. You knew all the answers already." He glances at my legs for the briefest second before he looks away. "Besides, you were distracting me."

My neck warms. "I thought you didn't like me because I wasn't smart enough."

"That's not true. Look, I don't think I'm what you're looking for." Sean clasps his hands and places them on his knees. "You're too popular. I wouldn't be able to keep up with you."

Interesting reason to turn someone down. A new wave of dizziness sets in, and I grasp at the unspoken message between his words. Behind him, a dozen European film posters crowd the wall—Godard, Truffaut, Fellini, Buñuel, Bergman—names I've absorbed through sheer osmosis. I watched every one of those movies in Ray's home theater with Raymond himself and all twelve speakers (because he insists on full surround sound for everything), but the one I remember most is *Belle de Jour*. Catherine Deneuve wears a stiff blond wig and plays a housewife who secretly moonlights as a prostitute. People project whatever they want onto her. "I get it now. What you meant by 'popular' is that I'm easy."

I rub my temple where a headache is manifesting. My phone buzzes again.

"What? No! That's not what I meant. You have loads of friends and everyone likes you. Honestly, it's me."

Usually the *it's not you it's me* excuse happens at the *end* of a relationship. I gesture at the air between us. "I don't usually do this . . . chase after boys. I like you. I've liked you since freshman year."

"Thank you for telling me that." He holds my gaze and says, "And this isn't about me thinking you're shallow, or stupid, or anything like that."

"But you're still saying no."

He straightens himself. "I'd like to stay friends."

None of his reasons make sense. This situation is so excruciatingly hard. My satin dress is at the ideal length, showing off three provocative inches of bare skin on my thighs. My makeup is immaculate, winged eyeliner perfectly symmetrical with slim traces of shimmer beneath my eyes, and my hair is a dark river of dreams. What more does he want?

A wave of nausea rises out of nowhere. I put a hand over my mouth.

"You all right?"

"Not really." I push myself up, tired and upset, suddenly impatient with this conversation. "I'm going home. Consider yourself off the hook. Message received."

"How are you going to get home? You can't drive like this."

"I have enough sense not to drive, thank you. I'm going to walk."

"You're going to walk," Sean repeats. "In those shoes. At midnight."

"Yes. It's one of my special talents." I brush past him and head out of the room, or at least try to. The door is locked, and I keep turning the lock in the wrong direction until Sean reaches over to open it for me.

Please, let this night end already.

Running down the flight of stairs, I push through sweaty bodies, bump my shoulders against everything in the way, and try not to trip over myself. For once I don't feel like posting snippets to my story.

"I'm guessing the plan didn't pop off as you hoped. You're leaving?" Raymond asks as I hustle past him and hand back the key.

"Yeah," I say, breathing hard to push back emotions. "I'll text you tomorrow."

Before I head out, I set upright the toppled snake plant—apparently chosen by Ray's parents because it thrives on neglect, much like their parenting—beside the front door and get ready to leave my epic fail behind.

A hand taps me on the shoulder. "Let me walk you home," Sean says.

Half of me is annoyed at him for being nice, because I want to focus on being mad at him right now. Half of me struggles to keep the hurt under wraps. My place is only fifteen minutes away, but late at night, drunk, and in heels isn't my favorite way to wobble home alone. I shrug, and Sean takes that as a sign to follow me out the door.

The chilly night air hits me, soothing my burning humiliation. The sky is dark with no stars. Aside from the sound of my heels clicking on the pavement, we walk in silence, and Sean matches his pace with mine. I don't feel like talking to him anymore. His hands are in his pockets as he stares far ahead.

The city is nestled between the water, wrapped in mist most of the year, and on nights like this, I get the hype. Most of our class lives in the suburbs, where the houses are small and dainty. The closer you get to downtown, the taller the buildings rise above the hills. Raymond and I live on this side of the bridge, just a short drive from downtown Seattle, close enough that the skyline is always on the horizon, even if it's hardly a tier-one fashion capital.

I breathe in the night. Trees and rain, a scent I never get tired of. The fresh air almost makes up for the nine months of gloomy skies.

"You're probably going to tell everyone you rejected me," I say.

"I promise I won't tell anyone."

I should've listened to Madison and not been so direct. The drinking-game buzz has waned but it's still acting like a truth serum. "How am I ever going to face you in school again?"

"You don't have to worry. I won't make this weird for you." He turns to me, the streetlamp casting shadows along his jaw. He scratches the back of his neck. "We'll never speak of this again, but for now—thank you for telling me. It can't be easy, being honest like that. You made me feel special."

My heart constricts. It almost hurts. He has no idea the effect he has on me. "Well, you *are*. Special, I mean. And trust me, it's harder for me to *not* say anything."

I catch his eyes and his smile deepens.

"Hey, can I ask you something?" I lean in. "You *are* the creator behind CourseView, right?"

In freshman year, some unknown genius designed a platform where students can get a clearer idea of what electives are worth taking. It's far superior to what the school provides, which is a list of classes with high-level (useless) descriptions. CourseView tracks past grade trends, workload changes, and which teachers are the best (read: breeziest) by pulling insights from buried forum posts and Discord chats.

But no one knows who made it. The most obvious suspect is Sean, but he flat-out denies it every time.

"No," he says now. "Why would you think that?"

"Oh, come on. 'Schrödinger's Elective: Simultaneously easy and hard until you take it'?" Whenever there's not enough data to suggest whether an elective is worth taking, CourseView slaps that rating on it. "Who else would come up with something like that but you?"

"Anyone with the barest understanding of quantum superposition?"

My point exactly. "Also, I saw you downloading old syllabi for Nutrition and Wellness: Baking. There's no way you'd take that course in a million years."

"Since I'm so mysterious, I could be a wedding cake baker for all you know."

I say nothing, waiting for him to crack under the silence. As my mom would say, lulls can be very effective in making people open up; don't try to fill them all. The silence stretches out effectively.

"Okay, fine, it's me."

I turn to face him full on. "Of course it's you! But why would you keep it a secret? It's the single most brilliant thing this school has ever seen. Without you, I'd still be agonizing over whether to take Introduction to Fashion and Textiles or Principles of Fashion and Textiles. I got mostly As because of you."

"Glad it helped," he says. "Jake transferred late freshman year, and most of the decent electives were full. I threw something together to help him with the options left, then figured I might as well expand it and share it with the whole school. But features like Rate My Teachers could get me in trouble, so it's easier to stay anonymous. It's really not that big of a deal."

Not that big of a deal?

A data-driven platform to refine the process? Taking proactive steps to improve the quality of student life? I can practically hear my dad selling the heck out of this at one of the pharmaceutical company-wide town halls he hosts on a regular basis, which inevitably end with some corporatey nonsense like "solving real-world problems with innovative ideas."

Plus, Sean didn't build it for credit or recognition. Mysterious, altruistic genius right there.

"Imagine creating something so impressive but not being able to claim it." I sigh on his behalf. "I'd brag about it every chance I got. And after you graduate, you won't be able to pass on your legacy."

"I'll put it on my college application."

"We *have to* rename the platform to something legendary. How about . . . Foster Select? And then all the incoming freshmen would be like, wait, *you're* the Foster behind Foster Select?"

He laughs.

"Seriously, it's got a nice ring to it," I continue. "The name alone gives off a premium, high-end feel, like a curated list of luxury hotels or something, but it's literally an elective course database."

"You're hilarious. I'll keep that in mind."

"Anyway, this is one of the many reasons I have a crush on you. That, and because you're ridiculously good looking." My mouth moves faster than my brain. "And you're a great tutor. You always know what I'm going to ask before I do, like you're steps ahead. And you play varsity basketball, which should make you a hotshot, but you don't act like it. Not in that typical jock way. It's like the millisecond I decided I liked you, everything you did after kept proving me right."

Sean doesn't respond right away. "I don't know what to say." His gaze drops, just for a moment, and his voice is quieter now. "You're making me sound a lot cooler than I actually am."

My building comes into view much too soon, a sleek tower of glass and steel reflecting the glow of distant streetlights. Floor-to-ceiling windows flicker with muted lights. The entrance is still, and the only sign of life comes from the concierge desk, where Greg is scrolling through his phone.

"You *live* here?" Sean says.

"Yeah." He's staring at the building with a mixture of awe and intimidation on his face, so I attempt a joke to relax him. "You can still kiss me good night, though. The doorman won't tell my parents."

He laughs, flicking his gaze back to me. "Maybe next time, when you're not drunk."

I arch one eyebrow. "Is that a promise?"

He lowers his head to avoid answering, but I can still see his smile. That's good enough for now. "Thanks for walking me home."

"My pleasure."

"Good night."

"Good night, Flora. Hope you're not too hungover in the morning."

He looks cuter than ever standing there with his hands in his pockets, smiling, his eyes soft in the dark, his hair rumpled by the wind.

I love "good nights." "Good mornings" are vibrant with energy while "good nights" are quiet and intimate. Hearing a "good night" from Sean makes tonight kind of worthwhile even if he did reject me.

CHAPTER TWO

Sean

If this is how a typical party at Raymond's unfolds, then I've been missing out on *a lot*.

By the time I get back from Flora's condo, my brain in overdrive, Josie's already by the car, twirling the keys between her fingers. "The designated driver is tired. Let's find Jake and Dylan and go."

We pile into her car. I take shotgun, Dylan claims the back, and Jake fumbles for his seat belt but doesn't bother to click it before he pipes up, "Broski, what was that all about?"

Good question. What *was* that? It's not every night that the most beautiful girl at school looks you straight in the eye and tells you she can't stop thinking about you, then proceeds to praise the bare-bones Python platform you built, along with providing a running list of reasons why she likes you.

Not sure my fragile male ego is equipped for that level of validation.

"Nothing worth talking about," I say.

Josie plugs in her playlist, and some unfamiliar indie song spills from the speakers. Whatever she picks, we listen. Being the lead singer of her band gives her that authority. I turn up the volume, hoping it'll shut down this conversation.

Dylan leans forward from the back seat, raising his voice over the music. "Seriously, man. What was so important that she had to drag you upstairs? You were gone for a while."

"Yeah, that's a long time for *nothing*." Jake finally clicks his seat belt. His grin is wide enough to fill the rearview mirror. "Very suspicious behavior. You can't expect us to let that slide."

"Leave him alone," Josie says, eyes on the road. "Healthy boundaries, guys."

"I *knew* Flora liked you," Jake says. "Remember that one time I hung out with her? She kept trying to steer the conversation back to you. 'Are you close with Sean?' 'Is he secretly a softie?' At some point I started dropping your name randomly to mess with her. And she was *riveted*, dude. Funniest thing ever. I told you, right?"

"Yes, the evening of, and the next day. And the week after."

"I also told her you disabled the parental controls on my laptop, and she couldn't be more impressed."

"Of all the things you could've said about me . . ."

Dylan snickers. "Imagine Jake being a stepping stone because Seany is too intimidating to talk to."

"Yeah, to be *used* like that," Jake agrees. "Truly humbling experience. Man, I understood . . . *all too well*." He starts to sing, and Dylan, because he has no shame, jumps in on backup vocals.

I rub the bridge of my nose. "Jacob. Please." That's not his real name, but I use it when he annoys me, which is daily.

"She's way too chatty, by the way," Jake says. "It's like we were competing for an invisible microphone. I'm just waiting to tell my story, which is way funnier than hers, and she keeps cutting me off with more questions like, 'Has Sean ever had a serious girlfriend?'"

"Hey, play 'Love Story' next," Dylan says. Josie may know all about obscure bands but she's not above some mainstream fun, so I suffer through the bros bellowing in harmony about Romeo for the next four minutes. Nothing bonds them tighter than making fun of me, especially when they can do it at maximum volume.

I try to steer the conversation elsewhere. It takes three tries before I finally get them talking about the latest *Elden Ring* expansion. Jake's house comes into view, we drop him off, and then it's just the three of us heading back to Cedarbrook, the neighborhood we grew up in together. The farther we drive, the more reality settles in. The streets narrow, and the houses shrink block by block.

"You know what they say about Flora, right?" Dylan says. *This again?* "Just so you're prepared for all that drama."

Josie scoffs. "None of that is true."

"Not saying it is. Just want our boy to be aware." Dylan pulls out his phone and scrolls, then shows it to me over my shoulder.

I'm in at least twenty-five different text groups, and I mute twenty-four of them, leaving only our core squad open. I rely on Dylan and Jake to relay anything truly worth knowing. So far, that hasn't happened. These chat groups are, at best, white noise, and at worst, truly vicious, like the one staring me down right now.

Anonymous 453: *Search up Lakeridge High, she's literally under "Things to Do."*

Anonymous 17: *Flora's your basic cheerleader. Easy and desperate for attention.*

Anonymous 226: *Pretty sure she's been with half the football team. Maybe more.*

The words land like a punch to the gut. For a second, the thought flashes through my mind—tracking their IPs, finding out who's hiding behind those cheap shots. Then Dylan's reply pops up.

DylanReyes: *Talking trash behind an anonymous post? Pathetic.*

I hand the phone back, tension still burning under my skin. "You should leave that group. It's a cesspool for cowards."

Does Flora know? I hope she never finds out.

"There's a lot of talk about Flora because guys catch feelings, and when they realize she's not into them, they trash her reputation," Josie says. "In this day and age, you can't be an attractive and approachable girl without people misinterpreting the vibes. In any day and age, actually."

"Sure," Dylan says, "but let's not pretend all Flora does is hang out with guys and pick daisies together. Sometimes there's more."

"So?" Josie shoots back. "I don't see you calling Jake out for his drama."

Jake's notorious for his sexcapades, and never apologizes for them, nor does anyone expect him to.

Dylan raises his hands in surrender. "Look, we all like Flora. She's cool, and she always picks up the tab. I'm looking out for you, Seany. Don't get too caught up."

"I'm not. I get why people gravitate to her, though. She's . . ."—*disarming and hard to ignore*—"She's sharp. And funny."

"Sure, man. Not caught up at all."

"It's an *observation*," I say.

Josie pulls onto our street. Dylan gets out first, heading to his place just a few doors down. Josie parks in her driveway, and I get out with her since I live next door. Before heading inside, she pauses, giving me the best-friend look that says *I know there's more.* "Anything you want to get off your chest?"

I hesitate. Part of me wants to spill, but I promised not to tell anyone.

"You should hear it from Flora."

Josie nods like she expected that answer. "Yeah. Thought so." She turns to head inside. "Don't let other people make up your mind for you, okay? Flora's worth it."

The night air feels heavier without the distraction of their voices. The house is dark when I step inside. My family is asleep, and I creep upstairs, avoiding the floorboards that creak too loudly.

It's past midnight and I'm in my room now, but sleep isn't coming. My brain churns like an endless algorithm. There's something about Flora, an allure that's effortless and overwhelming. Her eyes are huge, and her face keeps flashing through my head like a glitch. *And those legs.*

Why would someone like her want to spend time with me? We're on different wavelengths.

Restless, I flip open my laptop to check my MIT prep. My dream school. *The* dream school. My grandfather was a physics professor there before he retired, and I can't wait to go to his alma mater. He makes it sound like more than a school, that it's the place where you prove you belong.

I scroll through my Schoolhouse profile. Over one hundred hours logged tutoring students. Then I check the due dates for all my homework and update my planner with the weekend's study goals. Lastly, out of habit, I click on the MIT admissions website, even though I've memorized every word.

This goal has been years in the making. I can't afford distractions. I'm not ready to be dazzled by Flora. She's too pretty, too flirty, too far out of my league.

Focus.

MIT wants risk-takers. People who know how to balance. One of the essay questions literally asks: *Tell us something you do simply for the pleasure of it.*

What if I went on *one* date, one casual date, to see what Flora Morgan is all about?

It wouldn't ruin me, right?

CHAPTER THREE

Flora

The next morning, I lie in bed browsing my Instagram feed. I've analyzed Sean's behavior eight billion times already, but guys are mysterious creatures. He said he wants to be friends, yet he drank for me *and* checked out my legs. He rejected me, then he walked me home *and* said I make him feel special. He might've even flirted a little.

A group call is in order. I need help from my friends.

Madison Jenkins, my best friend, picks up first. While I show my love by letting her take the back spot when we take a selfie (so her face appears smaller and her angles sharper), she shows hers with insults and brutal honesty. Her yearbook quote would likely be *It's fine to be a bitch as long as you stab people in the front.*

Josie hops on next, yawning. She checks every box on the high school cool list: fronts a rock band, types on a MacBook Pro, and has two news articles written about her. The fact that she's Sean's next-door neighbor/childhood friend doesn't hurt either. A girl needs all her resources, and it's crucial to have someone on the inside.

Carmen is the last to join. To balance out my daily dose of negativity from Madison, I need the Hallmark Cards girl in our clique. Carmen Belle brings in some much-needed virtue, since Madison is mean, Josie is jaded, and I'm (adorably) vain. She's my go-to when I need encouragement, and she even pretends to share my enthusiasm for Sean.

After a debriefing from me, Madison starts with, "What's with the obsession? Sean's not as hot as you make him out to be. You're interested in the challenge, not him. He's an animal head you want to mount on the wall."

Gosh, Mads doesn't disappoint.

"Jake is cuter," she goes on. "But you already dated Jake, so there goes the thrill of the chase. You're hung up on Sean because he's hard to get."

I sputter. "That's *so* not true. And I went out with Jake *once*, okay? To *Shake Shack*."

"Sean's great, so if you're not serious, don't mess with him," Josie says.

Who is she, his *agent*? Josie is definitely more Sean's friend than mine.

"I like people," I say. "I won't put my social life on hold to wait for him. But I *am* serious about him."

It's true. Even though I adore all mankind, I save a special place in my heart for Sean, like I do the presidential suite at St. Regis. I let him stay there in peace, undisturbed by the meaningless flings that come through the hotel lobby.

Madison snorts presumptuously.

"Walking you home sounds like Sean," Josie says. "That's the gentlemanly thing to do. I wouldn't read too much into it."

"What do you think, Carmen?" I ask her partly because she says nice things, but mostly to make her feel included in the conversation.

"He'll come around!" Her voice is unnaturally bright, every word laced with forced cheer. I can practically hear the exclamation points through the phone.

So helpful, this group. The most promising young women our school has to offer, who always seem to have it together, yet they're nowhere close to figuring this out.

After I hang up, I open my contact list. I could call Raymond for a guy's perspective—or text my mom. Maybe. I tap on our last conversation, which is still left on Read from nine hours ago. The text before that says *In a meeting*. Mom's away on a business trip in Madrid, and with the time difference, we're talking even less than usual.

Ray it is.

Before I can find his name, my phone vibrates in my hand. My pulse shifts from a casual stroll to a full-on stampede.

Sean Foster: *Hey, can I call you?*

Stay calm. Stay calm. I breathe through my mouth, like that's going to help. I stare at the screen for too long, then—whatever—tap his profile picture and hit Call.

Think of a fun, witty, sexy opening line.

"Hi!" I squeak the minute he picks up.

"Hi." He sounds calm, in control. "How are you feeling?"

"Oh. I'm great!" *Real smooth. And here I thought I was an expert at flirting over the phone.* "Um . . . how are you?" *Perfect. Even worse.*

"Fine, but I couldn't really sleep last night. How badly does your head hurt?"

"Not at all."

"That's good." A pause. "Did you get in trouble with your parents?"

"Actually, no. My parents weren't even home."

"Ah. That explains why you went so hard last night. If they were home, you probably would've taken it easy in case you got caught."

"Yeah," I say, panicking. Here I am, letting him carry the entire conversation on his own. He's going to hang up in a second. I order myself to come up with something—*anything*—as I visually rummage through my room. My designer handbags stare back at me, offering no inspiration. Sean won't care to learn the differences between the Chanel 2.55 Reissue and the Classic Flap Bag.

"Well," he says, "glad you're fine, I was just calling to—"

Oh no. That's his exit line! My mouth opens on its own. "Please don't hang up. I'll think of something interesting to say soon!"

Excuse me? I'm done. *Done.*

The back of my neck prickles when Sean's light laugh comes through. "I was going to ask if you want to meet for coffee, if you're not doing anything later. I figured I owe you a coffee after stealing your drink last night, but I didn't want to ask you out over text."

And now, after nine failed attempts at small talk, five uneventful group dates, one tutoring session, two shared classes, and one drunken confession, I'm finally going on a first date with Sean Foster.

* * *

Sean waits for me in front of the coffee shop he suggested, the Pavement, with sunlight in his hair. One look at him and I forget all the first date questions I googled. I melt like caviar on an epicurean's tongue.

"Hi! You're here," I say unnecessarily. "Sorry I'm late." Ten minutes late, which isn't technically *too* late, but I know my manners.

We're standing across from a tree-lined park, where birds trill from branches overhead, and the steady splash of a fountain echoes somewhere in the distance. Sean glances over at me, taking in my blush silk cami with delicate straps and my floral skirt, a soft watercolor print that flutters just above my knees, then pushes open the heavy wooden door.

"You're worth the wait."

Yes! Off to a good start.

The café has an industrial feel, with exposed metal and weathered wood, and sunlight flooding through tall windows. "Is this okay?" he asks, as a whiff of freshly ground coffee hits my nose. "I'm here a lot. To do homework."

This is where he hangs out.

"I love it!"

Except maybe it's too quiet for my taste. The only sound is the humming of the coffee machine, while I prefer places with music and chatter, where I can laugh out loud. Never mind that, because I'd agree to whatever Sean says, even if he suggested bird watching.

"Do you want anything to eat?" He points at the glass showcase that holds desserts. Everything beckons to me, from the glossy pecan cheesecake, to the golden apple strudel with its flaky crust, to the rows of freshly baked cookies.

"I can't decide. It's a tough call between cinnamon roll and blueberry muffin. Everything looks amazing. I guess . . . cinnamon roll?"

"Sure. And coffee?"

"Chai latte. Wait, I changed my mind. Blueberry muffin."

Sean nods. "Find us a seat? Let me get this."

Should I fight with him over the bill? But maybe this is important to his male ego, so I let him pay. I sit down at a table near the back and watch Sean at the counter.

He likes his coffee black, my brain notes furiously. Poor kid also doesn't own a wallet. He has all his cash clipped together with a metal clip, which is awfully . . . *sophisticated.*

From now on, money clips and black coffee are the definition of cool.

Sean comes back, balancing the tray. I push aside a tiny ceramic vase to clear space for him. He places the drinks on the table first, then lifts two plates and slides them in front of me—one with a blueberry muffin, the other with a cinnamon roll. "Try both. I'll eat the rest if you can't finish."

The cinnamon roll is the fluffiest I've ever had, with vanilla cream glaze swirling in my mouth. The blueberry muffin is fresh and buttery, packed with juicy bursts of flavor. *Out of this world.*

"Do you like it?"

I nod, too busy to answer. When I swallow, I let out a satisfied sigh. "I *love* this place."

Sean's shoulders relax. He smiles and looks . . . relieved? Somehow that makes me a bit relieved as well, knowing he's not entirely cool and collected about this. Between bites, my mouth carries out conversations on its own.

"Do you have any pet peeves?" I ask, after learning that he's a dog person, his favorite place in the world is his bedroom, he enjoys bass fishing on Lake Sammamish with his grandad, and that if he won the lottery, he'd still go to school the next Monday.

"People who blame everyone but themselves for their problems. Also, drivers who switch lanes without signaling. How about you?"

Note to self: stop whining and use the blinker from now on.

"I hate it when I buy ice cream and the scoop isn't a perfect sphere. Or when it starts dripping at the bottom halfway through. That irritates me to no end."

Oh god. Can I change my answer?

"I hate that too," Sean says, "and when it melts too fast and runs down the side of the cone. Sometimes they only give you a tiny piece of napkin, which does no good other than sticking to the cone."

"Yes! And then you try to peel if off and it tears apart."

He chuckles, picking up a fork as I push my unfinished baked goods his way. There's a raw spot on the skin around his thumbnail that I didn't notice before. He cuts into the muffin, the fork making a soft clink against the plate.

"How does it feel to be the star of the basketball team?" I ask, as if I'm interviewing him. To be honest, Sean isn't *that* good, but I don't mind giving him a little confidence boost. Guys like that.

"The *star?*" His eyebrows rise. "Have you paid attention to our games? You mean Jake." Jake plays small forward, and we all expect him to be sent off to college in the loving arms of D1 scouts.

"I wasn't watching Jake during the games."

His fingers pause around his coffee cup for half a second. "Good to know."

My heart thuds. I don't care much for the rest of the team, although it's a tried-and-true fact that hot guys travel in packs. If they were movies, then Jake Lancaster would be *The Dark Knight*— everyone's default favorite, just like how everyone agrees Jake's one great-looking dude. Dylan Reyes, Sean's other friend, with the buzz cut, tattoo, and habit of swearing every other sentence, is one of those cult films, like *Pulp Fiction*—dedicated fans, but not mass appeal.

I can't tell what kind of movie Sean is yet, but he'd be the kind I never get tired of watching. Every time I replayed it, I'd notice something I didn't before, and I'd always be at a loss for words when I tried to describe what was so special about it.

"Do you dream of playing pro someday?" I ask.

"Never. Basketball's good exercise, and I like hanging out with my friends. I have other interests."

"Such as?"

"Well," he says as he picks at his cuticle with his index finger (so that's how he gets that raw spot). "I like physics. I'm prepping for the USAPhO."

"The what?"

"The United States Physics Olympiad." He utters the name slowly, his voice growing quieter. His eyes stay on the salt and pepper shakers on the table. "It's a physics competition. There are a series of exams to select the national representatives. If I do well on the first test, I get invited to the semis, and then . . . Sorry, I'm boring you."

"No, no. It's fine. Physics is so useful." I rack my brain for something intelligent to say. "Like in pool games, right? Something to do with Newton's second law and collision and velocity?"

He nods as if he doesn't just hear the dumbest take on physics ever. "I can predict where the balls are going, and in theory I can plan my shots, but I can't actually make it happen."

"Too bad."

"I'm good at teaching people, though. Dylan has a pool table at his place. I can show you next time if you want."

There's a next time. He's not tired of me yet. Like sinking into a warm bath, my body uncoils inch by inch. "I'd love that."

"My grandad used to set up these science challenges for me when I was a kid. Stuff like building engines from scratch or launching a balloon rocket across the room. That's what got me hooked on physics in the first place."

"Out of all the projects you did with your grandad, what would you say was the most—" *Complicated?* No way, I wouldn't understand a thing he says. "Fun?"

"Probably the Rube Goldberg machine." He watches my reaction, then adds, "You know what it is, you just don't realize that's what it's called. Ever seen one of those YouTube videos where a ball rolls down a ramp, knocks over dominoes, hits a lever, then starts a pulley that rings a doorbell?"

I *do* know what it is. "It's doing something simple in the most roundabout, complicated way possible?" *Like me flipping over backward to end up sitting across from you now, watching your lashes flutter.*

"Exactly. I enjoy adjusting, fine-tuning, and eventually, the predictability of it—how everything falls into place after careful planning. My grandad taught at MIT before he retired, and I got to see some truly incredible machines there."

"Is MIT your dream school?"

"Yes." No hesitation. A light sparks in his eyes, and he stops picking at his cuticles. "It's what I've always known I wanted. That's why I take so many AP and honors classes, like you pointed out—eight billion of them. I started entering STEM competitions in middle school, participated in robotics camps, and I play varsity basketball. I enjoy all of it, but I won't lie, part of it is because it makes my application look better."

"The last time I heard someone talk like that, it was my mom," I say. "My parents work at a pharmaceutical company in Seattle. My dad's the global marketing VP, and my mom just got promoted to senior VP. She's always talking about changing the world and improving patients' lives. And the way she plans her career—every move feels so intentional." I shake my head. "She makes it all look so easy."

"Your mom sounds remarkable."

Nearby, a family chats quietly, and a group of students tap away on their laptops. A comfortable silence settles between us as he finishes everything on the plates and I drain the last few drops of my chai latte.

"But they're on business trips all the time," I say. "They just launched a new cardiovascular drug, which is why no one was home last night."

"I thought you had an older brother?"

"Yeah, Jeremy. He's at Harvard now."

Sean takes a sip of his coffee. Most people either envy my freedom or joke about throwing a party without parental supervision, but he asks, "Do you like being alone in the apartment all the time?"

"I get to do whatever I want, but if I could choose, I'd pick a family brunch over anything. I don't care how lame that sounds."

"No, I get it. I'm lucky, my dad cooks every night."

"I wish *my* dad cooked. Or at least ate at home. We have a gigantic kitchen, but it only ever gets used to boil water."

When was the last time I sat down and ate with my parents? I can't remember. Sometimes I try to conjure up an image of my mom's face, but all I can picture are her scarves. They're always silk, soft and delicate, patterned with prancing horses or Parisian streets. She often comes home, drapes one over the quartz countertop, and then forgets to take it with her on her next trip.

"Is that why you go to all those parties? Because you want to get out and see people?"

"Weekend parties are a must. I read somewhere that in parts of the country where there are no bars, the incidence of violent crimes more than doubles. People need to blow off steam, you know," I ramble. "I got invited to a college bonfire tonight—"

That's *not* the kind of thing to say to impress a guy like Sean. I add, "Oh god. I promise I'm not trying to hook up with some college guy or anything—"

That's enough, Flora. Kindly shut up now.

Sean's expression remains stoic.

"Would you like to go with me?" I suggest, in a feeble attempt to turn things around.

"Nah, hooking up with college guys really isn't my thing."

Okay, that's some pretty dry humor, and I also want to die. My heart has sunk all the way past the table and onto the floor, flopping about like a fish out of water, when he adds, "But if you need a ride home, you can call me."

My head snaps up. "Seriously?"

"Yes. But maybe don't get drunk?"

Don't get drunk. It's not cute.

"You're afraid I'll puke in your car," I can't resist saying.

Sean puts down his coffee and lifts his eyes to meet mine. His gaze is simultaneously firm and tender, steady but not intrusive, allowing something soft to curl up inside me.

"No," he says. "I'd be worried about you, friend."

* * *

Seven hours later, I'm firmly planted in the passenger seat of Sean's Honda Civic. Night has fallen as he sweeps me away from jazz music, a small patch of sandy beach, and grassy hills, where a bonfire is starting.

"I wasn't expecting your call so early," Sean says, eyes on the road ahead. His navy-blue bomber jacket creases slightly as he shifts, the cuffs snug against his wrists. Around us, the city wakes with lights. "It's only nine thirty. What happened to the college bonfire thing?"

I sneak a peek at his profile. "I decided it'd be more fun to sit in your car instead."

"Oh. The pressure is on."

It's the first time I've been alone with him in his car, and I savor every second. I observe the way he checks his mirrors and flips the turn signal. He puts both hands on the steering wheel, of course, and brakes well ahead of time. Even the fake leather seats are endearing in their own way. We're so close, cut off from the rest of the moving world outside.

He stops at a red light and turns to me. "Want to do something together?"

I rack my brain for second date ideas:

1. Go somewhere for food. *No, I'm too jittery.*

2. See a movie. *But we won't be able to talk. Plus, he has questionable taste—he thinks* The Avengers *is a classic.*

3. Wander the bookstore? Visit a gallery? *Let's not pretend to be someone else. No clue how late those places stay open anyway.*

I take the bold way out. "My parents aren't home. Want to come to my place?"

Sean doesn't respond right away. Passing headlights illuminate his face, emphasizing his presence beside me, and I envision going back to my apartment, alone on a Saturday night. The floor-to-ceiling windows are gorgeous when the sun filters through them, but in darkness, they turn to huge black holes.

"I'm not propositioning you. It's nice to have someone in the apartment with me, that's all."

The traffic light turns green. "Sure."

Two dates in one day. I'm too lucky. Time to donate to charity to keep my good karma flowing.

✳ ✳ ✳

"Hi, Greg, how's it going?" I greet our doorman as we enter. He not-so-discreetly checks out Sean before pushing the elevator button for us. We ride up, the elevator doors slide open to a hardwood double door, and I turn my key.

Sean halts and sucks in his breath.

Our great room gleams from the coffered ceiling to the marble floor. A see-through fireplace sits on one side as a divider. Behind it, a crystal pendant hangs over the dining area; its pieces set off a shadow of constellation along the wall. Sean takes all this in, then casts his glance at the stainless steel kitchen appliance. "Your apartment is stunning. And huge."

"Because it's empty." I give him the grand tour as we sail past a shelf full of souvenirs from around the globe, rattling off features like a Realtor. The old-world French vibe my mom's going for in the den (he's careful not to step on the cream-colored rug). The lacquered rosewood cabinet in the hallway, filled with fine china we never use. A small ink-wash painting, mounted in a gilded frame like a museum piece, positioned with careful negative space around it. Then we stop in front of my room.

"Give me *one* minute." I crack the door open an inch. My god. It's in its usual state of disarray: an erupted volcano of clothes, shoes, and beauty products. A black bra is strewn across my full-length mirror.

I shake my head. "Meet me back here in an hour."

"Is there a body behind the shower curtain?"

"Don't check the closet either."

He laughs. "Oh, come on. Let's see it."

Sighing, I step aside to let him in.

"Wow." His eyes crinkle at the edges when he smiles. "What interior design style is this?"

I eye him with my chin up. "Minimalist. Can't you tell?"

He laughs again. Tapping on my phone, I select a song from Josie's band, Fishnets, and her voice comes through the wireless home speaker. Josie's lyrics are dark, but she sounds like a Disney princess. As she sings ". . . *leave before your cat learns the horrible truth* . . ." with all the teenage angst she can muster, Sean manages to clear a space on the floor. He sits down and leans his head back against my bed.

"Want anything to drink?" I ask.

"I'm good."

"How's the temperature? Too hot, too cold?"

He stretches out his legs. "Nope, this is perfect."

Now what? I haven't thought this through. Now that Sean is in my room, his presence impossible to ignore, I'm suddenly at a loss for what to do next.

"What's that?" He points to the tapa cloth hanging on my wall as art. The fabric is deep brown and off-white, woven with geometric patterns of diamonds framed by intricate borders of crosshatches.

"It's a masi," I say, grateful for something to talk about. "I got it during our family trip to Fiji. It's made from tree bark, isn't that cool? They soak the bark, then pound it until it's soft enough to turn into cloth."

"That's fascinating. I've never even been out of the country. Was it a good vacation?"

"Oh yeah." I pull a photo album from my bookshelf. "I actually have some photos here. Want to see?"

"Sure. You have them in print?"

"I like physical copies."

I sit down and he scoots over, his shoulder rubbing against mine. He doesn't pull back, so I don't, either, and I take the chance to breath in the warm, clean scent of his cotton shirt. He makes all the appropriate noises of interest when I show him our luxury resort, over-the-top breakfasts, and translucent water, until I flip to a new page. There's me lying in the sand, and my thighs are smooth, which is great, but a random guy (Alex? Adam?) is lying next to me, which is not that great.

Out of reflex, I flip to the next page. More Alexes grin at me. Blood rushes to my face and I snap the album shut.

"It's okay. I didn't see that," Sean says calmly beside me.

I stand up. "This isn't interesting to see. I mean, Fiji is just an island . . . with lots of water surrounding it."

He nods. "Yeah, I believe that's the definition of an island." I don't miss the teasing glint in his eyes, which reminds me of the lagoons in Fiji under an overcast sky. "We could look at something else?"

"I could show you the one where I went to cheerleading camp?"

"That's something I've got to see."

My fingers pause over the album. For sure there were no guys there.

Wait. Madison's then-boyfriend visited and brought a friend, who hit it right off with me. It was strictly platonic, of course, but it might not look innocent on film. Maybe the photos I took back in the days of St. Margaret's would be fine. It's a private girls' school after all.

No. We had dances with St. John's.

I sigh.

"Not safe either?" Sean asks from the floor. It's impossible to tell if he's more turned off or amused.

I drop down beside him, folding my legs underneath me. "Look. I need to be honest with you." I knit my fingers together.

"I have a lot of friends, and at least half of them are guys. They're just friends."

"Hey, it's okay. You don't need to explain."

"All that is BS to me," I say, scanning his face. *"Before Sean."*

He gazes at me, then his face breaks into a grin. Relief blooms in my chest. "You have a cool life, I'm not judging you."

He stands up and wanders around my room, stopping to glance at a few snapshots lining my shelves. Seven-year-old me in a tutu. Eight years old, clutching the reins of my favorite horse, Sammy. Ten, in baggy black sweatpants from my hip-hop phase (a style choice I've never revisited). Middle school violin and fencing, where I lasted all of six months before giving them both up. None of it stuck. I have tried everything under the sun yet somehow ended up feeling no closer to figuring out what I'm good at.

"You have so many talents," Sean says. "And no surprise there, you were a cute kid. Seems like you've been beautiful all your life."

"That's actually my one and only talent," I say without thinking. It's a joke, but also true. Aside from applying nail polish with my left hand, there isn't much else I've mastered. My brother, Jeremy, once told me that with me what you see is what you get, since my face is the only thing worth mentioning about me. Wanting to direct the attention from myself, I swallow. "I bet you've been beautiful all your life too."

"Not really. I was a scrawny kid in middle school and wore braces."

I refrain from telling him that even if he had them now, I'd still totally kiss him.

My bookshelf is crammed with magazines I started collecting when I was younger. Even with influencers dominating the scene now, there's something about glossy pages that I can't let go of. When

I try to stick my photo album of Fiji back into place, a leather-bound scrapbook tumbles to the floor. A couple of buttons roll out.

"What's that?"

Picking up the buttons, I hide my face behind my hair. "It's silly. It's kind of a fake magazine I put together when I was little."

"Can I see?"

Why Sean's interested is beyond me, but I hand over my scrapbook. Let's just get it over with. He'll make polite comments and I'll joke and deflect. He unbinds the leather wrap, and my face heats like he's undressing me.

The pages are brittle with age, yellowed around the edges. Swatches of fabric are taped in crooked rows, alongside magazine cutouts of haute couture dresses. Three whole pages are dedicated to buttons, glued on in messy clusters. My childish handwriting fills the blank spaces with commentary—*Fabulous!* or *Efferevansce!* (an enthusiastic attempt at *effervescence*, apparently) or *Don't know what to think about this yet!*

There's even an entire section devoted to Met Gala events. Next to each outfit, I'd scribbled critiques on how it could improve—*Lose the necklace* or *Different hairdo, please*—followed by snide remarks and analogies only a younger me would think were clever.

Next to one particularly unfortunate white dress with embroidered green patches, I wrote *Toast with mold???*

Sean laughs at that one. He flips through the pages gingerly and smooths a crease.

"I like fashion," I offer as an explanation.

"Yeah, I wanted to ask you at the coffee shop. Is that what you want to be, a designer?"

"Oh, no, I'm not that talented. I can't even draw. I'm more interested in, you know, fashion trends and cultural influences. Things like what works and why. Why are some things classic while others go out of style? What do people's outfits say about them?" *Also, why does Sean only wear neutrals and still look incredible?* "That sort of thing."

He rubs his chin with his thumb. "I've never thought of any those questions before."

"The spare buttons come with the clothes I buy, so I collect them." I open my palm to let him see. "These are flat buttons. You usually find them on dress shirts. They seem insignificant, totally interchangeable, but they're not. A plastic one with the wrong depth can cheapen a look instantly, but switch it to a high-shine mother-of-pearl one? Timeless. It's a detail that people don't think about, but they feel it. And that's not even getting into jeans studs or toggles."

I catch myself. This is a guy who'll go on to build a rocket for NASA, while I'm here obsessing about *buttons*? How much more frivolous can I get?

"Anyway." I force a laugh, then slip the buttons back into the scrapbook, close it, and set it aside. Then I settle back down on the bed next to him, but look at the crystal knobs on my closet doors.

"Very cool," Sean says. I check to see if he's being sincere. "No, really. I'm not that interested in buttons, but I like hearing you talk about them."

No teasing glint, no smirk. His eyes are kind.

I turn the music down and we keep talking. When the playlist reaches its end, he stretches his arms over his head and says, "I'm getting déjà vu."

"How so?"

"This is the second night we've ended up sitting together in a bedroom."

Without knowing why, my lips curl into a smile. My cheeks tingle as I try to control it.

"What's so funny?" Sean asks.

"I'm just . . ." I peer at him through my lashes. "I'm happy. I've wanted this since forever, to talk to you, and tonight is one of the best nights of my life."

His eyes soften. "Flora—"

"You know how you can have a crush on someone, but when you get a chance to know them better, it feels wrong? Like, *what did I ever see in them?* But sometimes, they turn out even better than you imagined, and you want to freeze that moment and relive it over and over again? I'm really happy now. Thanks for keeping me company."

In movies there's always a climax leading up to a kiss. Maybe it's a heated argument, or a reunion after a long time apart, or that perfect ending moment when the saxophone swells, snow starts to fall, birds sing, and you know everything is going to be okay.

In my case, it just happens.

He moves in closer, I shut my eyes, and the kiss falls into place.

It feels right. *Destined.* I've imagined kissing Sean Foster many times in my head, but every version was wrong. It's so much better in reality. Intoxicating and warm and devastating and firm and soft and tasty and all the good stuff thrown together. His kiss reminds me of cotton candy and mint and starlight and the first ray of sunshine, like spring and summer rolled into one.

Before I know it, we're on the bed and I'm on top, his chest muscles taut beneath me. Despite the part of me that is getting carried away, part of my stunned brain is running a news report about the fact that it happened. Sean Foster *kissed* me. Sean Foster is *still* kissing me.

I've kissed boys before, but this is on an entirely different level. He knows how to do this.

"Wait," he says, pushing me away.

"What? What's wrong?"

He reaches behind him, fumbles around, and pulls out a high heel. The velvet shoe I tried on before going to the party. He holds it up, scrunching up his nose. "I can't concentrate with this digging into my back."

I snatch it from him and toss it to the floor. With a playful shove, I push him back on the bed, and that's when we both break into laughter. His body trembles as he wraps me in a hug. I bury my face against his chest, drowning in mortification but also giddy excitement.

When the laughter dies down, he brushes my hair away from my forehead and lifts his face to find my mouth again. This time, without the distraction of my shoe, it's heaven. Sean might be reserved on the outside, but his kisses aren't. We continue, stretching it out for as long as possible, and he keeps his hands above my waist.

When we finally stop, both of us breathless, I gasp, "You're the best kisser *ever.*"

"Hmm. Was it a tough competition?" He squints at me then smiles, and my heart kicks into a gallop. He seemed so serious at first glance, and now the contrast is amazing. I've cracked open an ice door to find a garden blooming.

Sean is my Wonderland, and I've tumbled down the rabbit hole. It's a long, hard fall, and there's no way I can climb back up again.

CHAPTER FOUR

Sean

Sunday brunch with my family has been a tradition for as long as I can remember. Every other weekend, after paycheck Friday, we squeeze into the same sticky booth by the window at our usual hole-in-the-wall breakfast spot, where the scent of warm maple syrup and spiced chorizo hangs in the air. The menu never changes. I typically refill my coffee at least three times to hype myself up for the day ahead, which is usually a combination of working out with Jake, two tutoring sessions, and catching up on any studying I feel shaky on from the week before.

Today, I might need four cups.

My lips still tingle with the feel of hers. It's ten in the morning. I wonder if she sleeps in.

"You came home after midnight two nights in a row," my mom says. Her tone is calm, more of an observation than a lecture. If anything, she's usually telling me I study too hard.

"It's just back-to-school stuff. You know how it is."

"Make sure you're getting enough rest." Dad flips through the menu, like he's ever going to order something other than the frittata with extra salsa. "You look tired."

"He's just ugly," my kid sister, Lindsey, says, and my mom reprimands her. Middle schoolers are insufferable.

Grandpa, across from me, stirs cream into his coffee. When Grandma passed five years ago, he left Massachusetts for Washington, trading New England snowstorms for the endless gray skies of the Pacific Northwest. His eyes flick to me over the rim of his mug. He never misses much. "Anything good happen this week?"

Making out with Flora on her bed for hours while losing every last scrap of self-control I thought I had. I stare at the worn wood grain of the table. "Made a lot of three-pointers at practice."

"Lame," Lindsey says, practically bouncing in her seat. "I got first place in the regional creative writing contest!"

"Well deserved." Mom ruffles her hair, even though we've known since the night she found out, and she hasn't stopped reminding us. Dad joins in with more praise, and Lindsey launches into an info dump of her world-building. I tune her out after elf politics come into play. To be fair, I read the story and it's good, just not *hear about it three times* good.

Text her. I never touch my phone during family time, but then again, I've never been kissed like that before either. What the sorcery, really.

Under the table, I scroll through Flora's Instagram. She has 8,946 followers. She posts almost daily, and I can't even reach the bottom of her feed. Every post is greeted with at least a hundred comments. The latest pictures are from the bonfire last night, where she was glowing. Before that, a mix of lake house photos, luxe lunch spots, European vacation highlights. Capri. Côte d'Azur. I was spot on when I told her she has a glamorous lifestyle.

Madison, Josie, and Carmen are in most of them, plus a revolving door of new faces. She wasn't lying. She has enough friends to build an army.

Raymond Corbett makes frequent appearances too. There are

pictures of them attending some fancy black-tie event, and even a couple of them on a . . . *yacht*? Her hair whips in the wind and her sun-kissed skin is flawless.

And then I see it.

A photo from summer. Cheerleading camp and basketball practice before school started. Flora and me, standing together, her in her cheer uniform, me drenched in sweat, a basketball tucked under my arm. I forgot this existed.

"Addicted to your phone much?"

I flinch. Lindsey leans over and tries to pry it from my hand.

"Cut it out." I pull back, but not fast enough.

"Oh my god. Are you thirsting over a girl right now?"

"Lindsey, seriously, back off."

Too late. She lunges again, and in the struggle her thumb double taps the screen. A bright red heart pops up.

I freeze.

"Oh no," Lindsey says gleefully. "What now, should I unlike it?"

I yank my phone back, my face flaming.

Grinning, she pulls out her own phone and wastes no time searching Flora's handle, then, like a traitor, turns it to the group. The adults merrily peruse Flora's feed and bond over my agony. Mom seems particularly impressed by a rose-colored drink at a café where Flora was biting into a croissant.

"Stunning girl," she says. "Is she a friend from school? Wait, Josie's in this one."

I shift in my seat. "Yeah, we're all friends. We've been hanging out a little, that's all."

"You're hanging out with people in a different tax bracket now?" Grandpa chuckles.

"Et tu, Grandpa?"

Dad, without missing a beat, lowers his voice into a deep narrator tone. "And on this day, Sean vowed never to play with his device in the presence of his meddlesome family again."

Lindsey snorts, always appreciative of Dad's humor. "I wonder what filter she uses. Her skin looks perfect."

"That's exactly how she looks." A lie. If anything, the pictures don't do her justice. They don't capture how the light shifts in her hazel eyes and the sound of her laugh.

Our food arrives.

"Phones away. Time to eat," Dad says, snapping his napkin across his lap. He reaches for the hot sauce while Mom passes out forks and knives.

With how many followers Flora has, my accidental Like will drown in a flood of notifications.

I pull my plate toward me. My phone buzzes in my pocket.

Ignore it. But my heart's already racing.

Five minutes. Wait five minutes and—

"Be right back." I slide out of the booth and head to the bathroom, ducking behind the corner to check my phone.

Flora: *Stalker*

Thumbs flying, I type: *Who's the mysterious heartthrob next to you?*

The reply is almost instant.

Flora: *He's an incredible kisser too. Can't wait to see you again. Can we hang out?*

The corner of my mouth twitches. I lean against the wall, typing. *I want to see you too. I can't today, but we have a practice game tomorrow after school. Come see me? We can get dinner after.*

Flora: *I'll be there. See you at school*

Sure. Enjoy your day. I hesitate for a second. Then I type one last message: *P.S. You're a cute button.*

She hearts my message, and I slide my phone back into my pocket and head back to the table. My eggs are cold by now, but I don't care.

CHAPTER FIVE

Flora

There's no cheerleading on Mondays, which works out perfectly. I drag Carmen to the bleachers after school. Varsity basketball practices are usually closed, but today they're running a mock game in which they split into two teams and play against each other. Madison and Josie couldn't be less interested.

Fifteen minutes in, Carmen drops the polite pretense of watching and dives into her book. Emily Brontë—for fun! It's not even an assignment. She deserves no less than a guy who'll write her love letters with a quill and seal them with wax. On the court, Dylan passes to Sean, and he barely catches it. I smile at the way he fumbles, but then he shoots and scores. He casts a glance my way, and I wave.

Carmen finishes a chapter and closes the book on her lap. "I'm so happy for you with the way things turned out."

"I texted Mads to say we kissed, and she had to ask who I was referring to. Unbelievable!"

Carmen's curly dark hair bounces when she laughs. I take out a box of Pocky from my leather backpack and hand her a stick. "Did you do anything fun yesterday?"

"I typed up an editorial for the school paper. You?"

"Went to the mall with Charles. You know, my friend who lives in Portland?"

She nods, taking a bite. "Okay. But I thought you and Sean—"

"Oh, it wasn't a date. With Charles. He's in town and wanted to hang." I point my chin at the basketball court. "*This*—is a date."

She sighs good-naturedly. "Yet here I am."

"Because you're the best!" I link my arm with hers and rest my head on her shoulder. "I can't sit through the whole game alone in silence. You're a saint for putting up with me."

"Hey, you were the nicest person to me when I transferred from Louisiana," Carmen says. "If I can be here for you and watch Sean miss his free throws, I'm all in."

I laugh and nudge her with my elbow. When the game ends, Sean heads straight for me. His jersey, WOLVERINES stitched across the chest, sticks to his body with sweat. He pushes his damp hair from his eyes. "Hey, Carmen," he says, polite as always, then smiles at me. "Thanks for waiting. Can you give me thirteen more minutes to shower and change?"

"So precise," I say. "I'll time you."

Carmen bolts up as soon as Sean disappears to the locker room. "Great, my shift is over." Grabbing her stuff from the seat, she winks at me before leaving me alone on the bleachers.

I've watched Sean play basketball eight billion times, and he never so much as glimpses my way. Now I'm the only person left in the gym, waiting under the structural metal beams, waiting for Sean because he *wants* me to. I apply a fresh coat of lip gloss and forget to time him.

My phone vibrates, and Ray's text pops up. *Fort Sean crumbled in 24 hours? Wild. You spent two years laying siege, and it turns out the gates were unlocked the whole time. One good push and he's in your bed.*

Before I can think of a snappy reply, Sean comes back out in black joggers, hair still damp at the edges, and we leave together to get food. He picks the fast-food joint near our school, and I watch him wolf down his fries. So adorable. He seems pleased with the meal, like he's having a bowl of truffle soup at Guy Savoy.

"What do you want to do later?" I ask.

"See a movie?"

"Ray says there's nothing worth watching aside from the Fincher one, and I saw it with him already." As a certified movie buff, of course Raymond refers to movies by the director.

"Oh, okay." Sean's eyebrows rise briefly. Then he chews on a fry. "How about the Viewpoint, then?"

"Absolutely yes!" He means the park up on that steep hill, the one with an unobstructed view of downtown. There are always tourists and locals snapping selfies up there, but in high-school boy code, it's where guys go hoping to make out under the pretense of stargazing. The only sight they're interested in checking out is a bra.

I find comfort in the predictability of it. It's nice to be desired.

On the way up, Sean stops to get coffee for himself and a caramel latte for me. When we reach the parking lot, snippets of lights pierce the bushes, but there are cars all around. The smell of weed is almost stronger than the pine needles. Not the most romantic, but okay. Sean kills the engine and leans over, and I wait for him to cup my face and kiss me, but he grabs the door handle and pushes open the door on my side.

We're not making out in the car?

He rounds the car and holds out his hand, and I take it. "I know a better spot, but we have to walk," he says. In a daze, I let him lead me away from the crowded lookout point. We do a five-minute hike uphill.

The trail opens up. The trees clear and an illuminated night landscape stretches out beneath us. A sprawling sea of lights sparkles like Swarovski crystals. Ruby red, amber orange, emerald green, and amethyst purple gems dot the darkened land, flickering like flames. The lights take it in turns to breathe.

"Spectacular," I say.

"Right?"

We watch the city in silence. Faint laughter drifts through the air in the distance. The night breeze is gentle as satin, whispering secrets as it stirs my hair. Sean sits down first, then tugs on my hand and pulls me down beside him. I sip my drink, eyes on the lights reflecting off the water around the bay. I smell the sea, and I also smell the pleasant scent of his skin. He reminds me of clean laundry and fresh air.

He catches my eyes, and his gaze falls on my lips before he turns away. "We're so lucky with the weather."

"Yeah, and you can kiss me already. Skip the small talk."

"Oh, I have to. At least for five minutes. It's common courtesy."

I laugh.

"Seriously, though. I like talking to you." He brushes my hair with his fingers. "You're witty. Your sense of humor is the sexiest thing about you."

I'm a girl who's been called beautiful all her life. I'm used to getting daily reminders about how my nose is too flawless to be real, but here's this perfect guy who sees beyond that, who thinks I'm *witty*. A warm glow expands in me, and it's not the caramel latte settling in my stomach.

My phone lights up with a message. "Josie wants to know how our date is going," I say. "What should I tell her?"

"She texted me, too, when I was getting us coffee. I said it's going really well." He bumps his shoulder with mine lightly. "You better tell her the same thing to keep our stories straight, button."

This guy. This guy totally made out with me, gave me a nickname, and now grins at me like we're in on some inside joke together.

"I'm going to say it's even better than I expected," I say.

"She's always telling me to get to know you."

"Really?" *Thank you, dear Josie.* She claims she doesn't want to play matchmaker, but she put in a good word for me after all.

"Yeah, she thinks you're great. That day you offered to help create an image for her band? That was the highlight of her freshman year."

Josie's band is awesome, but they lacked something to connect the group visually. These days, it's all about branding. Since they're called Fishnets, I bought fishnet accessories for everyone—tights, long black gloves, scarves, and wraps—and threw in a crash course on basic makeup. Not that I didn't have an ulterior motive.

"I have a confession to make," I say. "This was two years ago. After I'd known Josie for a few weeks and felt the friendship was solid, I said something like, 'Josie, you know how much I value your friendship, right? You're a wonderful person and I'll never regret this,' and she's like, 'Are you breaking up with me?' and I'm like, 'I want you to know what we have is real.'

"I told her that I noticed her because she's friends with you. But that was just in the very, *very* beginning. I said to her, 'Once I got to know you, I can't *not* be your friend. And Mads adores you too.' I threw in Madison to make this friendship more appetizing, although Mads would never say she adores anyone in a million years."

Sean laughs. "I bet Josie took it well. She never said anything to me."

"Yeah, she was superchill about it. She admitted she wanted a free makeup tutorial, too, in the beginning, so we're even. And to be fair, I never bug her about you. Everything's on a need-to-know basis."

Some girls get a sense of pride when they give guys a boner, which I completely understand. I get my pride from seeing Sean laughing with his eyes bright. He pulls me close.

"I should've asked you out sooner," he says. "You're so interesting and easy to be around. I can listen to you talk for hours."

If my life were a movie, this would be the part where I realize things can't possibly go this smoothly. Something bad is bound to happen, otherwise how are they supposed to fill ninety more minutes?

But this is my life, so I snuggle against Sean's jacket and savor the touch of his hand on my upper arm. And then we totally make out. I figure I've earned it.

* * *

After the Viewpoint date, the next two weeks fly by. Sean and I spend every spare second catching each other between classes and after school, and squeeze in as many kisses as possible. Each one makes it a little harder to let him go. We couldn't hang out as much as I wanted since he has a packed schedule, but he made his best effort. When he wasn't available, he sent the dorkiest texts to make up for it.

Exhibit A:
Sean: *Here's a biology fun fact: no two Holstein cows have the same spot patterns. They're unique, like snowflakes and fingerprints*
Sean: *You're my Holstein's spot because you're one and only*

Swoon.
On the plus side, my parents are finally spending more time at

home after their product launch, and Jeremy's back for the weekend. This evening we're all in the family room, a rare sight in the Morgan household. My parents are on the sectional with me, and my brother is hunched over his phone, tapping away.

"Are you doing well at school, Jer?" my dad asks, a Kindle in hand and a glass of Cabernet Sauvignon on the coffee table. Every so often he stops to highlight a sentence.

Jeremy barely looks up. "Uh-huh. Fantastic."

"And you, sweetheart?" My mom is swiping through emails on her company phone, deleting one after another. Despite the tired redness in her eyes, she still manages a smile. "How's your dating life? How's Sean?"

"He's dreamy. He tells me everything—what he's been up to, what his calls are about if he answers in front of me. I never have to wonder where he is, he doesn't disappear for hours without responding. And if he's driving and a text comes in, he asks me to read it for him. It's like he has no secrets."

"I love that." My mom nods. "Reliability is undervalued these days. Your father's the same. He tells me everything, sometimes more than I need to hear. Honestly, there are moments I wouldn't mind a little silence."

"But I want to tell you!" my dad says.

"He studies a lot, though," I add. "He says normal people don't have time to date on weekdays. He volunteers to tutor online, but he also takes on loads of paid sessions to save for college."

Sean is, technically, not under desperate financial pressure. Sure, he may think Great Wolf Lodge is peak luxury and a Costco run counts as "splurging," but his parents have solid jobs, nonprofit admin and city maintenance management. He just likes to help out where he can. Save for a decent laptop, cover some tuition, and, occasionally, a preppy shirt that makes him look like he summers somewhere.

"Good thing we've got you covered," my dad says, but he doesn't ask me where I want to go to school, which is just as well because I have no idea. It's always been the same—Jeremy, the obvious prodigy with his ironclad career goals, and then there's me.

Growing up, my mom wanted me to feel comfortable, to blend in, and maybe that's why I always feel like I'm supposed to be fine, like they don't need to worry about me because I'll figure it out eventually.

My mom sets her phone on the coffee table with a resolute thud, a sign she's decided not to check her emails anymore.

"We had an interesting meeting this morning." She picks up my dad's glass and takes a sip, frowns, and sets it back down in favor of her own mug of genmaicha. "We were reevaluating how to streamline our mentorship program. The issue is that some mentees struggle with relationship building and effective communication. Typically, we match them with someone higher up the ladder— ideally, someone who's done the same role before—to help them navigate challenges through firsthand experience."

My dad lowers his Kindle, already engaged. They love talking to each other, and work-related topics rank high on the list, right up there with strategizing ways to maximize our passive income.

"That makes sense," he says. "I tend to connect high-potential talent from our affiliates with global counterparts in the same function. It sharpens their technical skills and expands their network at the same time."

"True, but that can lead to siloed thinking," my mom counters, rubbing the bridge of her nose. "Sometimes pairing someone in a technical role with a managerial role offers a fresh, outside perspective."

"But there's a risk." Jeremy cuts in from the leather swivel chair, eyes still on his phone. "Someone from the commercial side won't always grasp the nuances of a medical role, and that disconnect makes the mentorship ineffective."

He's such a smart-ass.

"Good point there, Jerry," my mom says, and I wish I'd come up with that myself. They continue the debate for a while, making valid arguments as smart people of this family.

No one asks my opinion.

"Is this mentor-mentee thing set in stone?" I say finally. "You all make it sound like an arranged marriage, but it should be like speed dating—let mentees talk to several mentors and see where the chemistry is. There's no guarantee that you'll match with someone of the same function, sometimes opposites attract. People will only be willing to share when they like each other."

My mom laughs, and Jeremy snorts under his breath. "Morganite, is dating all you think about?"

"That's certainly an unconventional perspective. Very interesting," my dad says in that *I'm a professional marketer and I'll humor you* tone of his, the one he uses when he hears something stupid.

"I just remembered I have to finish a paper." A sharp sting creeps behind my eyes. I get up before anyone can say anything else and head to my room to call Sean.

*　*　*

Sean picks up on the second ring. "Hey."

"What are you doing?" Two weeks ago, I never would've imagined calling him whenever and basking in the certainty that he wouldn't mind. Sean would get it. He'd laugh at my speed-dating idea, but in that kind, amused, *you're smarter than people give you credit for* kind of way.

"Doing my math homework. Is everything okay?"

"Yeah, just needed to hear your voice."

A pause. "How are your parents? You finally getting some quality time together?"

"Wait till you hear this. They're—" Now that the perfect opening is here, the words snag on the edge of my throat. "We're hanging out at home. It's nice having them back."

What's the point? As far as Sean knows, my mom's a powerhouse, climbing the corporate ladder faster than anyone else, a feat made even harder by the fact she's a woman of color, and my dad's the youngest VP in company history. They're everything success looks like on paper. Honestly, Sean would fit right in. The four of them could chat Ivy Leagues all day and pat each other on the back.

"I know how much you miss them," Sean says. "Were you going to say something?"

He might pity me, which is even worse. "We're going to this restaurant tomorrow that's usually booked out months in advance. I'll tell you all about it."

"Please do. Hey, I want to ask you something." He stalls, and inhales on the other end. "Want to go to the homecoming dance with me?"

I can't help but smile, my eyelids already lighter. How sublime it is to be wanted. I drop my voice and try to sound as grave as possible. "Cutting it close, Foster? It's two weeks until homecoming. I'm usually booked out months in advance too."

"Oh." Even without the visual, I can hear the disappointment. "Sure, if there's no way, I get it. I just—I really want to go with you."

"Of *course* I'll go with you! I'd be so heartbroken if you didn't ask. But I thought dances weren't your thing?"

Sean laughs. "Until now, there wasn't anyone I wanted to dance with."

I sink into my pillow, close my eyes, and sigh. If I could travel back in time, I'd tell freshman me to dream big, aim for the stars, floss your teeth, eat your vegetables, and everything will be all right. One day, Sean Foster will take you to homecoming.

My phone buzzes. "Wait, I'm getting another call. It's Raymond. I'll call him back later."

"No, it's okay," Sean says. "Take it. I should probably get back to my homework."

We say a hurried bye, and I swipe to answer Ray's call.

"Ah, hello there," he says in a fake noble accent that lands somewhere between aristocrat and total nonsense. "Let me guess, family night went like running naked through a cactus field?"

"What gave it away?"

"Intuition. Jeremy is home, and sixty percent of the time, he pisses you off every time." He quotes *Anchorman*.

Here's someone who doesn't need the backstory of the Morgan family saga, but I give him a quick rundown anyway.

"Poor little rich girl," he says. "At least your parents *like* each other. The more mine try to demolish each other, the bigger the house gets. It's like every screaming match adds a bathroom."

When Ray's parents yell at each other and, on occasion, fling plates across the formal dining room, he hides in his room and gets stoned. His current house is the third one I've seen him in.

"Poor little rich boy. At least you're an only child. No one to benchmark against. You can smoke pot and binge movies all day and still be the golden child." Movies are about as useless a hobby as fashion. Every year we watch the Oscars together (despite being appalled at the nominees), and boo the screen and chuck popcorn from his vintage popcorn machine at it.

"Golden child? Please, more like a hot potato with trust issues. Plus, neither of my parents have the slimmest idea of what a movie is. They probably think a montage is a fancy French cheese. At least your mom takes you to runway shows. Mine just takes me to family court."

We trade digs back and forth, and I say, "Fine. I'll let you take first place for most disappointing offspring to high-achieving parents."

"Happy to share the stage. Think of the speeches we'd give. Real tearjerkers. 'I'd like to thank my family for setting the bar so high I need oxygen tanks to reach it.'"

"And the crowd goes *wild*."

Ray snickers on the other end in that familiar way of his. Then he says, "What does Sir Seanathan think of all this?"

"Obviously that I'm this sophisticated girl who's traveled the five continents and always has a story ready, straight from a perfect family."

"Ah. So he doesn't know. *Shocking*."

"That's a twentieth-date topic. Besides, he doesn't have patience for people who complain, especially not when he's the one counting every dollar in his college fund."

I'm already so lucky, and I want him to admire my family as much as I do.

"Fair enough. Gotta be careful with these plebeians and their coupon-collecting egos," Raymond says, but his tone is not unkind. "Well, if you ever need to air out the dirty laundry, you know where to find me."

CHAPTER SIX

Sean

Flora is thirty-seven minutes late, somewhere between the margins of "running behind" and "completely bailed." It's homecoming night, and, naturally, my car is in the shop. She offered to pick me up.

I smooth the collar of my shirt and adjust the cuffs of my blazer. It wouldn't be so bad if I was waiting alone, but Lindsey is staring at the door, convinced that I'm bluffing about the "goddess from Instagram" being my date.

"She stood you up."

"She'll be here."

"Text her!"

"I'm not texting while she's driving."

When the doorbell finally rings, Lindsey's head snaps around so fast it's a miracle she doesn't sprain her neck. Through the window, Flora's silver car gleams in the driveway.

"She drives a *Mercedes*?"

Before I can answer, Lindsey shoves past me and yanks open the door.

Flora stands there in a green dress, radiant in a way that makes my front porch brighter. Her eyes, somehow larger than usual, catch the light, and today they're golden brown. With a wide smile she extends a hand to my sister. "Hi! Lindsey, right? I'm Flora."

Lindsey gapes.

"I've been dying to meet you." Flora's smile doesn't waver. "Sean told me you're in eighth grade?" They shake hands, and then Flora's eyes find mine.

I don't even like dances, but Flora makes it feel like maybe I could. I can't resist her even though my instinct tells me she's more than I can handle. My heart reacts to her like francium—unstable, volatile, and probably ready to explode.

I should be thinking about homework. Basketball drills. Anything else. But here I am, caught in the orbit of someone who's all shine and chaos. And her tanned legs are going to mess up my physics exams.

"Hi," she half whispers, like we're sharing some secret no one else could understand. Her eyes are half teasing, half innocent, like saying, *You have no idea what you're in for.*

That does *not* help.

"You look incredible," I say.

"Let me give you a tour!" Lindsey says, as if there's anything remotely worth showing around our house, unless Flora's conducting field research on the banality of middle-class charm in its most average form.

"I'd love that," Flora says, "but let me say hi to your parents first."

With that, Lindsey seizes her hand and drags her to the backyard. As a weekend ritual, my parents are grilling hamburgers. Dad looks up from the grill, wiping sweat off his forehead with the back of his hand, while Mom stirs a pitcher of lemonade at the table. Flora introduces herself. "You have such a beautiful house. It's so homey, and I love the art collage on your wall."

"Thank you, we add to it bit by bit over the years," Mom says. "It's so fun watching it grow. Are you excited for the dance?"

"Yes, especially because I'm going with Sean." Flora flashes a quick glance in my direction, and my heart takes off. "I'm sorry for being late, by the way. Traffic was worse than I expected."

Dad pauses midflip at the grill. "It happens. Friday nights can be brutal around here. Sean mentioned you live in that tall glass building near the interstate?"

Flora nods. "Yeah, the one shaped like a crystal. My parents call it the Shard, after the one in London."

"The lighting must be gorgeous," Mom says. "We remember when they first started building. It even made the news for bringing luxury high-rises to the suburbs."

They don't mention how those conversations always ended with *What kind of people can afford living there?* and I don't tell them I kissed Flora in her bedroom, and how it's the only place in the house that looks lived in, like all the warmth in the universe has been drawn in and condensed into that one small space.

"Well, the view is nice," Flora agrees. "But I love your sunroom, and this backyard is amazing! The smoke detector went crazy the one time my mom tried to cook frozen potstickers in our apartment. We don't get to have outdoor dinners like this."

"Did you get a chance to eat before coming over?" Dad asks. "Anyone feel like having a burger?"

"I'll have one!" Flora says without hesitation.

To my horror, my dad slaps a patty into a bun and hands it over with the barbecue clamps. Grease glistens on the surface as Flora reaches for it.

"Let me get you a plate." Her dress is way too nice for this.

She shakes her head. "Burgers are to be enjoyed with hands." With that, she takes a bite and munches. "Hey, Mr. Foster?"

"Yeah?"

"This burger." She points at it. "Is *out of this world*. I'm serious, this is really, *really* good."

"I know what I'm doing," Dad says over the smoke.

Flora's eyes flick over the bags of buns left. We're fully stacked. "Would it be greedy if I had another?"

"You can have as many as you want." Dad is already making her another.

Flora smiles at my mom. "Did you know Sean is at the top of our class? You must be so proud of him."

"We never have to worry about his grades, that's for sure." Mom pours her a cup of lemonade.

"And it's not just that he's smart, he's so nice about it too." Flora takes a sip. "*Delicious*. He explains things in a way that just clicks, and you wonder if it's always been that simple. Not to mention he's generous with encouragement and makes you feel good about yourself."

Heat crawls up my neck. "If you can't explain it simply, you don't understand it well enough." I quote Einstein as I accept the half-finished burger she hands me.

"Show-off." She winks at me. "My brother, Jeremy, is brilliant, but it's different. He has this way of making you feel stupid for not getting it fast enough. If I don't understand something in three seconds, he lets out this exasperated, dramatic sigh. It's so frustrating."

"That's *totally* how Sean acts around me," Lindsey says, and everyone chuckles.

We're the type of family that shops at Walmart and eats macaroni and cheese in front of the TV. Flora stands in our backyard, holding a paper napkin and a cup of lemonade, but it's as if a supernova has landed. My parents laugh at everything she says.

Lindsey gushes nonstop over her dress and makeup, and then somehow feels compelled to ask if she can touch Flora's purse.

Flora slides the strap off her shoulder and holds it out to Lindsey, who turns the tiny thing over in her hand like it's a baby bird. Her index finger brushes against the golden logo, one letter at a time, spelling it out. P-R-A-D-A. "This is the most beautiful thing I've ever seen." Lindsey sighs. "Can I look inside?"

Unbelievable. "For real, Lindsey?" I say.

"Absolutely!" Flora opens the clasp.

"Oh my god!" Lindsey squeals. I pray she won't pull out a condom in front of my parents. "Is this the new YSL lipstick? The limited edition?"

"Good spot."

"My friends and I are *dying* to get one, but it's sold out everywhere. Where did you get yours?"

"You know what?" Flora says, noticing the way Lindsey's fingers are still wrapped around the tube. "You can have it."

"Seriously?"

"Linz." Mom frowns. "Don't be rude."

"Honestly, Mrs. Foster, this color doesn't quite work on me," Flora says, then examines Lindsey's face. "Your skin tone is just right. You're doing me a favor if you put it to good use. Scrape off the end and it's good as new."

The last thing Lindsey needs is more encouragement. "Can you please come up to my room to check out my makeup collection?"

"I'd love to." Flora checks the time. "But I want to give you my full attention, and we're short on time now. How about the next time I'm over?"

A polite dodge. Lindsey is delusional if she thinks Flora has an ounce of interest in her measly middle-school collection.

"How about—" Flora taps on her phone. "Next Saturday afternoon? Wait, early afternoon. I'll get your number from Sean, and meanwhile I'll send you some influencers you must follow."

Lindsey nods like she might self-combust. Before we leave, out of nowhere, Dad pipes up. "Hey, let's get a photo together before you go."

I cringe. This isn't my first time trick-or-treating. "Dad, you're not making me look cool right now."

"Oh my god, we *have* to!" Flora says. "Can you take one with my phone too? And one with Lindsey?" She tugs on my arm and leads me to where Dad instructs, right by the masonry fireplace, then tilts her head to lean against my shoulder. The heat of her seeps through my sleeve.

She glances up at me and smiles before turning back to the camera.

I'm suddenly glad we took that photo.

* * *

After we're seated in her Mercedes, Flora drops her head back against the headrest and lets out a long breath. "That went okay, right? I was supernervous."

"Are you kidding? You made that look way too easy," I say.

"Hey, meeting my crush's family for the first time is nerve-racking, all right?" She turns and smiles. "But I'm glad I got to meet them. They're all so nice."

"Lindsey is a little brat."

"I like her."

It's already an hour and a half into the dance. "Sorry that took so long."

"No worries. Sorry I was late too. Ray was being dramatic about something, and then someone else came over. Not important. Let's go."

Flora steps on the pedal hard, and we thrust forward before I have time to dwell on whether "someone" is another guy. My seat belt locks, and I almost hear my neck snap. At the next red light, we screech to a halt at the last second.

"Whoa. Where did you get your driver's license?"

"What makes you think I have one?" Her grin is all mischief. "Kidding. I'm fully licensed and *extremely* skilled. What's the fun in driving if you can't speed a little? I bought my car for the gas pedal."

"You mean the engine."

"Yes. Can you feel it?" She guns it again, then lifts a hand, voice dropping dramatically. *"Quality."*

I laugh. "Yeah, and I have the spinal cord injury to prove it."

She chuckles and eases off the gas. The streetlights streak across her face, catching the gold in her eyes and the way her dark hair cascades over her shoulder. The world outside moves fast, but a strange calm settles over me. She's poised but reckless, thoughtful and daring all at once.

And she's with me.

* * *

The gym reeks of floor wax and punch, and a haze of cheap cologne hits every time someone brushes past. Music thumps through the speakers. After Flora greets what feels like half the junior class, she slides her arms around my neck. She smells like jasmine. The music shifts to something slower, and we fall into a lazy rhythm, ignoring the beat. Her hair tickles my face.

I never knew that dances could be this interesting.

"Do you know *everyone*?" I ask after yet another person stops by to say hi. We sidestep under a drooping strand of string lights.

"Most of them. Don't you?" She laughs, her face painted pink and purple by the lighting. "Aren't you kind of popular?"

"Not really. I have about three friends and that's it."

She tilts her head, eyes sparkling. "That's exactly what a popular person would say."

When we swing by the pink balloon arch by the entrance, Dylan and his on-again, off-again girlfriend, Sydney, spot us. Sydney is a year younger than us, and Dylan told me it was lust at first sight. His heartfelt confession of love was something along the lines of *You give me a boner every time I see you.* On good days they grope each other in public, and on bad days Dylan refers to her as "the psycho bitch from hell."

"Flora, can I dance with you?" Dylan asks. "I'm tired of Sydney."

"I'm more tired of you." Sydney stomps on his foot.

Flora's arms tighten around me. "No, I'm not done with my partner yet."

Sydney pretends to gag. Dylan smirks at me. "Seany, didn't think you had it in you." He shakes his head, and I move Flora away before he can say anything lewd to her.

Flora lifts her head, and her eyes draw me in like gravity. "I don't want to dance with anybody else. Unless you do."

"I don't either."

"Good." She rests her head back on my chest, and I place my chin against the top of her head. I wish we were somewhere more private, somewhere just us. But people are watching. A few even take out their phones.

Guess I finally did something worthy of being immortalized on a stranger's camera roll. Not sure if I'm supposed to feel flattered or hunted. Either way, I don't let go.

Madison passes by, her eyes scanning Flora from head to toe. "Green? *Bold* choice. I can tell you *really* tried."

"Sage charmeuse with a subtle champagne sheen," Flora corrects. "It's not for everyone, especially the untrained. They should stick to a boring color like cream or beige. You seem to wear those so well!"

Madison scowls. If an alien landed on Earth, they for sure wouldn't be able to decipher this as close female friendship. Madison flicks her gaze at me and curls up one side of her mouth. "How's it going with the catch of the day?"

Ouch. Flora's grip tightens around my arm. Without thinking, I say, "And here I thought I was more like Moby Dick."

"*Oof.* This one reads," Madison says.

Flora laughs. "Don't be jealous I found him first."

Madison tilts her head, her smile turning sly. "Nah. I'm just impressed you managed to reel him in. You two seem made for each other."

"Careful, Mads. You almost sound supportive." Flora turns to me, her voice playful but easy. "It's not a party until Madison makes a jab at her loved ones. If she didn't like you, she'd ignore you completely."

"Welcome to the inner circle," Madison says, as if I passed an initiation. They take pictures until the music cuts, and a loud crackle bursts through the speakers. "Time for the Homecoming Court announcement. Please give it up for your junior class representatives—Madison Jenkins and Raymond Corbett!"

The crowd erupts into cheers. Madison steps up, waving like royalty. Raymond follows, throwing a lazy grin to the crowd.

My hand slides off Flora's waist to take hold of her left hand, and her cool fingers curl around mine.

"How come you never ran for this?" I ask.

"Madison loves the title. Even though I was nominated, I dropped out. It's not worth it to fight with her."

"She was okay with that?"

"Obviously I said something like, 'I never stand a chance against you, Mads!' and I told her I hate the crown because I don't wear fake jewelry." She winks. "But between you and me, I'd totally win, right?"

I nod. "I'd vote for you."

Flora wants punch, and I offer to get it for her. She promises to stay put in front of the photo wall, where she's posing with Carmen and Josie. There's a small group forming near the beverage stand. The drink sloshes in its plastic cup as I dodge around seniors dancing in reckless circles. I grip the cups tighter, careful not to spill as I weave through the crowd.

When I get back, she's not there.

Then her voice comes through. "Tell me everything!" She's surrounded by a few guys from the hockey team, head tossed back as she laughs at something.

"You don't hang out with us anymore." William, the goaltender, leans in closer than necessary. "You have a boyfriend now?"

Flora shrugs, swinging her legs where she sits perched on the edge of the stage platform. One of her shoulder straps slips and she pushes it up.

"Are you coming to my party this weekend?" William asks.

"Maybe, we'll see." She spots me, waves, and hops off the stage. She takes one of the cups from my hand. After she finishes, she crushes the plastic between her fingers. "Hey. Want to get some air?"

* * *

We stroll around the empty campus holding hands. It's different at night, almost unrecognizable. The front lawn, where Josie blasts hipster music through full-size headphones at lunch, is quiet now, an open stretch of grass under the moonlight. The parking lot, where Jake always screeches in at the last second in his Jeep, is nothing but an empty grid of painted lines. The library looms nearby, a maroon block by day, now swallowed by the dark, fading into deep brown with no lights on. The trees are shadowless.

We pass the swimming pool, and Flora stops. Her face lights up. "Let's break in."

I only hesitate for one second. That gleam in her eyes when she gets an idea—how do I say no to that? "Only if you promise you won't push me into the water."

"I promise."

She leads me to the fence. I climb over first, the metal cold beneath my hands. Her fingers slide into mine as I pull her up, and as she steadies herself, her hand lingers long enough to trace the curve of my arm.

"Wow. Someone's been working out."

"Thank you for noticing."

"Isn't it nice? Like our own private pool party," she says as we sit down near the water. A row of backstroke flags crosses the pool, red and white and flapping. The greenish lighting casts an eerie glow over everything, and the sharp scent of chlorine fills my lungs. This couldn't be further from a pool party.

"It's very nice," I say, looking at her.

Flora wraps her arms around herself. "Tell me about your last relationship."

"No small talk this time?"

"We're past that."

"Olivia. We met while volunteering for a middle-school robotics league. We were creating a Daniell cell when she said my eyes were the color of copper sulfate. They aren't, but I went out with her anyway."

Flora bursts into laughter. "You *are* nerdy."

"Hey, are you supposed to laugh when I share my love life?"

Olivia and I dated until she moved away. Our kisses were polite, like all the others before her. Fine but forgettable. Sparks fizzled out before they even started. I'd rather be playing *Grand Theft Auto*.

Not like with Flora. Not even close.

"No, sorry." She laughs some more. "Clearly, you had a lot of *chemistry*."

"Your turn. Tell me about your last relationship."

She tilts her head up. "Nope. It's a conversation for another time."

"That's not fair."

She traces her fingertips over my knuckles. "How about I tell you about my next relationship?"

My breath catches. When I asked her to the dance, was it because I wanted people to see us together? I fight the urge to bite my nails.

"This is probably uncool to ask," I say. "Can we be exclusive?"

The moonlight shines down on the water, casting silver ripples across the surface. It's silent apart from the faint hum of the pool filter. She takes her time, long enough to make me wonder if I read this wrong. "I thought we already were? I like you so much."

I stare back at her, this beautiful, irresistible girl who makes my head spin like no one else ever has before. "I like you so much too."

Her lips split into a grin. "Say that again."

"I like you so much, too, Flora."

"This is the best night of my life. Wait, let me try it out." She gestures to me. "This is Sean Foster, and we're exclusive. Hmmm. I love how that sounds."

She smiles again, and I can't figure out why she's chosen me. We spend the rest of the night making out beneath the stars.

CHAPTER SEVEN

Flora

Ever since Sean and I agreed to date exclusively, I've been living inside a giant pink bubble. Giddy and energized, I feel like I'm drinking champagne all the time. I have no complaints. Well, *almost* no complaints, aside from the fact that he's obscenely busy. Once, he even texted me saying he related to how koalas are only social for fifteen minutes a day (and that he wanted to spend all fifteen minutes with me).

Personal space is important; therefore, outside those fifteen minutes, my days are filled to the brim with things to do and people to see.

When we *do* meet up, I try my best to plan the kind of date that blows his mind.

So far, to name a few, we've been on a hot-air balloon ride, played laser tag, cut German class to sneak off campus, and woken up at four to watch the sunrise from the top of my building. *That* was an epic date. I prepared everything: a cashmere blanket large enough for two, rich Mayan hot chocolate infused with cinnamon and chili, a playlist of romantic songs, and a bottle of Dom Pérignon. Sean took it all in with dazed wonder, either from amazement or lack of sleep. By the time the sun came up, he'd fallen asleep against my shoulder. Next time, I'm bringing espresso.

This afternoon, though, we're not doing anything original.

We're intertwined on my bed. His fingers skim somewhere between my sweater and my bra. Most of the time Sean wants to hear me talk, but today we're purely primal.

He brushes at the clasp on my skirt, and I place my palm over his. Pushing an inch away from him, I sigh. "There's something I need to tell you."

"Okay." He stops and looks at me. Sometimes I still can't believe the cutest guy in the Pacific Northwest is lying in my bed with his shirt off.

I struggle with my words and decide on the simple truth. "I'm not a virgin."

A few seconds later, he nods. "Okay."

"I thought you should know."

He rolls back a little and sits up. He gets this softness in his eyes, like he's waiting for me to say more.

"You already know, don't you?" I gasp. "Is that why you asked me out?"

"What? I didn't even consider it until you brought it up. I don't care either way."

"Look, I'm not going to have sex with you just because I've already done it. In fact, the first time was so underwhelming, I'm not exactly dying to go through it again."

He nods again.

"I mean it."

"Flora, I like you. I'm not dating you to get laid."

I cross my arms, tilting up my face. "So you *don't* want to have sex with me?"

"I—" His lips twitch, like he's not sure if he's allowed to smile. "I want to so badly, you have no idea. But that's not why I'm here. If you're not ready, I'll wait. I won't assume anything."

"Really?"

"I won't pressure you." Then, after a pause. "I might *encourage* you to, though, and I can be very persuasive when I want to be."

I chuckle. Sean always delivers his jokes deadpan, but he never fails to make me laugh.

"Do you want to talk about it?" He picks up his hoodie and throws it on. Alas. The dark pine-green fabric falls and covers his flat stomach. "Was that your last relationship?"

"It's not a cute story like yours." I comb a hand through my hair. "Do you know Zach Powell? He graduated last year?"

"He's an asshole."

"We hooked up once when I turned sixteen. My first and only time." I stare down at my hands, tracing the edge of my nail with my thumb. "I thought I was ready, and I said yes, but then it wasn't what I imagined. The sex wasn't bad or anything, but there wasn't any connection. I felt like I was just trying to get it over with. And afterward, I felt sort of empty. Like, that's it? That's what everyone's been talking about?" The words tighten in my throat. "What hurt wasn't the act itself, it was that he couldn't wait to tell everyone. I mean, *everyone*. I was a headline."

I try to swallow the burn rising in my chest, pushing it down with a weak laugh. "The most exciting event of the season. Really kept school life entertaining for everyone." I glance up, half daring Sean to judge me. "You've probably heard about it, too, right?"

"I don't pay attention to gossip." There's a shining light of affection in his eyes as he strokes my hair. "I'm sorry that happened to you."

"Carmen and Josie were so supportive. And Jeremy waited by Zach's car after school one day. I don't know what he said to him, but Zach never bothered me again." That's why I forgive Jeremy every time he calls me brainless, but this Sean doesn't need to know. "And Mads . . . we had a fight I barely remember. We didn't talk for three days. Then one afternoon, I overheard some girls in the bathroom trying to suck up to her, thinking my spot as her best friend was up for grabs."

Not that I blame them. People want to be accepted by Madison partly because she's mean, the same way there's always a huge line outside trendy restaurants where the servers have attitude problems.

"They called me a slut. Said I'd slept with the whole football team." I roll my eyes. "So disrespectful, right? It was *only* the captain. You'd think they'd get their facts straight."

Sean frowns. "It's okay to be upset, button. You don't have to joke about everything."

"And then Mads shut them down. Said she didn't associate with people who slut-shame, and that they didn't even deserve to carry my shopping bags. When I stepped out of the stall, she looked so embarrassed, like she didn't want me to know she had a heart."

"No wonder you're so loyal to her, even though she's terrifying."

"Yeah, Mads is the best. She said, 'That doesn't mean I forgive you,' and I said, 'Oh, but you have to! I'm in dire need of someone to carry my shopping bags for me.' And we never fought again after that."

Let them think whatever they want. The people who matter know the truth. They were there, and they saw me through it.

"Did you tell your parents about all this?"

"Sort of. Not in detail. They bought me that to cheer me up." I gesture at the Hermès bag on my dresser.

"They bought you a *bag*?"

"Not *a* bag. A *Kelly*. It's atrociously difficult to get one. But anyway, that's sort of the whole charade of my last relationship."

I exhale. Right after the story rolled off my tongue, I regret oversharing. Sean doesn't need to hear about the rumors or how my parents solve relationship problems. He won't get it. They meant well; buying something impossible to get their hands on was their way of making me feel better, to show they cared. But sometimes I wonder if they even understand what made me sad in the first place.

It wasn't just because it was a story for other people to tell. It was that I let someone in, was open, vulnerable, and got nothing real back. After that, I started keeping things light.

What's the point of dwelling on it? I'm fine now, and everyone loves me.

Sean pulls me into a tight hug. "I won't hurt you. Take as much time as you need to trust me."

I nod against his chest. He's warm beneath my face. The weight of his arms around me is solid, like nothing bad could reach me. For a second, I almost let myself sink into it. Maybe I don't have to keep it together all the time. He holds me for a while, and when I feel like I might cry, I squeeze my eyes to will the tears away.

No. That's not how I want him to see me. I don't need saving. I'm over it.

Sean needs to *desire* me, not pity me. Pulling myself together, I raise my head and narrow my eyes, challenging him. "Even if you need to wait for five years?"

He smiles. "I don't think you can resist me for five years."

I laugh.

He's literally perfect.

* * *

November rolls around with one of those rare warm days, the air sharp with the crisp scent of falling leaves. The clouds above are frozen still like they're painted on. I park outside a coffee shop I found online—one of those places everyone seems to be posting about but that I've never actually tried.

Sean's already there, settled at a corner table with his usual setup. This is his solution to my chronic tardiness: claim a table, order something strong, read, and wait for me. His caffeine addiction is borderline unhealthy.

The sight of him brooding over his laptop fills me with warmth. My heart faithfully skips a beat for him as I pull out a chair opposite him. He glances up and smiles. He's wearing a charcoal-gray crewneck sweater that makes him look effortlessly put together, even with disheveled hair and bloodshot eyes.

"What are you reading?" I lean over. "CNN?" I check the screen again to make sure it's not a porn site disguised as CNN, then catch a headline about climate policy.

"I want to know what's happening."

"That's what chat groups are for, you know."

"No thanks. I don't need updates on who blacked out at Raymond's last party."

Next to his laptop, there's a half-finished book, *Surely You're Joking, Mr. Feynman!*, a metal bookmark poking out. I make a mental note to google that later. His open notebook is a war zone of physics formulas, some scribbled out, others circled multiple times.

"This Feynman guy, does he have any funny lines?"

"'Physics is like sex: sure, it may give some practical results, but that's not why we do it.'" He quotes and heaves a sigh. "But I'm not having too much fun with it right now. I need to ace this physics Olympiad thing." He's too stressed. It's up to me to help him loosen up. "Want to order anything?"

I skim the menu and snort. "Who named these drinks? 'Midsummer Lament'? 'Velvet Remorse'? I want a latte, not an existential crisis."

Sean doesn't look up, but the corner of his mouth twitches. "You picked the place. Own it."

"I bet at least fifteen percent of the proceeds go straight to therapy."

A voice cuts in, smooth and warm. "Not a fan of our literary masterpieces?"

I look up. "Nick? Nicholas Ridge?"

"Flora Morgan! It's been a while."

"Nick, this is Sean. Sean, Nick." Standing up, I pull Nick into a hug. We met during Christmas shopping last year, when he gave me spot-on advice about which tie to get my dad. "I can't even remember the last time we talked. We need to change that!"

"Definitely. I upgraded my phone and lost half my contacts." Nick pulls out his phone, checking. Of course he doesn't have my number. I share it again, tossing in my Instagram handle for good measure. "Can't risk losing touch again."

"I'll call you when my shift is over. What can I get you?"

I glance back at the menu. "I usually go for a chai latte, but I'm up for something different. Which of these tortured-soul specials would you recommend?"

"Try our Solstice Reverie. Our bestseller and truly life-changing." He winks. "And it's on the house. Only for a special friend like you."

"You're way too nice. I hope the drinks are as cool as you." I hand the menu back to him, then eye his beige shirt, printed with tiny zeppelins. "Love the shirt, by the way."

He flashes one last grin before he leaves with my order. I turn to Sean, excited to share my joy of getting in touch with an old friend, but he's rubbing at his temples.

"Are you okay?" I ask.

"Yup." His tone is light, too light, like he's deliberately keeping it that way. Then he sighs and pushes his notebook away. "All right. To be honest, sometimes maybe you flirt a little too much with everyone."

My mouth falls open. "Come on, I was being friendly!"

"Why didn't you tell him I'm your boyfriend?"

"I—I didn't think. I wasn't even sure you'd want me to introduce you like that."

"Why wouldn't I want that?"

My fingernails dig into my thighs. *Get it together. Are you stupid?* This is the first time Sean has shown even a hint of frustration, and it hits hard. He's always been so patient—*indulgent*, even—and I let my guard down. I got too comfortable with his affection, so much that I forgot it wasn't something I was owed.

He's as mature as the dark-roasted coffee he drinks, while I'm a lollipop—bright, shiny, all sugar on the outside and empty calories underneath. I'm lucky to have his attention at all, and now is not the time to blow it.

Sean pushes his hair back with one hand. "I overreacted. I'm sorry. I've been so stressed lately, and I let it get to me more than it should have."

"I'll go back there and tell him you're my boyfriend." Through this whole mess, there's at least a small consolation that Sean acknowledges himself as that, *my boyfriend*. Sean Foster is my boyfriend. Intelligent, handsome, respectful, irresistible. He chose me, and I need to do better.

"Oh no, that'll be weird. Forget I said anything."

"How about we go social media official?"

"Like the grid and everything?"

I nod.

"If you're going to do that, at least let me approve the photo." His smile doesn't make cute crinkles around his eyes like it usually does. "No, you don't need to do anything. You did nothing wrong. I'm sorry I made you feel bad."

But the guilt is already sinking in. What can I offer him? How can I impress him?

There's only one thing in the world I know better than he does: *having fun.* So I playfully push the lid of his laptop down, determined to make him laugh, and remind myself to plan something exciting for later.

In my head, I review all the new rules on my imaginary list:

Stop being late. Drive slower. Follow CNN. Google Richard Feynman for insightful quotes. Don't flirt with other guys—no, don't even hang out with them, especially random ones you met eons ago. Plan more fun dates.

Make Sean happy.

November 17

Flora: *Sorry about today*

Sean: *Don't worry about it. I'm sorry too*

Sean: *I'm worried about the exam and I took it out on you*

Flora sent a photo

Sean: *Is that what you're wearing right now??*

Flora: *What? It's just a top*

Flora: *What are you doing?*

Sean: *I was studying,*

Sean: *But now you've turned me into quantum mechanics*

Flora: *What's that like?*

Sean: *Hard*

Incoming call from Flora

CHAPTER EIGHT

Sean

Dating Flora is the single most overwhelming thing I've done in my life. I'm in way, *way* over my head, but she's so hot she burns away every shred of my sanity.

We're in her room, and she wants to show me everything she bought this week. Once the ribbons are untied and the packages opened, she tries things on, twirling and asking for my opinions.

What can I say? She looks wonderful in everything, and I have a lot more interest in the body underneath.

"It's hideous. Please, take it off. *All* of it."

She laughs. "This one is my favorite." She slips on a red dress, the fabric falling around her curves. Red is definitely her color. "How was your day, by the way?"

"Great. I have an idea for my AP Chemistry project—"

"Wait, let's take a photo." She climbs onto the bed beside me and holds up her phone.

"What's the occasion?"

"I want everyone to know you're my boyfriend."

"Isn't that what the last fifteen photos were for?"

"They need a constant reminder." She presses a kiss to my cheek. "The world needs to know you're mine."

"I *am* yours, don't you worry."

It's flattering that she wants to claim me. At least now her fans can ease off on the DMs. With merely five mighty posts, I've never cared about social media, but there's this small part of me that does take some quiet satisfaction in the fact that she's not hiding me. The only person who still calls her nonstop is Raymond—but that's fine. They've been friends forever and she finds him hilarious.

She posts the photo, and I try to start again about the cloud chamber I'm building. Flora nods, but her focus is already gone, her fingers flying across her phone. I cut my story short and jump right to the conclusion.

It's ironic. She likes that I'm STEM savvy—finds it hot, even. But sometimes it feels like that's all she really wants from me: the label, not the substance. A random fact here or there? Sure. Dorky in small doses—*Sean, you're so cute, send me more.* But the second I go deeper, her attention slips away.

That's not her fault.

I'm a boring guy who's crazy about a girl who gets bored easily. Even when we're out with a crowd and enjoying ourselves, she'll announce that she wants a change of scenery. When Dylan broke up with Sydney (*again*) two weeks ago, Flora decided he needed a proper distraction. Instead of playing pool at his house as we planned, she showed up at his basement with the entire cheerleading squad from our rival school, plus a full bar setup, with shot glasses and all. The "breakup party" came out of nowhere, and by the time I caught on, she was taking body shots off me. I thought I'd be teaching her how to play pool, not lying half naked on the table with salt crystalizing on my stomach.

Jake's family runs a small wine import business, and he's usually able to get his hands on alcohol, but even he was blown away by the scale of it. He slung an arm around Flora, laughing. "You're a prodigy. Now I'm tempted to date someone just to break up and get this treatment."

"How did you even get them to show up?" I asked, still trying to process everything.

Flora shrugged. "Everyone likes a good party."

Now her phone buzzes. She checks it, eyebrows lifting. "Sydney texted—they got back together over Thanksgiving. Did you know?"

"Yes, didn't think it was newsworthy. It's a volatile situation."

"Time for a *so lucky to have you back* celebratory party?"

"You'll never run out of business if you throw one every time their relationship status changes."

"Fine. A simple double date, then. It'll be fun."

"You know they'll probably break up again before we even get reservations, right?"

I'm still full from Thanksgiving dinner and exhausted from all the family commitments, plus keeping up with my workload, but I don't say no to Flora.

* * *

The next evening we're at a dimly lit restaurant, crammed into a corner booth. We barely sit down before Dylan's already sticking his tongue down Sydney's throat.

"This is what you want?" I raise my eyebrows at Flora, who doesn't seem to mind one bit. "Dinner with porn?"

She shrugs. "Want to fight porn with porn?"

Somehow, we make it through the meal between make-out breaks and bickering over appetizers. After the two disentangle from each other, they suggest hitting a board game café. We order hot chocolates and initiate a game of Wingspan, chatting in bursts between turns.

Dylan flips over a card and narrows his eyes. "I lay three eggs, then tuck a bird under another bird? This game's got layers."

"It's called strategy." Sydney stacks her food tokens into a tower.

Between admiring the artwork and unsolicited trivia about migratory patterns, Flora takes over the role of talk show host and veers into couple dynamics. "What's the most romantic thing Dylan's done for you?"

Sydney squares her shoulders. "He beat up a couple of seniors for me and got detention. Also, we were stranded in the rain once, and he played guitar and sang to me until it stopped."

Not surprising. Underneath all the bravado and eff bombs, Dylan's the kind of guy who crouches to talk to little kids at eye level, helps grandmas carry groceries without making a big deal out of it, and chops vegetables for his mom, waiting up to eat dinner with her after she gets home from her law office.

Serenading? Checks out.

Sydney tosses the same question back at Flora, who blinks a few times. "Sean texts me the sweetest things?" She picks up her phone. "I love his texts. He sends me biology trivia, for example—"

"You don't need to show them," I interrupt.

Dylan leans forward and places his palms on the table. "I'm *intrigued*. Do share. Does Seany text you in Morse code?"

"Here's one about how zebras need their herd to feel safe, and he calls me Zebra One to his Zebra Two. And—oh, this one. 'I miss how you feel against my largest organ.'"

Sydney's eyes widen, and Flora clarifies, "Skin, Sydney. It's the skin."

Dylan smirks. "Yeah, that's not *my* largest organ."

"It's not as large as you might think." Sydney glares at him and he grins, then shakes his head at me. "Dude, you're embarrassing." This is premium roast material. I'll never live it down.

The things I do for you, Flora. I could be at home right now, in sweatpants.

We keep playing, swapping more couple secrets as I pretend to study the wetlands habitat bonus card, and I die a little more every second. Every new reveal is a fresh nail in my coffin, but Flora's having fun, so there's that. Glad my lameness counts as currency.

At one point, a waitress comes by to refill our water, wearing a shirt with a plunging neckline. When she leans down, the outline of her purple bra is hard to miss. Dylan, being a pal, kicks me under the table.

He could've been a little more tactful because Sydney catches it too. Dylan used to be a serial cheater, and even though he's pulled his shit together, the history is enough to keep Sydney on edge. Instead of calling him out directly, she goes for the jugular by bringing up his contributions to the game last Friday. "You only scored two points," she says. "It wouldn't even matter if you were off the team."

Dylan is his own worst critic, and he gets that look when he's beating himself up. He doesn't deserve to be dragged through the mud like that.

"He's the point guard," I say, even though I should stay out of it. *Flora would never do this to me.* "He's not supposed to shoot that much. His job is to set things up and create opportunities for the rest of us, not rack up points for himself."

"Exactly." Dylan perks up. "I pass to Sean and Jake, who are the primary scorers. My job's to get them the ball." He pauses to grin at me. "Sean's performance could be a little more consistent, though."

And that's the thanks I get for sticking up for him.

Sydney scoffs. "Then a point guard must be someone who sucks at shooting."

"Dylan has one of the highest free throw percentages on the team," I say.

"Yeah, Syd. Maybe you should shut up before people realize you're stupid," Dylan says. "Or is it too late?"

Flora's mouth falls open for half a second before she smooths it over with a bright smile. "Oh, come on, Dyl, don't be like that." She swings an arm around Sydney's shoulder. "And Syd, I *love* watching them play, don't you? They look so good in their basketball jerseys. Remember that buzzer-beater Dylan made last month? We're so proud to be part of the Wolverines family."

Flora's skills in diffusing tough situations are epic. She's familiar with our plays, can break down strategies, and makes insightful comments that surprise me all the time, but she dumbs herself down to lighten the atmosphere. My chest aches in the best way, and all I want is to take her home, away from these people.

By then, Dylan's chugging water quicker than rain absorption in the Sahara Desert so that our waitress comes by for refills more frequently. Finally, Sydney says, "Why don't you ask her for some duct tape so you can attach your face to her cleavage?"

Dylan shrugs. "If I had duct tape, I'd use it over your mouth."

Sydney picks up her glass and throws the water in his face.

Flora stands up. "I have to make a call outside."

Really? Abandoning me in the middle of the battlefield? After she's the one who suggested this? They're on the verge of a breakup right in front of me, and I'm left scrambling to keep the peace—and the plastic egg tokens—from rolling off the table.

My phone rings, and Flora says, "This is your rescue call. Come join me outside."

Dylan and Sydney are too busy tearing each other apart to care when I leave. I push open the door to find Flora laughing.

"Happy now?" I pinch her nose.

"How did we go from a wholesome bird-themed board game to—what the heck was that?"

"One of the duller episodes of *The Sydney/Dylan Show.*"

She puts her arms around my neck. We kiss for a while in the corner of the coffee shop, relieved to have a moment alone. No noise, no second-guessing if she's already getting bored. When we leave that evening, we're convinced we're the best couple in the world.

✳ ✳ ✳

About a week after the double date from hell, Flora and I are hanging out in her room. I'm on the floor flipping through my German vocab list while she sprawls on the mattress, scrolling through shorts about Korean skincare trends.

"What are we doing this weekend?" Flora asks.

"Can we go skating again?" I was so proud when I came up with the idea, because Flora had skied but never ice-skated. Seeing her delight as she clung to my arm, laughing every time she lost her balance, made me feel like I had given her something new.

"*Again?* But we already did that."

I swallow the disappointment and shift gears. "What do *you* want to do? I'm fine with anything." And it's not a lie. Flora likes arranging our dates, and I prefer leaving it to her, as long as we can spend time together. She's so fun and knows everything about everything.

"Let's go to a themed party!"

She's so excited I can't bring myself to refuse. If it was up to me, I wouldn't mind watching Netflix at home, but with Flora that seems to be the last resort. Deep down, I miss when it was just the two of us, grabbing coffee and talking for hours. Keeping up with her whirlwind energy is so far out of my comfort zone.

Doubt lingers at the back of my mind. Between her short attention span, the pull of her overflowing social life, the flood of unread texts lighting up her phone, and that natural flirt gene wired into her DNA, there's always that fear.

What if I'm not enough?

But I'm fascinated by Flora. Most of the time I simply give in and accept the fact that I'm one among her many fans. "If that's what you want to do, I—"

"Yay! Then it's decided. Oh, before I forget, I got you something. I saw this and thought of you." She hops off the bed and dives into the mountain of shopping bags piled in the corner. After rummaging through a few, she pulls out a small paper bag and hands it to me.

I have limited fashion knowledge, but this one I recognize.

"Gucci?" I ask, alarmed.

"You know? I'm so proud of you." Flora beams. "Open it."

I pull out a palm-sized key ring. It's metal, shaped like a heart, with intricate toothed gears inside, the exposed mechanics resembling the inner workings of a clock.

Flora leans in, studying my reaction. "Is it too girly? Gucci is all about maximalism and gender fluidity now."

"No, it's not that. But this had to cost a lot, right?"

She rolls her eyes. "Come on, this is the least expensive thing you can possibly find in the store."

"Thank you, baby. But I don't feel comfortable when you spend money on me."

"Please. This is nothing. Let's be happy you have a rich girlfriend, okay?" She touches my face and smiles, so dazzling that she should be in a Gucci ad campaign.

"I'm not dating you for your money."

"I'm not dating you for your looks, either, but I sure won't complain about them."

"Oh, I'm not so sure you aren't dating me for my looks."

"Busted." She laughs. "Oh, come on, it's to symbolize that you have my heart. I offer you the best two things I can give you"—she pauses dramatically before holding out her arms—"label, and love."

I should correct her, but I don't want to come off as too serious. I can joke too. "That's not the best you can give me. You can give me something that starts with a *b*—" . . . *and ends with job.*

"Bacon? Binoculars?" She frowns, pretending not to get it. "Ah, a baby! We barely know each other. Let's not get ahead of ourselves."

That part's true. We really don't know enough about each other.

She throws the best parties with a snap of her fingers, gives me expensive gifts, buys everyone caramel macchiatos at Starbucks as she pleases, takes me on the craziest dates . . .

But ungratefully, sometimes I worry. Even with all the science trivia in the world, I'm not interesting enough for her.

CHAPTER NINE

Flora

We're sitting in my bedroom the day before I'm set to leave with my family for Wyoming for vacation, and I set my chin against Sean's shoulder. "I'm going to miss you so much during the Christmas holiday."

"Me too." He strokes my cheek. "I'll call you all the time."

"Hopefully we have the same definition of 'all the time.'"

"Don't worry. Hey, you haven't opened my present yet."

The prospect of opening gifts is always appealing, though I've learned not to get my hopes up with guys. It's the thought that counts. Part of the fun is acting delighted when I'm inwardly horrified at their taste.

I open the tiny black box. *Jewelry is usually a bad idea.* But a pair of exquisite earrings are nestled against soft fabric. The metal is a soft, burnished bronze, aged with a timeless patina. Each piece holds an oval crystal, the facets catching the light with a subtle shimmer that evokes a vintage heirloom.

I'm speechless for a second. They're perfect. "Thank you, thank you, thank you, thank you! You have great taste!"

"Madison does. I sent her a bunch of pictures and asked her opinion. She's brutal, by the way. I'm terrified of her."

He shows me the texts:

1. *Tell me you sent that by accident. Do you hate her?*
2. *Is it a Christmas gift or a breakup announcement?*
3. *I'd rather receive a handwritten apology than this.*
4. *Slap yourself. Now.*
5. *Send me your location. I just want to talk.*
6. . . . .

I burst out laughing. "Mads is ruthless. I wish you gave me a heads-up about exchanging gifts, though. Now I feel bad I didn't get you anything."

"You gave me the key chain."

I scrutinize my room, tapping a finger against my chin. "That was only a trinket. Doesn't count. I'm sure I can find something among this mess to give to you." I rope him into a game of hot or cold, shouting out random temperatures to throw him off, until he pulls out a large Louis Vuitton paper bag from the back of my closet.

His fingers freeze over it. "Baby, please tell me you're using a Louis Vuitton bag to disguise something else."

"I'm offended. Do I look like someone who'd do such a tacky thing? Go on, open it!"

He lifts the gift like it might detonate—a duffel bag in the classic monogram print. I chose it for him because, even though I appreciate his simple style, a little glam wouldn't hurt. The deep caramel and rich tobacco tones add dimension to his usual cool-toned palette, an intentional contrast. Some people say it's too new money, but on him, it works. The right statement piece can elevate an entire wardrobe.

"Do you like it? You can bring this anywhere and travel in style!"

"I like it." He bites his lower lip. "But I can't accept it."

"Oh my god. I knew it. I had my doubts, but I thought since your clothes are so . . . understated, maybe something bolder would work. A single standout piece against clean neutrals. I should've gone with something more low-key, like Bottega Veneta, but this felt like a calculated risk."

"It's not that. I'm no fashion guru, but I know how much this must've cost."

I wave him off. "It's not that expensive."

(Okay, it kind of was, especially after I splurged on that tweed jacket for myself, but it was totally worth it.)

"I really, *really* appreciate it, but this is too extravagant." His face is all guilt and sincerity. "I'm more of a JanSport kind of guy. Can we return it?"

"No! How appalling. My family doesn't do returns." I cross my arms with a dramatic huff. "If you don't want it, I'll give it to Jeremy."

Relief spreads across his face. "Great, do that. He'll love it."

"And you shall receive *his* present, which is a mug with mug mittens."

"Please give me the mug with mittens!" His voice shifts into playful pleading as he grabs my left hand with both of his. "Ever since I was a little boy, that's all I've ever wanted for Christmas."

When Sean's this cute, I can't stay annoyed for one second. I chuckle despite myself. "Fine, you get the mug."

"How about I take some photos with my ex–Louis Vuitton?" he suggests to humor me. He holds the bag in his best model poses and pouts at the camera. I giggle with girlish delight, snapping photo after photo at my gorgeous boyfriend holding expensive leather.

* * *

As January begins and the date of Sean's USAPhO looms like a comet hurtling toward Earth, I see less and less of him. *Physics Olympiad* is a phrase I never expected to feature in my life before, but it's now making a frequent guest appearance. Sean abandons me half the time for studying sessions and the other half for basketball practices, but I try to stay positive, reminding myself that he's a rare blend of brains and athleticism. I should be proud. It still frustrates me to no end, however.

After school one day, we chat for about eight seconds before he announces he's heading to the library, *again*. Since Wikipedia exists, why would anyone need the library?

"I want to spend more time with you." It's been over four months since our first kiss, three months since we went exclusive. Thanksgiving and Christmas have come and gone, and my infatuation is *still* going strong. "Can I come with you?"

"No, I can't concentrate with you there." He leans against the brick wall, navy Herschel bag slung over one shoulder.

"I won't say a single word. I'll sit near you and do my own stuff."

Such as continuing my research on cloud chambers (it's a real thing, apparently). Sometimes Sean talks to me about his science projects, and I change the topic—not because I don't care, but because he'll realize how ignorant I am. There's only so many times I can ask him to explain it like I'm five before it starts feeling pathetic. And every time I sit there, nodding along, I wonder if he can tell I'm pretending to keep up.

"But I'll keep looking at you."

"It's just an English essay." I'm on the verge of tearing out my hair. "I don't get why it's taking you a week."

"School's important to me." His tone isn't patronizing, but somehow it lands that way. For my most recent paper, I wrote about fashion in Victorian literature and focused on ornate hats, velvet accents, fur trims, and lace details, and threw in a couple of Oscar Wilde quotes to round it out. I got an A minus with the comment "insightful," and I achieved that in two hours. Time management at its best.

"I want to get into a good university. I'll need a scholarship if I end up somewhere other than MIT," Sean says, like there's any real chance he won't get in. "Not everyone has the kind of money your family does."

"I can't control my family or circumstances."

"I'm saying you're very lucky, but sometimes I have more important things to do than go to the mall with you."

Kind of a low blow, isn't it? I never mentioned shopping—at least, not today. Rational me starts to crumble, and defensive me steps up fast. "You're suggesting I can't get into a good college, but I won't starve because my parents won't let me die on the street."

"No. I think you can do anything you want in life if you put your heart into it."

"I already put all my heart into getting the *one* thing I want in life," I say. *"You."*

He laughs. "Right. That's the easiest thing you could've done. I'm defenseless when it comes to you."

It doesn't quite soothe the knot in my chest. I feel like a dumb cheerleader whose only purpose is to entertain. I'm also mildly jealous that he's so driven. It'd be kind of cool if I could also associate myself with words like *academic* or *intellect*, but I have the attention span of a three-year-old who watches too much *SpongeBob SquarePants*.

Sean pulls me into his arms. When he strokes my hair, I catch the shadows under his eyes.

"Have you been getting enough sleep?" I ask.

"Not really. I've been staying up to finish homework after we hang up. And with the Olympiad coming up, there just isn't enough time."

My heart softens. *Poor kid.* "Sorry. I won't keep you, then. I'll find someone else to bother."

Don't be clingy—that's not sexy.

Before he leaves, he tugs me behind the building to kiss me. "I'm so lucky to have a girlfriend like you. You're intelligent, fun, interesting, witty, *and* supportive."

He pauses to kiss me after every adjective, and I laugh, somewhat relieved that he cares enough to offer me a half-hearted consolation. Even if, right now, I'm competing with the entire universe for a scrap of his time.

* * *

I join Carmen, Jake, Dylan, and Sydney for an afternoon treat. When no one has a better idea, we stop at Amber's, our go-to ice-cream place, and as usual, the smell of fresh-baked waffles and the red vinyl seats comfort me.

"Did you have a good Christmas break?" Jake scrapes the bottom of his bowl. "Bet you went somewhere luxurious again."

"I went to a resort in Jackson Hole with my parents." *And they talked to each other every day about value propositions and clinical trials while I played with my phone.* "You?"

"Eh. Me and my sister helped my dad renovate the bathroom. My mom picked the worst tiles. They're near impossible to remove." Jake has this way of smiling that makes everything seem like a private joke, like his eyes are always laughing. I wonder how he can be so perpetually happy.

"We didn't go anywhere either," Dylan says. He means him and his mom. Sean told me Dylan's dad flew for Alaska Airlines before he passed, and now Dylan spends as much time with his lawyer mom as he can. I ran into them at a restaurant once, and they were fully engaged in conversation in Spanish. She didn't seem bored, and he never checked his phone.

Apparently, highly educated professionals *can* have a decent sit-down dinner with their kid. Who knew?

Jake pushes aside his empty bowl and pulls out a deck of cards, grinning at Carmen like a magician warming up for his big trick. After three failed attempts, he shuffles the cards again and lets her pick one. The seven of diamonds.

"It's got to be this one, right?" He flips over the ace of spades with a flourish.

"Exactly!" Carmen claps. He beams.

I used to like our group gatherings, and I do like my friends, a lot, but without Sean it's not nearly as fun. What is it about crushing on someone that sucks out the joy of life? Shouldn't it add to it instead?

"Is Sean studying?" Carmen asks.

I nod, stabbing at my dessert.

"Is that even normal? No time for a sundae?" Sydney's eyes are innocent, but her lips twitch as if she's mocking me.

Dylan has his arm around Sydney's shoulders. "He's not bored with you, is he?"

"Hardly." I nearly break the glass with my spoon. "Sean's going places. Wait till he invents something."

Dylan laughs. "Someone's in a mood."

"That's just Sean," Jake says. "Let him do his thing and he'll let us copy his homework."

"Are you even in the same classes as Sean?" Carmen teases.

Jake shrugs and laughs. "We take German together. We're backpacking in Germany this summer. He'll probably memorize every train schedule before we even land."

Sean finally got a passport for this trip too. It's so him to pick the least fashionable cities in Europe. Munich and Berlin. Not Paris. Not Milan. Just World War II history and wursts. I told him if he brings me back Birkenstocks, I'm throwing them straight into Puget Sound.

"Can't wait to meet Europeans. We're counting on Sean to introduce us," Dylan adds, and Sydney pinches his shoulder. He snakes his hand up the hem of her shirt and rubs the small of her back. Sean says they're too intense for his taste, but she sure keeps him interested.

I think of Sean kissing me this afternoon and the sweet things he said. But all the kisses in the world can't silence the warning bell in my head. I worship and admire my boyfriend for his great ambition, but simultaneously, the exact same thing intimidates me. I'm standing on the edge of something I'll never quite measure up to.

That's the fear that keeps nagging at me, that he'll realize I'm not ambitious or smart enough for him, and I'm holding him back. I'm not the kind of girl who dreams of solving world problems. I want to live in the moment and have fun. What if I'm just another fleeting distraction before he moves on to better things?

Eventually, he'll get tired of me.

*　*　*

A week later, I'm having dinner with Sean on a beautiful Saturday night. We've been together for four months, through amber canopies of maple leaves, steaming mugs of cocoa, frost-laced windows, and melting snowflakes. Winter still has its claws in the city, but now it's the start of February, and I can almost smell spring (or wet mulch). While that may sound trivial, it's a significant milestone to me, one that I treasure.

It's our first proper date in weeks. Finally, a nice dinner without distractions where we can pretend he's not drowning in work and I'm not counting down the days until he's free again. He's even dressed up a little, which for Sean means upgrading his usual crewneck or hoodie to a soft knit sweater polo in an oatmeal color, with a subtle rim of blue lining the collar and sleeves. A hint of preppy, but still him.

When we're having coffee after the meal, he places a wrapped present on the table. "I'm sorry I've been so busy lately. Thank you for being an amazing girlfriend."

"Gosh, thank you! What's the occasion?" I love gifts, especially when they're unexpected. I run my thumb along the rich, dark ribbon. "I didn't know you could wrap gifts."

"Lindsey did it. And there's no occasion. I remember you mentioned it a while back and figured you'd like it."

I tear open the wrapper. It's a vintage-inspired newsboy hat in a distinct shade of herringbone gray, the very same one I showed him in an Instagram story.

"Not sure if it's the one, but it was the closest I could find."

"I *adore* it." I rub the material between my fingers, turning it over to admire it from a different angle. It'll contrast nicely with my dark hair, and I have three entire outfits planned around it already. *He paid attention.* "Isn't this expensive, though? You're working so hard to save money for college and your summer trip."

"Please. This is nothing. Let's be happy you have a rich boyfriend, okay?" He manages to keep a straight face while mustering my exact tone, and I laugh.

But his smile fades a second too soon, and his gaze shifts to his phone when it buzzes. He silences it without checking, but I catch the tension in his shoulders, like his mind's already drifting back to his to-do list.

"I should drive you home," he says. "I have to get back to studying—I'm behind."

Already?

I can offer something to pull him out of the fog. Something to make him excited again—much better than another designer gift he wouldn't use. "Wait. I have an idea."

He raises his eyebrows, waiting for my big announcement.

"Remember I told you about my parents' lake house? No one's using it on Sunday." Is there a more tactful way of approaching this? I swallow. "Maybe we can . . . you know . . ."

He studies me for a second. "Are you sure you're ready for that?"

"Yes."

"Because we don't have to if—"

"I've given a lot of thought to it. This is what I want."

He smiles, and it makes cute creases on his face, and then he's not smiling anymore. "Wait, you mean tomorrow?"

That's the beginning of all things unfortunate.

"Yeah, we can go tomorrow afternoon. It's got lake and mountain views. There's a deck, an outdoor Jacuzzi, a media room—"

"I have my physics test Monday morning, remember?"

"Exactly. It's on *Monday*." I laugh, even though my throat is dry, so it comes off as more of a cackle.

"Believe me, I want to, but I won't be able to concentrate the day before. I'll be freaking out about the test," Sean says, as if he ever freaks out about anything.

My stomach drops. All the anticipation and hope I built up crumbles. It shouldn't matter this much, but I feel stupid for planning it, for daring to think he might be happy about us being close in *that* way. That he'd see this as something special. "We can leave in the morning, be back by afternoon. You'll still have plenty of time to study."

"I need the entire day tomorrow. I'm so sorry." He looks at me like he knows he's letting me down, but it doesn't help.

Ever seen the movie *Carrie*? She's standing onstage, glowing, crowned prom queen, then in an instant, she's drenched from head to toe in pig's blood. That's me right now. "Are you serious?"

He nods and glances at his watch. He's already checked out.

If my life were a movie, I'd hit Pause, rewind, and stop myself from making a fatal mistake. I'd lecture myself about the importance of his test and how inconsiderately I'm acting. Remind myself not to take it so personally. Sex can wait. His education can't.

But staring at Sean across from me now, who has a *what's the big deal* frown etched on his handsome face, bottled frustration rolls out like a knocked-over jar of marbles. He's rejecting me despite all my efforts. I can't do one thing right. "I can't believe you're turning me down."

"Why can't we go next week? The lake house isn't going anywhere. This is a tough week, that's all."

"Sorry for the inconvenience." I have done everything since the beginning. I chased him. I waited for him. I planned every date, folding my backbone like origami. And I even offered *this*, but he sits there like some judge on a talent show and I'm out of tricks.

It's supposed to be different with him. A do-over. A chance to rewrite the first time the way it should have been, with someone who cares. But he's sighing like I scheduled a last-minute meeting on his Teams calendar and he's asking to circle back next week.

"I'm sorry, that's not what I meant. I want this, too, just . . . not tomorrow. Please understand that. Let's talk in the car," he says, already calculating how to minimize the time loss. "Come on."

He doesn't even reach for my hand as we leave the restaurant, and on the way back, his patience begins to fray.

"Flora, am I not allowed to have priorities? I'm doing everything I can."

"Of course. Your priorities are pretty clear to me."

He tightens his grip on the steering wheel, eyes fixed on the road ahead. "Look, I can keep apologizing if you want me to, but you're not listening anymore. I don't know what else to say. Maybe we should call it a night?"

It's worse than those PR-scripted celebrity apologies, the *I'm sorry if you were offended* kind. He's not sorry. He thinks he's right. And now he's done trying.

"Please take me home," I say with the most civilized tone I can muster.

In the back of my mind, I fantasize about him pulling over and kissing me until I forgive him, but knowing Sean, I'd have better luck wishing for a Godzilla invasion. He stops the car in front of my building, and I turn to face him. Maybe he'll come up with something soft now.

"Let's talk when you calm down." His expression is all serene and above me. "You're blowing this way out of proportion."

I throw open the door and get out, and then I slam it shut for theatrical effect.

* * *

On Sunday, Sean calls me once and gives up when I don't answer. It's for the best. If we talked we'd probably end up fighting again, and I refuse to be the reason his precious test scores suffer. He can focus on his stupid $F = ma$ equation and deal with me later.

That evening, I call Madison.

"Wanna come over?" she asks. "I'm watching cheerleading championship videos. Maybe we can talk through some choreography."

I groan. She takes this *way* too seriously. "No . . . why, Mads? Cheerleading is no fun without boys around."

Madison chokes on the other end. "You think I'm captain because I want to shake pom-poms for boys? I don't care about our stupid jock friends and their dumb games. Cheer is about *us*."

She always has to win. If she's not running for junior class president, she's plotting how to take our squad to nationals. I can't deal with this now. When I see Raymond's incoming call, I'm more than happy to take it.

Raymond is chaos in human form, but he's exactly what I need. He throws the best parties to which everyone's invited, but behind closed doors, he's a vicious hater who has an opinion on everything. If I need a laugh, I call Raymond.

"What are you doing home on a Sunday night?" he slurs, half drunk and probably freshly stoned.

"Nothing. Just sitting here, being angry at Sean."

"Why? What happened?"

"It's stupid. I don't want to get into it." Sean has three mistresses named Einstein, Newton, and Galileo. What else?

"Well, you wanna hang? It's creepy, you sitting home like a widow." He burps. "I haven't talked to you in ages."

"We talked, like, three days ago."

"Yeah, but I mean a real heart-to-heart, in person. Remember how much fun we had last summer? That was epic."

I laugh. Those mad summer nights of bad decisions and zero regrets. Thinking back, I kind of miss those carefree days of not stressing about pleasing a boy.

"If you're not doing anything, I can come over," Raymond says.

The suggestion is as innocent as a newborn kitten, but I stop to consider if Sean will like this. Raymond is an old friend, though, not some casual acquaintance who hits on me. I never flirt with him, and this certainly isn't a date.

Wait. Why do I care so much about what Sean thinks? He certainly doesn't care much about *my* feelings.

"Come on, you used to be so spontaneous," Raymond says.

"Fine, fine. Come over."

Raymond arrives with two six-packs and a joint. He set the cans down on my bedroom floor, cracks one open, and launches into a full-blown rant about everyone in our class—alphabetically, like they're a deck of library index cards.

"Marissa's eyes look like someone gave up halfway through editing them." Between swigs of beer, he comments while I giggle and agree. He brings out my mean, shallow side, the one I try my best to hide from Sean. It's kind of liberating to be exactly this version of myself for the first time in months.

Then Raymond turns on the TV and announces we're binge-ing every Coen brothers movie. Between his running commentary and overanalyzing, we finish the alcohol he brought over, and I bring out the good stuff my dad stores in his liquor cabinet. We might as well do this right.

"You're seriously one of the few cool people in our school," he says in a moment of sobriety.

"You're just here for the wine."

"Sure, I admit that's one of your redeeming qualities, but I do think you're all right."

I fan my face, pretending to blink back imaginary tears. "How touching."

"How's it going with Supreme Overlord Sean, by the way? You two good?"

"Yeah, we'll be fine."

His lips twist into a grin. "Why does he look so . . . worn-out lately? Too much sex involved in ruling Kingdom Flora?"

I shove him, and he collapses onto the floor laughing.

"Gross. Sean's decent," I say. "I'm sure that's a concept you're unfamiliar with—"

My phone buzzes. The sound is so muffled I'm surprised I even hear it. I dig it out from under a pile of clothes and see Sean (with a heart emoji) light up on the screen. Without thinking, I swipe to answer. "Hi, there." I giggle into the phone.

He pauses. "Are you drunk?"

"No, no. No." I shake my head, even though he can't see me. With one hand, I hurl a pillow at Raymond to shut him up as he snickers in the background.

"I want to see you."

"What? I thought you were studying."

"I was, but maybe I can come over?"

Suddenly I'm popular again. "This isn't a good time. I'm—" *getting wasted with a guy in my room, and he's smoking pot too.* "I'm out . . . with some of my friends from middle school. Jessica and Sarah. You met them once, remember?"

There's a beat of silence. "You're out?"

"Yeah. I need to blow off some steam."

Another short pause. It might've been longer, but my head spins, warping my sense of time. "Okay," Sean says finally. "Call me when you get back?"

"Yeah, sure. Good luck with your exam tomorrow!" I blabber when I'm drunk, and lying makes it worse, so I hang up before Sean gets suspicious. Not that I need to be guilty about anything. Picking up a half-empty can of beer, I drain what's left and get back to *No Country for Old Men*, then we pivot to *Attack on Titan* to keep the moral ambiguity and bleak vibe, but throw in some giant cannibals for good measure.

By the time Raymond is pretty much incoherent and we're too drunk to follow subtitles, I walk with him downstairs. He gives me a bear hug, and before he pulls away, he tries to plant a clammy kiss on my lips. I dodge and he gets the side of my mouth.

"Ew, Ray." I laugh, brushing him off. He gets weirdly affectionate when inebriated, and he would've kissed the lamppost if it was closer to him. He won't remember any of this, as alcohol wipes his memory clean the morning after. "You're a mess."

"Sorry." He rubs his face, eyes unfocused, voice suddenly quieter. "I'm so screwed up. Forgot to mention—my parents' divorce finally went through."

The buzz in my head dulls. My friend, whose idea of camping is staying at a Marriott, and for whom flying in premium economy is the most traumatic experience of his life, is truly grieving. I'm no Freud, but even I can tell he's too drunk and too sad to think straight.

"I'm so sorry, Ray." Stepping in, I put my arms around him. His grip is heavy, and we hold each other with no words. There's nothing else to say. After a while, I pat his back. "You be safe. I'm here for you."

He points a wobbly finger at me. "We should do this again sometime."

"Definitely."

I shove him into an Uber and head back up to my room. Something scratches at the edge of my mind, but I fall asleep before I can figure out what it is.

CHAPTER TEN

Sean

The streetlights are eerie this time of night, casting long shadows on the pavement as I sit parked across from Flora's building. The formulas were starting to blur, and I'd been rehearsing how to apologize for the past hour. Somewhere between calculating an electric field and setting up a rotational inertia problem, it hit me. She offered me something meaningful, and I brushed it off like it was nothing. I was going to tell her I didn't mean to be condescending, insensitive, or oblivious. That I miss her. And then I called.

But she lied. Jessica and Sarah—*sure*.

I sit behind the wheel and stare at the front door, picking my cuticles until one tears and bleeds. I shouldn't be doing this; I know how it looks. But I couldn't think, couldn't sit still, and I had to do something. I'm not even sure what I came for. I'm just here to . . . check. To prove I'm paranoid. There's this restless urge to peek at the answer, even though I already turned in the test. Like if I don't, I won't be able to sleep.

Maybe it's all in my head. Maybe she'll be back soon, and I can apologize in person.

When I call her again, she doesn't pick up.

And then I see it. It's like a volcanic eruption—I should run but I can't look away.

Flora floats down the flight of stairs, stumbling beside Raymond Corbett. The soft glow of the condo lights outline them. They're both wasted. They can barely walk in a straight line as they stagger down the steps of Flora's building, clutching their sides, each other, and laughing.

Every muscle tightens. It unfolds before my eyes, a cruel show for which I'm the designated audience.

Raymond pulls her into a hug, and she lets him. Then he *kisses* her. I sit forward so fast the steering wheel digs into my ribs. Flora smiles and leans in for another hug. Longer this time.

She's as beautiful as always, but right now this isn't for me. *Ray's so fun*, she tells me all the time. Subtext—he's everything I'm not. They can swap gifts from Gucci and Prada, trade inside jokes, and toast with Dom Pérignon in their multimillion-dollar residences.

I let her dazzle me, and this is what I get for not going with my better judgment. Flora is a mistake I was dying to make. I fell for her bit by bit and now it's too late. The way she doesn't take herself seriously and jokes at her own expense. The curious yet genuine light in her eyes when she talks. She has that naivety rich people have, but it comes across as well intentioned. And underneath all that glamor, she has a vulnerability that turns me soft inside, and I just want to hold her and make everything okay for her.

But if I can see that, so can Raymond; so can every other guy who laughs at her wit.

Even after they say goodbye, I stay frozen in place. My fingers ache from gripping the wheel. It takes everything just to focus on breathing, to stop my thoughts from swallowing me whole.

The cold creeps in. I turn the key and drive away before I can do anything I'll regret.

Tomorrow, I'll take the test.

And after that, I'll call her.

And I'll ask the question that's already sinking its teeth into the back of my mind:

Was any of this real?

CHAPTER ELEVEN

Flora

My mood is glorious when I get up on Monday. The air tastes fresher, my hair shines brighter, and even the Wi-Fi connection seems to be working better. Hanging out with Raymond turned out to be exactly what I needed, and thinking back, the fight with Sean was *totally* unnecessary.

I overreacted. I'll apologize, come clean about Raymond, he'll understand, and we'll sing a duet and ride off into the sunset.

I can't even remember why I lied last night—alcohol does make me stupid.

Sean calls me after his exam and basketball practice, and I suggest dinner. He comes to pick me up, and on the way to the restaurant, he barely says a word. A perfect blue storm forms behind his eyes.

Oh no. He must've bombed the exam. What if he thinks it's my fault?

"So, was the exam hard?" I ask carefully.

"No."

"Do you think you did well?"

He doesn't answer, and then he takes his eyes off the road for a second to glance at me. "Did you have fun last night?"

Abrupt change of subject. He obviously hasn't done well and wishes to drop it. Now's not the moment to bring up Raymond. "I had an okay time." I fix the hem of my skirt.

"How are Sarah and Jess?"

"Oh, they're fine. You know." I run a hand through my hair. "But I'd much rather spend time with you."

"Sure you would."

The silence that follows is thick. Even though I may have complained about his test quite a bit, I truly wish him success. Seeing the dark smudges under his eyes, my heart sinks. "Sean, what's wrong?"

He heaves a sigh, heavy and tired. "I can't eat like this." He pulls over to the side of the road. We're nowhere near the restaurant.

"Is this about ditching me for your exam? It's fine—"

"I did not *ditch* you." He turns to face me square. "Ditching you would mean we had plans, and I bailed. I've never done that to you."

"Pretty sure you took physics this morning, not the SAT verbal section." I attempt a joke, but it comes out strained.

"Everything always has to be about you, right? I told you that test mattered to me, and you had to give me a hard time. If the roles were reversed, I'd have supported you."

The tension coils in my stomach. "You didn't support me when I wanted to buy that Burberry coat," I can't resist saying, hoping he'd grace me with a smile. *A reluctant one will do, please.* Sean has never talked to me like this before, and my palms start to sweat.

"Quit trying to be cute. It's funny when you twist my words around to flirt, but I sure as hell am not flirting with you now."

His words hit me like a slap. I'm too stunned to speak. Tears well in my eyes, but I blink fast, refusing to let them fall. I don't know how to handle Sean like this. My stomach tightens, half out of fear, half out of a small rumbling ball of fury.

"I don't know if I'll get another chance, so I'm going to say everything I've wanted to tell you." His eyes flash. "You're a piece of work, Flora. You're self-centered and insensitive. It's exhausting trying to keep up with you. I really tried. I let you decide what we do, what we eat, who we hang out with, but that's still not enough for you. I can't drop everything to be with you every second, and even if I could, I doubt you'd be satisfied. I don't know what more you want from me."

My brain can't process so much information at once, so I randomly pick a sentence and respond to that. "I didn't ask you to drop everything!"

"Well, the minute I couldn't deliver, you gave up on me, right? You had to punish me."

Punish him? My mind scrambles for meaning. Because I lost my temper? I slammed his car door? I ignored a couple of his calls and—oh shoot. "I'm sorry I didn't call you back yesterday," I say, the memory clicking into place. "But it wasn't on purpose."

"Don't worry, I get it. You had more exciting company last night," he says, unusually sarcastic. "That's exactly the point. I'd never have forgotten to call you. When you have something better to do, you couldn't care less about me, but if you're bored, I'm supposed to show up instantly."

My chest tightens. That's not even close to fair. He's so far off base I can't think straight. "How could you say that? I care about you above everything else. I—I more than care about you. I love you!"

I didn't plan on saying it. I wasn't even sure I was ready to feel it. But now that it's out there, trembling between us, I know it's true.

My hand grips the edge of the seat. "I love you."

Sean's jaw clenches. "You don't love me. All through life, everyone has spoiled you, and you're in love with yourself."

When I imagined myself saying I love you to another person, I expected them to do one of the following:

a. *Say "I love you too."*

b. *Smile.*

c. *Tactfully avoid the question by kissing me.*

But Sean disregards my words as he has every thoughtful gift, every gesture, including the invitation for a night together at my parents' lake house. The sting in my chest twists, sharp and searing, until it erupts into rage. "What's your problem?"

"You don't take this relationship seriously. I took a chance on us, and I should've known better. I was so excited when we went exclusive, but now I'm disappointed," he says, each word dropping with weight, crushing me.

Why's he doing this to me?

He has more purpose in life and more important things to do, I get it. I'm a dumb, pretty cheerleader who lucked out and got his attention, and I've been flipping over backward to stay on his good side. I tried my best to be understanding, to stay out of his way, and I already forgave him for the stupid fight on Saturday. But he's lashing out at me.

"I'm disappointed too!" My voice cracks. "And for the record, I put a lot of effort into this relationship. Too bad you find it challenging to keep up. I'm the one planning our dates because you sure can't come up with anything worth doing, and funny how that was never a problem before." I inhale, my breath shuddering. "You know what? Sorry to waste your time. If you're so miserable, maybe we should break up."

I say it out of spite, of course. One of those stupid heat-of-the-moment outbursts. I don't want to break up with him, not even for one second.

For a moment, it seems to snap Sean out of whatever drug he's on. His eyes flicker, but then something shifts. His expression flattens, and that small flicker snuffs out entirely. He runs his eyes over my face. "Yeah, maybe we should."

The words hang in the air. I must've heard wrong.

But his face is calm, unreadable. He means it. I can feel it in the pit of my stomach—the hollow, sinking certainty. My heart stops. For once it isn't because of how cute he is.

"Fine."

Getting out of his car, I slam the door. This is how we end every conversation lately. It isn't until I'm standing in the cold winter air that I register the hot tears streaming down my cheeks. Sean drives off and doesn't look back.

* * *

With great difficulty, I scrape up the broken pieces of myself, Uber home, and call Madison and Carmen to join me, but I hesitate about Josie. Maybe she has to be Sean's friend right now.

All three of them show up together, and Josie wraps me in a hug as soon as I open the door. Carmen holds a box of chocolate chip cookies and cartons of ice cream (vegan options included for Madison). I break down the moment I see them.

"I don't understand," I say between hiccups. "I thought we were going great!"

"Technically, *you* broke up with *him*," Madison offers as a consolation. "So you can tell everyone you dumped him." In her world, the first thing to clarify after a breakup is who ended it.

Carmen rubs my back as we sink into the couch.

"Is this whole happy-couples thing my illusion? How could he blindside me like this? He called me spoiled, self-centered, and insensitive!"

"I get it," Carmen says, although I doubt she does. The girl has never had a boyfriend in her sixteen years of life (not that there's anything wrong with that). "It's bad enough when the relationship is going stale, but to break up with no warning makes it that much harder."

Madison crosses her legs. Her hair gleams in polished waves, brushed out to that perfect Old Hollywood finish. "You only dated for a few months. He turned out to be a jackass, but you got out in time. There's no use crying over a high-school jock. Even stray cats are more likable than they are."

Josie shakes her head. She always says she can't represent two parties with conflicting interests. "Sean's usually not like this."

"He blew his test and took it out on you," Madison says.

"Sean would never do that," I say. "Blow his test, I mean. He's a genius on the way to a Nobel Prize." I shift my attention to Josie again. She's the mutual friend, after all. "Jo . . . can you ask him? And your earrings are awesome."

"Aw, thanks. Even when you're sad, you appreciate the bling. I already called him on my way over. He said it's none of my business and that he doesn't want to hear anything about you." Josie rakes her hand through her tousled, blunt-cut bob. "He's never this moody and sullen. I can call him again if you want. Really, I'm happy to do it."

"I just don't understand. Any insights you might have—did he break up with all his exes this way?" As my dad says, past behavior is the best predictor.

Carmen hands me a tissue and grabs one for herself.

"Sean's pretty unmotivated about dating," Josie says. "To him, it's like riding in a boat floating downstream. If the weather's nice and the water's calm, then sure, but he has no interest in an upstream battle against currents. Usually the girls ask him out, and he goes along with it until it's not convenient anymore, like when she moves away or—"

"Or gets in the way of a physics test," Madison finishes.

I chased Sean too. I threw myself at him, and I guess he *accepted* me. But not anymore.

"To be honest, he hasn't talked to me much ever since you guys got together," Josie says. "I think he spends all his free time with you. It feels different this time. And I don't know if you need to hear this, but he did say he's crazy into you and you're the most beautiful girl he's ever seen."

Madison makes a disgruntled sound at the back of her throat. "No, she doesn't need to hear that."

"Maybe I should call him myself. Maybe if I tell him I'm sorry—"

"Honey, *no*. I'm glad I'm here to save the only remaining thing in your dead relationship." Madison grabs my phone out of my hands. Her gaze is harsh, but there's also a thin veil of worry. "Your dignity. You told him you loved him, and he spat in your face. That would've done it for me."

The dark memory cuts through me, splitting me in half.

She's right.

She's trying to protect me. How much lower can I get? I'm already at basement level. For months I've been staring up at him on his throne, worshiping him, yet he didn't hesitate for even one second when he threw my love back at me.

Madison eats the food Carmen brought over, not even stopping to check the ingredient list and calories. She cares enough to pause her diet. And Josie, even though I'd never ask her to pick a side, I feel like she has. Whenever I cry, Carmen cries almost as hard as I do.

I need to pull myself together. I assure them I'll bounce back in no time, and convince them that they did a good job comforting me. Madison stays with me after Carmen and Josie leave, then sleeps in my bed with me.

In the middle of the night, her eyes are closed. I curl up into a tight ball, my body shaking as the tears fall. I miss Sean with every shaky breath I take.

The sky unveils and unveils, changing from the color of dark seawater into the underbelly of a fish, the light casting different shapes on my windowpanes.

It's okay to put dignity aside for one more text, right? I stare at the screen for an eternity before I type:

Flora: *I'm sorry about everything. Forgive me. I miss you*

I should've been more supportive. His test is crucial, and I shouldn't have gotten mad at him. It's all my fault. I should've been more considerate, more understanding, and overall a better girlfriend.

Immediately, the three dots appear, flickering across the bar, then stop. After a pause, they start again, only to halt once more. The cycle repeats, until finally, the message comes through.

A fresh wave of tears follows.

Sean: *Goodbye. Take care of yourself*

* * *

The next two weeks at school, I avoid him like a clearance sale. Everyone knows we broke up. I make sure my appearance is impeccable, proudly embracing the role of the dumper, but at home, my tears drop faster than a snapped pearl necklace.

If my life were a movie, this would be the part where I dye my hair a bold color, head to Bali to cleanse my soul, and return transformed. In reality, I pull myself together with a fat check from my parents, a list of the saddest movies from Raymond, and a seething hatred for Sean Foster. That hate propels me forward. If he were to beg me to come back, I'd toss my hair in his face and laugh my head off.

The first post-breakup encounter takes place at my locker. It's after school, mid-February, and he walks up to me wearing a button-up shirt without a single wrinkle, and he's every bit as unaffected and composed as he's always been. A couple of sophomores mill about, whispering and pointing at us. Everything is gossip around this place. In that moment, I wish something awful will happen to him, like being made to sing the morning announcements while everyone snickers.

"How can I be of assistance?" I ask coldly, trying to sound smart.

"I've been thinking a lot. There's something—"

"Flora, I heard you're single again." We're interrupted by Liam Turner, a senior and the captain of the basketball team, and also one of the few people Sean doesn't like.

"I certainly am."

"Then maybe you'd go out with me?" He sounds like he's doing me a favor.

What kind of person does this in front of an ex? And they're teammates! Liam is clearly a douche. "Fill out the form," I say. "There happens to be a line."

"Text me the link." Liam laughs as he backs away. "And I'll get right on that."

"Don't go out with him," Sean says.

"I don't remember asking for your opinion."

"He's the kind of person who gives athletes a bad name."

"You're in no position to judge what I do and who I do it with," I remind him. We're no longer together, and he's still acting like he owns me. "You're not my boyfriend anymore. I can finally breathe again."

He narrows his eyes. "What does that mean?"

"You bore me to tears. I can't believe I wasted four months of my life on you. What do you want?"

He opens his mouth to say something but then shuts it again. He watches my face, the same way he did before he agreed to break up with me, and it's almost like he's trying to remember my features. With a shake of his head he reaches into his backpack, pulls out his keys, and then unlatches the Gucci heart key chain. He studies it for a few seconds before holding it out to me. "You can have this back."

The lump in my throat makes it hard to breathe. It was my gift to him, and now he doesn't want it. He doesn't want my *heart* anymore.

I grab it from his hand and stride to the nearest trash can. The key chain makes a dull sound when it lands where it belongs, and I walk back with my head held high. "There. All taken care of. Anything else?"

There's a watery light of sadness in his eyes. He squares his shoulders, and it's gone. "No. That's all. We have a lot of mutual friends, so we should try to be civilized around each other."

I laugh. "What makes you think I can't be civilized?"

Does he think I'm emotionally immature? I can handle a breakup fine.

Two days later, I start dating Liam Turner.

CHAPTER TWELVE

Sean

There have been countless times when I pulled up my phone to draft a message. *You cheated on me. You broke my heart.* And every time, I erased it.

I dissect the breakup over and over, trying to make sense of it, until I finally drag myself to her locker. And what does she say to me? *You're not my boyfriend anymore. I can finally breathe again.*

What's the point? She clearly doesn't care. She got tired of me—just like I always knew she would. I could drag it out, demand an explanation, but to what end?

No, I refuse to give her that. I won't stand there and ask for details I don't even want to know. How long it's been going on. Whether we ever meant anything at all.

I thought I wanted the truth. But maybe I'd rather burn than beg.

She doesn't get to see how much she's hurt me.

So I bury it all. The questions. The humiliation. The part of me that still wants to believe in her. If this is how she wants to play it, fine. *I can breathe now too.*

* * *

After the charade with Flora is over, I retreat to a dark place of solitude where I study with a newfound intensity.

By some improbable stroke of luck, I didn't bomb my physics exam, and qualify for the next round. At least now I can list "USAPhO semifinalist" on my college applications. Physics, at least, hasn't betrayed me.

March arrives in a whirlwind, wedged between the end of basketball season and the USAPhO semifinals, right when I'm also taking the SAT. The timing is relentless, and Flora being out of my life is just my luck. Imagine having to deal with her now, amid this chaos. She did me a favor, really.

Jake and Dylan take every opportunity to remind me that I've officially joined the ranks of Flora's trophy boyfriends. Ironically, it comforts me. Maybe the whole thing is something to laugh over.

The hardest part is this: admitting we weren't special after all. Our love was nowhere near epic. It was the most predictable high-school relationship, a clichéd nerd-and-cheerleader one, no less, doomed to end before it outstayed its welcome in the gossip mill. I was a designer bag she got tired of having on her arm.

My stomach twists every time she crosses my mind. As the air grows thicker with sunlight and warmth each day, the thought of her becomes more like background noise. I think *of* her, not *about* her. I'm going to be fine.

It's only a matter of time before I get over her, and I practice hard.

I practice not caring when she flaunts her new relationships in my face. First there's Liam, and then Ethan, and then Andrew, until I accept that I'm merely another name on the list. I practice not glancing over at the bleachers where she sits in her uniform, laughing with her mouth wide, showing off all her pearly teeth. When we play basketball against our biggest rival one afternoon, I practice keeping my focus.

The gym is alive with a flurry of noise and motion. Dylan fires a pass my way, and I barely catch it. Coach is screaming. He's been screaming at me a lot lately.

At time out, Jake grips my arm. "Are you okay? Do you need a break?"

"I'm fine," I say through gritted teeth, shrugging him off.

Jake doesn't buy it. "You sure? You look—"

"I said I'm fine."

The whistle blows. Play restarts.

I steady myself, then run toward the opposite end. The basket is right in front of me. The crowd roars. Flora stands on the sidelines but I don't look at her.

She's watching.

I jump off my left foot and make a shot.

As soon as the ball leaves my hand, I know it's going in. A clean arc. It sinks into the net without touching the rim. Then I land, and a sharp pain shoots through my right leg.

I hear the snap before I feel it.

Junior year basketball is over for me.

* * *

Jake and Dylan sit with me in the emergency room. "If it's any consolation," Dylan says as we wait, "the season's almost over, so you won't miss much. You picked a good time to bust your knee."

Jake nods. "Yeah, we only have one big game left. We can still win."

The AC is too strong and it's drilling a hole through my skull.

"That's what I'm afraid of. You'll realize you can win without me."

Dylan claps me on the shoulder. "Dude, we know you're a shitty player. We still love you."

The hospital isn't unfamiliar. Jake's sister had her chemo sessions here when she was diagnosed with Hodgkin lymphoma. All the doctors and nurses thought Jake was the sweetest angel when he shaved his head with her. Dylan's dad spent his last days here too. Dyl barely said a word through it all, just paced the corridors, fists clenched, hoodie up like he could disappear into it.

Now it's my turn. For something much smaller, much less important. But I've never quite noticed how cold this room is or how the humming and the beeping fill every corner. The sharp scent of disinfectant and alcohol pads clings to the air. My knee has swollen to the size of a baseball, and it stings like a beehive. I'm caged in, locked away from everything I take for granted.

Upcoming games. Driving to school. College visits. Our summer cycling trip to Germany. We were supposed to stay with Jake's uncle in Munich, ride through the countryside, and "take on Europe as the Three Musketeers," as Dylan put it.

I grit my teeth. "I can't go to Germany with you guys."

"Yeah, don't stress," Jake says. I wait for him to tell me they'll send pictures. "Let's reschedule."

Dylan nods. "We won't go without you."

"Hey, don't cancel because of me," I say, and it comes out a bit croaked. The way that they're so certain and quick to reply, like it's not even a question worth considering, makes my throat constrict. Being in the hospital really messes with my head.

"One for all and all for one," Dylan says. "No big deal."

The curtain pulls back and a doctor steps in. He tells me they're seeing signs consistent with an ACL injury, and without that ligament to stabilize my knee joint, my treatment options include crutches, rehab, physical therapy, and the possibility of reconstructive surgery. "We'll need imaging to confirm the extent of the tear, and when your parents are here, we'll discuss your options in more detail." My knee throbs even more after hearing all that.

When the curtain swings aside again, a huge batch of balloons enters my vision first, followed by Josie, Madison, and lingering a few steps behind, Flora. Flora with her glossy dark hair, luminous hazel eyes, and the annoying click of heels that disrupts my heart rhythm. She stands as far away from me as possible.

"We wanted to see how you're doing," Madison says. This is probably the first time she's spoken to me without hostility since Flora and I split. No one knows the real reason behind the breakup, not even Josie. It's fine, and I've accepted being wronged and taking the blame, but they're here now. The upside of this injury is Flora's gang is semifriendly to me again.

"Speak for yourselves. I'm only here to run into some hot doctors," Flora says. She shifts her gaze to my knee, stares at it for a second before she glances away. "Does it hurt?"

"It looks worse than it is."

"Will you still be able to play?" Josie asks.

"Not for now, but I'm hoping I'll be back next year." I go through the whole spiel again about the prognosis and treatment options. Maybe if I keep saying it out loud, it'll magically suck less.

Josie shakes the balloons she's been holding in front of my face. They have giant Albert Einstein faces printed on them. "Hey, we brought you these."

Flora takes a step closer. "I—we picked them out for you before coming over. Thought it'd be nice to have your dream man leering at you when you sleep tonight. These weren't easy to find."

For the first time since I fell, I laugh. "Thanks."

She's here. That fact alone consoles me. My injury must've made me weak.

"I hope they let you out of here soon," Flora says. "It's true what they say about hospital gowns. They're ugly as hell. But wait." A gleam comes to life in her eyes, and it brings back a wave of memory and nostalgia. My heart hurts as much as my knee. "Is this the kind that opens in the back? In that case, would you mind getting up and closing the blinds over there?"

I miss the days when she flirted with me. "Don't harass the patient," I say.

Her words pull me under, right back to where I don't dare revisit. The afternoons tangled in her sheets. The way her hands on my skin set fire to every rational thought. Late-night phone calls that stretched until midnight, followed by homework and shots of espresso until my hands shook. I missed her as soon as I dropped her off at her door, and I texted her even when I didn't have anything to say.

Flora shrugs. "Never mind. It's nothing I haven't seen already."

Dylan groans beside me. "You guys should date again and get each other out of your systems. All this sexual tension is hurting my brain."

I clear my throat. "Actually, the brain itself can't hurt because there are no pain receptors."

"See?" Flora rolls her eyes. "That's *exactly* why I can't stand him."

She examines her nails and then only addresses Madison. Before they leave, she tilts her face and our eyes lock for a second. I can't look away. There's too much to read in them, like stumbling upon a brilliant book at the library that I must return, but for now, I want to devour every line. There's sadness, tenderness, and maybe even longing. I want her to stay.

She leaves, and then a minute later, runs back and dumps a warm hospital blanket on my chest. "It's freezing in here. You can't get better if you're an ice cube."

Her jasmine perfume strangles me like a scarf before dissipating in the air.

I'm trapped.

Trapped with a nonfunctioning knee and blind infatuation for my ex-girlfriend. She's all kinds of trouble and no good for me.

But who ever wants what's good for them?

CHAPTER THIRTEEN

Flora

Madison shoots me a warning glance as soon as we part ways with Josie. We're standing in a hospital corridor near a row of ugly plastic chairs. "Are you seriously not over him? You were practically drooling over him in there."

"I wasn't. I was trying to take his mind off the injury." Sean clearly hated talking about surgery, especially when he mentioned things like "autograft" and "arthroscopic procedure." The balloons made him smile—I'd been right to insist on them.

"What do you care, anyway? I thought you wanted him to suffer."

It's true that whatever love I had for Sean has fermented into hatred, but I never wanted him in physical pain. "By suffer, I meant crying himself to sleep every night thinking about me. Not suffer through a busted knee. What if he can never play basketball again?"

Madison scoffs, cold as the cucumber salad she ate for lunch.

"His knee looks awful. Maybe I should get him a brace? I wonder how much his medical insurance covers."

"Honey, he's not your problem anymore."

"There must be something I can do for him. Maybe—"

"Stop right there." She turns to face me square on. The usual arrogance drains from her eyes, replaced by concern. "It's been *weeks* since you broke up. You have to move on. He. Doesn't. Care. About. You. I'm sorry, but it's the truth."

Madison is all about brutal honesty. She doesn't do fake smiles, just like I don't do knockoff bags. Everything she says is true, but it doesn't make it any easier to accept.

I tried moving on. I dated my way through the senior class, but no one made it past the second date. I'd mentally grade the new guys, giving them tiny black marks every time they did something uncool, or in other words, un-Sean-like.

I miss him. I loathe him but I miss him. I want to drive him to class and carry his books until he gets better, but the burn behind my eyelids reminds me that I don't have that privilege anymore.

When Madison leaves, I sink into one of the chairs.

I'm not ready to go yet.

"Flora?"

Lindsey's eyes are red rimmed, her usual brightness dimmed. Beside her, Sean's mom stands with that familiar warmth. A sob rises in my throat. They worry about Sean as much as I do, if not more.

I stand up, and, obeying an impulse, wrap my arms around Mrs. Foster. "He's going to be fine." My voice wavers, but I blink back the tears.

When we pull apart, she squeezes my hand. "It's so good to see you. How have you been?"

"I've been better," I admit.

"My dad keeps asking when you'll be back for his famous burgers," Lindsey says.

I manage a smile. *Probably never.*

"I still use that highlighter you gave me," Lindsey adds after a pause.

"The pink one? Told you. It makes you glow from within."

"Lindsey had so much fun that day," Mrs. Foster says, referring to the afternoon I played personal stylist/image consultant and gave her tips based on her undertones and color theory. *God, I'm such a pro.* "By the way, she's starting high school this fall."

I turn to Lindsey. "That's exciting! We'll have a great year together. You know you can come to me for anything, right?"

Lindsey tugs at the end of her hair. "I wanted to text you, but I wasn't sure you'd want to hang out since you . . . since you and Sean . . ."

"Hey, I'm still your friend," I say, meaning it. "That hasn't changed."

When we wave goodbye, she's smiling.

CHAPTER FOURTEEN

Sean

With my knee, my summer plans were as blown out as my joint. My grandad got me an internship at a physics lab, where I spent my days playing with lasers and radio frequencies. On the side, I managed to land a few freelance contracts as a web designer. Josie drove me everywhere. Jake and Dylan worked as lifeguards, and most evenings after their shifts, they dragged me to the park for drills, making sure I didn't slack off.

A typical training session started with lateral shuffles, followed by acceleration sprints, where they timed me. Then came plyometric exercises, and if I didn't do them in perfect form, I had to start over. Those sadistic jerks also threw in a random "surprise of the day" for the sole purpose of making me suffer. We ended it all by making ten consecutive free throws—if they were feeling generous. By the end, I was near tears, begging to go home, but Dylan made me buy them burgers for "all the work they did," which mostly meant him blowing his obnoxious whistle at me and Jake making endless comparisons between me and his grandma. At least they were there for me, in their own way. They didn't even bring up Germany—made it sound like it was a better idea to go before college anyway. When we'd legally be able to drink, Dylan joked.

I'd been off crutches since late spring. My knee improved a lot between rehab and "Bro Camp," and I could jog for longer stretches of time. It was a quiet, drama-free summer, and by the time school starts, I'm fully back on my feet.

Josie sits next to me in world history, three rows behind Flora. Mr. Goleman assigns a written paper and an oral presentation in groups of two or three. After class, Josie rests a hand on my desk as we pack up. "Can I be your partner and not do any work? I have a battle of the bands kind of thing coming up and I can't afford to lose time. Besides, you owe me. I was your personal driver all summer when I could've been hanging out with my UW boyfriend."

She's been dating Brian, a college guy she met at a gig, for about a month now. Ever since, she's been acting like some kind of relationship expert, and she never refers to him simply by name.

"I guess?"

"My Asian ancestors would be proud of me for breaking the cycle." She picks up a fallen pen from the floor. "You'll get us an A, right?"

"I'll try my best."

"By 'us' I mean you, me, and Flora."

"What? No." *Absolutely not.* I learned my lesson with Flora—even microorganisms adapt to avoid swimming toward poison. And if I have to spend extra hours with her, my body will forget what my brain already knows.

"She'll be mad if she finds out I'm your partner instead of hers. It's best if we all work together. Besides, this has gone on long enough." She gives me a pointed look. "This assignment is a perfect opportunity for you to get over yourselves and be friends."

Part of me wants to remind Josie that Flora and I were never friends. But I'm already running late for my next class, so I let it go. Hers'll just be one more name on the project I'll end up doing myself.

What a way to kick off senior year.

The other unfortunate thing is that my kid sister has officially started freshman year as my sidekick. At lunch, we stand in line together while she rattles off reasons why she should keep sitting with me.

"I'm only hanging out with you for now. If I'm seen with seniors, I'll look cooler."

"Being a senior isn't an achievement. Stick around long enough, and you'll get here."

"They get hotter every day." She steals a glance at my usual table, where Jake and Dylan are waiting. Conversations between us are usually like this, where she ignores whatever I say and brings up a new topic. "Do you think they'd be into me?"

"My friends aren't exactly boyfriend material, and you're seriously too young for them."

She shrugs. Her high-school fantasies consist solely of parties, dating, and falling in love, which will all turn out to be bad surprises, if my own experience is any indication. I don't tell her that. She has four years to figure it out herself. "Anyway, if you don't start being nice to me, I'll tell Mom and Dad you're mean."

"You tell them whatever you want because I don't care."

She reaches for a plate of Tater Tots, and someone cuts in line. A subtle trace of jasmine perfume drifts past.

"Lindsey! I can't believe you're here and didn't say hi."

We both turn. Flora Morgan, bane of my existence, stands there in a ridiculously short skirt.

"Hi! I was looking all over for you," my sister says. Traitor.

Flora drapes one arm around Lindsey's shoulder, leading her away without so much as a glance in my direction. Now that my knee's recovered, she's back to treating me like radioactive waste.

"You must be so excited to start school! Care to join me for lunch? I brought my own today. Do not try the chicken rice from the cafeteria, it's blasphemy."

Before I know it, they're halfway across the room, and Lindsey is nodding at everything Flora says.

I grab Lindsey's tray, stack it on mine, and get my spaghetti before heading to my table.

"Congrats on finally ending your babysitting job." Dylan takes a loud sip of his Coke.

"I don't mind having your sister around." Jake smirks at me. "I forgot how cute she is."

He's only saying it to get a reaction out of me, but it works. He knows exactly which button to press. "Jacob. Don't even think about it."

"What are you gonna do, threaten me with your friendship? Tough choice." Jake holds out both hands like a scale, pretending to weigh the options, then lets one drop. "Sorry, I choose your sister."

Dylan snickers. "Lighten up, Seany. Jake's a real catch. If I had a sister—"

"Stay away from Lindsey. Both of you."

"Chill, broski. I'm kidding. She's way too young," Jake says. After a beat, because he can't resist: "But give it a few years—"

Dylan chokes on his drink. "Dude. Stop."

Jake shrugs. "But give it a few years, she'll be older, wiser, and I'll still be here, maintaining appropriate boundaries with non-creepy behavior, and treating her with the utmost respect. As I always do." He grins, pleased with his bait-and-switch of the day.

"And I'll bury you in the backyard if you ever forget that," I say.

Jake bows in musketeer fashion. "Yes, my good sir. I shall not bring shame upon her name."

My eyes travel across the cafeteria to where Lindsey sits with Flora's squad. I guess she's in good hands. Flora can be charming when she wants to be, and I thank her silently for taking care of my little sister.

Flora's text comes through. *Josie says we're partners for history. What a JOY. Literally jumping up and down right now.*

She could've talked to me in person a minute ago. Also, that's not what *literally* means. I text back, *You think I'm thrilled to do all the work?*

Flora: *You think I'm thrilled about dealing with your attitude? When are we meeting to discuss this?*

Sean: *Sunday at ten? The Pavement*

Flora: *It's not due for three weeks*

Sean: *Let's start early and get it over with*

Flora: *Whatever. Try not to be late*

Sean: *Right back at you*

* * *

When she calls me early Sunday morning, she proves she can be dreadful when she puts her mind to it.

"Good morning!" Her voice booms through the phone.

"What?" My eyes refuse to open. "What time is it?"

"Showtime! Let's tackle the much-dreaded history project."

It's a quarter past seven. I barely slept, thanks to a pulled quad that flared up all night, and now my head pounds from every direction. "We agreed to meet at ten."

"Sure, but I got back from an all-night party so I'm available now. Let's get this over with."

"I'm hanging up."

"Come on, I waited a whole hour before calling you. I'm at the Pavement."

I roll over, pulling the duvet over my head. "See you at ten."

"Sean Foster, if you don't show up in fifteen minutes, I'm coming straight to your house."

I take a deep breath and exhale into the phone. Knowing Flora, that's not an empty threat. "I'll meet you there."

"Perfect. But hurry up. I can't stay long. It's not going to take all morning, is it?" she asks, like I'm a kid pestering his parents for a trip to the park. "I have plans this afternoon."

For a moment, I can't remember anything I liked about her.

CHAPTER FIFTEEN

Flora

Fine. He wanted early? I gave him *early*.

Josie might be fine letting Sean do the heavy lifting, but that's her prerogative. I don't want any favors from him.

I sit at the Pavement, drumming my fingers on the wooden table. This is where we had our first date, back when he was still the adorable guy who polished off my cinnamon roll. Now, he pushes open the glass door, a mixture of exhaustion and wariness on his face.

"What's so hard about showing up at the agreed-upon time?" He drops his laptop and a stack of history handouts on the table. I brought nothing except my wallet on chain, having just spent the evening watching *The Cook, the Thief, His Wife, & Her Lover* with Raymond at his place. He obsessed over the gore and the grotesque violence, while I was captivated by Jean Paul Gaultier's stunning costumes. That was followed by a techno party, where I barely had time to sit down, let alone get any sleep.

You don't see *me* complaining.

"You're here already, so quit whining."

He casts a glance at me and shakes his head. Fake eyelashes probably aren't his thing. "Okay, what have you got?"

"Ginger latte. It's not bad."

"No." That look of controlled irritation is hard to miss. "For the history presentation. You must have some ideas already."

"*Oh.*" I chuckle. "I thought we were supposed to talk about what each of us has to do, and *then* I can start."

"What?" He pulls back. "I didn't expect much, but showing up empty-handed? *Impressive.*"

"*Hello*, did you mention anything about bringing research? I rely on clear instructions. You set up the meeting, so it's your responsibility to communicate what you expect to achieve. Obviously, we approach things differently."

"That's an understatement. Why bother meeting if you came unprepared? You're wasting my time."

Hard to believe that the last time we were here, all I wanted to do was kiss him. Now I want to smack my purse over his head. "Forgive me for not being well-versed in silent academic telepathy. Please, wow me with your brilliance."

Without further words, Sean turns on his laptop and it whirs to life. This guy has a folder full of files already, all in order, and I pray he won't go through each and every one of them. He clicks one open, and a dashboard with a taxonomy system pops up, where he's already highlighted key terms on medieval history.

I try concentrating. I *really* try. But five minutes in, I yawn.

He frowns. "All-night party catching up to you?"

I wave a hand. "Go on, go on, I'm listening."

He starts again. It's barely eight in the morning, but the place is filling up. In the back, a lady is adjusting the lapel of her tailored wool coat. Two tables away, a girl's beige calfskin shoulder bag hangs off the back of her chair. *Would that color work on me?* Maybe with a monochrome look—camel coat, cream knit, gold jewelry.

Sean snaps, "Nice of you to zone out after I did all the work."

For someone who's sleep deprived, he sure has a lot of energy for biting my head off.

"Look, I'm sorry, but your presentation is tedious. And for the record, I don't like this arrangement any more than you do, so you and your 4.0 GPA can quit acting like it's my honor to be paired with you. Be mad at Josie."

Sean goes still for a second. He lets go of the mouse and leans back in his chair. Then, in that maddeningly calm voice of his, he says, "I know you'd rather not be my partner. So how about this? I'll do everything myself. I'll write the paper, put your and Josie's names on it, and I'll handle the presentation alone. You just show up on the day, wear something hot, and we'll call it equal contributions."

It takes everything in me not to dump my ginger latte onto his lap.

Or laptop. Whichever hurts more.

"You're so condescending."

He exhales. "I'm getting coffee first."

I stifle another yawn. "While you're at it, get me a vanilla latte. I'll Venmo you."

He walks off, and out of habit I check out his butt before catching myself. I whip my head in the opposite direction. A guy at the next table pulls out a chair and sets down a leather duffel bag.

The bag.

The exact same one I tried to give Sean last Christmas. I even posted a bunch of photos of my gorgeous boyfriend holding expensive leather, only to delete them later (along with every other picture of him on my account).

Now my gorgeous ex-boyfriend sets a mug down on the table—hard—breaking me out of my reverie. In retrospect, it's no wonder we broke up. Every time I wanted to offer him something nice, i.e.

a night at my parents' lake house, a romantic date with a carefully planned itinerary, or a gift I spent hours picking to match his style, he made me feel stupid.

Sean pulls out his chair and sits down. The café hums with conversation, the clinking of cups, the occasional hiss of the espresso machine. It's all so normal, exactly like before.

"Do you ever think of how it was when we were together?" I ask.

Sean pauses, midsip. "Excuse me?"

"You heard me. Do you?"

He sets his coffee down. It takes him a long time, then finally he says, "I try not to."

"So you do."

When he remains silent, I press on. "What do you think about?"

"Flora, this isn't the kind of history I want to discuss. Can we get back to business?"

"Come on, it's been ages. We're seniors now. Surely we can talk about it and maybe have a good laugh? How we defined 'opposites really shouldn't attract'?"

My heart pounds and my fingertips grow cold despite the hot beverage. Nothing about us can be treated with a breezy laugh. I've stopped crying over him, but the feeling of being abandoned is left unresolved. The way he ended it was like shutting off a movie twenty minutes before the ending.

And I need closure.

"Okay." He reclines in his seat. "What do you want to hear?"

"I want to know if you were happy and if you regret ever being in a relationship with me." The words come out all at once, a rush of everything I've wanted to ask but never could.

I hold my breath.

"No, it was fun. You're entertaining in small doses." He answers straightaway, carelessly, as if I'm a silly YouTube clip of singing cats. "Why, do you regret it?"

I shrug. My breath hardens into a knot in my chest. "I guess not. There are only so many guys in our school. I would've gotten around to dating you eventually. Good thing to get it out of the way."

"Yeah, thanks for the honor." His voice is clipped, sharp around the edges. "If we're done reminiscing, can we get some work done? Don't want you running late for your next date."

My god, he can be insufferable.

I shake my head as he flips open his laptop. The old Sean is gone, and all the king's horses and all the king's men can't put us back together again.

CHAPTER SIXTEEN

Sean

We agreed to meet after school again after my practice on Monday. Flora glides into the student lounge with her usual flair.

Her dark hair is pulled back in a ponytail, showing the crystal earrings dangling below her jawline. The faint sparkle brings me back to last year when we were still dating.

"Nice earrings."

"Yeah." Her tone is frozen, matching my winter memories. "Someone who used to matter gave them to me."

Ouch. Her dress hovers several inches above her knees. She's probably going on a date later. *It's none of my business.* "Are you going somewhere after this?"

"No, I'm all yours." She pulls out the chair next to me. The end of her ponytail swings in front of my face as she sits down.

I inch away. I'm a sucker for long, glossy hair, and I don't need distractions.

She dumps a folder onto the table with a sharp thud, then pulls out a typed document and shoves it in my face. "Here, read this."

It's several pages long. An outline of our paper, fully typed up, footnotes and references included. Some paragraphs are highlighted. She *was* paying attention.

"This is impressive." I flip through the pages. "You did this in one day?"

"What do you care? I come fully prepared this time. I can hold a proper discussion, so you can quit acting superior. I'm going to earn my name on the assignment."

"I wasn't . . . Hey, I'm sorry I offended you yesterday."

"You offended me, all right. I thought we'd brainstorm first, but you treated me like a parasite leeching off your brilliant mind." Her hazel eyes flash. "History isn't rocket science. It's not even hard. I don't know how you can be so arrogant."

"Okay, I deserve that. I was tired yesterday, and I don't function well in the morning without coffee. I'm really sorry."

She flips the school's history textbook open with unnecessary force.

I try reading the document she handed to me. Her lips are drawn tight, her shoulders stiff. I pick up my pen and tap the end against her forearm. "Hey, are you going to forgive me? I can't read with this much hostility aimed at me. Don't be mad. Please?"

"Fine." A long pause, then she exhales a quiet laugh. "Stop it."

Thank god. We're stuck working on this for three weeks, and I'd rather not spend all of them fighting.

"But," she warns, "you can't laugh at my suggestions or make me feel stupid again."

"I promise."

She snaps the textbook shut and leans in. "Okay, then. I have an awesome idea about our presentation."

"Let's hear it."

"We should do a play."

"A *play?*"

A smug smile tugs at her lips. "Yeah, like a skit. Something immersive. We can dramatize a year in medieval times, with characters like a peasant, a noble, or Crusaders, and show how our lives were shaped by the period. The plights we faced. The social structure. How famine, plague, and war impacted us. Depends on which angle we want to emphasize."

Is this the back cover of an RPG game, minus the quest to locate hidden treasures and conquer the seven seas? I stall, scrambling for a rejection that doesn't sound like one. "I don't know? Mr. Goleman doesn't strike me as someone with a sense of humor. I seriously doubt he'll go for it."

"I'm not about to stand up there for fifteen minutes reading from a paper and boring everyone to death."

"Can I at least think it over?"

"Think of it like advertising. Same product, better packaging. A play lets us weave in tons of historical facts. It's way more engaging than PowerPoint. Imagine if TV commercials were just slideshows. People need to visualize things, you know?"

"Unless I'm selling a medieval castle here, I don't see how that's relevant."

She glares at me. Then a dangerous gleam enters her eyes. "Wait, I have an even better idea. You play the knight, and I'll be the girl who mysteriously falls from the sky."

My mouth drops open. "What mysterious girl?"

"I'm from the modern world, but one day—bam!—I get sucked into a portal and land in medieval times. Time travel is so hot right now."

This is spiraling into a full-blown nightmare. "Oh, perfect. Maybe we can even fall in love, and you'll throw away your entire life to stay with me," I say dryly. "We'll feast on soup-stew and rye bread for the rest of eternity."

Flora claps her hands. "Yes! Like that old Meg Ryan film. We have to add this. And Josie can be the all-knowing narrator—this prophet or priest as the voice of reason. She's perfect for this role." She scribbles *time travel movie* on her notes and underlines it three times.

I drop my forehead into my palms. "I just can't win with you, can I?"

* * *

A week later, Flora emails me the script with the title "Meeting Pre-reads." When we meet again in the library, she hands me a printout. "Josie emailed me her suggestions, and I've incorporated her input in this updated version. I trust you've had time to read it over?"

I have. Flora's idea isn't half bad. The plot is solid, equal parts educational and ridiculous, and while I don't want to boost her ego any further, I can't keep the smile off my face as she tosses me my updated lines.

"'I'm clean, I've been tested for the plague'?" I raise my eyebrows.

"Tell me you're not enjoying this."

"Totally. A knight trapped in a Hallmark movie, riding a paper horse and reciting medieval pickup lines? My lifelong dream."

She chuckles, and I melt at the sound of her laugh. I'd forgotten how fun it was when we weren't at each other's throats.

"And you're much better at organizing meetings," I admit. "That first one I called, that was a disaster. That was on me."

"Right?" She elbows me. "As my mom says, you must start with a clear agenda and end with a concrete action plan. Watch and learn, young grasshopper."

When we wrap up for the day, it feels too soon. She collects her things, sorts her notes into a neat pile, and snaps her folder shut. "I'm hungry. Wanna grab dinner?"

"Sure." As soon as the word is out, I regret it. Spending time with her is one thing, but this might be pushing it. It's too easy to get pulled in again and start wanting things I shouldn't.

"Great! I'm starving." Flora is all smiles. "Let's take your car."

We walk in silence to the parking lot. This is a step. A huge step. *It's nothing.* Just casual dinner. People eat.

I hold the door open for her. "Where do you want to go?"

"I'm dying for some raw, dead fish. There's a new Japanese place near the park."

I start the car, eyes fixed straight ahead, but I'm hyperaware of Flora in the passenger seat. Her perfume gnaws at me, and being crammed inside my car with her feels claustrophobic. My mind goes blank.

Luckily Flora is chatty enough for both of us. "How's Lindsey adjusting to high school?"

"Pretty good, I guess. She doesn't tell me anything, but she's been giddy lately."

She nods. "That's because she has a boyfriend."

"Already?" It's been two weeks since school started.

"Yeah, his name is Beckett. He's in her English class. Lindsey's declared that she'll marry him the second high school ends."

"Right."

"She's got it bad. It's a recipe for disaster, if you ask me. When you pour your heart out to a guy this easily, nothing good comes out of it. As Madison would say, let the guy do some work. Make him sweat a little, or he'll never cherish you."

"I hope you don't believe that."

"In theory. But I have trouble applying it. When I like someone, I can't shut up about it."

Her eyes linger on my face, and something in her voice still gets to me. I need to remember why we broke up. But it's hard to remember anything when she looks at me like that. Then the thought of her cheating on me lands hard, like a stone dropped into still water. I change the subject. "Thanks for looking out for Lindsey. She's lucky to have you as a friend."

"No need to thank me. I've always wanted a little sister to spoil, and in a way, she reminds me of myself. I was clueless when I first started high school, too, and I had my fair share of boyfriends who didn't appreciate me." She glances at me again as I pull up in front of the restaurant.

Once seated, I let her order for both of us. She's meticulous about dining etiquette, acting like she grew up in Tokyo just because she can say *arigato* to the server, who greets us with "*Irasshaimase!*" She asks for recommendations and then orders something completely different, but still thanks the server every time she comes to the table.

She watches as I pick up my chopsticks. "They should revoke your right to eat Asian food."

"Enlighten me, then."

She demonstrates how to pick up a slice of marinated radish, her hands shaking. The radish wobbles, then drops back onto her plate.

"Yeah, not sure I want to learn from you."

"Put your index finger *here*." She reaches across the table, taking my hand to adjust my grip. Her touch is cool, but my pulse spikes.

I withdraw my hand as subtly as I can. "I can teach myself."

"Let's see how that works out." She leans back. I practice, balancing the food, while Flora lounges in her chair, gloating. When she reaches for another radish slice, I move faster and snatch it right off the plate with my chopsticks before she can.

She stares at me with her eyes widened.

"You don't have to be so arrogant, Flora. It's not rocket science. It's not even hard."

She shakes her head, biting back a smile. "You have terrible table manners, Sean."

I finish my dinner while Flora fills my cup with green tea and the space between us with her nonstop chatter. By the time we leave, it's dark outside. We stayed too long. I enjoyed her company a little too much.

What is this, poking at a bruise to make sure it still hurts?

I shouldn't do this again. Next time she suggests dinner, I'll head straight to a McDonald's drive-through and toss her a Big Mac.

"Can I close my eyes for a bit?" Flora asks as we settle in my car. "I'm exhausted. I'll get my car tomorrow."

"No problem. I'll wake you up when we get to your place."

"Thanks. How do I lean the seat back?"

"There's a handle to your right."

She fumbles around and turns to me. "I can't do it."

"It's the same as every car."

"No, yours is stuck. Can you help?"

Her face is innocent, but I have a truckload of dirty thoughts. Adjusting the seat means reaching over and touching her. As I lean in to work the adjuster, we're so close I can almost feel the warmth of her breath.

Flora is a Siren in Odysseus's tale, and I have the self-control of a sailor with no wax in his ears.

"Better?" I ask, my voice coming out rough.

She hums, eyes already closed. "Much better. Thanks."

I turn the music down and drive in silence. When we stop at a red light, I grab my jacket from the back seat and drape it over her.

She doesn't stir. She's so at ease beside me. When I pull up to her building, she's still sleeping. I indulge myself in gazing at her for a few seconds more, memorizing the way she breathes, the way her lashes rest against her cheek. I'll never have the chance again. She's still the most beautiful girl I've ever seen, even though she broke my heart.

"I had fun tonight," Flora murmurs, still not opening her eyes.

I tear my gaze away. "We're here."

She stretches, arms overhead, then straightens up and hands my jacket back. "Thanks. You're very sweet."

"No problem."

"Well, see you tomorrow."

Our eyes lock. My heart rate picks up again. Then, before opening the door, she leans over and gives my shoulder a squeeze.

It's with the right amount of strength, playful enough to keep me guessing. She gets out of the car and heads up the stairs to her door.

CHAPTER SEVENTEEN

Flora

The second I get home, I call Madison. "You're never going to believe this." I chuck my purse on the floor and flop onto my bed. "I was on a date with Sean!"

There's a short pause, then, "Sean? Sean *Foster?* What were you *thinking?*"

Instant rage.

"We were going over the history project, and I asked him to grab a bite. It was nothing."

"Right."

I sigh, pressing my eyes shut. "But it was *fun.*"

"Honey, no. You need to stop this. I'm getting bad vibes. Don't tell me you still have feelings for that guy."

"I don't know, but—" I hesitate, then blurt it out. "*He* might still be into *me.* He looks at me like . . . like he wants me but won't let himself."

She scoffs. "No, *you* want him. Sean's the tiger from *Life of Pi.* Richard Parker, was it? You're seeing your own emotions reflected back at you."

"There were clues all over the place. He ate everything off my plate when I couldn't finish. That has to mean something."

"Sure," she agrees. "It means he was hungry and has no boundaries. Get a golden retriever if that's what you're looking for."

"But we're history partners. We *have* to spend time together."

"Keep it professional. Have you forgotten how you were after the breakup?" Madison's voice rises through the phone. "Look, I don't do sweet and useless like Carmen, but I don't want you crying over him again. Tears are boring."

Those first few weeks—sleepless nights, tears on the pillow, the gut-punch rejection when he acted like we'd meant nothing. How is it so easy for him? How does he just move on while I'm stuck here, unraveling? My throat tightens. "You don't understand what it's like being around him. Half of me wants to drag him to the bathroom and kiss him senseless, and half of me wants to stab him with my chopsticks. I might even be subconsciously trying to seduce him. I want him to fall for me again."

Madison lets out a sharp exhale. "Why in the world would you want that? He's a shitty boyfriend who'll bolt the next time you have a fight."

She's right, of course. But then, out of nowhere, a completely unhinged thought forms in my head. I run my fingers through my hair, pressing against my scalp like I can massage the logic back into me. "Maybe I can get him to fall for me . . . so I can dump him."

Madison falls silent. Every second drips with judgment. "You already dumped him the first time. Why do it again?"

"I said it in the heat of the moment, but I didn't mean it. He was the one who wanted to break up. I'll never get over him unless he understands how it feels to be left behind." The thought sparks, catching fire.

He needs to know what it's like to lose me. He needs to feel it, deep in his bones, the way I did. Sean thinks he can stand up and leave like I was some passing phase? No. He can't escape me. I'm back—vengeful and even more powerful in the sequel.

"I already know how it's all going to play out. Your plan backfires, and I spend the rest of the year listening to you wail about it."

"Please, I need this. To gain my power back. It's the only way to stop feeling like I lost."

"Or, hear me out, you could move on like a normal person. Go to therapy—"

"Madison."

She mutters something unintelligible. "You're insane. Getting revenge is something only *I'd* do."

"That's why I need your wisdom on the art of revenge! Teach me your ways, *senpai*."

Madison doesn't speak. I can almost hear the gears churning in her head, coughing up evil schemes. After an eternity, she sighs. "This is a terrible idea."

A pause.

Then, grudgingly, "But as your best friend, I'll support every single one of your terrible ideas."

* * *

Madison's first action plan is a group date. Our cover is the newly opened ice-cream parlor a block from school. We must check it out and see how it stacks up against our old favorite, Amber's. We tell the guys Carmen is writing a review for the school newsletter and needs extra opinions. (Not that we share our real motives with Carmen, for obvious reasons.)

The moment we step inside, we're greeted with the warm scent of freshly made cones. The place is all soft peach-colored sofas and floral cushions on one side, stiff-backed chairs on the other. It's cute, but trying a little too hard.

Sean falls in step beside me, waiting for me to pick a seat. I sink into a sofa.

"I have an idea for the school newsletter." Jake plops down next to me before Carmen can even sit. "You should interview me, Carmesan." He snags the menu from under my hands. Sean grabs another from the counter and takes the seat across from me, sliding it across the table.

"They canceled the Student Spotlight column ages ago," Madison replies in her signature authoritative tone, even though *Carmen* is the editor-in-chief. "Otherwise I would've had my feature already."

"No, not an article on *me* per se. People know I've been voted Most Gorgeous three years straight and I'm the best small forward this town has ever seen." Jake rakes a hand through his hair, as if mesmerized by his own achievements.

"Are we sure the votes weren't rigged?" I cut in. "I didn't vote for you once."

Jake grins good-naturedly. "We all know who *you* voted for, Ms. Morgan."

Sean flips through the menu, suddenly very interested in his options. Jake continues, "I meant using the platform to share my beliefs. Something like, how to get laid as a gentleman."

I snort. "What does that even mean? You hold the door open for her when you're done having sex?"

"It means embracing your sexuality." Jake spreads his arms like he's delivering a TED Talk. "I'm all for sex positivity. Mutual consent, open communication, supporting fluidity, whatever you're into—some might say I'm an advocate for healthy relationships. I don't see why people have to be so judgy. Flora, you get it, right?"

I choke on my water. "What? I don't go around having casual sex!"

"No, but you strike me as a progressive thinker." He steeples his fingers together, forming a mock-thoughtful triangle. "Write it like a guidebook, Carmen. Rule one: choose your partner with caution. Rule two: acknowledge women are sexual beings—"

Madison scoffs. There are no vegan options here, and she's stuck with a glass of soda water. "We're a school paper, not a BuzzFeed quiz called 'What Kind of Walking Red Flag Are You?'"

"That's, uh, an idea," Carmen says. "But I don't think it'll make it past the admin. They're never going to endorse it."

Jake shakes his head. "This is why nobody reads the school newspaper."

"Sadly, the average mortals simply aren't ready for your wisdom," Sean says, not looking up, as if he's heard Jake's pitch a thousand times. Which he probably has.

"Thank you." Jake presses his palms together and bows his head solemnly. "It's rare to be recognized by one's peers."

"I have an idea," I say. "How about a college admissions guide? And maybe alternatives, like taking a gap year—"

"Think about it, Carmesan," Jake says. "My message is important. If we shame girls for being open to sex, then we're cock-blocking ourselves."

Carmen laughs, and even though Madison rolls her eyes, he gets her attention. I shut my mouth. My idea is lousy anyway. This is senior year. Everyone already knows where they're applying and what they want to do.

"You were saying?"

Sean's voice blocks out everything else. Jake is still rambling about his rules, but Sean and me, we're in our own little world.

"Nah, it's stupid." I glance away. "Are you ready to order?"

"What do you want to do after high school?"

Attend a New York City school, land an internship, and become a fashion editor. But I don't say that because it sounds frivolous; at least, compared to the kinds of dreams that get taken seriously around here. It's not helping patients or changing the world with engineering—it's talking about people looking pretty and stylish. "I'm still considering my options."

We order our smoothies and sundaes. When they arrive, ice cream is running down the side of my glass.

Sean gets up and returns with napkins for everyone.

"Thanks." I nod toward his glass. "How's your citrus smoothie?"

"Not bad."

"Want to try mine?"

"No, thank you."

"Come on, one bite. I'm great at ordering desserts." I scoop up a massive spoonful of ice cream and top it off with a blueberry.

Sean reaches for the spoon, but I dodge, holding it out of reach. A challenge.

Neither of us moves. My eyes narrow. His stay locked on mine. A second later, he leans in, lips brushing the edge of the spoon as he takes the bite.

"I like it," he says, still looking at me.

"Knew you'd give in eventually."

Beside me, Madison says, "Let's all go see a movie later." She's extending this date for my sake, and she goes as far as suggesting a horror film, which she normally hates.

"I thought you only watched movies with subtitles," Jake says.

"I feel like watching a scary movie today," Madison says. It's an excuse for me to grab onto Sean. "I'll cover your eyes when the scary parts come on. Like when the blond jock gets killed in the first five minutes, mid-hookup."

"Unless the prom queen beats him to the punch and dies first," Jake dishes back.

Sean clears his throat, shoving his hands into his pockets. "I have to catch up on homework and be home for dinner."

"God, you're such a good kid," Jake says. "Do you say thank you to your homework too?"

"Always," Sean says. "Anyway, I can't go. You guys have fun."

Madison and I exchange a look, and she shrugs. Nothing throws her off. "That's okay. Hey, can we stop by your place real quick? Lindsey wants to burrow my curling iron, and I have it right here." She taps the strap of her backpack.

"I can give it to her for you," Sean says.

Madison tilts her head. "And you're going to show her how to use it too?"

* * *

Everything goes exactly as Madison envisioned. She stays in Lindsey's room with me until dinner and leaves the second Sean's mom invites us to stay. Now I'm sitting at their dining table, one big happy family, while soft jazz drifts from a speaker in the corner. The whole room feels cozy, like a house that's always had people to fill it.

Sean's mom beams at me as I ask if there's anything I can help with. "No, we're just happy to have you."

Sean's dad sets a basket of bread in front of me. "I hear you're working on a history project with Sean and Josie?"

"It's a lot of fun. I didn't think I'd ever enjoy a school project, but I got lucky with my partners."

Sean raises an eyebrow. "I'm recording this."

His mom laughs. "I'm glad you're having fun. Get my son to

relax a little! He works too hard. We even talked him out of taking AP World History. Surely a 4.72 weighted GPA is enough?"

His dad grins. "Yeah, the day he got an A- in German was the darkest day in this family. We almost held a vigil."

Sean frowns. "I need to show I can handle a tough course load."

How does Lindsey feel about having a brother like Sean? It must be exhausting, living in the shadow of his perfect grades. There was definitely a faint twinge of jealousy when Jeremy won the state debating championship, even though I'm not supposed to compete with him. Maybe it's the same for her, constantly trying to measure up to the untouchable golden child.

"Lindsey's the creative one in this family." Sean's mom lifts a fork of mashed potatoes to her mouth. "She writes the best stories."

"They're not bad," Sean agrees. "My favorite is the one about the Everest expedition." He glances at me and explains, "It's a survival story with supernatural elements and psychological tension. Gets dark fast."

"Mine's 'The Road Trip.'" His dad gets up, opens a drawer, and pulls out a handful of mismatched takeout napkins and tosses them onto the table. "I keep wondering what happens to those kids."

"That one's ominous too. Messes with your head," Sean says to me, catching me up, and my heart melts a little. Kindness like that is underrated; it sneaks up on you.

"I love a good psychological thriller," I say.

"It's not that great." Lindsey's face flushes against her dark ringlets. "I have these stories in my head sometimes, and I must get them on paper."

"I love reading all your writing." Sean's mom smiles.

My stomach churns, even though the food is delicious. Somewhere on earth, people eat dinner with their parents every night—parents who read their work and know everything about the courses they're taking.

"You guys really lucked out with these two," I say, and they laugh.

"Well, we never have to worry much about Linz." Sean's dad fills his glass with tap water. "But Sean has his cranky teenager moments. Remember how bitter and cynical you were in middle school?"

Sean grimaces. "Dad! I may doubt the world sometimes, but I was never *bitter.*"

"He's pretty bitter to *me*," Lindsey says. "Flora is the one who takes care of me at school."

"True." Sean nods. "Flora's been an amazing friend to Lindsey."

"Thanks, that's very kind." His dad sets a bowl of salad in front of me. "She's ecstatic to go to school because of you."

"I didn't really do that much." With or without Sean, spending time with Lindsey is easy. "I only sat with her the first week, now she's got loads of friends of her own. She's delightful and everyone loves her."

"I could say the same about you." Sean's mom places her hand on my wrist for one second, and I want to hug her. I want to hug this whole dining room.

A comfortable lull settles over the table. I take a bite of grilled salmon and sigh. "I went to this Michelin-starred place in Napa once with my parents, and they served the most incredible whole grilled sea bass. It was buttery soft and melty." I wipe my hands on the recycled paper napkin. "Mr. Foster, this salmon takes me right back. It's delicious."

He chuckles, eyes bright with amusement. "You're exaggerating."

Beside me, Sean shifts, smiling good-naturedly. "Maybe you should stop going to Michelin restaurants if you can't tell the difference."

"I don't lie about food," I say, "and home-cooked meals are such a luxury."

"I'd rather we get Chick-fil-A, to be honest," Lindsey says.

"No one in this house appreciates my talent." Sean's dad sighs. "You're welcome to dinner any time."

When dinner wraps up, Sean pushes his chair back and stands up.

I stand too. "I'll help clean up."

As the rest of his family moves into the living room to watch TV, I pick up a plate from the table.

"Hey, I've got it," Sean says, a teasing glint in his eyes. "You hate loading the dishwasher."

"Your mom was nice enough to ask me to stay, it's the least I can do. Thanks for having me," I say.

"No, thank *you* for staying. It's nothing fancy, but my parents like you. Having you here makes them happy."

We grab the same plate at once, and he looks at me when I don't let go. "And are *you* happy I stayed?" I ask.

"It's one more plate to wash, but I can tolerate it." He lets go and picks up the glasses instead. Then he sneaks a peek at the living room and lowers his voice. "So, I finally met Lindsey's soulmate. But only because they needed a ride to mini golf."

Fine, change the subject. "Let me guess, you don't approve of him."

He carries the glasses to the kitchen. "They sat in the back seat whispering and were all over each other while I drove in front like a chauffeur. If there'd been a glass divider between us, they would've pulled it shut."

"I'm surprised he didn't try sucking up to you. If I was dating someone's sister I'd make sure I was on good terms with the older, more popular brother. Maybe ask you pointers on how to get deltoids like yours."

"Oh, that's easy. Use crutches," he says, then smiles with a trace of affection as he pulls open the dishwasher. "Only you'd compliment me on my deltoids."

We lapse into a moment of silence.

Our fingers touch occasionally as we pass the plates, and my heart thuds each time it happens. *Ridiculous.* This is a boy I've done a lot of things with. I've touched plenty of places that are way more off-limits than his hands, and yet here I am, freaking out over our fingers grazing.

I clear my throat. "So, this was fun. Nice to take a break from the history play, even though that's fun too."

"Yeah, you said that. And you feel *lucky* to be paired with me? This is new," Sean says.

"I can change my mind, can't I?" I peer up at him through my lashes. "I appreciate that you put up with my ideas with mild amusement."

"Mild amusement? Try excruciating reluctance."

"When I get upset, you drop the arrogant act. And even though you can be intolerably stubborn, at the end of the day, you're willing to listen."

He makes a small sound between snorting and chuckling. "Is this a compliment or . . . ? Because all I'm hearing is *arrogant* and *intolerable.*"

"I'm saying I love working with you."

Our eyes lock. There's a certain softness in his gaze, the same way he looked when he used to call me button. He bites his lip, and my heart stumbles. It's so hard not to like him.

"When you look at me like that," I say, "I really, *really* want to kiss you."

He stares at me, eyes wide, beautiful, not blinking. I raise my chin and hold his gaze. Then he leans in, his lips parted slightly.

I close my eyes.

A soft, light peck lands. On my *cheek*.

My eyes snap open. "Whoa, a kiss on the cheek? Can I post about this and let the internet decode it?" I muse out loud. "Is he testing the waters? Telling me to stay away? Hallucinating and seeing his aunt?"

"It means you're cute." He laughs. "But stop flirting with me."

I scratch my chin. "Hmm. Then how do I say 'I think you're cute, too, but I want to keep flirting with you'?" Not giving him time to react, I lean in and kiss him back—also on the cheek. Then I draw back, frowning. "Wait, not sure I said it well enough. Let me try saying it more slowly this time . . ."

He chuckles, taking a step back.

"Maybe with a British accent?" I press on.

He picks up the dish towel and swats at me, laughing. I laugh along with him, trying to remember the last time I had such a marvelous evening.

CHAPTER EIGHTEEN

Sean

"You should've come with us yesterday," Jake says to Dylan after practice on Tuesday, tossing his sweat-drenched shirt into his gym bag. "You missed a great show."

Dylan slams his locker shut, then pounds on it twice for good measure. "I thought you didn't go to the movies."

"No, watching Flora feed Sean ice cream. She was really laying it on thick."

Dylan turns to me and whistles. "*Seany* . . . what's going on?"

"Nothing's going on," I say.

"You're holding out on me?" Jake says, mock offended. "Your mentor, who taught you everything about dating and hidden make-out spots?" He shared *one* chill location at the Viewpoint, didn't make me cite sources, and now apparently I owe him everything.

"And look how successful Sean turned out under your expert guidance," Dylan says, somehow landing a clean double kill like it's *Fortnite*.

I zip up my gym bag, letting their jokes roll off me. Maybe I'm not making strides on the dating front, but this exes-turned-friends thing? Huge progress. Holding a grudge over the whole cheating mess would've been easy, but that chapter closed long ago. It hurt, sure, but somewhere along the way, bitterness lost its potency and metabolized into a guilty pleasure. She flirts, I can flirt back. Having a friend is preferable to having an adversary. I can forgive and forget.

As long as I'm careful not to let her disarm me again.

"What's the point of getting back together? You've been *there* and done *that*." As usual, everything Dylan says has the potential to be obscene. "It's the surprise factor that counts."

"I'm not getting back with Flora, but your theories are totally unconvincing. How many times have you gotten back together with Sydney?"

"That's because you don't know the things Syd's capable of. Let's just say, nobody understands what I need the way she does." He smirks. "What? I meant emotionally. Like being listened to."

Jake laughs, ready to contribute his astute insights on the subject, but as we step outside, I tune him out.

The door swings shut behind us.

Up ahead, Lindsey leans against a wall, kicking at the gravel with her foot. Now that she has a boyfriend, she only talks to me when she needs a favor.

"Can you give me a lift home?" she asks in a small voice. Her eyes are red rimmed. She keeps her lips tight all the way to the parking lot, gets in the car, and fastens her seat belt without a word.

"Are you going to tell me what happened?"

Her chest rises and falls a few times. "You have to promise not to say anything to Mom and Dad."

A car honks outside, and my grip tightens on the wheel. "Please tell me you're not pregnant." Okay, maybe that was dramatic, but—

"No, it's worse." She lets out a sharp sigh. "He dumped me."

"Oh."

"Because I wouldn't do what he wanted."

I do not require specifics to grasp the situation. The way they behaved together—it was inevitable that he would eventually push for more. I should've said something sooner. But Lindsey isn't a kid anymore, and I figured she'd tell me if something was wrong.

Guess I was wrong about that too.

Before I can launch into how she dodged a bullet, Lindsey's face crumples. "Now he's telling everyone we did it and I was terrible at it. I'm not even sure how a girl can be bad at sex!"

As usual, her tears freeze my brain on the spot. This is how she got the bigger bedroom, by the way.

But beneath the sibling reflex to make light of it, something darker coils inside me. For some reason Flora comes to mind. Sitting on her bed, twisting her fingers as she told me about Zach Powell and how he broadcasted the whole thing like it was his to tell. Seems like you just can't win—whether you say yes or no, someone can still take your story and make you feel disposable.

"That's awful. I'm sorry."

"We had so many plans. My birthday, everything. He won't be celebrating with me now. I feel so betrayed."

"Have you tried talking to him?" *Right. Because that worked out so well for me with Flora.*

"He denied saying anything. There's nothing I can do." She sniffles, turning her head to the window. "You know how rumors are. I can't prove he started it."

He'll get away with it. But he's not my concern, not really. I only care what happens to her.

"Are you sure you don't want Mom and Dad to know?" They created her, after all. They shouldn't be allowed to sit out a crisis.

"No! I already know what they'll say. They'll tell me to focus on school. Like you." She finds the energy to roll her eyes at me.

A long pause stretches between us. If only I could turn into Flora for five minutes. She'd find some effortless, borderline-miraculous way to cheer Lindsey up. A couple of students ride by on bicycles, and Lindsey straightens in her seat. She turns on the radio, and we listen in silence.

She pulls her lips into a reluctant smile. "Hey, you know I'm only telling you this so you can beat him up, right?"

"Yup. Just tell me where. Face or gut?"

She rolls her eyes, but her grin lingers. "Yeah, right. Forget it. I'm fine."

Lindsey handling this with composure somehow makes it even more unbearable. The only thing worse than a bratty Lindsey is a nonbratty version. It's like losing my little sister in real time. I grit my teeth at the way she shrinks into the passenger seat and tries to pretend this doesn't hurt as much as it clearly does.

"Seriously, what can I do for you?"

She wipes her nose. "Nothing. I want to forget about it and move on."

"I'm here if you need me," I say, the words sounding foreign in my mouth.

"Uh-huh. Thanks."

"Do you want a hug?"

She stiffens, then she opens her arms and hugs me. We almost never do this. She pulls away after approximately 2.8 seconds, grimacing. "Ew. Bad idea."

"Agreed. Let's never do that again."

She laughs and taps on the steering wheel. "Come on. Let's go home."

* * *

The next day at lunch, Flora calls out to me in the cafeteria. Lindsey is sitting with them, shoulders slumped. She hasn't sat with Flora's group for a while, but maybe today's special circumstances.

"We heard what happened. Unacceptable," Josie says as she crumples a juice carton and drops it onto the table.

Madison says, "We're brainstorming ways to get even."

"No, *they* are," Carmen corrects. "I'm against this whole revenge thing."

Lindsey lowers her head. "Me too. I don't want to talk about this anymore."

"Grow a spine." Madison gives Lindsey's shoulder a firm pat. "How's a girl supposed to move on unless she has the perfect revenge plan underway?"

"How about leaving it to karma?" Carmen suggests.

Madison scoffs. "Karma is what people say when they're too lazy to be petty. Strong people take matters into their own hands. Now, Lindsey, we start a rumor too."

"Something so stupid, so bizarre, that it outlives us all," Flora says. "How about he's been secretly feeding a Sasquatch in his backyard? They're best friends."

Lindsey snorts.

"We're trying to ruin his life," Josie says, "not make him seem *enchanting.*"

Flora's eyes sparkle in that way that excites and scares me. "Forget the rumor—let's pull a prank. If we put our heads together, we can make his life *very* annoying."

Lindsey turns to me, mouthing *No.*

"Come on, you don't have to stoop to his level," I say. "The best revenge's moving on and living well."

Madison says, "You sound seventy instead of seventeen. Toss whatever self-help book you're reading."

Flora leans in, both hands on the table. "We call his parents and say he's been stealing cafeteria meat loaf. Get them to set up a meeting with the principal. Or—I read about something like this on Reddit—we post a Craigslist ad saying he's giving away *free alpacas*. Imagine people calling him day and night, demanding alpacas."

Lindsey laughs—because alpacas. They have that effect on people. Then she drops her head into her palms. "Can we *please* drop this?"

"Write a song about him!" Flora claps Josie on the shoulder. "Something like, 'Beckstabbing Liar,' or 'What the Beck Was I Thinking?'"

"Again, not trying to make him enchanting. Dude, do it the old-fashioned way and punch him. Or at least threaten him. Or ask your guard dog Dylan to do it—he'll throw hands for you, no questions asked." At this point, Josie's just here for the chaos.

"Violence works like a charm every time," Madison seconds.

"I'm not going to hit a freshman," I say.

Flora shakes her head at me like I've personally let her down. "Chivalry is dead. You won't even defend your own sister?"

I don't answer. I could, technically, shove the kid against a locker and tell him to keep his mouth shut, but what would that change? Lindsey doesn't need revenge. She needs perspective. One failed relationship doesn't define her. High school can scar you, but it can also give you something real—friendships, memories, the kind of moments that stay with you long after you leave.

Besides, if we *really* wanted to annihilate him, it wouldn't be hard. Between Flora's friends and mine, between our social reach and whatever I can dig up online, we could make his life a lot worse than a few alpaca calls. But no one's said that, not once. Maybe because we all know the goal isn't to kick him down. It's to lift her up.

If only I could find a way.

CHAPTER NINETEEN

Flora

"Look, I need your help."

A few days after our inconclusive revenge convention, Sean finds me at my locker. I didn't think he'd come to me again so soon; we just completed our history presentation this morning. Josie absolutely crushed it as the prophet. She threw on an oversized black hoodie that hid her face, and every time she slammed her cane against the ground, the room erupted with laughter.

(We're all getting As, by the way.)

"Do you think we could plan something for Lindsey's birthday?" Sean rocks back on his heels, eyes scanning the corridor. "She's still upset even though she won't admit it."

"Obviously!"

"You throw such great parties. You did it for Dylan last year—"

"Did I?" I tilt my head, pretending not to remember.

He averts my eyes and mutters, "You did tequila shots off my stomach?"

I bite back a smile. *Oh, we're bringing* that *up now?*

Sean clears his throat, shifting his weight. "Anyway. How about a surprise party?"

Something about him standing here, needing me, asking for my opinion fills my chest with warmth. He's so self-conscious about it too.

"You're such a softie. *Awww.*" I stretch out the word, watching him squirm. "You sweet, *sweet* child. What's next, are you going to start a Pinterest mood board too?"

He scratches the back of his neck. "It's stupid, right?"

"Are you kidding? I'm going to throw her the best party *ever.*"

Sean looks up, a smile spreading across his face. "You will?"

"The end of September is less than two weeks away, though. We're on a tight schedule, and keeping this a secret makes everything doubly hard. Let's begin with the end in mind and work back from there." I whip my phone from my back pocket and open a new note.

Sean reaches out, pressing a hand over my forearm. "Wait. Before we start, can we go over some ground rules? No alcohol, no drugs, no noise complaints—"

"No fights, no summoning demons. Great, let's throw a lame party. If you want my help, then I'm going to call the shots."

"Sure, but you also need to know my budget."

"Budget?" That's one word I loathe, along with phrases like *garage sale, thrift store,* and *economy class.*

"Can we keep it under a few hundred bucks?" He winces as he says it. "That's all I have."

"But a good DJ costs at least a hundred per hour, plus a caterer, and decorations. Wait." I squint at him. "You're not thinking of opening a few bags of tortilla chips and playing music from your phone, are you? With all due respect, what's the plan—attract people with your charisma? Maybe five people will show up."

Sean leans against my locker door. "How dare you. I'd estimate about a dozen. Look, the point is to get her mind off the rumors, it doesn't have to be a huge thing."

"Then maybe you should invite a couple of girls over, have them braid each other's hair, and call it a night."

"Fine, Flora. Do it your way. Work your magic."

That's a supercute smile.

Don't get distracted. Now's not the time to marvel over his hotness. Sean wants a favor, and I need to milk his desperation for all it's worth. "Hold on a second. Why am I doing this for you?"

"Because you care about Lindsey too."

"I do, but this will take up a *tremendous* amount of my time. I'm retaking the SAT, I have cheer practice, and my schedule is dreadfully packed. If you want to hire me, you have to pay a price."

Sean's eyes widen. "You want to charge me? There's no way I can afford you."

As Joker says, if you're good at something, never do it for free. But there's no point in taking advantage of Sean's measly budget. Before I can answer, a student trips nearby, sending a pile of books and documents flying. Sean steps back as a pencil rolls toward him. I bend down, gather the scattered papers, and hand them back. The girl hurries off.

Straightening, I smooth the front of my skirt and face Sean. "I want . . . three wishes. You have to do whatever I ask. No objections."

He studies my face to see if I'm kidding. When he sees I'm not, he says, "You can get *one*."

"Then ask someone else. Raymond throws a banger too."

He flinches. I wonder why. Ray's parties are legendary, and they're also the only ones Sean ever goes to. He exhales and says, "Fine, you get two wishes. Take it or leave it. I don't want to throw Lindsey a party that badly."

"Deal." I hold out my hand to shake on it, but he keeps his at his side.

"No loophole wishes that multiply into a thousand ones, like I have to do whatever you say for the rest of the senior year."

"It goes without saying."

"And no illegal stuff or anything that'll get me expelled. Also, nothing embarrassing like asking me to wear a costume. I'd like to keep the five fans I have."

"Honestly, Sean, if there's *this* little trust between us, why are you even asking me for help?"

He grabs my hand and gives it a quick shake. "Forgive me for being wary. I tend to be cautious when I'm making deals with the devil."

* * *

At lunch the next day Sean and I take the corner table. I unveil the master plan—my vision: the ultimate birthday bash, not only an event, but an *experience*.

Guest List: Carmen got Lindsey's list of favorite people by pretending it was for a sociology project. Genius.

Event Coverage: Daniel, Madison's boyfriend (newly onboarded and fresh off his ninety-day probation), will take photos of Lindsey under the excuse of a photography contest. Let's hope he understands the assignment and meets management expectations.

Theme and Dress Code: Winter Wonderland, because it's easy. Light blue, white, and silver. Not the most original, but I like fairies in snow, and that's enough reason.

Venue and Logistics: Sean's house. His parents will be conveniently busy that night because I got them tickets to a jazz concert. My parents *happened* to have these, but *tragically* can't go, so the Fosters—being the kind, selfless people they are—agreed to take them off my hands. Genius, again.

Décor and Atmosphere: Ice sculptures on the back patio, silver streamers, white and blue balloons, a disco ball, lanterns, and a projector casting snowflakes and stars.

Entertainment: Josie's band, Fishnets, will be performing live. We'll also have a Polaroid station because nothing says *elite party* like instant-film proof you were there.

Food and Drink: A white-chocolate fountain, designer cupcakes with sprinkles, cookies with frosting, some light-blue drinks like Calpis and sparkling soda water, and maybe a cotton candy machine.

Signature Mocktail: A stunning, elegant, one-of-a-kind creation called The Arctic Kiss of a Frostbitten Celestial Goddess (or Arctic Kiss for short). It's basically blue lemonade with edible glitter, but branding is everything.

"I kind of want pizza at the party." Sean glances at the cafeteria line, but he takes one look at me and clears his throat. "Never mind. Doesn't go with the theme colors."

"Now we're on the same page." Scanning the room, I take in the glorious display of high-school cohabitation. Plastic chairs scrape against the floor and people shuffle in and out. "I'm breaking stereotype cliques and including everyone, regardless of race, religious beliefs, and whether they look good in khakis. How's that sound?"

"Sounds like there's going to be a lot of people." Sean dips a potato wedge in ketchup. "How many are we talking?"

"Oh," I say airily, "around a hundred."

He stops midbite. "I said thirty, max!"

I wave a hand. "Please. A tight dance floor is crucial. Otherwise, people won't let loose without alcohol. Thirty people staring at each other from across the room won't cut it. We need density. Flow. Energy."

He takes a long sip from his apple juice. "How can you keep this a secret with a hundred people involved? And you seriously know a hundred people well enough to invite them?"

"You have to know someone *well* before you can invite them to a party?"

"You're not using this as an excuse to invite all the guys you like, are you?"

I put down the celery stick I've been chewing. "Sean Foster, I'm putting *serious* effort into making this a memorable event, and you don't appreciate it. I don't know which is more insulting, that you think I'm using this for my own benefit or that I need to throw a party to get a guy's attention."

"I apologize. That was a bad joke." When I don't smile he tugs on my sleeve, first downward, then side to side. "Forgive me. Please."

I chuckle uselessly. "Okay, I like it when you grovel."

"I'm really sorry. I can't tell you how grateful I am for your help."

"Now stop before you get grease on my clothes." I shove him lightly on the shoulder, and he goes back to chomping on his potato wedges. "By the way, I found a way around the DJ and caterer. I know this guy, Xavier, whose mom is a caterer, and then there's this other guy . . . anyway, I'm pulling strings to fit everything under your budget, so don't worry."

"Hmm." He tilts his chin up, then wipes his hands on a napkin. "On second thought, I'd rather we pay. I'll get the money."

"Oh Sean." I rest my chin in my palm. "You sound so cute when you're jealous."

He fidgets. "I'm not. But it feels like I'm hosting a Flora Morgan ex-boyfriend support group."

"They're not my exes."

But you are. The only boyfriend who shattered my heart, and I keep forgetting I'm throwing this party for revenge, not because I enjoy it.

I cross my arms. "Two jokes about my dating life in under a minute?"

Sean leans back, sighs, and bites his lip. "Fine. I admit I'm a little jealous."

A flush creeps up my skin. Before I can reply, the click of a camera shutter distracts me. Madison and Daniel are a few tables away. Daniel is adjusting the settings on his DSLR, pointing it at a sad-looking plant near the window. He's quiet, eccentric, and plain weird, but Madison excuses everything by explaining he's an artist.

Over the summer, he even rented an exhibition space downtown, and Madison dragged us to see his work. All his paintings were aggressively abstract, and at one point she proudly announced that she was his muse and had posed nude for him.

We nearly died laughing.

"I feel so much closer to Daniel now," I'd said, wiping away tears. "He's an average teenage boy after all—"

"Who would say anything to get you naked," Josie had finished, and Carmen lost it. We pointed at random circles and kept bugging Madison to tell us which one was her nipple, then took selfies with the painting (obviously tagging her).

Ah, good times.

I still don't know how to respond to Sean admitting he's jealous, so I whisper this anecdote to him instead. My elbow rests on the table, my other hand on his shoulder as I lean in, and his laughter shakes his body beneath my fingers as our heads bend close together. It feels divine to make Sean laugh.

Then *click.*

Madison stands before us, and Daniel snaps a few more pictures of her and of me and Sean.

"Taking some shots of the planning committee," Madison says. *The audacity.* The only thing she's planned so far is what she's wearing, but at least she's convinced Daniel to help. "What are you two laughing about?"

Sean and I exchange a look. "Nothing," we say in unison. Then he catches my eyes and smiles.

CHAPTER TWENTY

Sean

At lunch the next day, Flora stops at my table, already midsentence as she pulls out a chair. I slide it the rest of the way for her.

"Dyl, Jake, I forgot if I told you about our party," she says. "I've talked to so many people, and you guys are obviously invited, but I can't remember if I actually mentioned it."

"Yeah, we know," Dylan says. "Sean told us. But as soon as we heard there wouldn't be a keg, we blacked out from boredom."

"What's the point if we can't get wasted and embarrass ourselves?" Jake asks. "But sure, we'll drop by. Moral support."

Flora leans in across the table. "Actually, I need more than that. Can you guys help keep an eye out? If you see any gate-crashers or someone sneaking in beer, shut it down. No alcohol. No drugs."

"We can't even bring our own booze?" Jake throws up his hands.

"Don't worry, I'll handle it," I say. Flora wasn't even on board with this at first, but now she's making sure it happens. For my sake. "These two can't be trusted with anything."

"You can't do everything yourself. In times of need, this is what friends are for." She gives the guys a pointed look. "It's called team-work. *Collaboration.*"

"We're the kind of friends who laugh when he fails," Dylan

corrects her. "Not the ones who show up to his baby sister's birthday wearing party hats."

Flora exhales, pushing a hand through her hair. She starts to describe her winter theme and dessert table. *Terrible idea. These guys won't humor her like I do.*

"Hmmm. The fairies and the enchanted forest sound fantastic, but you know what else is missing?" Jake pretends to chew on the idea, then lifts his head as if struck by an epiphany. "A unicorn."

"And spin the bottle," Dylan adds. "Oh, and a booth for painting toenails."

"I love fortune tellers too," Jake continues. "Please tell me you're hiring one."

"Guys, cut it out," I say. Beside me, Flora's smile is frozen, her jaw tight. She hates being mocked when she's serious.

"Jake, I don't need a fortune teller to predict where you'll end up in five years," she snaps. "You'll be pumping gas for my Porsche."

Jake clutches his chest, wincing. "*Oof.* Harsh. I thought we'd be flipping burgers side by side at Burger King."

Dylan laughs.

"Hey, stop. It's not funny," I say, though it kind of is. "Flora's only doing this because I begged her to."

Dylan shakes his head. "Dude, that's what you get for asking a girl to throw your party. Just buy some pizzas, order a few kegs, and you're all set."

"Oh, totally. And while we're at it, let's toss in a sticky beer pong table and a broken speaker. That'll really elevate the vibe." Flora sighs. "I need everyone to do their job. Madison's handling the Polaroid booth, Carmen's running the mocktail bar, and—"

"Wait, there's a mocktail bar?" Jake interrupts. "Tell me it has one of those fancy bartender flippy bottles."

Flora glares. "No, but it does have edible glitter, which you're banned from touching."

"The no-alcohol part was my idea," I say. "It's not cool, and you don't have to come if you don't want to, but Flora's put a lot of effort into this. Give her a break."

Dylan gasps in feigned hurt. "Are we being uninvited?" He turns to Flora and smirks. "Sean gets real pissed when we pick on the girl he likes."

"We don't pick on people," I say flatly. "Is it necessary? Is it kind? No. Don't forget to bring your own unicorn."

"Sure, Seany." Dylan's eyebrows waggle, and Flora's eyes are on me. I pick up my milk carton and take my time drinking. Kindergarten teachers must be exhausted, if this is what they deal with. No wonder they get summers off.

"We were messing with you, Flora. You know that, right?" Jake grins, shoving a handful of fries into his mouth. "Of course we'll be there."

"We'll keep an eye out like you asked," Dylan says. "And if you need anything else, say the word."

Flora's face brightens instantly. "Thanks, guys! I knew if I dug deep enough, under all that false pretense there are hearts of gold."

"Right. After all these years of digging, I haven't found anything," I say. "But I have gotten myself really filthy in the process."

They all laugh.

Jake leans back. "Why are you so uptight about drugs and alcohol? You've played drinking games with us before."

"Because the party is at my house. For my fifteen-year-old sister. If something goes wrong, it's on my parents, not just me. I'm not putting them in that position."

Jake shakes his head, grinning. "Such a good boy. Always so *proper.*"

"I need to make a confession at Church Sean," Dylan says solemnly. "I forgot to kiss my mom this morning and tell her I love her."

I drink my milk. "I hope you find forgiveness."

"Amen," Jake says.

CHAPTER TWENTY-ONE

Flora

After confirming Dylan and Jake's commitment to the party, everything is pretty much set. That afternoon, Sean and I stay after school for another progress update.

Pulling out my phone, I open the group chat, scrolling through to show him who's doing what. "I've got someone handling the RSVP list, and there's a team taking care of the decorations and setting everything up. Oh, and the parking situation. They can't park in the driveway because it'll ruin the surprise, so we're directing them to park at the community lot. I'm also coordinating carpooling for people who are coming from farther out."

I tap the screen, and the pinned message at the top expands. *By being added to this group, I acknowledge and agree to the terms and conditions of the party, which include: maintaining the confidentiality of the event, refraining from bringing any contraband, and understanding that failure to comply will result in Madison personally hunting you down. Please promptly leave the group if you do not wish to follow these terms.*

Then I add Sean to the chat. "Meant to add you earlier, but I wanted to make sure everything was under control first. For your peace of mind."

His eyes soften as he looks at the screen. "You're not just

organized with the fun details; you thought of the logistics too." His voice is full of sincerity. "I don't know what to say. You're doing all the work. How can I help?"

"I didn't do that much, honestly, aside from barking out orders. Turns out everyone's weirdly willing to contribute." If I wasn't already the most popular girl at school, now I definitely am. Party planning is a blast.

"You're doing this so we can save money. I can't thank you enough." Words like *help*, *free*, and *contribute* sure make Sean happy. Apparently, the key to a man's heart is through guarding his wallet, or in this case, his money clip.

"To tell you the truth," I say, my voice quiet, "I'm glad you asked me for help. For once in my life, I feel like I'm not completely useless."

He stills. "Wait. What was that?"

"Okay, *useless* isn't the right word." I shift in my seat, avoiding his gaze. "Sometimes I feel . . . well, unaccomplished compared to my friends. I'm all fluff. I'm a cloud of pink cotton candy. Looks good enough to eat, but no real substance. Josie's a small celebrity with her band. Madison's kind of a tough nut, but she's so wise and wins every competition she takes part in. Raymond watches all those films and can quote every line, and Carmen's both well-read *and* the editor of the school paper. And . . . I always feel inadequate next to you. What I'm good at pales in comparison."

My face flushes. He's the last person I should be admitting this to. He's the smartest, most ambitious and determined person I've ever met, and he'll have the brightest future out of all of us.

I plaster on my sweetest cotton candy–adorned smile. "Not that I don't think I'm fabulous the way I am, of course."

Turning my attention to my phone, I let my hair slide down one side so I can avoid his gaze, which is for sure full of sympathy. No, thanks. He doesn't need to feel sorry for me or even say something nice. I've never been the type of girl who needs people to worry about her. I'm the entertainment provider in designer jeans and perfect hair.

Sean lays his hand atop mine, and his fingers curl gently. "Flora."

Heat spreads from my neck down to my back.

"I never knew. I can't believe you think like that. Self-doubt happens to even the best of us, I guess." His tone is kind and empathetic, without any trace of mockery. "There's something very valuable about you. You were born with it. You have—"

"Family money?"

"You have awesome people skills. You have the power to inspire people, and everything you mentioned—you've helped them, right? Madison's campaigns, Josie's band image, and Carmen's newsletter? You're part of all of it."

"Yup, I'll always be the cheerleader." I throw a fist in the air, pretending to wave around a pom-pom. "Rah."

"And *me*. Look at how you wrangled this party together from scratch. You pulled it off in, what, a week? You're persuasive, and you get people on board, like . . . you're a team player *and* also a leader. The kind of work you do is harder to measure, but it's not any less impressive." After he says this in one breath, he stops and swallows. "You get what I mean, right?"

If only my parents could hear this. They're always stressing how leadership is equal parts strategy and execution. For once, they might realize that's exactly what I'm doing, too, even if it's party planning, not coordinating scientific disclosures at medical conferences. Maybe if I called it project management, they'd finally approve.

"If you put it like that . . ." I shrug, inhaling extra hard to stop my nose from running. My fingers are trembling. I embrace the rebirth of a familiar feeling, something warm and fuzzy expanding in me, like the first time he told me I'm witty and my sense of humor is sexy.

Not cool, Flora. You were supposed to make him fall for you, not the other way around.

"Well, thank you." I bow my head, slipping my hand out from under his. "But don't assume you can get out of paying by buttering me up. I told you, I'm not doing this party thing pro bono."

His mouth twists. "I'm your fairy godmother. How dare I forget?"

CHAPTER TWENTY-TWO

Sean

Three days before the party, Flora asks me to accompany her on an errand run. We sit in her car going over last-minute details. On the day of the event, she'll take Lindsey on a shopping trip while I oversee the preparations at home. She gives me the rundown once again.

"We start with hit songs the first hour, then the ceiling lights dim and we light up the lanterns. At ten, you give a short speech, thank everyone for coming, talk about how amazing I've been, and then we bring out the cake."

She goes on to describe the flavor and custom toppers, and I try to focus on her words, not on her lips.

"At midnight, we cut the power and send the house into darkness for about two minutes, so we have a Cinderella feel." She rolls down the car window, and a gust of wind lifts her hair. "The party ends at midnight—except it doesn't. The lights come back on, and Josie's band plays for one more hour."

"Why not move the whole thing up to ten? That way we get the surprise without going too late. These are freshmen."

She pauses for a moment. "That could work. Okay, ten. Good call."

"Can you plan my next birthday party too?"

She smiles and leans her head back, letting out a whoosh of breath. "Everything has to be *perfect*. A party isn't like your meticulous physics answer sheet. There's too much room for error," she warns, holding up her index finger. "If Lindsey's tears don't fall in three seconds, I'll murder you."

"It's just a party. We'll have a good time no matter what."

"It's not just a party, it's *the* party. People will refer to it simply as *The Party* long after we graduate. And Lindsey will land right at the top of the social ladder."

"Okay, okay." I raise my hands in mock surrender. "I'll make sure Lindsey cries. If she doesn't, I'll pinch her. *Hard.*"

Satisfied, Flora starts the engine and drives to my street. We make the rounds to all the neighbors and inform them in advance, determined to do this right.

"Should we notify the police department as well?" I ask when we're back in her car, my tone flat. "In case things get out of hand."

She rolls her eyes, but there's laughter in them. Reaching over, she ruffles my hair. "Fear not, my friend. We'll survive this together."

As she hurtles through the streets, my thoughts wander. "What we learn from history is that we don't learn from history," as Hegel supposedly said. We're destined to repeat the same mistakes, fight the same arch nemeses, lose the same battles, and fall for the wrong girl twice. She sets my heart ablaze when she lets her creativity run wild, when she flirts with her eyes gleaming, when she gets competitive and slams down her history homework, and when she's cranky one second and laughing the next. Nothing beats sitting in her car, watching her hair fly all over the place in the wind.

While she steers the wheel, phone calls keep coming in. Speaking into the Bluetooth earpiece, she rattles off instructions—spray-paint the branches white, ditch the multicolor string lights, prep snowflake-shaped cookies.

I go grab us coffee, and when I return, she's wrapping up by appointing someone head of the cleaning crew. "You sound professional," I say.

"Let's see how it turns out. Hey, can we stop at the park? I need to find some 'flourishing branches' myself. George has no idea how to set up a white forest."

We stroll through the park, coffee in hand, chatting as we go. With silent understanding, we stop at the pond in the center. A group of ducks swims under the sunlight. I pick up a pebble at the edge of the water and skip it across the surface. It bounces five times before it veers to the right and sinks.

Flora gasps. "Wow, teach me!"

"Okay. First you have to find a flat, round stone. Flick your wrist and spin it as you throw."

She bends down and makes her selection. "There must be a cool theory behind this."

"Suppose there's no loss of momentum when the stone interacts with the body of water. When it touches the surface, the force pushes the stone up, and it has to overcome its weight. You need to give it the minimum velocity required—" I stop when I catch the spark of amusement in her eyes. "You just can't resist a chance to summon my inner nerd." My cheeks flush, and she laughs.

"You have no idea how cute you are." She throws her stone and it sinks immediately. "Hey, this is harder than it looks, but you make it seem so effortless."

"I could say the exact same thing about your party planning techniques."

"Oh, I do what I can." She tosses her hair in my face and laughs over her shoulder. The sun reflects off her eyes, and there are gold flecks among the amber. "You know I'll do anything for you, dear Sean."

It's early autumn, and the trees are showing the first hints of yellow. The air is cooling but the sun still has warmth, basking her in a pool of gold. When she smiles, it's like a sudden burst of light. She has the most radiant smile that makes everything else fade—past mistakes, arguments, the breakup, all of it.

In this moment, everything is exactly as it should be.

I wrap my arms around her from behind, holding her loosely and inhaling the soft, floral scent of her hair. "Flora, thank you. Thank you."

She shifts, gazing up from my embrace. "You've already thanked me eight billion times for the party. If I could collect a dollar each time you do, we'd have enough money to serve caviar."

"It's not just for the party. It's for you being you, and for being here with me right now."

She leans her head back on my chest. "Well, in that case, thank you too."

I rest my chin on top of her head and close my eyes. She lets me hold her for a long time.

There are only a few perfect moments in my life that I wish to remember down to every detail. This is one of them.

CHAPTER TWENTY-THREE

Flora

On the day of the party, I take Lindsey shopping. I need to get her out of the house and glam her up, so we make a pit stop at my place first, where I layer shimmer and glitter on her eyelids, and then we hit the department stores with the prospect of finding her the best dress "for future events." A secret weapon sits hidden in my bag: the Swarovski tiara my parents gave me for my fifteenth birthday.

"You never know when you'll need a party-ready silver dress covered in this many sequins," I say, holding the glittering garment up to her body. "Please try it on! This is dream material."

"I can't think of a single occasion when I'd need this." Lindsey heads into the changing room.

"I can think of at least five." I tap my foot outside the door. When she emerges, I pretend to wipe away a fake tear. "You look fabulous!"

Not everyone can pull off sequins. It's a fine line—too many and it veers into tacky, but with the right cut, fit, and the right person, it illuminates the room. Lindsey adjusts the hem and observes herself in the mirror. "Are you sure I don't look like a giant disco ball?" She twirls, and the dress catches light from all directions.

"It's festive, fun, and the hue complements your skin tone. The silhouette is clean, so we won't overstyle it. No jewelry. Let the dress do the work." I snap a photo and show it to her. "But the most important thing is whether or not you feel amazing in it."

She strokes the sequins back and forth, watching the color change. "I love this." Then she flips the price tag and gasps. "Wait. Maybe not."

"Allow me, birthday girl." I pay for the dress (thankfully, she's not as weird about accepting gifts as Sean is), and we find the perfect strappy heels to go with it. Afterward, we head to a café for snacks. We both put on oversized shades as we take our seats outdoors, and we take eight billion photographs and try out all the Snapchat filters. When the tea and cakes arrive, we pretend we're influencers and take turns rating the food. I convince her to put the dress on, and we snap another round of photos.

"That was so much fun!" Lindsey says between breathless giggles as we head back, her face flushed. "I had the best birthday of my life!"

She's so easy to please I wonder why we're going to the trouble of a surprise party. The glow on her face warms me, and her laugh fills my chest with pride. We get in my car, and I text Sean: *the eagle lands in twenty minutes*. No reply.

There isn't a single car in the driveway when we pull up in front of their house. This is fine, but something feels off. The house is completely still. No lights, no movement behind the curtains. No way there's a hundred people behind that door. Lindsey chats away as she gets out of the car, her glitzy dress sparkling under the streetlamps, and my mind reels with six different ways to kill Sean. Has he completely blown this?

She slides the key into the door and turns the knob.

And then—boom.

Lights flood the room. Music blasts in my ear, and as I squint against the brightness, smiling faces swarm me. Everyone yells

"Happy birthday!" The room is an arctic dream, with magical lights and snowflakes twinkling across the ceiling. My head spins. I'm on a merry-go-round ride, and all that surrounds me is glamor.

Lindsey turns to me and her tears fall instantly. A sob lodges in my throat, and I blink away my own tears. This is the most beautiful thing ever. It's well worth it, every minute, every cent. This moment will be frozen in time, tucked away securely in my memory bank.

She covers her mouth with her hand. "Did you plan this?"

"It was Sean's idea, but everybody pitched in." I pull the tiara out of my bag and place it on her head. "Happy fifteen, Lindsey. *Now* you have the best birthday of your life."

*   *   *

Once the party is in full swing I slip outside to change in my car, peeling off my clothes to reveal the costume underneath. Cinched into a white satin corset, my featherlight tulle tutu flares in soft layers, barely covering anything. Garter belts clasp my thighs, and pearls drape down my collarbone. I grab a set of fluffy wings from the trunk, strap them on, and head back inside.

Snow flurries swirl across the dance floor, pumped from the machine Ray bought after a pretentious Icelandic film inspired him to shoot a short in his backyard. He dropped it off along with a crate of silver candleholders and crystal vases. He's not coming, obviously. A dry, miserable, middle-class gathering is beneath him (his words, issued with a shudder).

Sean stands beneath a veil of clear tinsel that glimmers like a frozen waterfall. He's actually put in the effort to dress for the theme, and wears a dove-gray blazer tailored to his frame paired with a Prussian-blue bowtie. *Not bad, Foster.*

"Glad to see you went all out with your outfit." I tilt my chin at him.

"Not as much as you did." His eyes flick away. I'm basically in lingerie.

"Me? I wear this to bed every night. But it's a pain sleeping on my back with the wings."

He laughs. "What exactly are you supposed to be? I thought you said fairies in a winter wonderland. Fairies don't have that kind of wardrobe."

"This is a Victoria's Secret angel-style fairy. Do you like it?"

He swallows. "I can't talk to you when you're wearing something like that."

I chuckle, stepping closer. "Why? Do I make you uncomfortable?"

"You make it so I can't think."

He doesn't glance away anymore. Instead, he gives me a slow once-over, and my skin burns. Maybe it's his gaze, or maybe it's his smile, but something stirs in me and makes me weak in the knees. "I'm ready to collect my first wish," I say, as a spur-of-the-moment idea hits me. "Let's go make out in your bedroom."

His lashes flutter. "What?"

"I said, let's go make out in your bedroom."

He turns to do a quick look around, making sure no one overheard. "I have to supervise the party. In case things get out of control."

Isn't that Dylan and Jake's job? Jake is currently bedazzled in edible glitter, and Dylan's trying to start a conga line with a group of freshmen—business as usual, basically. The only things getting out of control are Sean's hormones.

"Fine." I put my hands on my waist. "Then let's make out in the living room. You can still keep an eye on the party."

He exhales as if I asked him to donate his liver. "Why are you doing this?"

"You owe me."

Madison swings by and I call, "Mads, would you mind covering for us? Sean and I have urgent business to attend to."

"Sure." She smiles like the evil fairy-tale stepmother she is. "You kids have fun."

* * *

Inside his room, Sean sighs. "What's this about?"

"What do you mean?" I straighten my back. The wings are heavy.

His bedroom is pretty much the same as I remember. The duvet is a wrinkled mess on the bed, textbooks are stacked on his bookshelf, and trophies from basketball games and science tournaments clutter the top of the dresser. In one corner, sagging against the wall, are the Einstein balloons I got him.

He still has them.

"You know what. Feels like something's going on here."

"I just want some fun."

His eyelids droop, and he says quietly, "I thought you'd had your fun with me."

"The fun isn't over until I say it is. Please hold up your end of the deal." My gaze unfaltering, I raise my eyebrows. "What are you afraid of?"

He stares back, taking the challenge. One wish, one more step in my plan. That's it. My heart pounds despite my resolve to conduct this in a professional manner. After about an eternity, Sean steps closer and stops before me. "Close your eyes."

I do as I'm told. He moves in closer, but he's in no hurry, making me wait until my mouth goes dry. He brushes my hair aside and tilts my chin up. My breath hitches.

Then his lips land on mine.

He tastes *exactly* as I remember. He's warm and gentle, and applies the ideal amount of pressure. He takes his time, neither rushing nor stalling, and it brings me back to before.

I miss everything about it. I miss this so much I almost catch a sob rising. The weight of wanting him is unbearable, and I realize how sad I've been, how much I've wanted him, how much I *still* want him. I've been desperate to use my wish this way, hoping it'll remind him of us.

His hand moves to the small of my back and rests there, burning a patch on my skin, while his other hand runs through my hair, tugging at it, and then he pulls me in close.

I wrap my arms around his neck, struggling against the wave of nostalgia as the memory of our first kiss overlaps with this one.

He pulls me in even closer until my body is pressed tight against him.

I hate how much I still like him. I wish I never had to stop kissing him. The past few weeks we've worked together have been the happiest I've been in a long time.

And then it hits me. I can never win with Sean. It's a battle I'm bound to lose, and if I continue this stupid heartbreak operation, I'll only end up hurting myself. I can't control him, and I can't make him feel the way I do.

Why is revenge not all it's cracked up to be?

It's not satisfying, just empty. Instead of bringing closure, all it does is create more pain and confusion.

So I push him away. "Thanks, that's enough," I croak, my throat tight. "Glad to know your technique hasn't gotten rusty."

He stares at me, dazed, lips parted slightly, waiting to be kissed again.

"That's one wish done and one more to go," I say. "I let you off pretty easy, don't you think?"

A shadow of sadness crosses his face like a cloud drifting through daylight. "Flora . . . why?"

"We'd better get back to the party."

He reaches for my wrist, blocking me. "Tell me why you wanted this."

"I'll let you know what else you need to do."

With that, I push past him and leave.

* * *

"Did you really expect him to fall in love with you after one kiss?" Madison hisses after I pull her aside and fill her in. "He's not a Disney princess. He really hurt you and you're letting him do it all over again."

"I know what I'm doing."

Even though I have absolutely no idea anymore. This was supposed to be simple. Make him fall for me, then crush him like he crushed me. The end. Except this is the kind of movie that insists on a twist no one asked for.

"Sean has a powerful effect on you. I'll never understand your obsession, but let's admit he's an admirable opponent and drop this before it's too late," she says. "He's not worth this much of your headspace. You might be using this revenge thing as an excuse to spend time with him."

The truth stings. Maybe that's exactly what I've been doing. A weak justification to be around him, to feel close to him again, only to fail miserably as I fall for him.

"After the first bout of Sean-itis, I've got immunity now." I pick up a cupcake from the side table and inspect the frosting.

"Whatever you say, honey. You're too soft for the malicious revenge game. By the way, this turned out well, right?" Madison nods at one wall of the living room.

Several black-and-white photos are hanging there, and it's undeniable that Daniel knows what he's doing. Lindsey smiles like a movie star in her portrait, and the room now resembles a sophisticated photo gallery. There's also an absurd number of photos of Madison, filling up an outrageous amount of space, of which she says, "Hey, Dan's the artist, he decides what looks good up there." She points. "There's one of you too."

A small picture, about one-tenth of the size of the other portraits, is tucked into the corner.

It's of Sean and me in the cafeteria, sitting together. My head is thrown back and I'm laughing, mouth opened ridiculously wide and showing far too many teeth. Sean's as handsome on film as in real life, and he's gazing at me with unguarded affection. A tolerant smile tugs at his lips that seems to say, *I don't know what to do with you, but please stay the way you are.*

I'm speechless.

If that's not love, then I don't know what is.

CHAPTER TWENTY-FOUR

Sean

When the power cuts at ten, someone comes up behind me and taps me on the shoulder. It must be Flora messing with me again. When the lights flicker back on, Lindsey stands beside the fireplace. "I want to thank you."

"You're welcome. You should thank Flora, though. She did everything."

She nods. "Already did."

"Happy birthday. Are you having fun?"

She laughs. In the corner, a small mountain of presents has gathered, including a giant teddy bear—courtesy of Jake and Dylan—with a tag that reads *From Your Second and Third Brothers*, a handmade wreath woven with faux flowers and silk ribbons from her freshman-year friends, and stacks of books and enough pastel stationery to last her all four years of high school. "This is *much* better than Craigslist llama."

"Told ya. The best revenge is moving on."

"Sure. Look, listen carefully, because I'm never going to say this again for the rest of my life." She takes a deep breath, her eyes on the silver ornaments hanging on the fake tree. "You're a great brother, and I love you."

"I disagree. You'll probably say it again many, many more times in the future."

She giggles. "Hey, wanna know what my birthday wish is?"

"Find another boyfriend and get married before Christmas?"

"Ha-ha. No. I wish you and Flora would get back together."

Through the crowd, Flora leans against a table, her wings fluttering as she chats with a group of guests. Eyes bright, not a single strand of hair out of place.

I want to pull her aside and ask her what the kiss meant, because I never dare assume anything with Flora, but she doesn't spare me a second of her attention. She's fully back in event planner mode, circulating around the room to make sure no one's bored.

When our party dwindles and my parents finally kick everyone out, Flora barely acknowledges me as I walk her to her car. She's draped a trench coat over her angel costume, but I remember what's underneath. I can also taste her on my lips.

"Good night." She lays a hand on her car door handle, and it unlocks automatically. "I hope you had fun."

"I did. Thanks again. None of this would've happened without you."

She offers a cool smile. "You're welcome."

My heart hammers. What happened in my room, anyway? I knew exactly what her wish would do to me. It would give me hope, and the smallest sliver of it was all it took for me to fall completely. "You wasted one wish tonight."

"I don't think so."

I scratch at my palm, my nails digging in. "I would kiss you even without the wish."

Her eyebrows rise, her lashes casting delicate shadows on her cheeks, like palm tree leaves on sand. "You like my costume *that* much, huh?"

I swallow hard. "I like it, but the truth is . . . I like you."

I said it, finally. Once the words are out, there's no turning back. She'll have complete control over me. "Flora, I really like you. You know, *that* kind of like."

These were the words she'd once said to me. Now the roles are reversed, and with the confession out there, it feels like something cracked open. With no alcohol in me to bolster my confidence, my body can't decide whether to flee or stay. Every beat of silence stretches, and I brace for whatever comes next.

She's hurt me before. She can do it again, easily.

Her eyes stay on my face for a minute before she lets out a peal of laughter. "Who doesn't?"

I stand rooted to the ground. Flora's up-front but never cruel.

"Honey, are you ready to go?" Madison pulls up in her car and yells out of the window.

Flora whips around to wave. "Yeah, in a sec." She gets in her car, but her gaze lingers on me through the window. Then she rolls it down halfway and asks, "Why are you telling me this?"

"I don't know. I like you but I'm also afraid of you."

"Afraid of what?"

That you'll hurt me. But I don't say it, because there's nothing in her eyes I recognize. This can't be the same girl who wrapped her arms around my neck earlier, kissing me like she meant it. I was so sure there was a connection. "I don't understand. Did I imagine everything?"

"What did you imagine?" There's a hardness in her that seems to feed on my humiliation.

"I thought the past few weeks meant something to you too. It felt like we were getting closer, and I thought—maybe I'm wrong—but I thought you might . . . you might feel the same way."

Her expression remains blank. I bite my lip and wait, knowing she isn't going to grant me a good night's sleep. Her silence isn't the good kind, and with each passing second, the heat of mortification rises more in my chest.

What did I do wrong? Please, just tell me.

But I have to let her off the hook. "It's okay if you don't feel the same. I'm not asking for anything. I just want you to know how I feel."

She smiles, but it doesn't comfort me. "Good night, Sean. Get some sleep."

Then she speeds off into the night. The party isn't the only thing that's ended tonight.

* * *

Being ignored by Flora is somehow worse than breaking up with her a year ago. Back then it was ripping off a bandage with brutal force. This time, it's a dull ache that sinks into my bones. I tried talking to her all week after the party, but she radiates an air of icy indifference. Every text I send is left on Read.

Since she stops sitting with me in our corner at lunch, I've been joining Josie instead.

"J, *hypothetically*, if I'd been flirting with a girl, and after we kissed and I told her I liked her, she laughed and started avoiding me, that means I should back off, right?"

She stops in the middle of peeling open her sandwich wrapper. "Sean Everett Foster, you're a horrible friend. You don't tell me anything!"

"Come on, I'm telling you now."

"I'm not helping unless you tell me all the details. You only talk to me when you need someone to play live at your party."

"That's not true. I talk to you when I need to borrow money too."

"Is it Flora?" She squints at me. "It's Flora."

I shrug.

"I knew it!" Josie slams her hand on the table before taking a bite of her sandwich. "Wait, hold up. A lot of things are starting to make sense. No wonder it's been eternal sunshine in Floraland lately."

"What does that mean?"

"She's chirpy all the time. I thought it was because she liked planning the party, but now I get it. She was planning it with *you*. Tell me the situation one more time. Don't leave anything out."

I tell her everything I can think of, with her interrupting every two sentences. "She says she was only talking to me because we were working on our history presentation and Lindsey's party. Now that they're over, she has no reason to 'desperately hunt me down for conversations.'"

"I have a pretty good idea what this is about." For some reason Josie thinks she knows so much more about relationships than I do. "She needs more reassurance because you were horrible to her."

"What?" I draw a sharp breath. "What have *I* ever done to *her*?"

"You were so hard on her. You broke up with her after she threw *one* tantrum. She was devastated! That relationship was pretty one-sided if you ask me. You took her for granted."

"You don't know the whole story, J."

"Yep, and why do you think that is?" She jabs a finger into my shoulder.

"Anyway, at the time, it felt like the right decision, but now I'm not sure anymore. I was—am—crazy about Flora."

Josie leans back, taking her time with her sandwich. When she puts it down, she looks at me, all wise and profound. "Flora said she loved throwing this party, but let's face it, she has better things to do than asking freshmen for help or visiting your neighbors. She did all that to make out with you in an angel costume? She told us you're the best kisser ever, but surely you can't be *that* good."

The memories play themselves like a slideshow. Flora sitting in front of the laptop carefully reviewing the guest list. Picking branches with me, studying the alignment to make sure they were perfect. Staying for dinner and cleaning up with me. Calling me at midnight to confirm we could shut down the power in my house. Begging people to stay sober. Kissing me the way she did, like she refused to let me go.

"Dude, you're so clueless, no way you can survive in the dating jungle without me," Josie says. "I should start charging for relationship consultation."

"But why's she acting like this now?"

"She wants to feel special too. When have *you* ever made an effort?" She crumbles her carton of orange juice, folding it into a neat square. "She chose you, and all you did was . . . agree. Not to mention you broke up with her the moment it got a little bit hard—for *you*. And now, after everything, after she threw you the party of the century, you were like 'I like you but I don't know and I'm not asking anything.' Do you expect her to take it from there again? Maybe show more determination and less hesitancy, not act like you're waiting for her to convince you?"

"Maybe I pushed her away."

"Exactly. You need to show her you're committed. Make your intentions clear. Even though you've never chased a girl in your life."

A shadow falls over us. Dylan is at our table, and as his usual way of greeting Josie, he smacks her over the head. She glares at him. The three of us have been in school together since first grade, and some things never change. Jake appears a second later, pulling up a chair.

"Last time I checked, Flora was clinging to you like a sloth in a rainforest tree, but now she's all the way over there." Jake points across the room with his chin. "Did you two get into a fight?"

"Something like that," I say. "But I'm going to fix it."

"Give her flowers." Dylan is always eager to offer his unsolicited advice. "I give Syd flowers whenever I mess up."

"She'll be opening up a florist shop any day," Josie says.

Jake bites into his burger. "Write her a poem. I can even let you borrow one of mine. *Roses are red, violets are blue, forget about poetry, let's just screw.*"

"*Roses are red, violets are blue, Flora's mad at you, what are you gonna do?*" Dylan adds.

"*Better fix this fast before she finds someone new.*" Jake's on a roll now.

Josie presses her lips together. "Surely you can do better than that?"

CHAPTER TWENTY-FIVE

Flora

"Would you stop staring at Sean like you're on a police stakeout?" Madison snaps. I wrench my gaze from his table with brutal force, and then adjust my seat so I have my back to him.

"I still don't understand why you can't give him a chance," Carmen says. "You're clearly into each other. Why insist on torturing him?"

Madison scowls at Carmen as if she said something ludicrous, like *Crocs are acceptable footwear.* She already knows I'm over getting revenge, and couldn't be more relieved. "He'll hurt her again, that's why."

Ever since Sean's confession, I've been stuck in some weird emotional purgatory. There's no master plan after the party, only the weight of my feelings and the need to ignore him for the sake of my self-preservation.

Carmen shrugs. "Any guy sweet enough to spend five hundred dollars on his kid sister's surprise party deserves a second chance."

"He didn't spend five hundred dollars," I correct her. "I saved him a ton, and he thought the cake cost ninety dollars when it was in fact three hundred." Sean has no clue how much a customized cake with a Lindsey figurine is worth, and I lied about losing the receipt. "Anyway, I'm so over him. I'd rather be alone with a cactus."

Carmen kicks me under the table. Sean stands beside us, the top two buttons of his shirt undone, giving me a glimpse of the smooth skin underneath. He sits down and steals a piece of diced pear from my lunch tray.

"We weren't talking about you or anything," I say defensively.

"Of course not." He greets everyone, my friends respond to his small talk, and we all act as amicable as a group of old people playing bridge.

Sean seems . . . *different.* More self-assured? He drapes his arm along the back of my chair and helps himself to the rest of my unfinished lunch. After wiping his fingers on a napkin, he turns to me. "You're done? Let's walk to history class together."

"Are you my guide dog? I don't need you to walk with me."

He smiles. "Oh, I know you don't need me. But I need you. History is my favorite time of day."

"I thought AP Chemistry was your favorite subject this semester," I say, standing up. "You get to exchange smart-people talk with Mr. Miles."

"History isn't my favorite subject. I said it's my favorite time of day."

My insides shiver uselessly, and I hide it by ignoring him all the way to the classroom. It's difficult to concentrate knowing he's sitting three rows behind me and slightly to the right. Halfway through the class, my phone alerts me to a text from Sean.

Sean: $(x^2 + y^2 - 1)^3 - x^2 y^3 = 0$

Sean: *Can you please solve this for me?*

What is he up to? I text him back. *That looks like math beyond my algebraic jurisdiction.*

He replies almost immediately. *Want me to walk you through it?*
I text back. *No, just tell me the answer . . . or don't.*

Sean: *All right, if you insist. Would've been a lot more romantic if I showed you on Desmos, impatient young grasshopper*

He sends a picture, and I open it to reveal a graph. Sean's equation produces a looping curve that stretches outward in both directions, symmetrical across the y-axis and tapering to a sharp point at the bottm. It forms a perfect heart shape.

This is his idea of romantic?

Ugh. *Flora, why are you so weak?*

I turn to shake my head at him, and he rewards me with a grin.

Not going to lie—the old Flora enjoys the attention and hopes he'll keep up his antics, although the new, sensible Flora wishes he'd leave her alone. Kind of.

*　*　*

When I open my locker on Tuesday, there's a photocopied periodic table. Underneath it, Sean has printed in that goody-goody handwriting of his:

Barium Beryllium Yttrium Oxygen Uranium Rhenium Copper Tellurium

I can't decide if it's more considerate or condescending of him to attach the periodic table for my reference. Picking up my pen, I translate his encrypted message:

BaBe YOU'Re CuTe

I bite the inside of my cheek. Smiling at a chemistry pickup line in the crowded hallway isn't good for my image. He's *such* a dork.

* * *

After we endure another round of history class, Sean comes over. He takes the seat in front of me and sits down backward, placing his legs on either side of the chair. He gestures to my arm and holds up a pen.

"We're going to be late for our next class."

"This will only take a sec." He reaches for my forearm. "Besides, your next class is right across the hall."

"But you'll be late for yours."

"I can run fast." He scribbles along the inside of my arm, while his other hand lingers over my wrist. The warmth of his fingers sears my skin. What he's writing begins with *www.*

"Couldn't you have texted me this?"

"Where's the fun in that?" He finishes writing and looks up. "You don't have to use it if you don't want to, but I designed a blog for you. It's a style blog."

"A style blog?"

"Yes, so you can put your talent to good use. Write about what you wear every day and offer fashion tips. Rip apart this year's Met Gala too."

"Why would I want to do that?" This is the exact kind of thing I might do.

"You want to be a fashion editor. Not sure how the fashion industry works, but I figure a blog won't hurt, especially if yours takes off. Your book of buttons is incredible, but it's good to have reach with a digital platform. You could cross-link it to your Instagram handle as part of a broader online presence."

God, how is he now doing everything right? He's so good at this, making me want more than I should. Better not to get sucked into this. I pull my arm away from his grasp.

"Show-off." I get up to leave. "You just want to prove you can build a better web page than anyone else."

"I don't know if it's better," he says with a sunny grin, "but I made it with love."

* * *

On Wednesday at lunch, Sean swings by my table and drops a jumbo pack of Hershey's Kisses on my lunch tray. When he saunters back to his table, I pick up the plastic bag and weigh it in my hand.

"That's a lot of kisses," Carmen says.

"That's a lot of *calories*." Madison narrows her eyes. "What's that about?"

I shrug, suppressing the bubbles rising inside me. Sean is basically declaring himself in front of my friends. "He's been doing a lot of cute things lately."

Carmen tears open the bag.

Madison makes a face. "That's considered cute? You'd probably find it cute if Sean gave you a toilet plunger."

"Give him a break," Josie says. "He's in uncharted territory. First time he's ever chased a girl."

We share a few pieces (while Madison glares, since Sean didn't offer a vegan option), but there are too many. As the self-appointed goodwill ambassador of Lakeridge High, I get up and hand chocolates to everyone nearby, slowly working my way over to where Sean is.

I stop in front of him. "Sorry, Sean. No kisses for you."

He shrugs. "That's okay. I don't want anything less than the real deal anyway."

My brain freezes. He's declared himself in front of *his* friends, who're all snickering like they're some sort of deranged woodland hyenas. "Dare to dream."

"Oh, but I already did." He gets up to walk me to class, and I blush furiously underneath my makeup. Behind us, Dylan makes a guttural animal noise like it's supposed to mean something, and Jake fake-whispers, "They grow up so fast."

We head for history in silence, but my mood is light. I still ignore him, but Sean smiles at me when we reach the classroom, holds the door for me, and as always, gives me breathing problems.

* * *

On Thursday during history class, Sean sends a paper airplane sailing onto my desk. This might not have been a big deal coming from someone else, but Sean is a compulsive note taker. The idea of him pausing in the middle of the lecture to fold a paper plane is unbelievable, and, of course, everyone watches as he flies it at me.

Written on the wings of the plane is: *Please pass on to Flora Morgan if I missed.*

Sean and his precautions. I unfold the plane.

I want to be yours.
Please. I'll do anything. I miss you.

Chills run down my arms and a lump forms in my throat. Tears prick behind my eyelids without warning. Back when we were together, he used to say he was mine, that he belonged to me, as if it'd make him sound less possessive. I blink, fighting the emotions rising to the surface. It's not only that I miss him, but the ache of wanting to be someone he can't let go of.

When class is over, I push the plane aside. "Are you in third grade? A paper plane?"

"Hey, I'm out of tricks," he replies. "And if I was in third grade, I'd put little yes-no boxes underneath and ask you to respond ASAP."

I laugh despite myself.

"What's your answer?"

I pick up my books. "You're a smart guy, figure it out."

* * *

And then, *nothing*.

All through Friday, Sean does nothing. No cute notes, no texts, no walking to class together, and no snacks at lunch. I check my phone again, switch it to airplane mode, then back on just in case. When the last class ends, I search my locker for the fifth time to make sure there isn't any love letter stuck in a corner.

"What have you been up to lately?" Sean asks.

My heart jumps. I forget if I should be mad at him or pleased that he showed up. He leans against the locker next to mine in his varsity jacket, his backpack slung over one shoulder. The ultimate high-school dream.

"You know, the usual." I fumble with my number lock. "Staying at home, knitting, writing a symphony, that sort of thing."

"Interesting," he says. "Hey, I was wondering if you could help me with a relationship problem. I met someone. I've never felt this way before."

"Isn't that nice—"

"But after we shared a scandalous kiss, and there's even a pair of ridiculous wings involved, she's ignored me for two weeks," he says, deadpan. "To be exact, it's been thirteen days. Thirteen *agonizing* days. The question is, do you think I should try harder? Or should I stop because I'm beginning to feel like a stalker?"

I smile even though I don't want to.

"Or maybe she's too busy writing a symphony?" he presses.

"Maybe you kissed lousily."

He scratches his chin, pretending to consider, then he shakes his head. "Impossible."

I laugh. I'm seriously too weak. "Maybe you should try harder."

"Okay, Flora. I'll try harder." He stares straight into my eyes, and I just about crumble to a puddle of pink pulp around his feet. He turns, pulling open the zipper of his backpack, and takes out a large envelope. "This is for you."

Inside is a framed photo. It's the one Daniel took of us in the cafeteria, with me laughing and Sean gazing at me. It made me emotional the first time, and the second time isn't any easier either, especially since it's from Sean. He understands what's captured in that picture too.

"I look hideous," I say, trying to act nonchalant.

"You're beautiful."

"And look at you." I tilt the picture. "It's clear. Admit you're into me."

"I already told you I like you," he says. "You're all I think about."

And there it is. All the questions I tormented myself with, all the doubts I fed into my own head—they vanish. Why did I waste time anguishing over winning and losing? Why did I bother making him prove he wants me? I could spend a lifetime figuring out how to keep my heart safe, but I just want to be with him. I want those late-night conversations and text messages filled with corny lines. I want to hear him laugh, even if I'm always the one who cares more.

Fine, he broke my heart before. Maybe it'll happen again. I'm probably still not good enough for perfect Sean. But this. *Him.* He's right here, and I'm done pretending I don't want him. I'm down for whatever lies ahead if I get to have him, for as long as I can, even if it's only until he gets tired of me. His smile, his touch, and his kiss will always be stuck in my head like one of those annoyingly catchy songs.

"Hey, I know what I want for my second wish," I say, the words slipping out before I can stop them.

He swallows. "Okay?"

"Go out with me tomorrow. You can't leave until I say so."

"Am I a date or a subscription service with no cancellation policy?" He smiles, then it falters. "Wait. This seems overly easy. You help me throw a party, and I get a kiss and a date? What's the catch?"

I shrug.

He nudges me with his elbow. "Come on, admit you like me a little too," he says, glancing down.

Oh, who am I kidding? I'm smitten. "Fine, I like you. I like you a lot. I thought it was pretty obvious. I just thought that, maybe, you should make an effort. I feel like I'm always the one to initiate things, and . . ." It sounds so stupid when I explain it out loud. "You know what? Never mind."

"Fair enough, but I'm initiating *this*." He puts one hand on the locker door next to my face, and the other lifts my chin. Then he lowers his head to kiss me.

A locker kiss!

This is as public as it gets, and Sean, who hates attention, doesn't seem to mind. He's kissing me like there's no one else in the world. People are staring, but I'm too caught up in the moment to care. My head spins. This is long overdue.

"Wow." I gasp after he pulls back, my arms still circling his waist. "Wouldn't something as tacky as a locker kiss ruin your reputation?"

"Why would kissing the most beautiful girl in school ruin my reputation?"

He kisses me again.

CHAPTER TWENTY-SIX

Sean

Flora has never been known for punctuality, but her Mercedes appears outside my window at 9:59 on Saturday morning. I throw on my coat and hurry downstairs, stepping out the door before Lindsey can intercept her.

The sky is overcast, and the air feels damp. The street glistens with moisture. Flora stands by her car, waiting. As soon as she sees me, she runs up and pulls me into a hug. Her cheeks are flushed pink from the cold, and for a moment, we stand there in silence, holding each other.

She tilts her head. The vintage-looking cap I gave her suits her. Her dark hair falls over her shoulders, brushing against her leather jacket. "You look amazing."

"Thanks. Should I say hi to your family?"

"Please don't." I nudge her toward her car, and she laughs. Every minute is precious.

She starts the car and says, "I have the whole day planned."

We haven't said anything concrete about getting back together, but it's the direction I'm heading for. Does taking me out mean she's considering it? I'm ready to take whatever she tosses my way. *Give me a sign, please.* I even miss the way she speeds and how my body jerks forward at every red light.

"Ta-da." She pulls into the parking lot of the science museum. "This is where people like you hang out, right?"

"I've actually never been to one outside of field trips."

She planned this for me. When we get out of the car, she links her arm through mine and drags me to the ticket booth. Moments later, we're in the exhibit hall, surrounded by skeletons of dinosaurs.

The museum is massive, with high ceilings that stretch toward skylights. The walls are lined with polished glass displays showing off fossils, rocks, and scientific models. It's a quiet, contemplative space, filled with the soft hum of interactive exhibits as people move through the halls.

Flora seems *really* into me today, and I feel drunk already. She touches my face and smiles a lot, and she clutches my arm when we ride up the escalator, her fingers brushing over my skin. After enduring two weeks of her cold avoidance, this delicious whiplash leaves me completely undone.

We pass through an energy demonstration showing how wind turbines convert wind into green energy. She asks, "Why do you want to be an engineer?"

"To create things that move, like a robotic arm. Or a plane engine that roars to life."

"And you like physics so much."

"I like the clarity of it. When you finish a problem, you know whether you're right. It's straightforward." *Which is exactly what we aren't right now.*

"I like ambiguity. Like fashion. No right or wrong, only what makes you happy." She jabs at a button that triggers an avalanche simulation and then gasps when a rush of snow surges toward her.

All my previous "relationships" were like melting snow— light and fleeting, evaporating before the chance to transform into anything substantial. But Flora. Flora is an avalanche that crashes into my life.

"Science is fun!" she says. "But it's mostly because I'm here with you. I like you so much, I might combust."

We need to talk about why we broke up before. But maybe not in the middle of her taking a rare interest in scientific wonders. What if it triggers a major fight? I can't risk ruining it when we're finally good again.

No, better than good. When Flora likes me, it leaves me powerless. I take her hand when we walk through the earthquake simulation. Never thought I'd get this back, to have her fingers intertwined with mine, and when she smiles at me, I can forgive and forget everything because I want her too much.

"What's this?" She tugs on my hand.

The whisper dishes are set up with two identical, concave plates positioned across the room from each other, designed to collect and reflect sound waves.

I explain the setup, and Flora urges me to head to the opposite side. "Can you hear me?" she asks from her end.

"Yeah, but it's muffled."

"This is a dream come true. To date you again and kiss you wherever I want."

"Probably not *wherever* you want. There are kids around."

She laughs, her voice swirling around me like a galaxy of lights. "Say something nice to me."

With my heart thumping, I say the only thing that has circled my mind all morning. "I want to get back together."

"What? I can't hear you."

"I want to get back together."

"You want to what?"

"To get back . . ." My face flames. Eyes turn toward me, the room seeming to hum with awareness. I step sideways from the dish, and Flora smiles slyly at me across the room.

I hop off my platform and move toward her, but as soon as I take a step, she takes off running. By the time I catch up, she's sprinted all the way to an empty stairway, and we crash into each other, both laughing, breathless. I corner her and trap her with my forearms. "I know you heard me."

She laughs, and she's heart-stoppingly beautiful. "I forgot what you were saying. Say it again."

I lean down and whisper, my voice low, "Please be my girlfriend again. *Please.*"

"Yes." She kisses me. "Yes. Yes. Yes . . ." Each *yes* is interrupted by a peck landing along my chin and jawline. On the fourth one, I pull her closer and kiss her properly.

I don't even care why we broke up anymore.

CHAPTER TWENTY-SEVEN

Flora

My relationship status is officially back to being Sean Foster's girlfriend, and I want to shout it from the rooftops of the science museum.

Or maybe I'll just tell Instagram.

We find a small booth to ourselves where they show documentaries on a screen. Sean presses the button, and a couple of Greenland huskies appear on the monitor. He fumbles with the controls, but there's no sound. "Maybe the speaker's broken."

Who cares? I grab his face and kiss him savagely.

He lets me roam around his mouth for about four seconds before he pulls away. "I want to kiss you, too, but this so-called 'private' spot really isn't as secluded as you think."

I trace his jawline with my knuckles. "I can't help it. You're so incredibly cute."

"We'll find the next dark corner." He wraps one arm around me, and I lean back on his chest.

The huskies run around the ice field in silence on-screen, their white fur quivering in the arctic wind, and the faint thrum of Sean's heartbeat is beneath me. He draws circles on my shoulder, and we watch the animals, not talking. Being with him here is one of the most compelling moments of my life.

When the short film ends, I sigh. "This is so romantic."

He pretends to grimace. "The science museum? You're such a dork. I can't be seen with you."

"It's not about the location. It's because I never thought we'd get back together. You're perfect, even though you only have three pairs of shoes and I'm tired of all of them."

"You're perfect, too, even though you're filthy rich and you can't stop posting on social media."

Without me needing to ask, he presses Replay on the screen.

We're obviously soulmates.

* * *

We sit down in the museum café for Sean's hourly caffeine fix. A woman at the next table is desperately trying (and failing) to keep her two kids under control. One of them is banging his toy horse on the table, while the other is drawing and tossing crayons in every direction. When both start screaming, Sean stills for a second before he lifts his coffee.

Of course he won't stare; that's him being nonchalant and sexy as usual.

The mom grabs an empty water bottle from her bag and tries to open it with one hand while her other hand keeps the crayons from hitting the floor.

I lean across and catch her eye. "Hi, need some help?"

"Actually, yeah, I was hoping to get some water, but they're having a rough day."

"I'll get it for you," I say. "And if you need anything else from the café, let me know."

Her face softens with relief. "Thanks. You're such a sweetheart."

My mom calls me sweetheart, too, but she's never flustered like this in public. To her, she's an executive first, a wife second, and a mom third, and she gets everything done right. I don't mind the order, but I sometimes wish the percentages were weighted a little differently.

"Do you want to wait for me here?" I ask Sean.

He sets his coffee cup down, finished. "Let's meet at the gift shop later. There's something I want to get."

* * *

Sean examines the stone and mineral collection. After paying for his purchase, he borrows a pen from the cashier and writes. The cashier says something to him, and he smiles. It's the detached kind he forces out to fit in, but when he sees me, he smiles with the edge of his eyes crinkled up. The kind he reserves for me.

People like him because he's smart and good looking, but Sean doesn't do the whole *nice to everyone* thing. Although polite and respectful, he's always a little aloof. When he chooses to open up, it's because he decides to truly let someone in.

I'm not some random person getting the same treatment as everyone else; I've earned it, unlocked a level few get to reach.

I wander over to the postcard section and pick one with an octopus (it's such an intelligent species, and it even has mood swings), then write him a quick note. *Please remember this day with a smile and know that once upon a time, you made a girl ridiculously happy.*

Sean catches up to me and hands me a small paper bag with scribbled words on top. "Please don't laugh."

To the mysterious girl who fell from the sky: you hit me harder than a meteor. Inside the bag is a chunk of fake black stone.

"You're so cheesy."

I *adore* it.

Meteors are a girl's favorite kind of rock.

* * *

After the museum, I drive us to a pristine lake with a hiking trail around it. The drizzle has finally stopped, but the sky remains a soft gray, with sunlight beginning to peek through. The view is glorious. We complete the walk and get back to my car, and I pop the trunk, taking out the picnic basket I prepared for a late lunch. I made it myself—sandwiches with truffle cream, chilled Mariage Frères tea, and Valrhona chocolate-covered strawberries.

"Thanks for putting so much thought into this." Sean eats the last strawberry I feed to him. He tilts his head back, letting the sunlight fall on his face.

I collect the plates and put everything back in the basket. "Are you bored? Wanna get going?"

"No, I like it here."

"Don't you want to do something fun?"

He rolls over and props himself on his elbows. "There *is* something fun I have in mind. Lots of high-school couples are doing it every day, and I've always wanted to do it with you."

"No, thanks. I don't want to study together."

He laughs. "Can we not do anything other than be with each other? This is really nice." He pulls me down so I'm lying in his arms, and I play with his fingers.

Up in the trees overhead, a bird chirps. There's a gentle breeze and leaves rustle as a response.

I say, "Tell me the *worst* thing you've ever done."

Sean's eyes spring open, and he looks at me with mock disbelief. "You can't keep quiet for even two seconds."

"It must be something painfully mild, like abandoning groceries in the wrong aisle. Or cheating on a few tests in middle school."

"Actually, I never cheated on tests."

I gasp. "You should be ashamed of yourself!"

"In seventh grade, there was this bully at my school. I hacked into his game account and stole all his weapons. I felt terrible about it afterward."

Sean says this in such a serious manner, like he genuinely regrets it, and my heart flutters. He's so *pure*. "Were you bullied yourself?"

"No, but every morning on the school bus, he'd torment this other kid. Call him names, get the rest of us to laugh along. Even Dylan chimed in once or twice. Not making excuses, but Dylan lost his dad around that time, and he took it hard. He was angry all the time, lashing out at everything. I hated watching it happen. One day I told him he's better than that, and he stopped and even wrote an apology card to make amends. That's why my mom calls him a sweet kid and why my dad told you I was bitter in middle school."

"But it sounds like you stood up for this kid."

"No, I didn't join in, that's all. I could've done more. Sometimes I wish I had, but I generally hate confrontations. I'm the kind of person who never says anything when the server gets my order wrong."

But he called me a piece of work. He said I was in love with myself. His eyes are clear and innocent now, and I can't wrap my head around it.

I swallow, fighting the knot in my throat. "Can I ask you something?"

"Anything."

"Why did we break up last year?"

He holds my gaze, and slowly, he says, "Flora, you cheated on me."

The sentence doesn't register at once. Of all the possible reasons, this has never crossed my mind. I'd be less surprised if he told me he was an undercover assassin and only did it to protect me. "What? No, I didn't!"

"Don't lie." Sean pulls away from me and a muscle moves near his jaw. "This is part of the reason I said nothing before. I didn't want to hear you lie to me again."

"I'm not lying. I never even *considered* cheating on you."

"With Raymond Corbett."

I've hung out with Raymond eight billion times, but we're merely friends who goof together, not to mention cheating on Sean with Ray is a *preposterous* idea. Isn't that like cheating on Bradley Cooper with that funny bearded guy in *The Hangover?* Come on.

"The night before my physics test," he says with difficulty.

It takes me a second, but the memory clicks. "He came over, we drank and hung out. I didn't tell you right away because we were fighting and you had your test. I planned to tell you later." My head spins. "But that's all we did! He brought beer, he smoked, we gossiped, then he left. He tried to kiss me goodbye, but it meant nothing. He kisses everyone when he's drunk, and that night, with his parents splitting up, he was especially out of it. He doesn't even remember it."

Sean's face blanches, color draining like petals wilting under a cold front.

"It's true. But you were studying. How did you know about this—and why would you *ever* think . . . ?"

"I staked out your apartment. Not proud of it. Honestly, I hate that I even went there. I was spiraling and didn't know what else to do. I kept telling myself I was being paranoid, but you lied on the phone, and I wanted to prove myself wrong. But I saw you together, and the next day you lied again to my face."

"I'm so sorry you had to see that. And I'm sorry I lied, that was wrong. I thought I'd wait for a better moment to bring it up, which was terrible judgment. But I never cheated on you. I would *never* cheat on you."

"I assumed . . . *that's* what happened?" His voice is unsteady, eyes wide with panicked realization. "So you never cheated on me," he says, testing the sound of it on his tongue.

"No."

After inhaling and exhaling several times, he closes his eyes. "Then I was fucking wrong about everything. We broke up over nothing."

His words land with the force of a slap across my face. A surge of anger engulfs me, and my heart dives into a Jacuzzi of hot sauce. "That's why we broke up? *That's* why we broke up?"

Countless sleepless nights, tears, and confusion over such a stupid reason.

How could he be so *stupid*?

"Flora, I don't know what to say. I'm so sorry. I thought I saw you kissing and I jumped to conclusions."

The heat rises in my chest, a tide of frustration and hurt. Tears well up and tickle the edge of my eyes. I stand up, and he rises to his feet too. "You don't trust me at all! And you thought I was a cheater! I may not be a saint like you, but I've never cheated in my life!"

"I wanted to trust you. But why did you have to lie to me?"

"Why didn't you just *ask* me?"

Sean lets out a frustrated grunt. He tugs on my wrist, but I step back.

Does he know how many times I cried for him? How I replayed our broken relationship, picking it apart shred by shred, trying to figure out what I did wrong? I spent my days shifting blame, first onto myself, then onto him, then back onto me again.

I drifted through summer in an empty shell, wondering if I was nothing more than a mistake to him. And when he got injured, I wasn't allowed to be near him. I was forced to fret in silence, when no one was watching.

The tears spill freely. Sean apologizes about eight billion times between my angry sobs and accusations, until it sounds like a mantra. "I'm so sorry," he says again. "It's all my fault. I made a mess of everything."

"It *is* all your fault!"

He tries putting his arms around me, and I let him, too exhausted to push him away. "I didn't ask because . . ." He lowers his eyes, and his voice cracks. ". . . because it hurt too much to talk about it. I'd never fallen this hard for anyone, and I was terrified that I meant nothing to you. I couldn't handle it. It freaked me out, being that vulnerable. I didn't want the details. I wanted to walk away with whatever dignity I had left."

A hot guy with a little bit of insecurity is so . . . hot.

"And when I finally decided to approach you," he says, "you told me I bored you to tears and you wasted four months of your life on me. Then you tossed the key chain and started seeing Liam Turner. Two weeks after we broke up. That's why I never brought it up. It seemed pointless."

"I was . . . I dated Liam to get back at you," I mumble. "I assumed you'd gotten tired of me, so I had to act like I didn't care."

"I went through hell trying to get over you."

"Me too, Sean. Me too. I was so hurt, I even tried to get revenge on you." I take a deep breath, and my speech comes out in a cascade of sentences as I share everything about my stupid plan. ". . . but halfway through, I aborted it because I like you too much. That's why we kissed at the party, and why I ignored you after, because I realized I could never win with you. I needed to get over you, move on."

He sighs, pressing his palms over his eyelids. "That's why you were acting so strange. If this is about getting even, about *winning*, then you already won. I was never any match for you," he says, his voice tinged with sadness as he gestures at the air between us. "Are we—is this still part of your revenge?"

The little-boy look in his eyes softens me instantly. I can't remember ever wanting to hurt him. "No. This is the real me. No schemes, no ulterior motives. I want to be with you. I always have. That's never changed. Not since we were freshmen."

We lapse into silence, each absorbing the newly gathered information. "Wait. So you were willing to get back together even though you believed I cheated on you?"

He nods. "I can't stay away from you. When you say you like me, it's the best feeling in the world. I'm sorry about everything."

"I'm sorry too."

He takes my hand with both of his. "And you were willing to forgive me even though you had no idea why we broke up?"

"What can I say? You're a really good kisser."

He chuckles, pulling me toward him, and I fall into the comforting warmth of him. "I really missed you," I say against his shirt.

"I missed you too. All the time." As his arms tighten, I think of snow melting, water carving its way through rocks, and mountains crumbling, their edges worn soft by years. I think of glaciers running into cool streams. It's like getting over a long war and eventually returning home.

"You don't know how happy I am right now," he says.

"I think I do." I put my arms around his waist. There's still a lingering bitterness in the corner of my brain that he was so quick to misjudge me, but strangely, I also feel closer to him. We were both scared, but we risked ourselves to get here. "From now on, please tell me everything. If you're ever unhappy, you have to let me know."

"Well, there's just one small thing. This picnic you prepared is awesome, but I can't survive on cold sandwiches and chilled tea alone." His lips brush my ear, and he speaks in such a cute, pleading tone, there's absolutely no way I can refuse him. "I'm *so* hungry. Can we please go get some cheese fries?"

"Sure, anything you want."

"Anything?" He cocks his eyebrows. "Then I asked for the wrong thing."

I laugh and hit him. He really knows how to push his luck.

* * *

After hanging out together all afternoon, I'm not ready for Sean to leave. We finally cleared the air, and I want to make up for lost time.

"Can you stay with me tonight?" I ask.

"I can try," he says. I let him drive my car and set the lake house address on the GPS, and the day swerves into evening. As he mulls over what excuse to give to his parents, I order pizza delivery on my phone.

The sky stretches dark and vast, adorned with scattered stars. The glow from passing lampposts flickers and blurs, and my mind is a jumble of fragmented thoughts. What if we'd done this a year ago? If I hadn't gotten into that fight with Sean over his physics test, maybe things would've turned out differently. Then again, maybe not. We could've fought over something else and ended things in the heat of the moment. Maybe every path would've eventually led to the same destination.

"I should've tried harder." Sean breaks the silence. "Last year, it was my mistake to let you go. I didn't even give you a chance to explain. Instead, I got angry and defensive, lashed out, and said things I didn't mean. That wasn't fair to you, and I see how that must've blindsided you. I'm sorry."

"It's okay," I whisper. "It's all in the past."

"After everything you did for me, I ran away. Put my pride before you." His jaw tightens. "I feel like I betrayed you."

I turn my face to the night because I don't want him to see me cry, *again*.

Sean gets me, after all. He knows I need to hear this, even though he isn't the best at pouring out his heart. The breakup seemed like an unfair twist of fate at the time, but in retrospect, maybe it was a blessing. A second chance to fix things. Perhaps we were meant to be apart for a while, because making up is too good.

Sean steers the wheel with his left hand and takes my hand with his right one. "Baby, I'm sorry." He holds my hand all the way to the lake house, like making a silent statement.

It's as if a part of him has opened up, and for the first time in our relationship, I feel completely understood.

* * *

I went to Rome with my family once. When we visited the Colosseum, our tour guide told us an anecdote about how they'd starve the lions for a week then rub the smell of meat on the gladiators to provoke them.

I only saw the ruins, but I remember the weight in the atmosphere, that strange, electric intensity—which is how the air feels right now. When we get to the lake house, pizza is already waiting on the doorstep. I lead Sean inside, but he barely glances at the décor. His eyes are on me.

I offer him the pizza, but he pushes the box away. "Pizza can wait."

When he leans in, I close my eyes and welcome his lips. It feels, as always, like a first kiss. Like no one else mattered before him. There's a hint of urgency and resolution behind his usually calm demeanor. We make out until the pizza gets colds, and it doesn't stop there. Not that I want it to. Sean sets off an array of firecrackers everywhere he touches. His lips fall on me like leaving a bookmark in a page he wants to keep visiting.

"Are you sure?" he asks, pulling away just enough to meet my eyes, respecting the moment. His pupils are wide, like he's waking from a dream.

"Yes. I want this." My voice is steady as I give a firm nod. "Are *you* sure? Or would you rather pause and solve some last-minute physics problems first?"

"No, thank you. Not this time." He chuckles, low and breathless, and kisses me again.

I've never felt closer to anyone in my life. The space between us barely exists. Not just physically, but in the way he looks at me, like he sees all of me. It's intimacy in its purest form. We don't break eye contact, and he never stops kissing me.

And it's perfect. A completely different experience.

What can I say? Aside from the most crucial things—consent,

protection, and safety—he's a physics genius who knows all about force, speed, friction, collision, and *angles*. I have no complaints.

We finally microwave the cold pizza, though neither of us care about it anymore. We share a couple of bites, laughing over how it's not nearly as good as when it was fresh, then we kiss the night away between snippets of conversation. I ramble breathlessly about everything I like about him. He tells me how much he's missed me and wanted me. I don't remember when I fall asleep.

***

When I wake up, Sean is still sleeping. Sunlight filters through the blinds, casting striped shadows across the bed and painting his back in soft patches of light. Through the window, the leaves are a mix of bronze and gold, and beyond the western hemlocks, the lake melts into the surrounding cerulean mountains, with clouds lacing the sky like a chiffon dress. I slip out of bed, head to the kitchen, and make a cup of espresso with our new coffee maker, plus a latte for myself. I bring them to the nightstand so he'll wake up to his favorite drink. I want to slide my fingers into his hair, but hesitate to startle him.

He's angelic. His face is partly buried in the pillow, eyebrows arched at the perfect angle. My heart is bursting at the seams with love for him. I love him, and it's for so much more than just how beautiful he is.

His lashes flutter and his eyes open. They settle on me, and he smiles. "Hey, button."

"Good morning."

"You're still here. Then yesterday wasn't a dream."

I lean over to stroke his face. "You can't get rid of me that easily."

He grabs my hand and kisses my knuckles. "I had the best day of my life, and I woke up next to you. And you made me coffee. It smells so good." He rubs his eyes and sits up, reaching for the mug.

"Did you sleep well?"

"Better than I have in a long time." He squints at me over the rim with his eyes soft. "I don't think I can go back to my own bed now."

Good thing he doesn't know how much our mattress cost. He'd never relax on it again.

As Coco Chanel once said, the best things in life are free; the second-best things are very, very expensive. I've forgotten how wonderful the very best thing in my life can be. He wraps his arms around me, and it reminds me of all the pure and lovely things. Warm sun, budding flowers, mist rising off the lake at dawn, and the earthy scent of rain-soaked pine trees.

"There's something I need to tell you," I say, pulling my knees up to my chest.

"What?"

I take a deep breath. "We're supposed to have no more secrets left, but . . ." I sigh. "There's one last thing I've been keeping from you."

"What's that?" He sits up straight, the duvet slipping to his thighs.

"I don't know how you'll take it, so promise me you won't freak out."

He exhales, running a hand through his messy hair. "I'll try."

"Okay, here it goes . . . wait, no, I'm nervous about your reaction."

"Jesus, Flora! Just tell me."

"I know this is uncool, and probably too soon, but . . ." I pause a few long seconds for effect. "I love you."

It's his turn to be silent. His body tenses as he leans back, creating distance between us. There's no joy on his face. "I wish you hadn't said that."

This guy doesn't know how to respond properly! My face flares with heat. "You don't need to say it back or anything. I just want you to know how—"

"Why do you have to initiate everything? It should be *my* turn to say it first." He shakes his head in mock disapproval before breaking into a gorgeous smile that stops my heart. His smile is the best-kept secret in the Pacific Northwest. "I love you too. I love you so much, you have no idea."

I laugh, swatting him with a pillow. "Why are you so annoying?"

He tackles me and we roll over on the bed, laughing. "I love you, Flora. You make me deliriously happy."

"When did you realize that?" I ask when we break apart. "When did you start loving me?"

He doesn't answer right away. When he finally does, he says, "I'm not sure of the exact moment. But thinking back, ever since your confession at Raymond's party, I can't remember ever *not* loving you."

His eyes are calm and sincere, and he'd never lie to me. I roll back into his arms and smile until my face hurts.

CHAPTER TWENTY-EIGHT

Sean

We're still at the lake house on Sunday. The two of us are lost at the end of the world, content with the isolation.

"What do you want for lunch?" I ask.

Flora sighs, as if eating is hard labor. "I'm not that hungry. Maybe check the fridge to see if there's anything edible."

There are rows of bottled mineral water inside, a block of cheese, and not much else. Like the one in her apartment, the kitchen is gleaming white and fully equipped with stainless steel appliances. The marble countertop is shiny and spotless, and sitting on top, there's an assortment of high-end gadgets, including a rice cooker and three different types of toasters.

"My dad would kill for a kitchen like this. How often do you guys come here?"

"Every two or three months, I think. Jeremy stops by occasionally. We don't really use the kitchen, but we have stuff just in case. My parents want me to feel comfortable when I have friends over."

It must be cool never having to worry about things like scholarships and scraping by for a trip. But despite having everything handed to her, Flora remains so kind and genuine. Her parents must know what they're doing to trust her like this. I sift through the shelves, finding a pack of pasta and a can of tomato paste wedged between a bottle of soy sauce and a half-used jar of chili crisp. "Want to have pasta?"

"You can cook?"

"Not really, but let's find a recipe online. Shouldn't be harder than a chemistry experiment, right? There's more room for error." And I feel bad that no one uses this nice kitchen.

As I put a pot of water on to boil, Flora leans against the island in a silk robe, the fabric clinging to her in a way that doesn't leave much to the imagination. I add the spaghetti to the pot as the water comes to life with bubbles. The package says it takes seven minutes. On another stove, I heat up the tomato sauce. She makes an exaggerated sound of appreciation when she tastes it.

She hops onto the counter, crossing her legs. I drop the wooden spoon, and she wraps her legs around my waist, tugging me closer. I cup her face and kiss her.

The timer goes off. *Right. The noodles.*

"I should turn off the stove," I murmur, not really caring.

She responds by kissing me harder.

The noodles are getting limper by the second while I . . . well, I'm not. If we keep this up, we'll never eat. I pry myself away, and she heads to the living room to lounge in front of the TV. When I bring out two plates of spaghetti, she digs in.

Dropping her fork, she nods as she chews. "*So* good."

I take a bite. It's completely overdone.

"We need some good wine with it," she says.

"To be honest, good wine is a waste on me."

"You need to awaken your senses! Let me enlighten you." She heads back to the kitchen. There's the sound of a cork popping, the clinking of glass against the counter, and the faint sound of liquid sloshing before she returns. "I have two glasses. One of them is from a bottle of Chianti, and the other is cheap supermarket wine Josie left behind."

Only Flora would spring a wine tasting on me out of nowhere. What I wouldn't give to have a can of Pepsi right now.

"Close your eyes. Okay, the first one." She lets me smell first, then the cold glass presses to my lips. I take a sip.

"Do you like it?"

It tastes like . . . *wine*. "Yup."

She feeds me again. "How about this one? Which one do you prefer?"

There's no difference, so I take a random guess and open my eyes. "The first one."

She sets down the glass with a sigh. "Sean, it's the same glass."

"That's unfair. It was a trick question!"

"I love you so much, I couldn't bear to give you cheap wine."

I smile. "I don't care. Cheap wine suits me fine."

She exhales with a frown. "You don't appreciate the finer things in life. It breaks my heart."

"That's not true," I protest. "I appreciate *you*. You're the finest thing in my life."

"But this is part of me." She gestures to the wine bottle. "As well as designer clothes, gourmet food, extravagant parties—these are the things that matter to me."

"Come on, you're so much more than that. You're not just about money."

"No, it's not about money. I knew you'd say that because you don't get it. It's about developing *taste*," she says, her frown getting deeper. "If you never try new things, you'll miss out on a lot."

Some of us don't have the luxury to try new things all the time, and I'm still in high school. Besides, I'm so broke after Lindsey's party, I can't even afford to try old things right now. But why worry about money when Flora cares about my opinion? She just wants to share her interests with me.

"I'm sorry. Let's try again. Tell me what's so amazing about this wine so I can impress everyone at my next dinner party." I make a big show of searching for a piece of paper, preparing to jot down notes. "Now, what's this supposed to taste like?"

She rotates the glass counterclockwise, letting the dark-red liquid coat the sides before it runs down in slow stripes. "Chianti is like the little black dress of wine—elegant and timeless. The Sangiovese grapes give it acidity, which is why it works so well with tomato sauce. Do you get hints of flowers or berries or minerals? Think earth notes, like truffles."

Truffles? Flora made me truffle cream sandwiches yesterday, and it was nothing remotely similar to this. "Are you sure you're not just reading off the label?"

She narrows her eyes, even though her lips are curving up. "It's not on the label. Don't insult my extraordinary taste buds."

"All right then. You mentioned flowers. What kind of flowers?"

"What do you mean what kind of flowers?"

"Can you be more specific?" I place the pen over my notes. "In case you don't know, I'm a model student, and I need full comprehension."

"This isn't a written test. But if you must know, I'd say violets."

I cross out the word *flower* and put *violet* underneath. "What kind of minerals?"

"You're impossible." She shakes her head and laughs. Her laugh is the part that sticks with me.

✶ ✶ ✶

Josie is sitting by herself on the lawn when I arrive at school on Monday, headphones wrapped around her head. Instead of joining the other girls for their giant lattes, this is her version of breakfast. She feeds herself on enough rock and roll to get her through the day.

"I got invited to see this band, Birch Grove, perform at the Crocodile on Friday. You know, that grungy venue near Belltown," she says when I sit down next to her. "Wanna come?"

I'm her go-to whenever Brian is busy at university. A week ago, I would've agreed right away, but now I hesitate. "Let me ask Flora if she's up for it," I say, even though it isn't her cup of tea.

Josie doesn't miss a beat, and the realization clicks into place on her face. She'll stop asking me to hang out since I'm back in a relationship. "Of course, ask Flora to come! And congrats, by the way. Finally, the pair of you came to your senses."

"Yeah, and now you know everything."

"No need for me to point out the obvious. If you had confided in me, *at all*, at any point during junior year—"

I groan. "I get it. I brought this on myself. In the future, I'll report everything to you firsthand. Want to subscribe to our newsletter?"

"No, thanks, I've got limited space on my email server."

"I still can't believe I have her back." Flora was my first thought this morning and has stayed on my mind ever since.

Josie pats me on the shoulder. "She's one step away from tattooing your name on her forehead. Glad to see you're taking this seriously too. But also, you're different people at the core, and it's important to develop common interests—"

"We have common interests. You wouldn't believe what I did this weekend. I was wine tasting. I'm now an expert on tannin and oak notes."

"Well, I'm happy for you." She couldn't fake that smile of genuine approval even if she wanted to. Josie is the greatest friend I could ever hope for, even though I sideline her whenever I'm in a relationship.

"Let me know if you need my advice on anything. Picking out a baby name, for example."

"We've got that covered. Flora will name it Christian. Middle name Dior."

She laughs. "If you hurry, you can catch Christian's mom before class."

* * *

Flora is hanging around Madison's locker with Carmen. I seem to have developed tunnel vision—she's in the center, and everything else defocuses.

"I heard Flora took you back," Madison says as I approach. "How wonderful. I mean, recycling is good for the environment."

"Congrats!" Carmen, ever the balance to Madison's negativity, beams. "It's great you guys worked things out."

"If you hurt her again"—Madison jabs a finger at me—"I'll make sure you regret every second for the rest of your miserable life. And let me clarify the question on everyone's mind—how *stupid* could you be? I thought you were a cruel jackass, but now it's clear you're just an idiot. You owe us all a massive apology for the emotional turmoil you put us through."

"Okay, I deserve that," I say. "But can we do a onetime roast and get it over with? Instead of reliving this every time you see me?"

"Way to make this about you, Mads," Flora says, smiling. "Don't you need to go eat some small children or something?"

"Small children are hardly vegan." Madison chuckles anyway, like an afterthought. "I meant to say congratulations too. It came out wrong because I'm a bit allergic to happy people."

"Thanks." I'm too happy to come up with a comeback.

Flora grabs my elbow and waves goodbye to her friends. "Excuse us. We need to go and *be happy* now."

When she leads me over to the side of the building to kiss me, I don't protest. We've become the kind of annoying couple who makes out in public, but considering everything, we've earned it. For three days, at least.

It's not easy to pull apart but we manage. I have to remind myself she's going to class instead of to war. I walk her to her classroom even though I'll be late to mine.

"See you at lunch," she says.

The bell rings. She leaves a whiff of jasmine on my sleeve.

* * *

My life begins to be divided up into fragments, and the chunks of time in between become irrelevant, lost in the static. It's transformed into a conveyor belt of waking up, catching Flora before class, a blur, then lunch, then history class, where I stare at her chocolate-colored head from three rows behind. Another blur, class ends, and we spend every last drop of time together. The boundary of reality dissolves into a field of jasmine.

We went to the show with Josie. We attended the homecoming dance together, dancing exclusively with each other, staying true to our tradition. My dad snapped another photo before we left, which I shared on my account, bringing my total posts to six.

One day in history class, Flora and I text each other until my phone runs out of power.

Flora: *Dear Sean, it's very difficult for me to concentrate with you radiating heat from 3 rows behind. I want to serve you in your chamber*

Sean: *Dear chambermaid, we're on page 213. Stop fantasizing about my hotness*

Flora turns to wink at me, and all the words from page 213 melt away.

* * *

"What *is* it about Flora that keeps you crawling back for more?" Jake asks at lunch a few days later, and Dylan gives me a look that can only be described as inappropriate. "If you're willing to branch out, I hear some juniors are very into your whole broody, tortured energy."

"Jacob, I don't have tortured energy. And no, thank you."

Right then, Flora slides into the seat next to me, trailing a hand along my shoulder blades. "What are you guys talking about?"

"I'm telling him he can do better than you." Jake grins. "I'm sick of all your friends. I was hoping Sean could bring some fresh blood into this group, but we're stuck with you again."

Flora swipes a handful of fries off my tray and pelts him with them. Jake laughs, ducking just in time.

"Are you coming to my place Saturday night for the game?" Dylan asks me. It's our custom to watch NBA games together, especially the important ones. This year Dylan's basketball captain, and his obsession with strategy is even more intense.

"Saturday?" Flora checks the calendar on her phone. "Saturday's fine. We're free."

"I didn't invite you," Dylan says. "Nothing personal, it's a bro thing."

"You're watching the live broadcast?" Flora picks up a fry and nibbles at it. "Then that means you're not interested in free tickets."

I arch my eyebrows. "You have tickets?"

"No big deal, but they're lower-level sideline seats. Close enough to see the sweat." She shrugs, her diamond earrings catching the light as they shimmer through her hair. "My dad's client—anyway, I'm going to sell them online. Seems like watching TV is the cool way to go."

"Take me! Please!" I place my hand over hers. "I'm not friends with these people."

She must have more than two tickets. Flora doesn't flaunt unless she's offering.

"How many tickets do you have?" Jake asks.

"It depends," Flora says, "on how nice you are to me for the next five minutes."

I try not to smile as they scramble to butter her up. How is it even possible that being Flora's boyfriend keeps getting better?

"I'll end you if you ever break up with her." Dylan points a steady finger at me, a firm show of loyalty to Flora, the ticket holder. "You'll never know peace again."

Jake nods along. He puts a hand over his mouth and whispers loudly, just so she can hear and laugh. "Break up with her *after* the game."

CHAPTER TWENTY-NINE

Flora

Sean. Sean. Sean. Sean. Sean. Sean.

He fills my head the moment I wake up. If only I could stitch him into the embroidery on my shirt collar, carry him with me everywhere. We gave each other space before, but now we neither need it nor want it.

If being a good boyfriend was a job, Sean would already be in the C-suite. Ever since he uttered the *L* word, nothing holds him back. And I'm no better. This love spreads like a snag in a pair of pantyhose. One tiny break in the fibers and the tear races outward, unraveling everything in its path. There's no stopping it, no mending it.

Madison is the first to call me out. We're sprawled on her bed, scrolling through our phones, when she says, "Let's play a game. The first person to mention Sean buys everyone caramel macchiatos."

Carmen and Josie don't say anything, but they exchange a *finally someone said it* look.

My mouth clamps shut, but inside, I fume. I do *not* talk about Sean that much. And what are best friends for if they can't let me gush? It's only been two weeks. Not to mention I've been paying for caramel macchiatos for the past three years.

Tonight, Sean's away for a basketball game. I only cheer at home games, so I stay in and examine my shoe collection, waiting for him to come back. Normally, this would be the kind of night I'd call Raymond, who's free as a cheetah in the savanna, thanks to his parents never keeping tabs on him. After the divorce, they care even less.

But that was before Sean declared Raymond should be exiled for life.

Okay, those weren't his exact words, but he did say something along the lines of *I'm entitled to hold a grudge. He's the reason we broke up.*

I shook my head. "No. *We* are the reason we broke up. It's adorable that you've decided to pin it all on him."

"Of course I blame him. He knew you had a boyfriend and still went to your place and came on to you. That says a lot about his sense of morality."

I almost laughed. "Sean, you're morality personified. We're all sinners in front of you."

Needless to say, he didn't appreciate me "taking Raymond's side." I tried to explain that hanging out with Ray was completely innocent, but Sean wasn't having it. He clarified he wasn't asking me to cut Ray out of my life, but some "adjustments" were needed.

"Don't you think drinking with a guy in your room is . . . intimate?"

"Would you feel better if I drank with a *group* of guys in my room?" I joked, but the second he didn't smile, I regretted it. "Look, I'm not attracted to Ray, but I like our movie nights too much to give that up. He's my movie knowledge pipeline!"

I decided to end my argument with an analogy.

"I'm not a science nerd, but I know at least this much: no amount of catalysts can force a reaction that wasn't meant to happen in the first place. You have nothing to worry about when it comes to Ray."

Sean raised his eyebrows. "Impressive. But he's an unstable compound prone to spontaneous reactions. Given the right conditions, he could undergo an irreversible transformation, and once his molecular structure degrades, there's no predicting the chain reaction that might follow."

Ugh. Why did I bring up science?

When we still couldn't reach a unanimous agreement, Sean tackled it from another angle. "Okay, how would *you* feel if I invited some girl to my room?"

I tilted my head, considering the unlikely scenario. "I wouldn't be overjoyed, but that's different."

"How?"

"Because." I rolled my eyes. "You're not like that. You don't even let Josie in your room. If you suddenly wanted alone time with another girl, I'd know something was up. It would be out of character for you. But for me, it doesn't mean anything because that's what I do. Which is why we should have customized rules to suit our different personalities."

"You just used five sentences to describe double standards."

I can't debate with him. He's too good. He has a valid point, and he sticks to his boundaries. But I'm not wrong either. We're fundamentally different people expected to fit into the same mold. I have my own idea of how close I want to be with other people, yet Sean wants everything to be equal and standardized.

So now I find myself sitting in my room alone. I rearrange my closet. Run the jade roller over my face to feel productive. Post an entry in the style blog Sean made for me. Learn a new hair trick off YouTube and attempt a side fishtail braid.

Just as I'm about to shrivel up and die of boredom, my phone rings.

"Whatcha doin'?" Raymond sings.

"Braiding my hair and waiting for Sean."

He makes a dramatic gagging noise. "Wow. Riveting. Come over to my place."

"I can't. I'm in a relationship."

Silence. Then, "Okay. And?"

"And I mean I can't hang out with you."

There's a long pause, like he's trying to reboot his entire brain. "Wait. Are you saying that because you have a boyfriend, you can never see me again? Ever? Do I need to submit a formal request? Get a permission slip signed?"

"Well, we can hang out, but not like this. We can gather a few more people and meet at the mall. Or a movie theater."

"A movie theater?" He sounds like I've invited him to clean out an elephant's cage at the zoo. "Have you *seen* my home theater? And you think I'd trade that for sticky floors and seats with mystery stains? Hard pass. Also, I hate everybody. They all annoy me."

I laugh. Ray could write an encyclopedia with all his pet peeves.

"Wow," he mutters. "So this is it. The great Flora Morgan has fallen. Next thing you know, you'll start saying things like *We love that show* and *Our favorite restaurant.*"

"Stop being dramatic," I say as he starts to fake sob.

"I got hold of some Czech beer that's supposedly good. Let's invite Sean to share with us. I guess I can tolerate your boyfriend if that's what it takes."

Wow, he *really* wants my company. "That's nice of you to offer, but too much beer will damage Sean's valuable brain cells."

"If he's as smart as you claim, he should have plenty to spare."

"Actually, Sean says intelligence has more to do with the folds and grooves of the brain than the number of brain cells."

Raymond makes that disgruntled noise again. "I get that you worship him, but you quoting him all the time is seriously testing our friendship."

Gosh, he sounds like Madison. I decide to share the reason Sean and I broke up, just so he doesn't assume I'm blowing him off for no reason.

"*What?* I didn't hit on you!"

"You tried to kiss me, and he saw it. Now you're on the blacklist."

"But how's that even possible? I don't like you like that!" He seems offended, like I insulted his exemplary taste.

"I'm telling you, it happened. There's a good reason Sean doesn't want to hang out with you, and, like, can you blame him?"

"I'm sorry," he says, even though I never blamed him. "You're my friend, and I know how much you like him. I really didn't expect my actions to cause full-scale diplomatic tensions. I'll apologize to Sean too. Maybe send him a fruit basket. Seriously, I feel bad."

"No, he didn't want me to tell you. He's embarrassed about the whole thing." Sean and his ego refuse to let Raymond have the satisfaction of knowing he came between us.

"But I don't want him to hate me." It's amazing how Ray has no trouble hating everyone, but the idea of *being* hated is unbearable. He has this unexplainable urge to stay on everyone's good side.

"Forget it."

"Well, I can't apologize to him, I can't invite him to hang out, so what does that leave us? Are we just . . . done? Is this it?"

Oh god. I was never in a relationship with Raymond, but now we're breaking up.

"We can still say hi at school. And I'll like every one of your Instagram posts." I try to lighten the mood. "That's what friends are for, anyway. To make you feel popular on social media."

He grunts. "Well, if you'll excuse me, I'm gonna hang up now and check if you've actually liked any of my posts."

I let out a long breath, exhausted. The doorbell rings, and I sprint to answer it, nearly tripping over a pile of shoes on the way.

Sean stands before me in a (very huggable) eggshell-white hoodie, his backpack slung over one shoulder. In the back of my mind, I picture opening the doors of a cathedral, where the organs play and the angels sing. A halo surrounds Sean and *fine*, I worship him.

So what?

"Button." He tugs on my fishtail braid. I step aside to let him in, but he bends down to kiss me first. His lips are soft but firm, and waiting for him was totally worth it. He tastes like chocolate.

"Did you put cookies in my backpack?" he asks.

"Yeah. In case you got hungry during the game."

He pinches my cheek, already heading toward my room. "You're the best. I ate most of them before the game even started."

"Did you win?"

"Yes." He flops onto my bed. "How was your evening?"

"Um, Raymond called. Do you want to drink beer with him?"

"What?"

"It might be a good idea if we all hang out together. Maybe you'll learn to like him!"

"No thanks. What if he tries to kiss me?"

I chuckle. "It'd be great if you guys got to know each other better."

He cringes. "I don't know."

"I told him I can't hang out with him the way we did before. He wasn't happy about it, and I feel like an awful friend."

"Josie never gives me attitude for that. She gets that some things have to change."

But do they? This is such an absurd system. I don't care at all that Sean has Josie, but he gives that up simply for the sake of being fair. "You know how crazy I am about you. You shouldn't be threatened by other guys at all."

"I'm not threatened. It's like eating a meal with flies buzzing around. I'm not threatened by the flies, but they still annoy the hell out of me." He sighs, rubbing his temple. "Look, I'm not here to control who you spend time with. I trust you, and I know you'd never intentionally cross a line. And again, I'm sorry for how I jumped to conclusions last year. But I won't pretend I'm comfortable with you drinking alone with another guy in your room. Seeing him come on to you before—that image is seared into my mind. You know where I stand, but ultimately, it's your decision. If this is something you're not willing to adjust, maybe we need to ask ourselves whether we see relationships the same way."

Sean isn't being unreasonable with this airtight monologue. He's not making demands or issuing ultimatums. He's just laying out his feelings in the calm, levelheaded way he always does. Honestly, he's not asking for much.

"We can talk about this more if you want," he adds, even though it's clear he'd rather deep dive into why Goyard bags are coveted.

I don't want to push it, especially not after waiting for him the whole night. I already know I'll cave; it's just a matter of whether I let him convince me now or later. His love matters more than my entire collection of guy friends. If he decides we aren't compatible, it'd be worse than being forced to wear secondhand clothes for the rest of my life.

It's simple. I'll do anything to please him, even if it means changing into someone easier to love.

I wrap my arms around his waist, savoring the warmth of

his body beneath my fingertips. Moments later, all thoughts of Raymond are out the window. In the summer, Sean's skin is tanned like roasted almonds, but now it's winter-fair and smooth, flushed against my lips. He doesn't roll away when we're done. Instead, he pulls me closer to press a kiss to my bare shoulder.

I love the way the mattress dips when he shifts beside me, the subtle scent of his deodorant, the way he strokes my hair while I ramble, and how comfortable he is around me. There's an endearing, casual side to him, with an added dash of innocence. It reminds me of a lion cub yawning and chasing after a ball.

Later, as Sean absentmindedly folds the clothes on my bed, I bring over a bottle of burgundy nail polish from my desk.

"Want to help me paint my toes?" I'm half joking, certain he'll refuse, but he takes the bottle from my hand and unscrews the cap.

"Sure you want to trust me with this?"

"You can try."

He bends over, and the cute concentration on his face is overkill. He squints as if he's designing a space shuttle. "Uh-oh."

"You built a crime scene." My toes belong on a horror movie poster. But the effort deserves to be immortalized, so I frame the shot to catch a sliver of Sean's very concerned expression, with my tragic toes blurry in the background.

Caption: *Nailed it (not really)*

#truelove #hetried #michelangelocouldnever #youareluckyyouarehot

By the time he leaves, I've racked up 412 likes and 59 comments. I usually don't do this, but I check. Raymond isn't one of them.

CHAPTER THIRTY

Sean

As my Flora-themed life unfolds, she remains at the center, and I fit everything else around her. I understand her better now than I did in junior year. After we got back together, her parents were gone for a *week*. I've taken my dad's home-cooked meals, my mom's warm encouragement, and Lindsey's whining for granted. Flora's life, in contrast, is one black hole after school and cheerleading practice. She needs an exit for her excessive energy.

It's my responsibility to become that outlet. I start taking her home, and she brings us wine from her parents' collection. Sometimes she gives my mom flowers. After dinner, she offers to clean up, though all she really does is sit on the counter, dangle her toned legs, and flirt with me.

Some nights, we retreat to my room and try to stay quiet. Other times, I drive her back to her place, where we can really "blow off steam." The routine is all I could ask for. I nurture the dark circles under my eyes, which Flora finds sexy. She says they make my eyes bluer. Homework begins only after she sleeps, while espresso becomes my life-support system. We wear each other down like a meteor tearing through the atmosphere.

The real wake-up call comes one night when I accompany Flora to a Lanvin runway show. Her mom is one of the VIP invitees, and

Flora gladly takes her place. The show runs longer than expected, and by the time we get back to her house, it's late. We make out for a while—no matter how exhausted I am, the adrenaline rush keeps me going—then she curls up under the covers, barefaced, and I sit at the edge of her bed, holding her hand. My brain is running on fumes, grasping at some vague thought in the back of my mind. Something I was supposed to do.

"You're so wonderful to me."

The way she says it, soft and unguarded, is enough to override every rational instinct. The feeling of being needed is overpowering.

"Good night, button."

The next thing I know, I'm jolted awake by the cold. It's 3 a.m., my phone is dead, and every muscle in my body aches. The next morning, I oversleep and barely have time to shower, let alone eat breakfast. When I sit down in AP Chemistry, it hits me.

The thing I forgot to do.

Mr. Miles asks us to hand in our assignment after class. My answer sheet is blank. This can't happen to me. I don't forget my homework. I always check it three times.

Am I going to get detention? Detention is as foreign a concept to me as Lanvin once was.

When Mr. Miles turns to scrawl formulas across the blackboard, I force myself to focus. Chemistry is one of my stronger subjects, but today, the words dissolve before my eyes like salt in an undersaturated solution. Too tired to think, I curse under my breath.

Carmen slides her homework onto my desk. It takes me a second to register it.

"My answers are correct," she whispers.

I nod. "Thanks."

My back burns with remorse, but there's no time for that now. There's plenty of time for that two days later, when I get my German pop quiz back. German pronunciation is a struggle, but written tests are usually a breeze, so when I see the red numbers slashed across the paper, my first instinct is that this isn't mine.

Sixty-eight.

Sixty-eight.

I don't remember ever getting a mark below ninety. My eyes dart around the room, scanning for reference points. Maybe the test was harder than usual. Maybe everyone failed.

The first mark that meets my eyes is a whopping ninety-four.

I shuffle to my next class like Hester Prynne from *The Scarlet Letter*, a giant embroidered 68 scalding the front of my button-down shirt.

Flora is less than sympathetic.

"Wow, what a story to tell the grandkids, right?" she says on the way to cheerleading practice.

"Flora." I try keeping the irritation out of my voice.

"It's *fine*. It's one test, and German isn't that useful anyway. Everybody in Germany speaks English, including Einstein." She tousles my hair.

"My grades are slipping. I'm not as smart as you think. I've always had to work for it. This shows I have to put in more effort."

"One pop quiz isn't going to tank your GPA."

"It's not the test per se. It's a warning sign, I forgot to do my chemistry homework too."

"Didn't Carmen save you in time?" We reach the football field, and she's losing interest. "I have to go to practice now. Blame me later."

"Baby, I'm not blaming you, but we need to make some changes.

Let's talk after practice, okay?" I'm so drained I don't even have the energy to explain.

Her lips are set in a thin line. "Sure."

"Can you go to practice now and get mad at me later?"

"Getting mad at you won't interfere with my practice. I'm a pro at multitasking."

We stare at each other for a second before breaking into smiles at the same time.

"You're so hot in your cheerleading uniform, no one can argue with you and win." That sounds like something Flora would say. Well, two can master this art.

She gives me a proper smile, one that washes away my worries like waves erasing drawings in the sand. "I'm sorry about your test. Call me later?"

With a small wave, she jogs over to join Madison.

CHAPTER THIRTY-ONE

Flora

Sean comes over in the evening. My parents are back from their business trip to Buenos Aires, but they're still downtown, dealing with some corporate crisis.

Usually, he pulls me into a kiss the second I latch the door, but this time, he brushes past me and heads straight for my room. He sits on the floor, stretches out his legs, and delivers his grand opening. "We need to talk."

My heart lurches. "Am I getting fired, or what?"

"I'm crazy about you. You know that. But we can't go on like this."

"Like what? Being in love with each other?"

"You're acting defensive before I even say anything."

"Fine, go ahead. I won't interrupt until you finish."

"We have to establish some rules. I'm exhausted all the time. I thought I could juggle everything, but I've realized I can't study, date you, play basketball, and prep for college all at once, on top of getting five hours of sleep every night."

He does look like he's drowning in fatigue. *Poor kid.* My heart plummets from the treetop and hits every branch on the way down.

"My personal statement is a mess," he continues. "Mr. Miles agreed to write my recommendation letter, but he wants me to draft a brag sheet, and I haven't even started. Every time I sit down to work on it, I end up too tired to think."

There it is. Something has to give, right? He plans to sacrifice me. I'm the first junk he throws overboard from this sinking ship.

"Being with you feels like a vacation," he says, "but a vacation eventually has to end—"

I blink.

"—and it's time we start building a real life together. Don't get me wrong. You're too important. Ever since I got you back, I've been thinking about how to make this last, which is why I can't burn out too quickly. I want you in my life for as long as you're willing to stay."

He smiles at me, and how many people can resist Sean like that? My insides turn into mush.

"I hope that's what you want too . . . you know, a steady long-term relationship," he mutters, as if it's embarrassing to admit. "Because if you want a winter fling instead, I'll undress you right now and you can forget everything I said."

I laugh. "I want a long-term relationship too." My face heats up. Somehow, getting serious makes me shyer than getting naked, and it stirs up bubbles in my stomach.

"Great. Glad we're thinking the same." His smile lasts for a few seconds, serving as the sweet opening before he gets serious. *Using the sandwich feedback method on me, Foster?* "First, we should spend less time together and limit our phone conversations. I can't text you in class anymore because I'll wait for you to text back. I need to concentrate."

Getting serious doesn't seem to offer much, and wait, there's more.

"I have to finish my homework before we can hang out. And I

don't know if I can meet the early action deadline, so the next two weeks are critical. I need extra time to work on my essays."

Whenever Sean talks about his dream of getting into MIT, it fills my heart a little more with pride (and mild panic). A few days ago, he let me read one of his essays. If I was the admissions officer, I'd have admitted him on the spot, but Sean deleted the whole thing because "it wasn't compelling enough." There's the familiar fear that sprouts in me, warning me I'm not half as smart or driven as he is. And everything he's saying is irrefutable.

"Don't get mad at me when we spend the weekend separately," he goes on. "I have brunch with my grandad, and I need to hit the gym. I haven't been in two weeks, and I'm afraid I'm losing these."

He lifts his shirt, revealing his abs.

I lean forward to trace the faint lines on his stomach. "They're very much intact, all six of them."

"I do this for you, you know. You're very, very superficial."

"I'm superficial and proud of it." I raise my chin. "Is that it? Is this the part where we slash our palms and make a blood oath?"

He scratches his chin as he plays along. "I was aiming for written consent, but if you want to go hardcore . . ."

"Why don't we draw up a prenup while we're at it? You're not getting half of my shoes if we break up."

"I don't want your shoes. I want you." His eyes sparkle with a warm glow, like a heated pool on a sunny day. "Thanks for putting up with me. You're so understanding."

"No worries. You're good looking, so you're allowed to be difficult."

He sprang the Declaration of Independence on me. For the past two weeks our love has been *fabulous*, the kind of montage-worthy romance where our scenes overlap with emotional music playing in the background. A split screen might even show us both on the phone, falling asleep with matching grins on our faces.

I didn't expect the sappy phase to expire so soon. Flirting with Sean was like standing outside a bakery, breathing in the sweet air, staring longingly at the cute cupcakes in the display window. Now that I'm finally inside the shop, he's telling me to cut back on sugar and drink a glass of water instead.

Sean stretches, then climbs into my bed. "Can I sleep for a while? I'm exhausted."

"Sure. I'll go tweeze my eyebrows."

"No . . . can you come here instead? I want you beside me."

I slide in and lie down next to him. He places his head against my shoulder, positioning his arms around my body. "I don't know what I'd do without you." His voice is soft, falling over me like rose petals. "I feel better whenever I see you. You don't even need to say anything."

Here it is. The final positive feedback part of the sandwich method, and it works. This guy is *good*. I run my fingers through his hair. I don't speak, because I'll ruin it if I do.

"Baby, I need you," he murmurs. His body grows heavier as he relaxes against me. Underneath Sean's cool, composed exterior, he's pure Bambi-level sweetness.

"I need you too," I say. "Hey, I forgot to mention. My parents want to have dinner with you."

He nods with his eyes closed. "I can't wait."

CHAPTER THIRTY-TWO

Sean

Flora's parents are the least parent-like figures I've ever met. Some of it's because they're so young, with practically nonexistent lines around their eyes, but mostly it's because of the way they carry themselves. It's easier to regard them as Taylor and Alice, two polished, charming executives who make you believe their lives must be spectacular.

Her dad has a perfectly calibrated handshake, paired with just enough eye contact to seem engaged, but I get the sense he meets too many people to remember them all. Her mom speaks with practiced ease, like someone who has refined these lines to perfection. Still genuine, but detached enough to stay in control. Her brother, Jeremy, seems self-assured and laid-back. There's a cool glint in his eyes that says *I'm exceptional, but I won't hold it against you.* He has Flora's eyes.

"You're the first boyfriend I've gotten to meet." Jeremy rises from his seat, offering a handshake with an easy grin. The grin disappears and his tone turns ominous. "My dad handled all the previous ones. One of the bodies is still unaccounted for, but we don't talk about that."

"Shut up." Flora shoots him a glare. "I really like Sean. Don't scare him off."

Run, Jeremy mouths.

"Sweetheart, we're happy you got back together." Her mom brings up our breakup as casually as if she's recommending a new coffee shop in Capitol Hill. She smiles at me. "Flora's told us so much about you. All good things. We're thrilled to finally meet you!"

There's a round of hugs before we sit down again under the giant ceiling light, an extravagant fixture made up of countless gold spoons. Everything sparkles, from the silver utensils to the wineglasses that are as thin as eggshells. We're served a bread assortment, accompanied by three different types of butter, shaped like a pyramid, a cookie, and a tangled mass of yarn respectively.

The menu arrives, and they all barely glance at it before ordering, as if they've memorized it already. Flora's mom asks about a special venison dish that isn't even listed. I've always thought my vocabulary was broad enough, but it falls short in the culinary world.

"Have you been here before?" Taylor asks. "This is our favorite restaurant in the city."

I peel my eyes away from the prices on the menu. "No, thanks for inviting me. This place is incredible. I feel like I should have dressed nicer."

Alice smiles. "Don't mention it. At the end of the day, it's just a restaurant with better tableware."

"And servers who deserve Academy Awards," Jeremy adds. "They act like they're genuinely excited about our dinner choices. I always have the urge to ask what would be a not-so-excellent choice."

Apparently, there's no such thing. Every bite is exquisite, from the lobster and langoustine ravioli to the turbot bathed in a soup of flowers and herbs and the mini glass of raspberry parfait meant to cleanse the palate. I never knew people ate like this—a collection of heavenly ingredients boiled down to a single drop of sauce.

When Taylor asks me about school, Flora launches into full grandma-brag mode, gushing about my grades as if she's showing off baby pictures. "If MIT was smart, they'd *beg* him to enroll."

Taylor nods. "Impressive. What field do you want to specialize in?"

"Either electrical engineering and computer science or mechanical engineering with a focus on robotics," I say, and they nod in approval, like I answered a test question correctly.

"That's a lot to juggle—varsity sports, AP classes, and extra projects," Jeremy says. "I've been there, still trying to repress the memory."

"It's wonderful to hear how well you're doing. You're goal oriented," Alice says to me, then she flicks her gaze over to Jeremy. "Jer was valedictorian of his high-school class. We're all so proud."

"Sometimes I feel like I'm barely keeping up," I say as Flora fidgets beside me. "Any insights on how you got into Harvard?"

"Let's see, perfect GPA, elite-level hockey, debate nationals. Yeah, it was basically a done deal. Not gonna lie, having some family advantages didn't hurt." Jeremy leans in, mock sympathy all over his face. "But I had one less thing on my plate—I wasn't in a relationship. Dating my prima donna of a sister has got to be . . . *character building*, right?"

Flora kicks him under the table.

"Oh, for sure. Trying my best to cope," I joke. "But in all seriousness, Flora is the best thing to happen to me in high school."

Jeremy smirks, clearly unconvinced, and gives me a *you don't have to lie* grin. "I've got to warn you—there're no hot girls at MIT.

But they do build some impressive robotic cheetahs, if you're into that."

"Keep it up and I'm feeding you to the robotic cheetahs," Flora says.

"But don't fret, there are plenty of choices at BU and Wellesley. I'll email you the details later. *Just in case*." He winks at me to irritate Flora.

"Sounds like you've done extensive research," I say.

Jeremy shrugs. "Gotta be thorough. That's part of what I did when I was applying for college. It's all about planning ahead, right?"

Taylor chuckles, finally chiming in. "College applications *are* daunting. Easily one of the top two most stressful times of my life."

"What was the other one?" Flora asks.

He gestures to Alice, who simply swirls her wine with an amused smile. "Marriage."

"Hey!" Alice says. "Want to try again?"

"That extended business trip to Shanghai." Taylor pauses to take a measured sip of his white wine. "Incredibly impactful, lots of key takeaways and growth opportunities, but it was a challenge being away from you all. I was fortunate to have such a strong support system." He places a hand over Alice's.

"My dad had to stay there by himself for a year," Flora explains. "My mom had just started a new role, so she stayed behind to take care of us."

"Stepping into that role meant transitioning from an individual contributor to a leadership position." Alice shakes her head, and her straight dark hair shines. "It was a learning curve for all of us. There's no such thing as work-life balance. You learn to prioritize and make trade-offs."

Jeremy shrugs good-naturedly. "We have more than enough. No complaints."

"And look, we turned out all right," Flora adds.

Alice leaves the table to take a call, and when she sits back down again, she apologizes profusely. "I'm so sorry. That was one of the investigators from our phase three trial, but it's all taken care of now." She sets her phone on Silent and tucks it into her bag. "I did clear my schedule this evening, because I really want to get to know you, Sean. Flora told us you designed an app?"

Taylor leans in. "Tell us all about it!"

"It's nothing groundbreaking, but we use it for some of our physics projects. It organizes thermophysical properties of fluid systems. It has built-in formulas, unit conversions, calculations for specific heat capacity and thermal conductivity. Flora can't believe how nerdy it is."

Taylor doesn't let me off the hook, and Alice jumps in with more questions—how I came up with it, why I chose the interface, what the biggest challenge was, and how I'd refine it with unlimited time and resources. I do my best to answer.

When I finish, Taylor raises his glass to me. "Sounds like you've got your dream school in the bag. Make sure you highlight this in your application. Schools don't just want to see what you built; they want to understand how it's being used and who benefits from it."

I nod, taking mental notes. He's right. I've been so focused on the technical side that I hadn't thought much about how to frame the app's impact. Their questions make me rethink my approach to my essays.

Before I can say more, Flora turns to her parents. "Hey, you didn't ask about *my* SAT scores and where I want to apply."

"It's not going to ruin my appetite, is it?" Taylor chuckles, setting down his fork. "I'm looking forward to dessert."

"You don't need a good score," says Jeremy. "Just send the admissions office your best feature, your photos."

"Maybe I should pick my twelve greatest shots and make a calendar." Flora doesn't even sound sarcastic.

Jeremy nods. "Solid strategy. No surprises beyond the surface, anyway."

Everyone laughs, including Flora. Maybe it's an inside joke, and I should go along with it. But it doesn't sit right. At the risk of sounding overly serious, I say, "I don't know, I feel like I keep discovering new layers. It's like dating an onion. But, like, in a good way. I find something new and amazing about Flora all the time."

Dating an onion? Not my best moment.

Alice smiles. "That's a lovely way to put it. She's full of surprises."

"For example, this new Bulgari bracelet I'm wearing. So pretty, right?" Flora lifts her wrist, tilting the serpent's head. "Anyway, I've been thinking about college. My grades aren't that bad, and if I retake the SAT, I might have a shot at fashion school?" She swallows, and her voice becomes quieter. "I'm not sure yet, but I want to be in the industry. I was looking into fashion buying—curating collections, selecting pieces that consumers will want to purchase—"

Jeremy nudges her elbow and grins. "So, more excuses to shop?"

"That sounds fun," Alice says, cracking open the dessert menu. "Whatever you choose, we'll support you. You have great taste, I'm sure it'll serve you well."

"Cool." Flora nods, folding the corner of her napkin between her fingers. By the time desserts are served, the conversation has shifted seamlessly to how delicious the blood-orange sorbet is.

* * *

Dinner winds down on a pleasant note. As we get up to leave, I thank Flora's parents for having me, while she and Jeremy exchange a long hug. I'm adjusting the cuff of my sleeve when his voice, although low, carries over. "Hey, Morganite. I give you a lot of crap, but you know I'd step in if I had to, right? He's treating you right?"

"Don't worry, Jemstone. He's not going anywhere," Flora says easily.

Jeremy comes over to shake my hand. "Fair warning, bro. If you break her heart, you'll have to deal with my dad. If you don't, you're stuck with her. So, either way, you're screwed."

"Good to know I have options."

He pats me on the shoulder. "That's the spirit."

With a final round of goodbyes, we step outside. The air carries a chill, and the pavement glistens with leftover rain. Flora tucks her hand into my coat pocket, catching hold of mine.

"So, that went well, right?" She beams up at me. "I knew you'd hit it off with my family."

"Yeah, I had a great time. Your family is impressive. So knowledgeable and truly charismatic." I mean it, but some of the conversations from tonight haunt me. "Do they always tease you about, you know, being pretty?"

She shrugs. "That's just how they talk. Everyone in my family goes to the Ivies, and my talent is, as you know, being beautiful all my life."

I stop in my tracks. "You don't mean that."

"Sean, it's no big deal."

"It *is* a big deal. You're more than just beautiful. How can you let yourself believe that?" So many things make sense now—why studying has always led to arguments, why she gets defensive whenever school comes up. She's been dealing with this at home. Her family barely asked about where she wants to go to college, yet they had endless curiosity about the basic app I built. No wonder she's upset.

Her smile falters. She looks away, then exhales softly. "Let's sit down."

We settle on the steps of a random building. Flora lets me hold her hand, and after a lot of coaxing, she finally starts to talk. "When I was little, Jeremy could sit in front of a black-and-white puzzle for hours, completely focused. I wanted to help, but he didn't want me getting in his way. I had a short attention span, and my parents decided early on that we were different. He did Kumon for fun, went to private schools, and had tutors, but they let me stay at Lakeridge High. Saved a great deal on tuition." She flashes her usual toothpaste-commercial smile, so bright it's sad to watch. "My parents are the best. They let me buy whatever I want, and they never pressure me to get into a top-notch college. They just want me to be happy. They have given me so much, and I can't be ungrateful."

You can appreciate your parents and still acknowledge that they've substituted material things for their attention. But I don't say it. Who am I to judge them and the way they express love? She's as delightful and magnetic as can be. They must know what they're doing.

"Do you *want* to go to college?" I settle on saying.

"Yeah, but I guess it doesn't matter where I go. They won't let me starve."

We lapse into silence. This conversation is bleak on so many levels. She's a sharp, capable person who could do so much more, but she plays it off like she's too cool to care. Happiness is having choices, the freedom to chase what excites you, yet she defines it in the shallowest way possible: my parents let me buy whatever I want.

"But becoming a fashion editor, that's your dream."

"That's what dreams are. Dreams are . . . dreams."

There's a reason why I never bring up her college choices. It's a sore topic, and she might make passive-aggressive remarks about being a brainless cheerleader, or that she can't score eight billion points on the SAT like I did. She could hire a tutor if she wanted, and it'd be so much easier if I stayed in my lane—her boyfriend, the guy she has fun with.

I can't even guarantee we'll still be together after graduation. Statistically, it's unlikely. I know this. I could shut up, kiss her, and let the moment pass. But I just can't stop myself from asking, "Can I help you study for the SAT?"

* * *

When I get home, my family is sprawled in front of the TV. Dad has two cans of beer balanced on his stomach, Mom's face is painted green with a thick facial mask, and Lindsey is absorbed in a graphic novel.

"Was it fun?" Mom has trouble speaking because she doesn't want to wrinkle her mask.

"You lucked out," Dad says. "Your mom's lasagna was awful. I took one for the team and ate it all, so you won't have to suffer through leftovers tomorrow."

My parents are nowhere as glamorous as Flora's. They don't work in sleek high-rise offices or stay in perfect shape. They probably don't know how to pronounce *Gruyère* or *Châteauneuf-du-Pape* either. But they know which classes I'm taking each semester, and they notice if Lindsey isn't home when she's supposed to be.

I tell them about dinner, how much I enjoyed everything, and how Flora's family is genuinely interesting. "But I like you guys better," I add on an impulse.

Three pairs of eyes turn to me like I have food poisoning.

"I can't afford to get you a new car," Dad says, "if that's what you're getting at."

I laugh. "Thanks, Dad. I already have everything I need."

CHAPTER THIRTY-THREE

Flora

Ever since that family dinner, Sean's been determined to pull me out of the abyss of self-deprecation. Lately he's more tutor than boyfriend, and *SAT* has replaced *sex* as the three-letter word dominating our dating agenda.

"This is how you do it." He picks up a pen, going over the mock test I did earlier. The few questions I got right are drowning in a crimson sea of wrong answers. He scrawls on a piece of paper, demonstrating how to solve the problems.

I never noticed before how he bites his lower lip when he calculates, and I don't understand how I could've missed it. It's so distractingly provocative.

He puts down his pen. "You're not listening."

"Sorry. It's not entirely my fault. Tutors aren't supposed to be this hot."

I thought he'd have the decency to smile, but no, he scowls. "This is important. You won't have time to retake the test. College application deadlines are around the corner."

Everything he says is true, but he could say it in a nicer way. Nowadays he's all about responsibilities and priorities, and I can't even recall the last time he touched me properly. He used to be a mechanic who checked every part of the plane, but now he's a pilot who jumps in the seat, sticks the key in, and takes off.

Obviously, if I was to contemplate this rationally, he's doing it all for *my* sake. He takes time out of his hectic schedule to help *me* prepare. But sometimes it feels like I'm not his girlfriend anymore but another project for him to fix. In the heat of the moment, when frustration over homework collides with the pressure of college applications, the gnawing fear that his infatuation is wearing off, and my parents' not-so-subtle pride over Jeremy, it all boils over. And another fight spins from there.

"I don't need to go to college." At this point, I'll grasp at anything. "Plenty of people do fine without it. The idea that you need a diploma to succeed is a myth."

"You don't have to go, I agree, but I'm not spending thirty minutes debating it. Don't try to convince *me*. Convince yourself. Are you sure you don't want to go, or are you just afraid to try?"

Is the brutal honesty necessary? Sometimes I only want to vent for a minute before getting back to work, but he makes it so easy to get mad at him.

"SAT scores aren't the only thing colleges look at." I put my hands on my hips, almost as if I'm accusing him. "Getting a perfect score doesn't guarantee anything."

"True, but that's not a reason to deliberately tank it." My argument is so flimsy he can dismantle it from any angle. "Besides, you still have time to improve."

The unspoken truth is he can't fix my GPA, and it's too late to sign up for volunteer work now. I always get defensive, and he turns sarcastic. The fights creep into our lives like the ugly mold on the classroom walls, but eventually Sean's softer side kicks in. It's amazing how I can clearly sense that moment. He understands I'm frustrated and upset, and his whole demeanor shifts, and he leans in to kiss my hair.

"Let's not fight, baby. You know we want the same thing."

I sigh. "Yeah. We want sex."

He laughs. "Sure, but that comes later." Pulling the test in front of me, he taps the paper with the confidence of someone who aced the math section. (He got a perfect score. *Shocker.*) "Come on, this is one of the few things in life that I know a little better than you do. Please let me help you." His face is all earnest, like he's asking for a favor.

I force a smile and nod.

"Are you serious about becoming a fashion editor?"

"Yeah."

"Do you know how?"

"Have amazing fashion sense?"

"Besides that. I did some research." The image of Sean googling fashion makes me swoon. He continues to explain everything I already know. "Intern at a magazine during college, or for a brand. Connections matter as much as talent. A journalism or a communications degree could help, but experience counts more. Your blog and Instagram already give you a head start, but you should pitch articles to fashion sites and build a portfolio. You might want to apply to one of the schools in New York—NYU, Pratt, Parsons, FIT, or Columbia."

Such blind faith. "Hello, Columbia? I don't think so."

"It's not impossible. Have you picked out the photos you want to send in yet?"

I smack his arm, and he laughs, grabbing my hand and holding it in his. "Hate to break it to you, but going to runway shows should help, too, especially if you blog about them after. If you ever need to see Lanvin's new collection again, you can drag me with you."

My heart expands. "You're supersweet, you know that? You care about my future."

"No, it's not about you. I love those tiny snacks they serve at the runway shows."

I chuckle, and he smiles. I wait for him to say more nice things, but his expression turns serious again. "You really need to concentrate now, okay?" He places a hand on each side of my face and directs me to the test. "You have eighty minutes to complete the math section."

I groan as he sets the alarm and goes right back to tutor mode.

He pats my head and leans in to whisper, "If you score over seven hundred, you can have sex with me."

That's the weirdest sexual fantasy I've ever heard. "Wow. I knew money could buy sex, but I wasn't aware SAT points could too."

His lips curl up. "Yeah, what kind of guy do you take me for? I don't sleep with just anyone."

I laugh and dive into my mock test. Having a hot tutor has its perks too.

*　*　*

One beautiful weekend afternoon, I grab lunch with my friends at a café near school. The place is always packed thanks to its aesthetic (if overpriced) smoothies and its willingness to let people loiter for hours without buying much.

It's been a few days since I got my SAT scores back, and I'm still riding the high of my academic makeover—like I emerged from a YA montage of flashcards, late-night cram sessions, number two pencils, and studying straight through Thanksgiving—while Sean practically went into cardiac arrest when he saw my score (pretty sure he was more stressed about it than I was). My math section shot up by well over a hundred points, and the reading section got a decent boost too.

It was the early-December test, the last chance of the year before college applications were due, and the relief was overwhelming. My parents gave me a nod and a quick "good job." In my family, "biggest improvement" isn't quite as impressive as "top performance." Still, I'll take it.

Madison and Raymond show up a little later, fresh from their meeting with the prom committee. I hang out with them because I miss them and refuse to be the kind of girl who forgets her friends once in a relationship—not because Sean is away at a basketball game.

"Is Sean busy today?" Josie stirs her metal straw in her iced tea.

"Let's just be happy Flora deigns to eat with us." Madison scans the menu before ordering an Impossible Burger.

Raymond pretends to shield his eyes. "You eat? You almost resemble a human today."

"Does that bother you?" Madison snaps.

"No, I approve," Raymond says. "No one likes a girl who survives solely on iced coffee and air."

"Guys are the biggest hypocrites." Madison stabs her fork into her food with righteous fury. "They say they like a girl who eats a hot dog and wears no makeup, but that only applies if she still looks flawless."

Raymond shakes his head. "Beauty is subjective. But speaking of which, can we all agree Ms. Hawthorne's new hairstyle is . . . a choice?"

Our school nurse recently got a wild perm, and somehow, it ended up lopsided. "It's like half the seeds got blown off a dandelion," Madison says, and Josie snickers into her drink.

"Mads." I clear my throat. "Are we being mean by secretly making fun of people?"

"Secretly?" She raises an eyebrow. "If she asked my opinion, I'd say the exact same thing."

"I don't make fun of people," Josie says. "I make observations. Can't promise they're always positive. And what's with this sudden moral awakening? You literally just blogged about the ridiculous outfits at the Venice Carnival ball."

"That's fashion critique, completely different. And Sean says . . ." I trail off when Raymond pretends to gag. "Anyway, it's not nice to laugh at people, even if they never hear it."

Carmen smiles. It's not easy finding someone who shares her opinion, but Saint Sean never disappoints. "Exactly! I've said it a million times—if you don't want to be talked about, don't do it to others."

But does keeping mean thoughts to yourself make you a better person? Or a fake one? Ms. Hawthorne totally resembles a ruined dandelion.

"I get nervous when people *don't* talk about me," Madison says.

Raymond slurps his drink, making obnoxious noises with the straw and looking at me funny. "You're changing, but you were pretty cool the way you were before."

"Come on, I'm still me. I'm Flora 2.0, with some bugs fixed and a few new features added."

Josie shrugs. "Oh, hey, by the way, congrats on the SAT. I heard you crushed it this time."

"Thanks. I worked my butt off. Now I feel like I might actually have a shot at NYU."

"I'm going to NYU too," Raymond announces, like his acceptance letter is already framed. "Cinema studies at Tisch. We can have movie nights all the time."

That doesn't sound terrible, but I'd rather sit in my dorm and

FaceTime Sean, especially if the unthinkable happens and he gets into one of his backup schools. They're all in California. I loathe the prospect of a long-distance relationship. I might die.

Sean says he doesn't need to wake up next to me to remember he's in love, but to be safe, I've checked out every school in Massachusetts. What if we got an apartment together? I may never need movie nights with Ray again. (Even though Sean either falls asleep halfway through or only watches stuff in which things explode every ten minutes.)

"Wanna go to the mall later?" Madison asks.

I do, actually. I'm in dire need of some new purchases, but I check my watch. Sean's game will be over soon. He'll call as soon as he's free, and I'll fly into his arms. I'm not placing him before her; it's only because he's busier and I want to be available whenever he has time.

Makes total sense, right?

* * *

But Sean sure doesn't act grateful for being chosen. When he agrees to go shopping with me, he says *okay* like he's authorizing a missile strike. His idea of the perfect date is one that includes me but doesn't involve dressing up or even leaving the apartment. One that is *comfortable*.

Translation: stay home, study, and have sex (optional).

Most of the time I go along with whatever he suggests doing (which, to reiterate, is nothing) to be supportive. But today I feel like boosting the economy.

"Do you really need five clones of that dress?" he asks, taking the bags from my hands as we walk through the mall.

Madison would get it. She'd understand why the cut matters, why one drapes better than the other, and why salmon pink and coral are worlds apart. She'd hype me up and we'd probably grab bubble tea after. Instead, I'm here with Sean, who calls it *five clones of the same dress.*

"Do you really need to lecture me on how I spend my own money?"

He clears his throat. "Your parents' money."

I pretend not to hear him. Lately, I find myself fighting with him over the most irrelevant things, caught in this endless loop where his opinion always wins. It's part of being the perfect girlfriend, even when I resent it.

Life has become a grinding wheel of "doing the right thing."

But today the plan is to blow off some steam. I did so well on my SAT, a break is duly deserved.

"Hey," I say. "There's a party tonight. Want to go?"

He squints at me, and as usual it's mind-numbingly cute. "Is this a trick question, or do I really get to decide?"

"We'll go only if you want to go."

"Okay, then, no." *Surprise, surprise.* "Why would I go to a party when I can hang out with you? Besides, I want to finish my essay tonight. You should do the same."

There. The real reason.

I sigh. "Sure."

On the way home, I drive the only way a Mercedes owner should, which is cutting in front of slower cars and rushing forward the second the light changes. If a driver hesitates too long at a turn, I'm not too hesitant to blast my horn.

"Why did you do that?" Sean asks. I hear his frown. "We're not in a hurry."

"I don't like it when other cars stall me. What has the world come to? Imagine owning a Mercedes and still having to breathe in the exhaust fumes of a Honda."

Kidding, obviously. I have nothing against Hondas (Sean drives a Civic himself), but as soon as the words leave my mouth, I remember how he feels about making (harmless) fun of people.

"How inconsiderate of the government. They should build an expressway specifically for Mercedes. No cheap cars allowed."

My lips tighten, a clear sign that his sarcasm isn't appreciated, but that doesn't stop him from excessive side-seat driving. "You didn't signal when you switched lanes."

"I forgot," I lie.

Didn't he used to find my recklessness cute? He'd smile when I gunned it and braked at the last second. But today, he's treating me like a liability. He doesn't shut up until I pull over.

"Why don't *you* drive, my sweet darling angel?" I ask, getting out. "Since you're obviously the superior driver."

"Can't object to that. I *am* a better driver than you are."

"You're not just a better driver"—my temper flares out of nowhere—"you're a better *person* altogether. Sometimes I want to do what makes me happy, and it isn't necessarily the right thing, and you—look, I don't need another parent."

He nods. "Right. Another parent? You barely have one."

I blink, and he reaches for my arm.

"I'm sorry, that came out wrong. I didn't mean—"

"You don't get to insult my parents. They're nice to you! Don't you *dare* imply they aren't doing their job."

"I'm not." He rubs the back of his neck. "I'm sorry. I swear, I like your parents. I think they should spend more time with you, that's all. You miss them, right?"

"Yeah, but now I have you. That's enough."

But is it?

I blow a strand of hair off my face. "Sometimes I feel like we're eighty, living in a retirement home. I miss when we were carefree and actually had fun."

"I can't be just about fun. There's a lot at stake, and I have to be responsible for both of us." He exhales, pressing his fingers to his temples. "If you want to go to a party, we'll go, but don't pretend you're fine with it and then pick a fight later."

Deep down, it's not even about the party. Maybe this is a phase, a rough patch after the honeymoon period. I test him now, push his limits, but I'll settle back into normal. We'll be solid. Permanent.

Even something as dull as water has three states. Surely we're more complex than that?

We stand there, neither of us moving, and something snaps in me. "You said you love the way I am. Well, *this* is me." I gesture to myself, my hands shaking as well as my voice. "I love hanging out with my guy friends, partying at night, spending money, and driving fast. I hate studying. I make fun of people, but I don't mean any harm. Why are you trying to change me?"

"I'm not—"

"Have I ever complained about anything *you* do? No. I love you for you. I even went to the science museum with you. I learned all those facts so we could speak the same language. But you"—my voice cracks—"you can't stop finding things wrong with me."

He sighs, then he's silent as his eyes darken, no doubt thinking up something to render me speechless. "I love the way you are, too, but—"

"You don't love me for who I am. You love me for who you can turn me into."

"That's ridiculous. I'm not changing you for *my* benefit. I ask you to drive slower because I need you to be safe. I push you about studying so you won't regret not living up to your full potential. And partying late? Getting drunk with other guys? You act like I'm trying to control you, but I'm just worried about you. Lastly, when you criticize people less fortunate than you, even if you don't mean anything by it, you have to realize not everyone's had the advantages you've had."

I take several deep breaths. "That's profound," I say, blown away. Why is Sean so good at persuasion? Why is he always right?

"That's from *The Great Gatsby*. First page." He tugs on my arm, eyes soft. "Hey . . . what's wrong with changing? Isn't love about adapting for each other?"

He's right.

"Of course." I nod, but a tiny voice nags at me from the back of my mind.

Why am I the only one adapting?

As usual, I don't say it out loud, because I love Sean more than chai lattes, Hermès, and Aman Resorts combined. He's already perfect, and if anyone has to change, it's me. *Duh.*

Sean makes me better.

So after the short argument on the side of the road, he gets behind the wheel, pleased to get his hands on my car. I let him drive us back to his place, where we have leftover mac and cheese his mom made (*shhh—it doesn't have any flavor*).

He's a wonderful guy and we love each other. How can that not be enough?

*   *   *

When I leave that night, everything is good again. I say good night to Sean with affection.

He's a simple guy who loves comfort food, playing basketball with his buddies, studying for his dream school, and me. I'm the luckiest girl on the continent.

"Text me when you get home?" He plants a kiss on my lips.

"Sure."

Striding into the night, I fight the urge to slam my foot on the gas. My phone lights up with a dozen texts and party invites. The breeze is welcoming, charged with possibility. It whispers of bizarre adventures, unfathomable wonders, and fascinating strangers, which I'll now steer away from. I'll drive straight home, otherwise Sean will worry.

And yet, as I cruise through the dark, I feel lost.

CHAPTER THIRTY-FOUR

Sean

My life with Flora continues, each day marked by her presence. Small moments take on greater significance, but despite our increasing proximity, our trajectories remain misaligned. From college decisions to trivial matters like where to eat or how often to text, everything is a negotiation.

One weekend, I agree to try molecular gastronomy at an upscale restaurant. I did my due diligence—checked the menu, planned for the cheapest entrée, and counted on tap water. I no longer tutor for free. Now every one of my sessions is for cold, hard cash. Even college admissions should recognize that I can't survive on altruism alone.

The server informs us there's no à la carte tonight, only "the experience," a multicourse set meal with dessert. Tap water is also off-limits as it "disrupts the culinary concept." The alternative is imported Italian mineral water.

The numbers are impossible to ignore. We could get a basket of fried chicken for a tenth of the price.

"You know I got this, right?" Flora says. "Think of it as tutoring payment."

"I can pay for my own food." *Can I, though?* I pick at my cuticles as I do another calculation, factoring in tips and the water surcharge.

"Sean, can you not stress me out?" She sighs as if she's the one facing financial ruin.

I relent, even though my stomach twists. The food arrives, each dish more unrecognizable than the last. Crab is restructured into neon turmeric custard, chicken is minced and molded into a marshmallow, and green basil foam lingers suspiciously at the edge of the plate.

This is certainly . . . an experience.

Flora catches my expression. "You never seem open to anything different."

"I'm willing to try, but that doesn't mean I have to love everything."

Her grip tightens on her fork as she pushes at a piece of saffron jelly. "It's safer to keep ordering the same thing, of course. No risk, no disappointment."

That's not true. The same thing is exactly what disappoints her.

"Why can't you go along with me for *once* and enjoy?" she asks.

I take a sip of my overpriced water, washing down the last of the chickmellow. "I can't even make a comment?"

"When do you ever gasp in amazement when I introduce you to something new? This is what I *love*, but you'll never see the magic in it the way I do."

She's been getting mad at me so much lately. The usual quick fixes don't work, and I'm running out of cute lines. "Hey, I'm sorry. Can you give me a smile? Rough day. Traumatized on the court, and now my girlfriend hates me."

"You must be doing something wrong if she hates you."

"She thinks I'm predictable." I hesitate. "But she used to like me that way."

The light shifts in her hazel eyes before she glances down. "I'm sorry. I still do. It's just that we haven't eaten out in a while, and I wanted everything to be perfect."

"It is. Being with you is perfect."

Her eyes soften, and she reaches across the table to touch my face. "Tell me what happened."

"We lost because of me. Some days I'm just . . . off, and I don't know why. Basketball feels completely out of my control." *And so does my relationship.*

"No one can control everything in their life."

"Ever since my ACL tear, I haven't been as good as before. Sometimes, midrun, I get this fear my knee will give out. I didn't get reconstructive surgery because I didn't want to miss senior year."

"You want to play with Jake and Dylan."

"Yeah. I could probably play in college, but it won't be the same."

I barely see them outside of practice anymore, and when I do, Coach is consistently yelling at me in the background.

"Hey, you're still the best shooter on the team," she says, which is generous of her.

The check arrives, and I grab it out of reflex. It's worse than I expected. Apparently, Flora's citrus and lychee mocktails are what's keeping this restaurant in business.

"Don't be silly." She takes the check from me and slides in her Amex without a word. My stomach twists again, a reminder that I'll always hesitate when the bill comes.

After dinner, we step into the alley behind the restaurant, and Flora kisses me. Her lips are fervent, and I kiss her back just as intensely to calm my nerves. She tells me she loves me, over and over, like she needs to hear it out loud.

As if she needs to convince herself.

When we pull apart, she asks, "What are we doing tonight? Should we go back to your place?"

It's been a long week, and the thought of anything but sleep makes my head throb. But I know better.

"Actually, let's go to a party."

Flora laughs.

"I'm serious. Do you know any good ones?"

"You don't have to do this."

I hold my ground. We go back and forth, and finally she says, "All right. Ray has a small group together. We can go there."

Since the breakup, I haven't spoken more than five words at a time to Raymond. He probably doesn't like me, since I'm the *possessive boyfriend* who doesn't get his and Flora's bond. And I don't like him, either, or the fact that she needs this emotionally supportive, generational wealth–funded best friend. I'd rather drink a foie gras shot again than step into his house, but Flora is already chuckling.

She sounds lighter, bouncier, like an intensified version of her. By the time we arrive at Raymond's house, she's laughing a lot.

That laugh is the highlight of the night for me. I'll never get tired of it, especially since it comes a lot less these days. As Flora works the room, I leave her to it and retreat to a corner.

She absorbs the atmosphere like a sponge, her energy bar recharging with every conversation. It's both impressive and mildly concerning how much happier she looks talking to other guys. She moves through the room like a caged animal finally let loose, and something tightens in my chest.

It's not jealousy—jealousy I can handle. It's the dark fear that I'll never be enough. She's in her element here, shining brighter than the chandelier overhead. We got together the first time because of a party, and the second time after planning one. Turns out, I fell for a party girl. And she's dragged herself away from her natural habitat for me.

When Flora returns, a tall glass of punch is in her hand. She sits down beside me. "Why aren't you drinking?"

"We can't both get drunk. Someone has to drive."

A faint frown crosses her face. "Are you having a good time?"

"The best time," I say, injecting as much enthusiasm as I can manage.

"You're a terrible liar."

"Don't worry about me. I don't mind being here at all."

She sets her drink down. "But you're sitting here like a chaperone. I can't relax knowing you're tired and miserable. You're probably keeping track of how much I've had too."

Three glasses down, working on the fourth. "Go have fun, Flora."

She shakes her head and lifts her drink again, taking slow, deliberate sips like she's saying goodbye to it. Then, with a quiet clank, she sets it down. "Let's just go."

Tugging on my hand, she pulls me outside with a force in her stride. We pass Raymond on the way out.

"Heading out already?" he asks, reeking of pot.

"Yeah." Flora brushes her hair behind her ear. "Just a long day."

Ray's gaze flicks to me. "You guys good?"

I nod. "Thanks for having us."

"Of course. You know you're always welcome."

They share a quick fist bump, and we're off.

The moment we step into the cool night air, I can breathe. The chill is quiet and soothing, like slipping under a cool blanket.

There's a small garden in the backyard. Flora sits on one swing, and I take the other. The paint on the wooden beams is chipped, and the frame creaks under my weight. She traces idle patterns in the grass with the toe of her shoe.

"I feel guilty for forcing you to come here," she says. "You tolerate the things I like and you're the sweetest, but I wish you genuinely shared my interests."

I take her hand. "I can try harder. Give me time."

"No, it's fine." She squeezes my hand tighter. Her eyes are darker than usual, like rare pieces of meteorite. "You're a simple, sensible guy, and I love that about you. I can do your thing."

When Flora tries to be the understanding one, I get twice as scared of losing her. Pointing out the obvious isn't easy. "Button, you're not happy doing my thing."

We're both trying to please each other, like pushing a plate back and forth, insisting the other take the last bite. Sharing food is easy. Finding common ground is a lot harder.

I like order. She thrives on chaos. I think things through. She leaps first, asks questions later. I rely on routines to keep my sanity, while she craves the rush of the unpredictable to feel alive.

We're not just different. We're complete opposites.

She rocks on the swing, watching people stagger in and out of the house. "We have nothing in common."

"We both like ice cream." I try to lighten the mood.

"Well, if that counts . . ." She tilts her head, letting a strand of dark hair fall. "We both hate it when it melts too fast and drips through the bottom of the cone." She stills. Swallows. "Have you ever wondered if it'd be easier to date someone more compatible?"

Her words crush the wind out of me. I love her too much to even consider it.

"It would be easier," I say, gazing at the face I wish to look at forever. "But I don't want easy. I want you."

Her eyes shine, and for a second I think she's going to cry. My throat tightens.

Please don't bail. Not now. Not when I'm all in.

She stands up, lifts my face, and kisses me. "I want you too. I want it to always be you."

A bug chirps. That moment on the swing feels like staring into eternity. I could type my hobbies into a dating app, let an algorithm find me a perfect match. Flora could walk back inside and pick anyone she desired. But it wouldn't be the same. Because despite everything, we put each other first. We make each other laugh. We get each other.

As unimpressive as that sounds, it's everything.

No one makes me feel the way she does.

She glows under the night sky, eyes twinkling, wind in her hair, and, if given the choice, I'd choose her all over again.

We stay outside for a long time, unable to decide if we want to go back in, and does it even matter?

Everything I feel that night, I know Flora does too.

That's more than enough.

CHAPTER THIRTY-FIVE

Flora

Lately, my brain's falling apart, but not in a floaty, sighing-at-the-rain, pressing-your-forehead-to-the-window kind of way you see in romantic period dramas. Everything sets me off, especially Sean. My aspiration is to be a rare blue parrot, soaring through the skies of Rio, and I get angry at him for being a house cat, content to stay at home and eat the same kibble every day. It's unfair to blame him for not flapping his wings.

Therefore, I tell myself, *Don't ask what your boyfriend can do for you, ask what you can do for him.* This is my new relationship motto, and here are a few things I (willingly) do for him:

1. I eat at his house and marvel over his dad's cooking. Sean thinks he's doing me a favor by bringing me home, and sure, his family is awesome, but what starts out as a warm gesture soon turns into a performance. They expect me to be a one-woman comedy special. Meanwhile, I'm itching to check my texts without looking rude.

2. Fine dining? Not anymore. The second Sean sees the price, he gets this panic-stricken twitch around his temple, then he stares, unimpressed, at the tiny portions, while I sit there, deeply offended on behalf of the sous-chef sweating in the back. Sean's palate is as adventurous as a kids' menu— chicken tenders, club sandwiches, buttered noodles. I tone

it down and take him to a perfectly affordable Indian restaurant, and he drowns the spice level in three gallons of water.

3. We've retired from parties. Couples don't need them. Parties are an excuse for drunk people to hook up anyway, and since I've "graduated" from Solo-cup life, what's the point?

4. I've started working on Sean's Christmas gift. At first I aimed for a Brunello Cucinelli wallet since it's classy with understated luxury, but he has no money to put in there. So I ended up—don't laugh—knitting a scarf.

Sean appreciates my effort, even though he constantly worries if I'm happy. I assure him that I am, because after all, what's there to complain about? We have everything a solid relationship offers: stability, trust, affection, and understanding, even though it lacks a few other things, such as possibilities, surprises, unlimited choices, and that sense of open-ended freedom.

Sean reminds me of stepping onto the balcony on a crisp winter morning, the air sharp against my skin, my breath visible in the stillness, then coming back inside, warmth settling over me, like it was always waiting.

Whenever he smiles at me, I still think he's the greatest guy ever and I'm beyond lucky to have him. That's when I remind myself, *forget choices.*

I've already chosen the best.

* * *

Two weeks before winter break, it's right before lunch, and Sean's in the hallway, heading for the cafeteria. When I call to him, he stops and waits. Every girl in the vicinity envies me. He's oblivious, but their stares heat my skin, a scorching spotlight tracking our every step.

Sean smiles at me, and *only* me. Ligands bind to specific receptors, and I'm the only person who melts the aloof front he puts up. A few steps ahead, Wayne, the janitor, exits the storage room. The door doesn't close all the way, scratching to a halt against the floor.

A sudden spark of inspiration hits. Even old married couples find ways to keep things exciting, and why shouldn't we? We'll make it work.

All we need is some spontaneity!

Before Sean can protest, I yank him into the storage room. I'm not even horny, but the thrill of doing something *bad* with him is exhilarating.

It's pitch-dark inside, the air thick with bleach and a hint of mold. It doesn't matter. I push him against the door, his body hot and solid against mine, familiar yet foreign at the same time. Muffled voices filter in from the hallway. Out there, it's bright, open, public. In here, it's dark, hidden, electric.

A long-lost rush of excitement floods my veins. My nerve endings crackle.

I find Sean's lips and kiss him hard.

"What are you doing?" His breath is warm on my face, and as usual he smells of soap and fabric softener.

"Isn't this fun?"

It takes him a moment to recover, but he kisses me back. My hand moves over his chest, and beneath my fingers, his heart pounds. He makes a small sound between a sigh and a groan, and at that, all my reserves fly out the storage closet.

He's sexier than a crime. My hand slides past his flat stomach, thrilled with what I find. "You like this."

He removes my hand. "Yeah, but that's enough. Let's go before anyone finds us."

"Come *on*." I kiss him again, fingers trailing along his neck to his collar. I fumble with the first button on his shirt.

"No."

I start on the second button, wanting to kiss his collarbone, but Sean pulls away.

"No," he says more firmly this time, and pushes me off him. In the dim light slipping under the door, he straightens his shirt, putting space between us.

The spell shatters, and humiliation creeps in fast. "What's wrong with you?" My voice comes out shriller than I intend.

"What's wrong with *you*? We don't have to sneak around like this."

"We're not doing anything wrong."

He exhales, and the faint light is enough to catch the hint of exasperation on his face. His tone remains neutral, but there's an air of icy annoyance. "I'm opening the door now, okay?"

He turns the knob. Light washes over me like a bucket of ice water. He takes my wrist and pulls me outside. "Let's go to lunch."

"No." I plant my feet, staring at him. I should drop this. I don't even know what I want from him. But I can't move.

Sean sighs. "I don't want to get caught. It's bad for your image."

"How's that bad for my *image*?"

"Well, you're a girl, and people are judgmental toward girls. They—"

"I was kissing my *boyfriend*." My voice spikes.

"But you know how people are. Give them the slightest material and they'll run with it. Especially when it comes to you." He stops, swallows, then reaches for my arm. "Come on, I'm hungry. Let's go."

I shake him off. "What does that mean? What do people say about me?"

"Nothing. I meant you're the center of attention, that's all."

"Tell me."

He shrugs. "Nothing."

"You promised you'd tell me everything!"

He hesitates, then finally says, "Just that . . . you dated around. There are implications. And lots of graffiti in the boys' locker room." His voice is low, but it explodes on my eardrums.

A sharp heat shoots up my nose, like vinegar. Sean's name is written in the girls' locker room, too, but his comes with hearts. I have a pretty good idea which body part is scrawled next to mine.

"Boys are filthy," Sean says. "They fantasize about you and attack you. It's not your fault."

"I may have gone out with some people, but nothing happened!"

"I know, baby. I know. I don't believe any of it."

"What have you heard? Give me *one* example."

He looks everywhere but at me. I wait. "Well, for example . . ." He lets out a reluctant sigh. "When you dated Liam Turner, he used to brag about how you let him . . . do things."

"I didn't even let him touch my car!" My blood boils, at Liam, at Sean, at everyone. "You know I went out with Liam to spite you. I bet you never defended me!"

"How was I supposed to defend you? You broke up with me. It was bad enough being on the same team with him. I had to listen to him bluff about how you said he was 'better.'"

The tears come fast. If anyone so much as catcalled at Sydney, Dylan would give them a ruptured spleen at the bare minimum, but Sean didn't do anything. He only *listened*. Didn't he tell me how he tends to avoid confrontation at all costs?

But he did specifically ask me not to go out with Liam, and I did it anyway. I remember flaunting my relationships in Sean's face, so smug about how easily I made friends, how confident I was with boys.

Turns out they don't necessarily *like* me.

I have a reputation. And I have no one else to blame but myself.

"I didn't let them . . ." My voice barely rises above a whisper. "I never did any of the things that we . . . that we . . ."

"I know. I don't care about that."

But he does care. If he didn't, he wouldn't have hesitated to date me in the first place. He wouldn't have assumed I cheated. He wouldn't be so wary about my friendships with other guys or so tense about people twisting our kiss in the storage closet into something worse.

"That's one more flaw I bring to the table. One more thing you have to fix."

He blinks. "What?"

The words claw their way up. "I'm sorry it humiliates you to be with me!"

His jaw clenches, and the irritation is unmistakable in his eyes. "Why are you saying this to hurt me?"

This is it. Sean hates public scenes more than anything, and nothing mortifies him like being yelled at in a crowded hallway. He won't put up with my mess anymore. This is the day he walks away. A few steps away, people are whispering and pointing at us.

A chill runs down my spine as I wait for him to break my heart. My tears are dry, but my eyelids still burn.

He takes a step closer and wraps me in a hug. "Please don't say things like that. I love you. I love you."

I tremble in his arms. He says it again, his voice as firm as his embrace, and I nod. "Okay," I whisper. "I'm fine now."

"You sure?"

I force out a smile. "Yup. Let's go to lunch."

"Do you need to fix your makeup?"

He's thoughtful, as expected.

While he waits outside, I step into the restroom to reapply my eyeliner. A wide-eyed girl in the mirror stares back at me, mascara smudged, and I almost don't recognize her.

Everyone agrees Sean's a great influence on me. I'm a bottle of Flora by Gucci perfume, diluted with his virtue. The same pretty packaging, the same black bow, but the content inside isn't quite the same.

I can't decide if that's a blessing.

But there's no question that I love Sean with everything I have. I love him inside and out, from his immaculate face to his kind heart and his grounded personality. I love the sweet boy he is now and the responsible man he's becoming. I love his strength and his vulnerability, his efficiency, his practicality, and the way he always knows what to do.

The more I know him, the higher I build the pedestal I've placed him on. I look up so much, I never notice how small I've become.

When I step out, Sean smiles at me as if nothing has happened. He takes my hand as we head to the cafeteria.

"I'm sorry," I murmur. "I'm really sorry."

He squeezes my fingers, a little tighter than usual. "Nothing to be sorry about."

I glance up at him and feel dirty. I don't deserve him because he's too perfect.

CHAPTER THIRTY-SIX

Sean

It's bad. And then it gets worse.

After our fight outside the storage room, Flora and I manage a few days of peaceful silence, no raised voices. Now she's lying next to me in my room, and I push her hair back to kiss her neck. She lifts her eyes and says, "I love you so much, I'm falling apart."

Oh no.

She pulls the duvet off and stands up from the bed. "I'm not cool anymore. I'm clingy, moody, and on the verge of tears all the time. When you're not here, I mope around waiting for you to come back. You'll stop loving me eventually, and I'll die a slow, painful death."

The changes she mentions are more obvious day by day, but I stay quiet for selfish reasons. I can't lose her. "You're still the same. Overly dramatic."

She's miserable. It's a plain, sad fact. Despite my intensive watering, this jasmine flower is withering right before my eyes.

She runs her fingers over items from my desk, but her eyes don't focus. "Are you getting tired of me?"

"Not at all."

She picks up the postcard from the science museum. It reads *Once upon a time you made a girl ridiculously happy.*

"Flora, the best moments of my life have been with you. You're everything I want."

At this moment, she drops the line to break my heart. It's not unexpected, but still hurts, and I let it sink in without defense.

"It's like I'm channel surfing. Even when I'm watching one channel, I'm wondering what else is on and what I'm missing. I hate myself when I'm with you."

What stings the most is that she's not trying to hurt me. For a second, I'm too choked to answer.

"You feel like that because you haven't found what you want to watch," I say. "If you did, you'd be fixated. You wouldn't want to miss a second. That's how I feel with you."

Her eyes lock with mine. Time stands still, until she throws her arms around me, her wool sweater rubbing against my face, and everything starts moving forward again at a mind-numbing pace. "I'm sorry. I'm so sorry. I didn't mean that."

The truth is lying naked before me. She claims I'm her destination, but she prefers the journey. The trailer lured her in, but now that she's discovered the movie isn't as interesting as she anticipated, she's forcing herself to sit through the whole thing.

"Please don't break up with me," she says between sobs. "You can't break up with me because I said *one* stupid thing."

Forever is no longer the dream. She should be set free, but I'm too weak to let go. I'll wait until she's ready to leave me. "I won't break up with you."

We're a radioactive isotope destined to break apart. No matter how much energy I pour into keeping us together, the decay is inevitable.

"Let go on a trip together," she says, voice still unsteady. "During Christmas. Three days together."

"Anything you want," I say.

* * *

Flora wants to go to Paris. *Three days in Paris? Seriously, who does that?* I suggest a road trip, hitting up delis, eating gas station nachos, and cranking the music. She says motel bed linens will give her a rash and that she can't stay anywhere below four stars.

In the end, we settle on New York City. She might end up there for the next four years anyway.

She flops onto her bed. "You'll come see me every weekend, right?"

"Of course."

I'm going to lose that privilege, dear Flora.

For me, this trip might be the last good memory we'll have together. Every second is a countdown.

She tosses me a list of luxury hotels to give the illusion of choice. Out of these, only the Four Seasons doesn't have a minimum age requirement to check in, so that's her decision made.

"I can't afford it." *Not even close.*

"I have a big allowance. I mean, *huge*. Rolling around in high-thread-count sheets won't scald your skin, Sean."

"I don't feel comfortable spending your money."

"Strictly speaking, it's my parents' money."

"Wow, now I feel so much better."

She folds her arms. "Why's it fine for me to eat at your place all the time, but such a big deal for you to accept favors from my family?"

"That's different. My dad's cooking anyway, with or without you. You don't eat much."

"Well, I'm staying at a five-star hotel anyway, with or without you. You don't take up much space."

"You make it sound so simple."

"I'll cover the hotel, and we can figure out the rest. Come on, let me spoil you." She strokes my face, chuckling. "We'll be together forever anyway."

My stomach clenches. While I'm waiting for her to break up with me, there's some secret bad news she isn't aware of yet.

"Hey, I almost forgot," she says. "I have your Christmas present ready."

I pick up my backpack from the floor. "I brought yours too."

"Can't wait!" She grabs the gift Lindsey helped me wrap, tearing open the wrapper. Her hands freeze. It's a puzzle, the cover showing a black-and-white photo of an old couple standing on rainy pavement, facing away from the camera. In the corner, there's a corner of the Eiffel Tower. It's an antique shot from the midcentury.

Flora sniffles, and her voice catches. "Thanks. You remember I told you how Jeremy didn't let me join in his puzzle time. We'll go to Paris together someday." She pulls me close, wrapping her arms around me. I let myself briefly entertain the slim possibility of that happening.

When we break apart, Flora says, "Ready for yours?"

Her smile is bright as she pulls out a Louis Vuitton paper bag from her closet. I offended her when I had to return the duffel bag she gave me last Christmas, but I hide my disappointment this time. "Wow," I say, keeping my tone light. "Louis Vuitton keeps coming back to haunt me."

My fingers meet something soft. A scarf—thick, knitted wool, blue with a touch of gray. It's full of holes.

"I knit it myself." Flora swallows. "I restarted three times, but I finally accepted this is the best I can do. As my dad would say, don't let perfect be the enemy of good. It's supposed to be the color of your eyes. But they're nicer, of course."

I run my fingers through one of the holes, unable to utter a word.

"The holes were unintentional." She fidgets, then snatches the scarf from me. "Gosh, what was I thinking? You're too cute to be caught dead wearing this. It's against every fashion rule in the universe. I'll buy you something else."

The lump in my throat slides down and my voice comes out scratchy. "I love it."

This is exactly what I want. I lean in to hug her, trying to keep my emotions in check as I speak into her hair. "Thank you. Seriously. This is the best present I've ever gotten."

"You like it more than Louis Vuitton?" She laughs. "Honestly, the best part of the gift is probably the paper bag."

I bury my face in her neck, holding her as tightly as possible without hurting her. "I mean it. Thank you. I'm going to wear it every day in New York."

"Oh no, you're not. Don't embarrass me like that at the Four Seasons."

* * *

I lie to my parents, telling them a bunch of us are going on a trip together. They buy it, for some reason, but Lindsey catches on immediately. She even offers to lend me the prize money she won in an essay contest. I take her up on it—every bit of help counts.

Our vacation is the wealthy version of New York City, and even though Flora's been here eight billion times like she claims, she's still enchanted—by the city itself, the holiday decorations, the high-end department stores and their elaborate window displays, the aroma of roasted chestnuts from street vendors, the constant hum of the streets, *the fineries in life*. She's *happy*, and I remind myself to gasp in amazement every now and then, even if she's just trying on shoes.

But to be fair, it's not all about money. We go to MoMA and make out on the deserted stairs. We take a walk in Central Park, breathing in the crisp winter air, and end up in a small-scale snow fight. We have incredible coffee in Williamsburg. At night we sit by the window, watching the city unfold below us, and she looks at me with such quiet love, saying we should do this every year. We take a bath together, the steam clouding the windows as she kisses me everywhere.

How can this end? I wonder in a daze as Flora leans in to wipe cream from the corner of my mouth. We're having cupcakes in a park, and she's sweeter than the red velvet cake. How can something I treasure so much slip through my fingers like this?

Flora and me, we're so good together on vacation. It's easy when we're planning parties, flying paper airplanes, on that over-night date at her lake house, when the world feels like it's all ours. It's easy when we're spending Christmas in this fabulous city. But then reality plods in, and our love loses its invincibility in the harsh light of mundaneness.

We'll go back home eventually. And that's when we'll be torn apart.

She brought her camera with her, and I take pictures without thinking—clouds, piles of snow on the curb, the cracked bricks of a nearby building, the reflections in windows, fire escapes casting shadows on the streets. Each minute is carved into my memory. But mostly, I take pictures of her laughing.

It's the best view in the city.

When our vacation ends and we part ways—Flora to St. Barts, me to Tampa, Florida—to catch the next segment of our vacation, I kiss her like it's the last time.

"Why do you look like you're about to cry?" Her eyes twinkle as she tugs her luggage behind her, her coat unbuttoned and flapping. "The Four Seasons is *sensational*, right? You'll never be able to enjoy anything else again."

"Yes, I'll never be able to enjoy anything else again," I repeat, looking at her. This is my perfect ending with her in New York.

CHAPTER THIRTY-SEVEN

Flora

It's logical to assume I, Flora Morgan, would *not* fare well in a long-distance relationship.

Every minute in NYC was sugarcoated with Sean beside me. Whenever I glanced sideways, he was there, tall, handsome, and very much mine.

It turned sour the second our plane landed in St. Bart's. Over the next few days, while my family unwinds at our luxury resort, I sit by the pool all day, missing Sean too much to allow space for anything else.

My parents are usually off somewhere, chatting and coaching each other on work stuff (it's both adorable and unsettling how much they love it), while Jeremy finds a new girl to hang out with every eight seconds. At breakfast, he'll launch into some "customer experience improvement" discussion, tossing around phrases like "from a consumer's standpoint," and my parents will laugh until their coffee goes cold.

Funny how much I used to crave their presence, but now that they're here, I don't feel any more involved. So I channel my energy into accusing Sean of not texting me enough. I'm fully aware of how unreasonable I am, but I can't stop; it's like when a character walks into a dark garage in a slasher movie.

"You can't even squeeze out twenty seconds to hit Send?" I ask after breakfast.

"Didn't I send you one right after I got up?" Sean sounds less patient every time this comes up. "I don't want texting to turn into an assignment."

Actually, if it *had* been an assignment, Sean would've aced it. Probably added citations too. After a few more rounds of back-and-forth, I slump at the edge of the pool. The call ends with me telling him I love him. It's genuine, but it serves more as a peace offering. He echoes it right back.

"You look bored." A deep voice interrupts my anxious, circular thinking.

I tear my gaze away from Sean's last message and my self-pity. A guy with an olive complexion and green eyes tilts his head. "Wanna go find the best tiramisu in town?"

I wrap my towel tighter around myself. "I have a wonderful boyfriend."

"What's that got to do with anything?"

He's wearing a midnight-blue polo shirt with a fox head stitched in one corner, leather penny loafers, and a Patek Philippe watch around his wrist. I wonder where he does his shopping. A familiar, dimly remembered sense of excitement bubbles up in my chest, like Aladdin's genie from the bottle. The blue genie nudges me with his elbow and wiggles his eyebrows, saying, *Look, this could be fun.*

Not to mention I love good Italian dessert.

But that was before Sean.

"I don't want to go, okay? Leave me alone."

As the guy walks off in a huff, I unlock my phone. *My dear darling boyfriend*, I type, *I miss you. I need you so much.*

Not even my texts are funny. I'm desperate, even clingy, and no wonder Sean doesn't bother to reply. He's spending time with his family as he should, maybe doing wholesome Christmas things like posing for ugly sweater photos in front of the tree (neither of which exists in my house). I toss my phone back in my tote and go back to my hotel room, alone but proud of myself. The old Flora would've flirted with the guy until he blushed, but I've outgrown that stage. I've matured.

Fifteen minutes later, I'm crying into my pillow.

It's not because of the tiramisu invitation, not directly. I live in a grand palace, surrounded by everything I've ever dreamed of. But as I stand on the balcony of my golden cage, staring down, I picture escaping to the field outside, where I can roll around in the mud and rain.

Here I am, on vacation in my string bikini with tiny gem embellishments, basking in the sun, freaking out because a cute guy talked to me.

That's when it hits me: the worst thing a girl can lose in a relationship isn't her reputation, her friends, or even her freedom.

It's herself.

To love Sean, I've lost myself.

* * *

My mom comes into my room later that day.

"How's your evening?" She stretches her legs out across my bed. Hanging out with my mom is like having a sleepover with a friend you don't see often, full of catching up, fashion tips, and zero lectures.

"It was okay. How was your dinner?"

The lines around her eyes soften as she recounts every ridiculous thing my dad said. He honestly isn't that hilarious, but his lame jokes are right up her alley. The pearl studs in her ears catch the light with a soft pink sheen when she turns her head. "And then we ordered another bottle of wine, and he—"

"Mom, how did you know Dad was the one?"

She stops midsentence, and I brace myself for profound wisdom. "I don't know. A part of me is still waiting for an Italian man on a Vespa to sweep me off my feet."

"You married at twenty-two! You must've felt *something*."

"Yeah, I started throwing up a lot, then Jeremy came."

"Mom, I'm serious."

She places her hand on my wrist. The rose-gold rings on her fingers are icy. "Sweetheart, what's wrong? I thought you had an amazing time with Sean in New York."

"We did. That's why . . . it's so hard right now."

Her smile fades. "Tell me all about it."

"It's a lot of things thrown together. I can't be sure of anything anymore. I rely on him for everything, but we don't have anything in common, and we've been fighting lately. He doesn't even like sushi!" I stop, catching my breath after sharing our top three most epic fights and the tiramisu guy incident. "But Sean's a great guy, right? He has a noble heart. It's like, there's nothing indecent or dirty about him."

"I seriously doubt 'teenage boy' and 'not dirty' belong in the same sentence."

"Mom!"

"Okay. I mean, no one's perfect."

"He's as close as anyone can get. I'm never going to do better than that."

"Sometimes the best isn't necessary the best choice." She studies my face for a long moment. "Are you happy?"

"I am . . . I think. I don't know." I let out a long breath.

"I can't tell you what to do, but remember you're allowed to make mistakes. If you need time to clear your head, then do it."

"Right."

"I wasn't sure if your dad was the one when I met him, but gradually, he became it after everything we went through together. All those memories, those are the things that make him irreplaceable, you know?" She makes everything seem so easy, even though she's got her own struggles—working in a white-dominated industry, balancing an identity that doesn't fit into clean boxes, and juggling urgent and important priorities like she's stuck in some never-ending four-quadrant career matrix. "After all, we raised two little rascals together. We bond through battling our common enemies. So, ultimately, I believe love grows through experience rather than a perfect match. You're really young. You don't need to solve the 'forever' question. You should be happy and carefree at your age."

"Sure," I say, nodding slowly. "I'll tell Sean the only way to solve our problems is to have a baby together."

My mom kicks me. "Hey, what did you mean when you said you rely on him for everything?"

I swallow as I check out the potted orchid on the table, trying to focus on something else. My parents are my heroes, and they've given me so much. I never want to accuse them of anything.

But they've also unknowingly wounded me countless times over the years. "Mom . . . did you know you and Dad spend more time traveling than staying at home?"

My mom winces and her nose scrunches up. "We're definitely thinking of cutting down. I'm—"

"I don't need you to choose me over your career. I'm proud of how you and Dad have fulfilling jobs and so many sources of meaning in your lives, and I'd never ask you *not* to prioritize that. But I want you to be proud of me too." My voice thickens. They never say it. They never really show it either. "When you're here, why do you only ask me about my relationships?"

Her mouth opens, then closes.

"Sean's the only one who values my opinions. It's like no one cares about what I want to do, or believes I can actually do it. He's carrying the entire weight of my future on his shoulders."

I want him to be my love, my friend, my parents, my mentor, my validation, my confidence—all while we're still very different people. I'm suffocating both of us.

"I understand," I say, taking a deep breath, "that Jeremy's the golden child in this household, but every now and then, it'd be nice if you asked about how I'm doing at school too. You asked Sean so many questions when you met him at dinner. I can't imagine what kind of wisdom you could give me if you helped me with my college applications. You say you believe in me, but I don't want passive support. I want to be challenged. I want you to be involved, to ask me what I'm working on, to help me figure things out."

My mom stays quiet for a long moment before she responds. "Your dad and I, we want to believe we're doing the best we can. We recognize we're absent a lot, and we get lost in our work, but we convinced ourselves that the autonomy and problem-solving we experience in our jobs were valuable lessons for you too. We assumed since Jer's fine, you'd be fine too. I didn't realize . . . I'm sorry. And I'm sorry you didn't feel comfortable bringing this up sooner. We should've noticed you wanted more. We were so focused on giving you freedom we overlooked when you needed guidance. That's on us. I don't want to keep making that mistake."

Red rims circle my mom's eyes. For once, she doesn't look like she's in total control, and I immediately want to make her feel better. "Well, I'm fine most of the time."

"No." She shakes her head. "It's not fair to you. And Jeremy isn't the preferred child. I admit we're more familiar with the path he's taking, and we didn't want to pressure you with your grades, but you're right to call me out on it. You can do anything you want to. Fashion, right?"

I smooth out the wrinkles on my sham pillow. "You don't think it's irrelevant?"

"Of course not. If I didn't ask more, it wasn't lack of interest but not knowing enough to comment. But that's still an excuse. I'm going to hold myself accountable and try to do better."

"Mom, that means a lot." I exhale, feeling a weight lift.

A few months ago, I wouldn't have said any of this. I would've laughed it off, convinced myself it didn't matter. But it does. I was raised to keep the peace, to respect my parents and be grateful, but I'm learning that honesty doesn't mean I love them less.

"Your dad needs to hear this too. Do you want to talk to him, or should I bring it up?"

"I'll talk to him."

"Okay. I've got an idea for a start." She sits up. "I *do* know where to find the best tiramisu in town. And it's still open."

* * *

When we get back from our vacation, I head over to see Sean at his house. After days of missing him, when we finally meet up, it's like playing a song after hitting Pause and then realizing I've forgotten the tune. Something feels off. He smiles at me, but I'm back to staring at him through thick ice.

I've brought the photos we took in New York. Sean wasted a lot of storage space shooting meaningless stuff, but I printed them all out anyway. We sit on the floor with our backs against his bed, flipping through the pictures together. I manage to look horrendous in most of them, especially when I laugh and my features twist like I'm midsneeze.

I swat him on the shoulder. "You caught me at my worst moments!"

"You're cute." He pauses on a picture of me standing on the beach in St. Bart's. "That one looks amazing. Was it fun?"

"Not really. Sorry for text-yelling at you so much."

He shrugs, smiling. "No worries. I can't sleep without you yelling at me before bed anyway."

Sean isn't one to make a big deal out of things, but I must've made his vacation terrible. How long can he put up with this before he reaches his limit?

I wasn't planning on saying anything, but the moment I open my mouth, the words tumble out. "Look, something happened there," I begin, and I don't stop until I've told him everything. He listens, not interrupting.

"And then I told him I had a wonderful boyfriend. And then I went back to the hotel room and cried."

Sean's too smart to not get it at once. "Your wonderful boyfriend isn't so wonderful if the idea of tiramisu made you cry."

We fall silent, the weight of that sentence hanging between us. We sit there for what feels like an eternity, measuring the silence, until I finally break it. "I'm not sure . . ." My voice is small, like I'm being called on in class to solve a math problem I don't know the answer to. "I'm not sure I can do this anymore. Maybe we should stop before I do something to hurt you."

There's no trace of surprise on his face. "You're doing it right now."

"I can see us going downhill, and I'd rather end it early than badly. I can't bear the thought of us ending badly."

Sean stays strangely calm, and like rehearsing a line, he says, "You have no faith."

"I want to be better for you. I need time on my own to figure things out. We love each other, but we want different things, and we're not good for each other right now. I need time to figure out who I really am, outside of you." By now, I'm rambling between hiccups, not even sure I'm making sense. "You're perfect and I love you, but you're not perfect for me."

"I'm not perfect. When you say that, it's a slap in the face because I don't know what I can do to fix it."

"There's nothing to fix. It's me, and I'm not ready. I don't know how to love you and myself at the same time. I don't know who I am anymore, and I feel like I can't breathe without you. I can't keep clinging to you like you're the only thing holding me together. It's not fair to you, and it's not fair to me. Can you . . . can you give me some time?" I wince at how selfish that sounds. "I still love you. I just need some time apart to clear my head."

"How much time?"

"I don't know. A short break."

He shakes his head. "No."

"I want a break, not a breakup."

"That's exactly the same to me."

Sean likes clear answers. It's either a serious relationship or nothing.

My eyes well up again. I expect this to hurt, but not so much that my insides turn over. I might puke. I can't be with him, but I can't be apart from him either. It's impossible to decide.

But then there's the alternative—we learn to resent each other. Or worse, we grow so far apart that we end up strangers.

"I guess we're breaking up," I choke out in between sobs.

"Are you sure?" he asks, almost serenely. "I don't want to break up, but once you decide, that's it. I'm not doing this back-and-forth thing."

Of course I'm not sure. But after an eternity, I nod.

"Okay. If that's your decision, then I accept."

He's composed throughout the conversation, as if we're discussing dinner options. There's no bargaining, no pushback. He just *agreed*, more undisturbed than a lifestyle coach saying they support my journey while my entire world caves in.

We sit and mull in silence. He picks up the photos I brought over again. This time he examines them more slowly, his head lowered, going through each one without saying a word. My chest is so tight I can barely breathe.

A teardrop rolls down his cheek.

My heart shatters. Sean's never like this. He's always so poised, so in control of his emotions. In that fleeting second, he's never looked nobler.

He's trying to make this easier for me.

A second later, he wipes his face with the back of his hand, and he's back to his usual self. "Sorry about that. I thought my tear ducts shriveled up back in third grade."

"Sean . . ."

He glances up. "Can I keep the photos?"

"Of course." My own tears fall, each one quicker than the last. "Those are for you."

"Thanks."

Even at the end, Sean remains the gentleman he is. There's no bitterness, no resentment. I can't find one bad thing to say about him. He's perfect all the way.

"Just so you know," he says, "I don't regret anything that happened between us. I still think the best time of my life was spent with you."

"Me too."

He doesn't answer. After a short while, he flicks his gaze to my face, and there's a lost little boy in his eyes. "When . . . *if* you think of me, can you remember the good times? Not that we fought a lot and I made you cry."

At that, a fresh wave of tears hits me, and all I can think of are the little things I love about him. The way he drives. The sound of his laugh. How he bites his lip absently when he does his math homework. The thoughtful gifts he gives me. How he's all about doing the right thing even though he can opt for the easy way out. He's normally calm, gracious, and confident, but his vulnerable side melts me. How he's cocky and innocent at the same time. His kisses. His nerdy jokes and lame pickup lines. He's the sweetest, most earnest boy I've ever known, and every moment spent with him has been the best.

He gets up and hands me fresh tissues. "Stop crying, Flora. My parents are going to think I did something to you."

I blow my nose. "Can we still be friends?"

He nods. "Sure."

CHAPTER THIRTY-EIGHT

Sean

Back when I was in third grade, we had a dog. Technically, it was Lindsey's dog, but she named it White Fang and then considered her responsibility complete. The name didn't stick, so we just called him Dog. I took Dog for walks all the time and fed him scraps under the table.

Dog got sick. On his better days, when he was in better spirits, he could still run around a little. I'd start thinking he might pull through, but then he'd relapse. It went back and forth, and we gradually lost hope, until it was just a matter of time.

Just because it was expected didn't make it any less painful when Dog passed. It's a terrible comparison, but sometimes I think Flora and I could make it. When we don't, I'm not shocked.

But it still hurts like hell.

* * *

The day after the breakup, we finish a basketball game in which we completely crushed the other team. I've done my part, scoring better than I have in weeks. As we're about to leave the gym, Jake slaps a hand on my shoulder. "What's wrong?"

"Nothing."

He scrunches his nose. "Your head's not in the game."

"I'm just tired."

"Bullshit." Dylan's voice is flat. "You're always tired, but you're not usually like this. Enough with the emo brooding. What happened?"

I adjust the strap on my bag. Telling them is inevitable, but if I sit with the information a little longer, it feels less real, like I'm stuck in some parallel universe.

"Flora broke up with me," I say, after a long pause.

They're bound to make jokes about it, since breakups are so common no one takes them seriously anymore. But then the smirk slips off Dylan's face and Jake shuts his mouth. After a few seconds Dylan says, "You'll get back together in two days."

"No. This is final."

"But why?" Jake asks.

Good question. I pick the simplest answer. "We're . . . incompatible."

"Physically?" Dylan insists it's a legitimate question. He's adamant that people split up all the time over this.

"No, not physically. Jesus, Dyl."

"Financially?" Jake asks.

"Not that either. At least, not entirely. I guess we want different things in life right now."

Dylan shakes his head. "You helped her study for the SATs, but she just wants someone to party with."

"No, it's more complicated."

So complicated that I'm not sure why it has to happen either. *She says I'm too perfect? She loves me but she's lost? She needs to "work on herself" before she can be with me?* Does it sound as absurd out loud as it does in my head?

Jake would probably say, *So she dumped you because she loves you and you did nothing wrong?* and Dylan would be like, *Bro, what? That's the stupidest breakup I've ever heard.* I spare them the confusion because it'll only frustrate me more.

As we walk out of the locker room, I search the parking lot out of habit.

Her silver Mercedes isn't there, of course. No one's waiting for me outside.

Jake catches me looking and steers me toward his car. "An era ended! You've destroyed my faith in high-school relationships completely."

Dylan whistles. "You can still bet on Sydney and me."

Jake glances at him before turning back to me. "You were the *one* couple I rooted for. I thought you were going to make it."

"Sorry we didn't try harder for you."

Dylan's less sentimental. "When it's over, it's over. You good, man?"

They both look at me like I'm a rabid dog that might bite. I've never needed them to comfort me, and I'm not about to start. "I'm fine. Don't look so concerned."

Jake studies me, like he's gauging whether it's safe to start cracking jokes. Then he tilts his head and spreads his arms. "Come here, bro. I'll hold you while you cry. I'll even stroke your hair."

"I'll play a sad song on my guitar and light a scented candle," Dylan adds.

They're so ridiculous that I laugh, surprising myself. "You guys are idiots."

Dylan throws an arm around my shoulders. "You love us. Now let's go. My place. We'll order pizza—or whatever else Flora wouldn't let you eat—and run *Call of Duty* until our eyes bleed."

We get wasted in Dylan's basement. Jake invents a drinking

game on the fly: take a shot every time we die on-screen or someone mentions a word that starts with *f.* Dylan tries *really* hard not to swear, and I avoid bringing her up. I wouldn't have, even without the rule.

They pester me about brushing up on my German, insisting we need to last more than five seconds in Munich before locals figure out we're American.

"This summer trip is our chance to blend in," Dylan declares. "We refuse to embarrass ourselves."

Jake nods solemnly, then ruins it by slurring, "You're literally our only shot at international success."

She isn't going to be in my life anymore. Neither are Paris or New York.

But I can still look forward to Germany.

It's not the same, but it's something.

* * *

"All right, let's get him up." Jake's voice.

Something shifts beneath me. Arms under mine. My legs lifted. My body tilts, dragged upward. Head lolling, too heavy to hold up. My brain is syrup.

A pillow slips under my head. A blanket drapes over me.

"I'll call his parents, let them know he's staying over." A pause.

"Hi, ma'am, this is Jake. Sean fell asleep at Dylan's. We were hanging out, and we didn't want to wake him. Would it be all right if he stays over?"

"Hey, Mrs. Foster." Dylan's voice.

A pause.

"Yes, ma'am. Thank you." Another pause.

"We're good," Jake mutters.

"You staying over too?"

"Yeah. In case he wakes up sobbing in the middle of the night. Can't leave you to deal with that alone."

The air mattress hisses as it inflates. Plastic scraping against carpet. Footsteps shuffle, then a heavy sigh.

"This breakup bullshit or what?" Dylan.

"Total bullshit." Jake. A beat of silence. "I don't know what more she could want from him."

The hum of the mini fridge fills the silence.

The last thing I feel is warmth. The weight of a blanket. The steady rise and fall of my own breathing.

Sleep pulls me under again.

* * *

Lindsey sticks a Post-it Note on my door every day. They're quotes about heartbreak, her way of telling me that I'm not alone. She also writes these ten-years-later stories, in which I'm happy and successful, living my best life.

It's not going to take me ten years to be okay, right?

"It's fine to be upset, you know." She plops down on my bed. "You talk like you're holding a press conference. Come on, vent away."

"There's nothing to vent about."

"It'd be easier if there was someone to blame, right?"

There's a reason people hate their exes. It's a defense mechanism, because getting over someone not at fault is so much harder. I picked a wonderful person as my first love, which is both the best and worst thing about my situation.

Flora wants to stay friends, and I try to keep that promise, just not in the way she imagines. I smile at her, make small talk at my locker, keep things easy for our friends. I never say a bad word about her. But I delete all her texts and stop responding to new ones. They're meaningless now.

After high school is over, I'll never contact her again.

Only a few months left to go.

* * *

The aftermath of a breakup isn't dramatic. It's slow, repetitive, and quite frankly, boring. Mourning *is* boring, so I do it alone.

I pretend to be as excited about the trip itinerary as Dylan and Jake are. I collect Lindsey's notes from my door and add them to the growing pile, not forgetting to reply with a smiley face. I listen to the playlists Josie carefully curates for me. I lay down a perfect report card in front of my parents, assuring them my grades aren't suffering, and neither am I.

But in the quiet moments when I'm alone, I mourn.

I miss her when I drive to school, stopping at the intersection, wondering if she remembers to flick the blinker. I miss her when I go to the movies and accidentally order caramel-flavored popcorn. I miss her in the early mornings, when the world is hushed and empty. I miss her when I shower, watching the water drops trickle down the drain after I turn off the shower. I miss her before I fall asleep, staring at the ceiling, fighting back silent tears, as I ask oblivion,

Dear Flora, how are you?

CHAPTER THIRTY-NINE

Flora

I underestimated Sean's determination to stay *friends*. We've become friends in the most meaningless sense, where he treats it like a professional courtesy. He gives me the forced smiles he reserves for random girls who hit on him, answers my questions politely but with that same detached tone. He's composed and distant, like a news anchor delivering a scripted segment.

There's nothing special left between us. And that, to be written off entirely from his life, hurts more than anything.

My friends try to be supportive, even though they don't really understand why I had to let him go. They now talk about Sean like he's some priceless piece of art at Sotheby's that I've been outbid on. Madison even goes so far as to say *Sean's not the worst* (although she immediately follows up with, *but I'll hate him if you tell me to*), while Josie encourages me to focus on myself. As for Sean's friends, Dylan quite bluntly stopped me one day before I could get to Sean and said, *Look, it's nobody's fault, but the breakup wrecked him twice already. Can't you give our boy some space?* Whenever I pass their table at lunch, I sense a wave of hostility, and the laugh that used to live in Jake's eyes isn't there anymore. It's probably all in my head, but I no longer feel comfortable enough to pull out a chair and join them.

Raymond calls one morning, waltzing right back into my life. "You need something fun to cheer you up. I'll take you out."

I make him promise to steer clear of anywhere that might remind me of Sean, so naturally, he takes me to an amusement park (after grumbling about standing in line with plebeians). When I get off one of the rides, the person in front of us turns and a strand of dark hair falls across his forehead. It's Sean's hair.

Raymond makes his trademark disgruntled noise. "You're not gonna cry, are you? Because if you do, I'm not the guy for that. I'm terrible at comforting people."

I turn my face away. "No."

"Good. I bet you're ugly when you cry."

Expecting anything sweet to come out of Ray's mouth would be pure naivety. If this was Sean, he'd be so flustered. "I miss him." My mood plummets faster than a roller coaster.

"Look, we can go home right now if you want."

"But we just got here."

He shrugs. "The whole point of coming here is to get your mind off him, but I see it's not happening. Let's go."

We're at the far end of the park, so we end up hopping on the tour train, which takes forever to reach the entrance. It's packed and the seats are stiff, so, predicably, Raymond complains the entire time. He makes crude observations about the man sitting in front of us and his smelly feet (he strongly suspects they are), tells me every joke he can think of, and even though he's not as hilarious as memory serves, the effort counts.

"Why are you being so nice to me?" I ask, since it's a long ride, with stops at all the major attractions. "Are you pretending to be my friend so you can swoop in and catch me at a vulnerable moment?"

He snorts, chips in hand, crumbs falling all over himself. There's never been a single ounce of sexual tension between us, but better to make sure.

"I'd feel so betrayed if you had a secret crush on me."

"*Pfft*. I don't. You know what they say—if you sleep with everyone, sooner or later you end up with no one to go to amusement parks with."

The train stops, and the man with the alleged smelly feet stands up, swaying. Raymond jumps out of his seat to grab his elbow. "Careful there. This thing doesn't come to a full stop. Have a good one!"

When he sits back down, he rolls his eyes. "I can finally breathe again."

Sean never makes fun of other people like that. I love that about him, but he won't offer help either. He's a bystander, mostly hanging back unless something directly affects his inner circle. It's part of his elegant charm, but it's not the only valid way to move through the world. While Raymond can be insincere at times, he doesn't hesitate to offer a simple act of kindness.

Sean also misjudged my friendship with Raymond. He's not always right.

Maybe Sean isn't perfect?

It's the first time I've really let that thought land. For so long, I convinced myself I was the only problem, that I had to be easier, quieter, and *better*. I backed away from conflict because I wanted his love too much. I avoided the big arguments but pestered him incessantly about small things like how often he texted. I never invited the real conversations, and I guess he didn't either.

The train lurches to another stop. Ray offers me the last chip, then pops it in his mouth without waiting for a reply. "You miss him. I get it," he says, reading my mind. "But don't sell yourself short like you're the sole villain. You're not *that* powerful. Pretty sure it takes more than one confused teenager to destroy the most iconic love story of our time."

I nod. It's hard not to carry all the blame, but maybe I can cut myself some slack. Maybe growth means not overcompensating and recognizing that Sean is still figuring things out too.

"And hey, at least now you can stop pretending to agree that Pepsi is the best drink on earth."

I laugh. A light jab at Sean without reverence. "Yeah, he doesn't just think Pepsi is okay—it's his top choice."

Ray grimaces. "You people have *so* much to learn."

* * *

Carmen pours two glasses of sweet tea and slides one across the counter. "Are you feeling better?"

"Not really." With my straw, I stab at the bottom of the glass where a clump of sugar has yet to disintegrate. "Everything is pointless."

As the days drag on, I sink into a constant state of sorrow. If the acute pain of a breakup is screaming in agony, the aftermath is writing a sad letter with no one to address it to.

Carmen has listened to me vent over lemonade, peach iced tea, root-beer floats, and mason jar Arnold Palmers as I've moped around all spring, insisting that a good Southern drink will make me feel less like death.

"Sometimes I wish I'd never started anything with Sean. All I have left are memories. Memories and an astronomical amount of pain."

"Just because it's over doesn't mean it was all for nothing. You were amazing before you met him—you're the kindest, most charming person I know. And now your grades are improving, your college application was submitted in the best shape it's ever been, and you even stood up to your parents. Most importantly, you're no longer willing to lose yourself to hold on to someone else. Sean is wonderful, but you made the right decision, even though it was hard and painful. That's admirable."

Her voice is soothing, and even though her advice is a bit high-level, it still makes an impact. I nod, holding back tears. She gives me space to think about what she said, and we finish the rest of our drinks in silence. It's the kind of silence that resembles a blank piece of paper, too impeccable to be ruined by any redundant words.

"Would you like to read a book?" Carmen asks.

I grimace. "You know I don't read much." Mostly the shampoo bottles in the shower when bored.

"Maybe it's a good time to start. Books are stories. How can you not enjoy a story?" She moves to one of the many bookshelves in her house, returning a moment later with a thin book by Françoise Sagan, *Hello Sadness*. "Sagan reminds me of you. She's been attributed with saying something like, 'Money doesn't fix everything, but if I had to cry, I'd rather do it in a Jaguar than on a bus.'"

"I love her already."

"She wrote this when she was a teenager, and it became an instant hit."

"Well, the length is perfect," I say, flipping to the last page. Only 127 pages.

"Yeah, you can finish it this afternoon. Tell me what you think later."

I crack it open. There's a paragraph about how sorrow feels, how it always seemed profound and almost noble, something heavy and poetic. But now it's different. It wraps around her like a delicate, silken web, soft and suffocating, setting her apart from everyone else, leaving her trapped in a world of her own.

How fascinating is this?

To find myself in someone else's words.

* * *

As senior year trudges on, I get better. The jigsaw puzzle Sean gave me has a bizarrely calming effect, like my brain's version of a spa day. I finish it in three weeks and, in a fit of newfound productivity, buy a couple more. Meanwhile, I keep building my portfolio through my style blog. I've posted a range of articles that I'm proud of, covering topics like the quiet luxury trend, how culture shapes style, how social media flipped fashion's power structure, and the psychology of shopping. Okay, so maybe these aren't exactly thesis-level masterpieces, but I did spend several hours in the library doing research—*actual research*, not relying on my trusty friend Wikipedia.

I've also started working part-time at a clothing store. When my first paycheck hits, I take my parents out to lunch. They've been making an effort to be around more, and when they're not home, they schedule one-on-one calls with me.

We settle in at a local bistro. Something nicer was out of budget. After taxes, social security, and Medicare, my paycheck isn't exactly impressive. This is the best I can do—my biggest act of generosity is sparing them a trip to the Cheesecake Factory.

Dad picks up the menu. "Is there a limit on spending?"

"Yes. You each have a forty-dollar limit. Including drinks."

Mom raises eyebrows. "With or without tax and tip?"

Dad grins. "This reminds me of pharma compliance rules. Dining with physicians always has a strict spending cap."

Mom nods. "Right, and alcohol can't exceed thirty percent of the bill."

"Exactly. Don't mess up the ratio," I say.

Dad pretends to look concerned. "So if I were to, say, order a steak . . ."

I tut. "Then you'd be violating company policy and washing dishes in the back. I suggest the soup."

They laugh. "We raise a daughter, put her through school, give her a good life, and the moment she gets her own paycheck, she feeds us soup."

As the food arrives, Mom steers the conversation back to my work. Neither of my parents have ever worked in retail, and they have loads of questions, starting with my dad: "How does the store track performance? Do they set individual sales targets?" and followed by my mom: "What's the biggest bottleneck in your day-to-day workflow?"

I lean back. "I said I wanted to be challenged, but for now, can you chat with me like my parents instead of giving me a performance review? Dial it back down a little, would you?"

"We're trying!" Mom laughs.

Dad adjusts his tone. "Fine. No KPIs, no metrics. Just casual parent-child conversation. So . . . what would you say is your biggest strength in the role?"

"Dad!"

"Okay, okay—serious question. Do you at least like the job?"

"I do. But I can't believe how much folding needs to be done. I'll spend an hour making everything look perfect, and then a customer walks in, grabs a sweater, unfolds five others, and leaves without buying anything. And don't even get me started on fitting rooms."

"You know, it's funny," Mom says, "considering how you never used to fold your own clothes growing up."

Dad nods sagely. "Turns out, the amount of clothes a person folds in their lifetime is constant. If you don't fold your own as a kid, karma makes you fold other people's clothes for them."

"Wow. That's profound," I say. "You should write a parenting book."

Dad leans back, satisfied. "I'll call it *The Unfolding Truth*."

"Subtitle: Why You Should Do Your Own Laundry Before Life Makes You," Mom adds. "Hey, has working there made you want to shop more or less?"

"Oh, being around all those beautiful clothes absolutely makes me want to shop. When things come in, I start mentally putting outfits together." I gesture at the plates on the table. "But I just blew my entire check on this meal because you insisted on ordering steak, Dad."

Dad pauses midbite, looking guilty but not really. He pats me on the shoulder. "Welcome to adulthood."

* * *

By the end of March, when I receive my acceptance letter from NYU, I've done four more puzzles. Carmen introduces me to a few more complex women, including Lady Chatterley, Madame Bovary, Eugénie Grandet, Thérèse Raquin, and Anna Karenina. She says we'll start with European classics and then move on to modern literature. Besides strengthening my bonds with my core friend group, I party a little, but no rebound relationships this time.

Heartbreak is something I must face on my own.

I call Sean to share the news. He congratulates me but refuses to take any credit for it.

"Can I buy you dinner, or at least coffee?" I ask. "To thank you properly."

"That's really not necessary."

"I miss you. I want to know how you are."

"I'm fine. Thanks for asking."

My stomach churns, but I try to keep it light. "You don't talk to me anymore. What have you been doing lately?"

There's a long pause before he speaks. He tells me he got in everywhere he applied to, *obviously.* "And I helped my grandfather build a boat. It's something he's always wanted to do. His health's not great, so the goal's to finish it before I go to college." Three sentences in and his tone shifts. "Honestly, this is a depressing topic for me. Let's drop it."

After a short silence, I try again. "I hear you're much better at German now."

He responds with a string of rapid German sentences. I don't catch a word, but his accent seems right on. "I have no idea what you said, but I'm guessing you're going to impress German girls with that."

"I don't need to speak German to impress them. Some things are universal."

For a fleeting second, he sounds like his old self. It's such a delight to hear.

"I've been taking AP Fashion History," I say.

"I heard. That's pretty cool. Taking it senior year, second semester, no less."

"It took some convincing to switch out my free period, but this is my first AP class ever. A milestone for me."

"Good for you. Just 7,999,999,999 more classes to go before you're on my level."

Ah, an inside joke.

We're going to be okay.

"Can we hang out?" I ask.

He's silent for a second.

Just when I think there's hope, he says, "Not yet."

CHAPTER FORTY

Sean

I'm coping well.

At least, until Flora called and told me she got into NYU.

Despite being happy for her, there's this sense of loss because everything's pointless now. We used to talk about a future together before it came crashing down. In the end, it doesn't matter where she goes to school. She'll go to Central Park and MoMA with some other guy, and I'll have no one to build a robotic cheetah for anymore.

After I hang up, I meet up with Josie. She offers to take me to a loud concert to numb my brain. I slide into the passenger seat of her car, and the radio is playing "I Wanna Be Yours" by Arctic Monkeys.

She switches it off.

"I've been thinking about what I did wrong," I say.

"What's the conclusion?"

"She changed a lot for me, but I couldn't do the same for her. There were things I was willing to do, but I had to draw the line somewhere. Flora was like, she could give up anything for me."

She gives me a noncommittal nod, signaling she heard rather than agreed. "And it's your fault you can't change for her?"

"Maybe? She wanted a break, not a breakup, but I couldn't do that either."

"Of course you couldn't agree to that. You'd just be waiting, overanalyzing, and torturing yourself. That uncertainty would eat you alive."

"You know me so well."

"Dude, I *literally* grew up with you." Josie adjusts her grip on the wheel as she merges into the next lane. "Flora was changing for *you*, not herself. She was trying to fit into your world, adopting your values because she felt she should, not because she actually agreed. That kind of shift doesn't last. In the end, you simply weren't right for each other. It's like a band with a great lyricist and a genius songwriter, but the sound just doesn't click, so you separate on good terms. It's not anyone's fault."

"I wish it was that easy."

"Ask yourself: If you could do it all over again, what would you change?"

Our moments together, each one more precious than the last, unfold as the fading sunlight spills like liquid gold across the dashboard. What could I have done to save us?

There are things that go against my core values that I wouldn't change. I'd still prioritize school, challenge her to do the same, and choose safety over spontaneity. I'd still hold my ground when it matters, even if it pushes her away, because I'd rather lose her than let her regret something I could've prevented.

But just because there's nothing drastic or fundamental to rewrite doesn't mean I did everything perfectly. Now that Josie's question hangs there with no background music, the truth becomes abundantly clear: There's no singular moment to undo, but I could've moved through it differently.

I could've listened more, been more curious, and given her the chance to speak instead of jumping in with a solution before she could finish a thought. There were moments when the words hovered on her lips, and I was secretly relieved when she swallowed them.

I wouldn't have stopped being me. But I could've made her feel more accepted for being her.

"I did what I thought was right, but I could've been . . . *kinder*. Sometimes I knew I was winning by talking her into a corner, not by changing her mind. Maybe—deep down—I liked that she listened to me. Like if she followed my lead, she'd be okay. And that's not partnership. That's—"

"Arrogance," Josie supplies.

"Yeah," I say. "The kind that hides under good intentions."

She nods. "Exactly. You offered logic, structure, and a plan, but she needed empathy. Not everything is yours to fix, but let's be real—you're Sean. You couldn't *not* care if you tried. Did you ever ask her how she felt about all this?"

"No, it was more like, *Here's what we're going to do, please trust me on it and agree.*" I cringe, realizing how it sounds. "I genuinely believed I was doing what was best, but in hindsight, I never checked if she was truly on board. Part of me was even a little proud of my talent for persuasion. And when she started pulling away, instead of addressing it, I'd smooth it over. Turns out, keeping the peace meant avoiding the deeper stuff. Guess I won the battles but lost the war."

"In a way, you were still avoiding confrontation," Josie says.

"Yes. Even during the breakup, I tried to be respectful by accepting without protest, but I didn't ask any questions either. I never pushed to understand what she needed from me. Maybe I was afraid to ask, because I couldn't give it to her."

She's quiet for a moment. "Even knowing all that, your fundamental differences are still there. So these realizations wouldn't necessarily have saved the relationship. It still might've ended like a

Shakespearean tragedy. You see the end coming, but you can't stop it."

"True. So we were doomed, huh?"

"No. Then you have no regrets. You both gave it your best shot. You cared, you tried, and both your lives are better because you met each other. The best thing you can do now is give it space, let her figure things out on her own, and do the same for yourself."

It puts a positive spin on things, makes them less pointless. And besides, I'll never forget a single moment with Flora. Those sparkling memories are snowflakes in a snow globe, perpetually preserved. I can shake them up and watch them fall whenever I want.

"And I think the problem is, you're treating this like a physics test. You thought if you put in enough effort, you'd get the result you wanted. But relationships don't follow a formula. Even if you do everything right, you can *still* fail."

The words hit somewhere deep. I've spent my life believing hard work guarantees success—grades, MIT, basketball—every step is a calculated input for a predictable result. But Flora was never a problem to solve.

"J, maybe you *do* know more about relationships than I do."

She raises her eyebrows and holds one hand out, as if to say, *You think?* "Maybe it won't last forever, no matter what you do. But the feeling of doing the right thing will last."

"And I guess an NYU diploma will last forever too."

"Exactly." The engine hums as she steps on the gas. Halfway to our destination, she stops at a red light. "It takes time, you know."

"To get to the concert?" I ask, even though I know better.

"Yeah, to the concert." She smiles. "You'll be okay."

* * *

Not long after, prom rolls around the corner.

"I assume you're not going with Flora," Josie says as we sit on the lawn, waiting for class to start.

"That's right. Who's she going with?" *None of my business.*

"She's making a statement and going solo." Josie looks at me. "How about you?"

Dances were never a big deal to me, but senior prom's different. It's important. And going with someone random doesn't sound right. "I don't know. No one comes to mind."

"How about we go together as best friends?"

I laugh. "You want to go with me? You should go with Brian." She's offering because she's worried about me. "Thanks, but I'm fine."

"Dude, I'm serious. My UW boyfriend's already done his senior prom. No need to drag him to mine."

"But don't you want him to pick you up in a limo?"

She snorts. "That's so lame. We're too cool for that."

"Don't expect a limo from me either."

"Take it easy. We'll just hang out."

"Are you sure Brian won't mind?"

"He doesn't care." Josie pops a piece of gum into her mouth, chews it for a moment, then adds, "You know what? I wouldn't date anyone who doesn't get our friendship. I've known you my whole life. He's totally cool with it."

"Well, then, sure. Let's go to prom together."

"Great! Who knows how many chances we'll get to hang out after graduation," she says, her eyes softening with a foreign light. The kind of look that comes with endings. A wave of melancholy hits, even though high school isn't over yet.

The bell rings. Josie stands, slipping on her headphones. I'm grateful for her friendship, especially considering where I am in this—the guy friend, the exact role I'm wary of when it comes to being a boyfriend, yet here I am, agreeing to go to prom with her.

That's some serious double standard right there.

*   *   *

Josie, wearing a gray tee and black leather pants, rings my doorbell. It's not what anyone would expect for prom, but for Josie, this is just another night of defying expectations. We grab a quick dinner, take her car to school, and join a small group of friends.

Jake, Dylan, Josie, and I huddle around the punch bowl, toasting to whatever comes to mind—Jake being voted Most Gorgeous four years in a row, Josie's single hitting ten thousand streams on Spotify, me securing the second-highest GPA, the cafeteria lady who always sneaks us extra servings, and Dylan and Sydney proving that high-school relationships can at least last until prom. I'm almost jealous. For now, they seem to be on good terms, treating us to a live showing of Parental Advisory: Explicit Content. We toast to brotherhood—Josie calls it "not inclusive." Dylan insists, "but you *are* a brother," and she smacks him upside the head. Then we move on to toast the Roman Empire, democracy, the American education system, the strong relations between Germany and the USA, and, of course, peaking in high school.

When Josie finally gets fed up with our shit and takes off to find Carmen and Madison, Jake raises his cup. "Seriously, though, wouldn't have made it through without you."

Dylan nods, lifting his drink. "Yeah, I fucking love you guys."

"Without you two, I'd have been valedictorian," I say. They both punch me on the shoulder. "Totally worth it, though."

And it is. These guys know everything I don't outright say.

By the time I spot Raymond moving through the crowd, I'm already tipsy on nostalgia. He's pulling a few shy, unsure girls onto the dance floor one by one. He does this a couple of times until no one's left standing alone. He doesn't make a big deal out of it, either, just throws them a smile and makes them feel like they belong. This isn't even his party.

It's something Flora would do. In some ways, they're quite similar. High school's ending, and I don't want to leave with any regrets, so I step forward.

He sees me coming and grins.

"Hey," I say, stalling for time while figuring out how to start this conversation.

He nods, wise and smug. "I know what you're going to say."

"Oh yeah?"

"Uh-huh. We don't run in the same circles, and there's been some misunderstandings. But we're cool now, right? No hard feelings."

"Right. Pretty much. And thanks for inviting me to all those parties over the years."

He shrugs. "My pleasure. Probably not the best time to say this, but for what it's worth, you're a good guy. And, hey, respect for the SAT thing. Flora's lucky to have you."

"She's lucky to have you too. I'm glad you're both at NYU and can have your little movie nights together." I grimace. "Can't believe I said that."

Ray's hands fly to his chest in mock gratitude, and a faint cloud of pot hangs in the air. "I've been waiting *years* for this. Your approval means the world to me, you have no idea."

"Moment of weakness. Won't happen again."

He grins wide. "Nah, I need this on record. Write it down for documentation purposes."

"You want a paper trail of me being nice to you?"

"Preferably with a time stamp. Maybe even a signature, if you're feeling generous."

I snort despite myself. Me, laughing at Raymond Corbett's jokes. The bass from the speakers thumps through the floor. "Okay, that's it. Have a good night." I turn to leave, then stop. "You might want to ease up on the pot, though. It's not good for you."

"Thanks, *Mom*. Anything else? Want to check my exercise routine? Make sure I'm taking my vitamins?"

Thank god he's not my responsibility. Imagine having to deal with all his life choices.

"Unbelievable. Just when I was starting to like you."

"You'll come around. They always do. By the way, post-prom party at my place. Please come." He claps me on the shoulder before disappearing back into the crowd.

* * *

A commotion at the gym entrance pulls my attention.

Flora arrives alone, fashionably late, as expected. She moves through the crowd like moonlight on water, leaving ripples in her wake. It's impossible to ignore her existence. She slows time itself.

I force myself to look away.

Or try to.

Her dress is bare backed, held together by a few absurdly thin strings. Josie is talking about a summer class she wants to take, and I try to focus, but it's like studying enzyme kinetics in front of a flashing neon sign.

Then Brian shows up in a tux, limo waiting outside. Josie laughs, actually blushes, and ditches me without a second thought.

Raymond and Madison are crowned Prom King and Queen—no surprises there. I scan the room again.

Flora stands at the drink table, pouring herself a glass of water. She sets it down.

Her eyes catch mine across the room, and the lights reflect off them. They're warm as chocolate, sweet to drink in and ultimately to drown in.

Turn away. Even cavemen learned their lesson after the first burn. But this is Flora, and when it comes to her, logic and self-preservation don't stand a chance.

I blame her dress, mostly.

My heart pounds against my ribs. It's reckless, maybe even self-destructive, but it's so wrong to end senior year without at least one dance with Flora.

So I make my way toward her.

CHAPTER FORTY-ONE

Flora

You know that moment in romantic comedies when the guy and the girl spot each other across a crowded room? Their eyes cut past all the irrelevant people, the background noise fades, and everything turns to slow motion. Strangers step aside in a trance to make way for them.

Yeah, that's not what happens. But Sean does find me from across the gym. And from the safety of this distance, I let myself stare back. He's temptation in a suit, and I am nothing if not weak. As he moves closer, my pulse quickens.

Is this a fresh start or our grand finale? Is he here to talk or just extending a polite courtesy—one last dance before we fade to black?

And now he's right in front of me, tall and lean, and the color of his tie even matches my dress.

"Would you like to dance?" His voice is soft, but it carries great power.

I can't speak. It's a simple sentence, but coming from him, it can unravel me. I place one hand on his shoulder, and he takes my other hand. We both halt at the touch. With us, everything carries an undertone of intimacy. A dance isn't just a dance, and fingers are more than fingers.

His other hand slides onto my back, resting below my shoulder blades. My body tightens as his palm warms my bare skin. We start moving to the music, and I relish being so rightfully close to him.

"You look great in silver, Flora."

I shake my head, deeply disappointed. "Sean, I expected better from you. This is gunmetal gray."

He smiles and it stops my heart. It's a real smile, the kind that's been in short supply lately.

"So this dance . . ." I gaze up at him. "Does this mean you're ready to be friends, or is this the last time you're going to talk to me?"

"If we're being honest . . . I want to be friends eventually, but right now I just want to dance with you. One more time."

"Okay." A letdown, although not unexpected. We move in silence for a while before I speak again. "I keep pushing for your friendship because if I didn't, you'd let us fade out. You'll go to college and never contact me again."

He doesn't answer. I'm right.

"Just so you know," I say, "I'm an *excellent* friend."

He gives me a faint smile and spins me around. "No doubt about it."

"If you need help throwing another party or picking out the right bottle of wine . . ."

"Or scoring front-row seats to another game."

"Exactly! It never hurts to have connections in very influential circles. And if you ever visit New York again, I'll give you suggestions on restaurants and attractions."

"I can consult my other friend, Tripadvisor." He glances at the overhead speaker and frowns, his lips twitching slightly. "When's this song ever going to end? You're annoying me."

His arms tighten around my waist. I tilt my head. "Weird,

considering you once said you wanted me in your life for as long as I was willing to stay."

"That's *not* what I meant."

"I can't stay in your life as a friend? We don't have to abide by the muscle fiber's all-or-none law."

"What?"

I sigh, pretending to be impatient. "Sean, don't you know *anything*? When you stimulate a muscle fiber, if the stimulus is strong enough to exceed the limit, then the muscle fiber *will* respond. It either responds fully or not at all. Like you. It's either 'love you forever' or 'never speak to me again,' which is silly, because you're a human being, not a muscle fiber. You should have at least *some* nuance."

He blinks, and then he starts to smile. "I seriously can't keep up with your science knowledge anymore."

"You might as well say yes now, or I'll keep nagging you."

"Okay, okay. I'll start by returning your texts. Don't push it."

We fall silent, wrapped in each other's arms. The rest of the world melts away.

This is why people love dancing. It's a chance to hold a hot guy who doesn't belong to you for a few shimmering minutes of heaven.

The song ends too soon, like a merry-go-round cut off mid-loop. Sean pulls away, taking the warmth with him. But I can't dance in his arms forever.

"Thanks for the dance," he says.

"My pleasure."

We've stepped apart, but he's still looking at me, like he's not ready to let go either. My head is filled with a tangled ball of thoughts, where every thread starts with his name. When I leave tonight, it'll be final. Right now, we're trapped in limbo, where nothing has ended and nothing new has begun.

I take a step closer. "Hey. Want to get out of here?"

* * *

He doesn't ask where we're going, and he's not surprised when we stop at the swimming pool. Entering without breaking again for old times' sake, a tribute to our first homecoming together.

He hoists me up, steadying me as I climb over the fence.

"Don't try to look up my dress."

He smiles and shrugs. "It's nothing I haven't seen already."

We sit by the pool, enjoying our private party. I kick off my heels, toss my purse onto a lounge chair, and dip my feet into the water. Sean shrugs off his jacket. With graduation looming so near, this might as well be the last night for everything, for recollection, for prospection, and for sneaking peeks at Sean with his tie loose and the sleeves rolled up.

"You're going to kill it at MIT."

"You'll love NYU too. You'll make friends in no time, but at first, it won't be like high school. You won't see the same people all the time. Everyone's on a different schedule and some days, it might feel like you're on your own." His eyes are unreadable under the dark lashes. "Just—make sure you enjoy your own company too."

"Solid advice."

He's worried about me. He still cares even though I'm not his problem anymore. I look up at the stars, missing him already.

"God, I'm sorry," he says suddenly. "I'm doing it again—telling you what to do like I have all the answers. I keep slipping into guidance counselor mode. Please ignore me."

"Hey, I don't mind some good old-fashioned *Seansplaining*," I tease, elbowing him lightly. He sounds genuinely guilty. "Whatever will I do without you as my Northern Star?"

"You'll cope, just like I'll survive without your *Florazzle-dazzle* every five seconds." He smiles faintly. "Seriously though, I'm sorry for always trying to fix things. I didn't know how else to show up for you. And I messed up a lot."

"You did show up. More than anyone ever has. And it's not your fault I idolized you, but you never abused it."

"Still, I benefited from it. I didn't pay enough attention to the silent sacrifices you were making. Sometimes I was overbearing, and I steamrolled you more than once. Thanks for indulging my savior complex." He exhales. "Anyway, this is my thesis on why I'm not as perfect as you thought I was."

"Give yourself some credit. I'm not exactly low-maintenance. I craved independence, but also admiration, approval, and constant attention. I was like, *Push me to be better, but gently and only when I'm in the mood!* Let's be real, that's a lot for anyone. You were seventeen, prepping for MIT on five hours of sleep, and tackling this relationship on expert mode. A lesser man wouldn't have been as patient as you were."

"You give me endless grace, Flora."

"No, I mean it. We had a good run. A plus for effort."

"Indeed. A plus for effort."

I hold out my hand, palm up between us, and he high-fives it. There is still camaraderie between us, and no one else will truly understand how hard we both tried. It's a cloudless night and the air is serene. The water ripples and moonlight casts a shadow along his jawline. How fortunate that it was him on this intense, messy journey with me, and we came out the other side with no bitterness, no regrets.

A spur of the moment idea hits me. Standing up, I beckon for him to join me. "Let me show you something I discovered the other day."

Sean gives me a wary glance but humors me. I lead him to the pool's edge, right near the deep end. The tiles are cool under my feet as I turn to face him, leaning in just a little. "Remember the first time we broke in here together?"

He nods. "Sure."

"Do you remember what you said to me?"

"I said a lot of things."

"You made me promise something."

"To date me exclusively?"

I flash him my sweetest smile. "No. Not to push you into the pool."

With that, I plant my palms on his chest and shove.

It's such a stupid, reckless thing to do, and I'd do it again if I could.

Not because of the sheer shock on his face or the way his soaked shirt clings to him when he resurfaces. Not because his dark hair mats against his forehead, making his eyes more enticing than ever. Not even because when he hauls himself out of the pool, he says to me in a harshly sexy tone that I should surrender myself now before he has to chase me.

And definitely not because of how easily he lifts me, arms clasped around my waist, before tossing me straight into the water.

It's because when we start splashing each other, he laughs.

And my heart takes off.

I'd do it a thousand times over to hear that again. Making him happy is one of the things that makes *me* ridiculously happy, and I watch his face with my chest full.

I love Sean. I love making him laugh. I can live without his kisses—probably—but I hope he'll always share his happiness with me.

"You're every bit as chaotic as I remembered, Flora Morgan." He helps me out of the pool and pushes his wet hair out of his eyes.

"At least I made sure your phone wasn't on you. That's proper etiquette."

We're both drenched, water dripping from our clothes as we make our way to my car. My dress, now practically see-through, clings to me.

"Did you drive?" I ask.

"No, we took Josie's car, but she left with Brian already."

"Then let me give you a ride."

"Thanks."

"You can dry off at my place if you want. We can head to Ray's after."

Sean stops in front of my car, running a palm along the hood. He doesn't say anything.

We spent so much time in my Mercedes. Late nights, post-game exhaustion, the quiet rhythm of his breathing filling the space between us. I used to pick him up after games and let him crash in the passenger seat, watching his chest rise and fall as he dozed. When he finally woke up, groggy and apologetic—*Sorry, I'm such a boring boyfriend*—I'd shut him up with a kiss and make out with him until he was thoroughly convinced he wasn't boring at all.

Then we'd go up to his room and make out some more.

"God, I miss this . . ." He pauses. ". . . car."

"You waste this car's potential. You drive under twenty-five miles per hour."

"I don't drive under twenty-five," he says, scowling. Then he smiles. "Only in school zones."

I laugh. "God, I love you"—I catch myself—"your sense of humor."

His hand brushes the door handle, hesitates. Then he pulls it back. "Actually, maybe I'll see you later at the party."

"Why can't we go together?"

His eyes are clear and honest, like a shallow pool I can see right through. "Because I still think about you in ways I'm not supposed to."

The words land between us unpolished. Not flirty. Not teasing. I can't remember the last time he was this blunt.

A hot, aching pulse runs through me, and for a split second, I almost reach for his hand. "We don't have to stay friends." It comes out quieter than I expect, like a door creaking open.

His hesitation is brief, and he gazes at me with so much tenderness. "I think it'll be best if you go to NYU without me holding you back. You've worked so hard to get here, and you should be free to do whatever you want. Explore the city. Make friends. Go on a few horrible dates so you have stories to tell . . ."

His eyes trace my face, like he's trying to memorize it, like he won't be seeing me for a long time. It's a goodbye in disguise. A lump rises in my throat. I blink rapidly, but the tears come anyway.

"I mean it," he says. "I still . . . you mean everything to me, Flora. This isn't me saying no to you. This is the best thing I can offer you right now."

"You're saying it like you want us to both move on and forget each other."

"I want you to be happy. I know this sucks right now, but you'll be okay. You'll be *more* than okay."

I want Sean to be happy too. I really do.

He steps closer then pulls me into his arms. The wet fabric of his shirt is cool against my cheek. I circle his waist, and he hugs me back, like pouring out every ounce of love he's allowed to give me.

I can't tell how much time passes. Seconds. Hours. A lifetime.

His lips brush my ear. "I'll never forget you. You're the best, baby."

The word *baby* breaks me apart. A shiver runs through me, and tears sting my eyes. I sob against him until I have no sounds left. He rubs the back of my head, then my back, then gives me one last squeeze before he breaks away. "Thank you for the perfect prom night."

I nod, unable to choke out a single syllable.

"But you ruined my suit and I'm sending you the dry-cleaning bill." His lips curl up and he looks cuter than ever.

This boy will forever be the death of me. As I watch his retreating back, the moonlight washing over his shoulders, it hits me. Sean never promised to stay friends or said whether I could contact him again. The strangest, most conflicting emotions crash against me, both equally strong.

One part of me believes I'll never get over him. That I'll wait until he's ready, and take whatever he can offer me—as an acquaintance, a friend, or something more. But at the same time, I imagine him as a beautiful deer in the forest, one that makes this world a better place simply by existing. I don't need to mount it on my living room wall.

I don't need to own him.

He doesn't need to be mine.

Sharing a part of myself with him, however brief, has been enough. Wherever he ends up in the world, I'll think of him with nothing but fondness, knowing I haven't wasted a single ounce of my love on him.

I start my car. My dress sticks to my body and I'm eager to get home to a hot shower. At the intersection, the road is empty. Not a single car in sight.

The light shifted from yellow to red only a millisecond ago. I can run it. I almost do, then step on the brakes hard. The car screeches to a halt.

I flick on the blinker.

As the *tap, tap, tap* of it echoes in the darkness, I scan the empty road in front of me and say to the night, "Thank you, dear Sean."

CHAPTER FORTY-TWO

Sean

Flora and I don't talk again after graduation. It seems we've exhausted all that can be said.

I spend the summer without her. At first, it's brutal. Thinking of her is like a broken rib that hurts with each inhalation. Gradually, I get used to it. It's a tolerable kind of sadness, the way fragrances lose their scent after a while.

At least I have the freedom to think of her all I want.

When summer is close to an end, a plane takes me and my unresolved feelings across the ocean. Germany is everything I hoped it would be. I write a postcard to Flora every day, even though the plan is to never send them. These postcards serve as an archive of my trip.

I write about how Jake smiles at everyone and insists on chatting up the people at the next table, how Dylan has to repeatedly explain the White House isn't in Washington State—he's never been so passionate about geography—how I order in grammatically correct German and always get replied to in English. How Jake's uncle is somehow even cooler than him—if that's even possible—and pulls off the *chill American in Europe* vibe so well.

How we braved Bavarian clubbing, jogged along the Rhine, plunged into the freezing hellscape that is Eibsee, and played public chess. How Jake and Dylan forced me onto a karaoke stage, where I butchered a song so badly that even the polite Germans struggled to clap, only for Dylan to go next and absolutely obliterate. How I jay-walked *once* and they refused to let my descent into lawlessness slide, insisting "our sweet, innocent boy is gone," and debating whether I should be banned from reentering the US. I swear, these two bond over tormenting me.

See, Flora? I *am* willing to try new things when it doesn't cost me an arm and a leg.

I tell her about the two Korean students who stayed up all night playing bridge with Dylan and me, while Jake was out doing whatever it is that Jake does. About the middle-aged Frenchwoman we met at a bar who's a small celebrity after one of her YouTube videos went viral. About the Jamaican obstetrician we met in the hotel lobby who decided to take a year off from delivering babies. And about the old lady who roped us into moving a couch into her apartment, and then made us the best grilled trout of our lives to thank us.

Writing is my therapy, to get over Flora, but also to hang on to her.

One evening, Dylan leaves the room to call his mom and Sydney, in that order. I'm sprawled on the bed, writing.

Jake asks, "Are you writing to Flora again? Anything dirty in there?"

"Yeah, you and Dylan. You can read it if you want."

He skims it, and smiles. "I like your writing. We're really having such a good time in Germany."

"Yeah. So where are we going next? Summer after freshman year of college?"

He doesn't even hesitate, like he's already been planning it. "Somewhere Spanish-speaking so Dyl can do all the talking and we can nod along and be useless."

Then, just to be annoying, he double taps my face in that obnoxious big-brother way. "I love you, but your German sucks."

* * *

After my first grueling semester at MIT, I come home for winter break. When I finish packing again, getting ready to leave the next day, Lindsey refuses to get out of my room.

She stands in the doorway, blowing her nose every few seconds because she's "crying tears of joy" and she "can't wait" to see me go.

I chuckle. "Would it kill you to admit you'll miss me?"

"Fine. I'm going to miss you," she says, sniffling. "Just a tiny bit."

"I'll miss you too."

She hands me my yearbook. "You forgot to pack this last time. Want to take it with you?"

There's a picture of Flora and me dancing in there. It feels like a cruel prank, and I skip that page every time. Josie says we were an epic couple, and it makes sense to have us in there, as a fragment of history, a UNESCO World Heritage Site of Lakeridge High.

Flora never signed my yearbook. When I got it back from the cheerleaders, I skimmed the last few pages. Every one of them had signed it except her.

I get it. We were too much to be summed up in a few sentences.

I touch the cover, breath held, and flip to the page with us dancing. A thin piece of paper slips out. Flora's handwriting.

Dear Sean,

I paraphrased below some sentences by Simone de Beauvoir. They conjure up what I'm trying to say:

What you gave me meant so much, it's mine to keep. Losing your love hurts, but I'll never lose the part of you that stays with me. Your kindness and friendship mean more than you'll ever know. I hope, so much, that I'll see you again someday, but I won't ask for it, not because of pride. Seeing each other again will only matter if it's what you want too. I'll be here, waiting. Whenever you feel like reaching out, it'll make me happy.

Your Flora
PS, I hope our story doesn't end here

My throat tightens. The letter digs up emotions I thought I'd buried, and it isn't just because my baby is now quoting Simone de Beauvoir. Lindsey leaves the room quietly. I read the letter again. And again. A third time.

She still cares. She longs to reach out, but she's leaving the choice to me. My eyes drift to the stack of postcards I've written her. We never lost contact.

Perhaps some differences can't be solved by negotiation, by compromise, by tears. Maybe we can't find a way to be together now, but maybe we still need each other.

Maybe we can try to be friends.

On impulse, I pick up the phone and press her name. It rings. Three times. Five.

"Who's this?" A peeved male voice picks up. "Flora can't come to the phone right now. She's in the shower."

I was wrong. I do *not* want her to be happy. Not this soon. She can't have replaced me this quickly. "I'm her—"

Laughter. "Sean, I'm messing with you. This is Jeremy," he says. "Flora's brother? You remember me."

My pulse slows. I exhale, unclenching my fist. "Hi, Jeremy. How are you?"

"Fantastic. Hey, Harvard is only two bus stops from MIT. Swing by and I'll show you where your future bosses went to school."

"Jeremy!" Flora's voice, horrified. Muffled sounds, wrestling over the phone and Jeremy laughing.

Then her voice, breathless on the other end. "Sean. Sorry about that. He's being a jerk, as usual." Just a few sentences in, and I miss her so much already. "Are you back home for the holidays? And how was Germany?"

I tell her about our trip, and she responds with enthusiasm to everything, even when all I'm sharing is how many miles we rode each day.

"I'm home too. My mom pulled some strings and connected me with an FIT grad who's a buyer for Moncler, and it's been eye-opening. Apparently, being a buyer isn't just shopping with a company credit card, which is fascinating but also mildly disappointing. I've also been looking into personal shopping, because, you know, if I can't be a fashion editor judging other people's outfits from a distance, I might as well fix their wardrobes up close. Oh! And I landed a summer internship at a fashion company, plus a local brand found my style blog and wants to collaborate. So yeah, branding, business strategy . . . I'm kind of a big deal now. Don't be intimidated. I have *so* much to tell you."

"You'll be great at whatever you do."

She pauses for a second. "If that's the case . . . I want to be your friend."

My eyes flick to the stack of postcards I never sent. "Listen, Flora—"

"I didn't mean to twist your words again. It's just . . . it's really nice to hear your voice. Can we keep talking? Please don't hang up."

I clear my throat. "I was going to ask if you want to meet for coffee, if you're not doing anything later."

Silence. A long one. My heart thuds hard.

"Flora?"

"*Sean.*" Flora laughs on the other end, in that flirty, charming way of hers I'll never get enough of. "See you at the Pavement in an hour. I thought you'd *never* ask."

ACKNOWLEDGMENTS

Kissing Is the Easy Part is a story close to my heart. I started writing when I was twelve, and over the years, my characters evolved with me as the course of the story changed multiple times. Growing up, I devoured countless love stories, but I always wondered what happens after the couple kisses and they get together. I've been eager to show that the hardest part of a relationship starts after the initial attraction.

In 2015, I took a leap of faith and posted it on Wattpad, hoping to find a few kindred spirits who enjoyed low-stakes, slice-of-life, coming-of-age YA with a realistic take on high-school relationships. Essentially, a story about love.

The story really took off once it emerged from my hard drive and hit the internet. First and foremost, thank you to my Wattpad readers, whose enthusiasm and heartfelt encouragement changed the trajectory of this story. Flora and Sean owe their ending to you. There truly is nothing quite like having an online community breathing life into a story as it unfolds. Thank you for your unwavering support, for taking the time to send personal messages, share your experiences, and write theses and character analyses in the comment section. The amount of real-time beta reading I've received is more than most writers can ever hope for.

To my writer friends—Em Slough, Chelsea Xena Tortland, Sevval Serdaroglu Yildirim, Gina Musa, Sandi Ward, Tessa Lovatt,

Katie Cruz, Tay Marley—writing can be lonely sometimes, and this would've been such a different journey without you. I'm extremely grateful to have met you along the way. Thank you for cheering me on, listening to me vent, giving me shoutouts, and offering advice. I think of our interactions with nothing but fondness.

I'm grateful to the Wattpad team for championing this story from the beginning through multiple programs and campaigns. I've always been met with kindness and professionalism whenever I needed assistance. A special thank-you to my editor, Deanna McFadden, for her rapid responses and helpful notes; to Delaney Anderson and Rebecca Mills, who helped polish this book into something I'm proud to put on shelves; and to Erika Turner, whose thoughtful feedback in the sensitivity review is greatly appreciated.

Thank you, Lindsey Alexander and Dana Burnell from The Reading List, for reading an earlier draft and offering the kind of constructive, honest feedback that made the final edit feel far less terrifying. There were times I wanted to tuck this whole publishing plan away, and your encouragement pulled me back in.

My sister once built an entire high school ecosystem with me on notepads and generously let me take charge of all the 'cool, popular' characters. That was the start of my writing journey, and we had a sprawling series of interconnected stories all planned out. These days, she's my legal representative and the person I trust most when it comes to character arc, narrative logic, and moral messaging. If my sister hates a book, I usually hate it too—if not more. I'm glad she doesn't hate this one.

Thanks to my parents, who instilled a love of literature in me from the start. Besides food, shelter, frequent reminders to wear a vest or a scarf, high (but achievable) expectations, and plenty of room-temperature, expertly cut-up fruit, I also never ran out of books to read. Thank you for pushing me to read Penguin Classics while also having the grace and flexibility to take me to the library to check out Sweet Valley High books by the dozen. I wouldn't be who I am today without you.

To my husband, who tirelessly endured questions ranging from "Is this a plausible reaction?" to "What would you say in a situation like this?" and "Help me think of a snide remark that's mean but not too mean"—to the point where he suspects every character is loosely based on him and feels comfortable enough to claim that he wrote half the book in spirit. Thank you for being emotionally intelligent, patient, supportive, understanding, and the reason I forget about all the fictional boyfriends the minute I put the book down.

My son has never read a single page of my writing but knows not to stand directly behind me and breathe into my hair while I'm typing. That's more helpful than you'll ever know.

And lastly, to my daughter, who read an early draft of mine, printed and held together with a binder clip, and told me she forgot it wasn't a "real" book. Thank you for asking every day if I was going to publish it. Sophie, we did it. Now let's go out there and tell the world.

ABOUT THE AUTHOR

Christine Duann, originally from Taiwan, holds an MD and is a former thoracic surgeon. She lives outside Indianapolis with her husband, two kids, and two rescue dogs. When she's not working, she's booking plane tickets, sipping unsweetened green tea, researching the mechanics of board games, and picking dog fur off her sweater. *Kissing Is the Easy Part* is her debut novel.